P9-CMT-303

RIZZO'S FIRE

Also by Lou Manfredo

Rizzo's War

LOU MANFREDO

RIZZO'S FIRE

Jefferson Madison
Regional Library
Charlottesville, Virginia

MINOTAUR BOOKS
NEW YORK

305181255

This is a work of fiction. All of the characters, organizations, and events portrayed in this novel are either products of the author's imagination or are used fictitiously.

RIZZO'S FIRE. Copyright © 2011 by Lou Manfredo. All rights reserved. Printed in the United States of America. For information, address St. Martin's Press, 175 Fifth Avenue, New York, N.Y. 10010.

www.minotaurbooks.com

Library of Congress Cataloging-in-Publication Data

Manfredo, Lou.
  Rizzo's fire / Lou Manfredo. — 1st ed.
    p. cm.
  ISBN 978-0-312-53806-4
 1. Police—New York (State)—Fiction. 2. Bensonhurst (New York, N.Y.)—Fiction. I. Title.
  PS3613.A5368R54 2011
  813'.6—dc22

                                        2010040693

First Edition: March 2011

10 9 8 7 6 5 4 3 2 1

To my daughter, Nicole Maull.
An extraordinary young woman.

ACKNOWLEDGMENTS

Thanks to my wife, Joanne, for her invaluable help.

The press, Watson, is a most valuable institution, if you only know how to use it.

—SHERLOCK HOLMES
"The Adventures of the Six Napoleons"

RIZZO'S FIRE

CHAPTER ONE

October

DETECTIVE SERGEANT RIZZO PARKED his Camry in a perpendicular parking space on Bay Twenty-second Street, in the shadow of the hulking mass of Brooklyn's Sixty-second Precinct building. He walked around to the front entrance and, once inside, waved a greeting to the desk officer and stepped to the keyboard positioned above the radio recharger.

After removing car keys from the hook marked "DET 17/22," Rizzo turned to leave. As an afterthought, he reached for a thin Motorola hand radio and slipped it into the outer pocket of his coat.

Back on the street, he scanned the vehicles along both sides of Bay Twenty-second Street, all the cars sitting with front wheels up on the sidewalk. He spotted the gray Impala, crossed diagonally to it, and unlocked its passenger door. He rifled through the glove compartment and removed a crumpled pack of Chesterfields. With one leg in the car and the other extended outward onto the curb, he spit the Nicorette gum he had been chewing into the gutter and quickly lit a cigarette. Drawing on it deeply, he frowned.

"A fuckin' junkie," he said aloud, shaking his head sadly. A fleeting thought of his wife and the promise he had made some three weeks ago now crossed his mind. "Sorry, Jen," he said. "I'm doing the best I can."

Joe Rizzo was fifty-one years old, a veteran New York City cop with more than twenty-six years of service. He had lived in Brooklyn since age nine and had first met his wife, Jennifer, when they were seniors in high school. Married for over twenty-five years, Rizzo, his wife, and three daughters resided in a neat, detached brick home located within the boundaries of the Sixty-eighth Precinct in the Bay Ridge–Dyker Heights section of Brooklyn.

Just as he finished the Chesterfield, the deep, rumbling sound of an engine caught his ear. Turning slightly, he watched as Detective Third Grade Priscilla Jackson swung her crimson red Harley Davidson Softail off Bath Avenue and onto Bay Twenty-second Street. She slowly nosed the bike into a spot near his Camry, straddled it, and reached down to kill the motor. Rizzo lit a fresh smoke and got out of the car, slamming the door behind him.

"Good morning, Cil," he said as he reached her. "Welcome to Bath Beach, the heart 'n soul of Bensonhurst."

Priscilla Jackson was a thirty-two-year-old Manhattan patrol officer and the ex-partner of Mike McQueen, Rizzo's last partner. She was reporting for her first day of field work as a detective third grade. While still in uniform, she had assisted Rizzo and McQueen on one of the last cases they had handled.

Now Priscilla pulled the black helmet from her head, shaking out her short, straight hair. She smiled, highlighting her beauty, eyes dark and wide.

"Hey, Joe," she said, "how are you? And I gotta tell you, brother, I just rode through this neighborhood, and I didn't see a whole lot of what I'd call soul."

Rizzo laughed. "Yeah, well, Italian soul, mostly. And when did you start ridin' again? I thought you had this thing locked up in a garage somewheres."

Priscilla swung a long leg over the rear bobtail fender, dismounting. "Yeah, well, I did. When I was renting over in Bed-Sty. But me and Karen have a place together now on East Thirty-ninth Street. A bike is a lot easier to deal with in the city. Karen keeps her Lexus garaged and it costs more than my old apartment rent did."

Rizzo stepped slowly around the Harley, examining it. "Nice lookin' bike," he said, expelling smoke. "Looks fast."

Priscilla shrugged. "It's not a pig, but it ain't a real hot rod, either. Fourteen-fifty cc motor. I spent a lot on doodads, like the Badlander seat and the drag bar on that high riser. The bullet headlight cost me a fortune. But don't it look cool?"

Rizzo nodded. "Yeah. Cool. Me, I figure my twenty-eight-mile-to-the-gallon four-cylinder Camry is cool enough."

"Whatever floats your boat, Partner," she replied with a laugh. "So, shall we go in and meet the boys and girls? Get this shit over with?"

Now it was Rizzo who laughed. "Sounds good. It'll be nice to have a steady partner again—that bouncin' around filling in for guys on sick or annual leave really screwed up my stats. I'd hate to end my stellar career on a downturn. I was planning on doing about six more months, but I think a year is more like it. I recrunched the numbers: a year from now, I'll be about maxed out, pension-wise."

Priscilla smiled broadly. "So I get a year out of you, same as Mike did. Maybe I'll get over to One Police Plaza like he did, too."

Rizzo tossed away his cigarette. "Not likely. That was a freak thing. Someday I'll tell you all about it, but it's kinda like how you got that gold shield."

Priscilla nodded, a serious look entering her eyes. "Well, I don't need to know all about that, Joe. I just know I owe you. Big time. The bump-up to detective pay let me do this move-in with Karen. At least now I can half-ass carry my weight with the finances. Thanks to you."

"You earned that shield. If it wasn't for your help, me and Mike would still be lookin' for Councilman Daily's runaway kid. All I did was make a call and explain that to him. Daily did the rest. The hacks over at the Plaza musta tripped over their own shlongs getting you that promotion so they could kiss up to him a little more." Rizzo's voice had hardened as he spoke.

After a moment he went on, his tone once again conversational. "Besides, you're gonna be my sharp young partner, helping me get my stats back up. Then, I go out a legend and spend the next couple a years cookin' dinner for Jen till she retires and we move to Drop Dead Acres in Florida somewheres." Rizzo reached up and tapped his temple. "I got a plan."

"You'll miss the job, Joe. You just won't admit it."

3

"Yeah, I guess. But it sure has changed. Twenty-seven years ago, you told me I'd have a black female partner in the Six-Two, I'da told you, 'no way.' And here we are."

"Not to mention a *gay* black female," Priscilla said, her eyes twinkling.

"Oh, we always had gays, Cil," Rizzo replied. "Not open, maybe, but we always had them. Women *and* men."

Priscilla nodded. "Damn right," she said.

"But the job's changed in bad ways, too. It used to be like a family. One big family. Now . . . well, maybe we got a few too many half-retarded cousins wanderin' around at the holiday meals. You know what I mean?"

Priscilla reached out and patted his shoulder. "Yeah, Grandpa. The good old days. I got it. Now let's go sign in. And I'm feeling a little hungry. Do detectives start the day tour with breakfast, or is that just uniforms?"

"Cil, we start *every* tour with breakfast. C'mon, I'll introduce you to the boss, then we'll get going."

RIZZO SIPPED at his coffee, rereading the blurry copy of the precinct fax he held. The two detectives were seated at a rear booth of Rizzo's favorite diner awaiting their meals.

"Son-of-a-fuckin'-bitch," he mumbled.

Priscilla looked at him over the rim of her mug. "Damn, Joe, readin' it over and over ain't going to change what it says."

Rizzo compressed his lips. The fax had come from Personnel Headquarters at Police Plaza, addressed to all members of the force and distributed to all precincts in the city. The police recruitment civil service exam scheduled for early November would result in expedited hiring. Due to an unusually large number of impending retirements, anyone successfully completing the exam could reasonably expect to be hired within six to nine months as opposed to the usual fifteen- to twenty-four-month window.

"This is exactly what I didn't need," Rizzo said. "My youngest daughter is taking this friggin' test. In six months, she'll have enough college credits to get appointed. I was figurin' on a hell of a lot more

4

time to talk her out of it. This jams me up real good. My wife is gonna freak on this."

They sat silently as the waitress delivered their meals. When she left, Priscilla spoke.

"Don't you have three girls?" she asked.

Rizzo nodded. "Yeah, Carol's the baby. She's almost twenty, a sophomore at Stony Brook. Marie is my oldest, she's twenty-four. She's in med school upstate. Jessica is twenty-one. She graduates from Hunter College in June."

Priscilla buttered her toast and winced. "What a tuition nut to crack," she said.

"I can't even dent it, let alone crack it. Everybody is borrowed to the balls."

"Well," Priscilla said, "you gotta figure one of them for the job, Joe. They're all a cop's kid."

Rizzo shook his head. "Bullshit. I told you, the job's changed too much. For the worse. These kids, all starry-eyed, gonna save the world. Ends bad for most of them. You know that."

She shrugged. "It is what it is," she said. "You make it work for you if you got the balls."

Rizzo leaned forward and spoke softly. "Let's just drop it, okay? This ain't your problem."

Priscilla smiled. "Whatever you say, boss. My lips are sealed."

They made small talk as they ate, discussing their individual relationships with Mike McQueen, who had partnered with both of them at different times, and what Priscilla might expect in Brooklyn.

"In case you haven't noticed," Rizzo said with a smile, "this ain't exactly that Upper East Side silk stocking house where you worked uniform."

"I noticed that as soon as I pulled my bike offa the Belt Parkway and hit the streets. Now," she continued, taking a last sip of coffee and patting her lips dry with a paper napkin, "let's go do what we're supposed to be doin': cruising the precinct, getting the lay of the land. I'm anxious to start raisin' those stats of yours, Mr. Legend."

Priscilla stood, stretching out her back muscles. "Let's go," she said again.

They left the diner, pausing outside for Rizzo to have a quick cigarette. Priscilla had made it clear: no smoking in the car.

"I don't want you stinkin' me up with that crap you smoke," she told Rizzo.

Rizzo had her take the wheel. As she started the Impala, he reached under the front seat, pulling out a bottle of green mint Listerine. Priscilla watched as he raised the bottle to his lips, swishing the liquid around in his mouth, then opening the door slightly and spitting into the gutter. When he was done, he replaced the bottle, then shifted in his seat and pulled on his shoulder harness. Feeling Priscilla's eyes on him, Rizzo turned to face her. Seeing her expression, he frowned.

"What?" he asked.

"What? You asking *me* what? What the fuck did I just see? You got a date, Joe?"

He shook his head. "No. Jen thinks I quit. If I gargle after every couple a smokes, my breath won't smell when I get home tonight. That's all."

Priscilla shook her head and glanced into the mirrors, easing the car from the curb. "Damn, Joe. Cops ridin' this car next shift find that bottle under the seat, they're gonna figure I'm givin' up some head for that shield you got me. Don't leave that shit there. Please."

He chuckled. "It's been awhile since I worked with a dame," he answered with a smile. "I forgot how all of you think."

"Besides," Priscilla said, "Jen isn't stupid. You come home all minty-breath, your clothes smelling like horse shit, she probably knows exactly what's going on."

"You could be right," he said with a shrug.

They spent the next two hours cruising the varied areas of the Sixty-second Precinct, from the bustling, thriving commercial strips of Eighteenth and Thirteenth Avenues, Eighty-sixth Street and Bay Parkway, to the nestled residential blocks, tree-lined and glistening under the October sunshine. Rizzo pointed out the trouble-spot bars and social clubs, the after-hours mob joints and the junkie haunts. Beneath the elevated tracks on New Utrecht Avenue, he pointed to a grimy, antiquated storefront, its plate-glass windows opaque with green paint.

"The Blackball Poolroom," he said. "It's nineteen fifty-eight inside there, Cil. Totally."

He showed her sprawling Dyker Park, with its adjacent golf course, and pointed out the bocce, basketball, and tennis courts. There multiple generations of neighborhood residents played their distinct games with equal intensity. As they cruised slowly along Nineteenth Avenue on their way back to the precinct, Priscilla slowed the car for a red light. Rizzo reached across and lightly touched her arm. When she turned to face him, he pointed diagonally across the intersection.

"Take a good look at that guy and remember him. The tall kid wearing the Giants cap and black coat. That there's Joey DeMarco, seventeen years old, future serial killer. About once or twice a year the house gets a call. This guy lures stray cats with food. Then he douses 'em with lighter fluid and sets them on fire. They run like hell, squealing like banshees. Usually they die in midstride. Time the uniforms get there, the thing is stiff and charred like charcoal. God only knows how many times he's done it and never got caught. He's a real sadistic little prick. So far he hasn't grabbed some kid or old lady to kill, but mark my words, it's coming."

Priscilla glanced up as the light turned green, and she eased the car forward.

"Why's he still out free, roamin' with the citizens?" she asked.

Rizzo shrugged. "Why you think? Every time they lock him up, he gets psyched over to Kings County Hospital G Building. The geniuses over there drug him and squeeze Medicaid, or insurance or whatever, dry for thirty days. Then they pronounce him *cured,* and he walks. The charges get dismissed, and Joey starts savin' his nickels to buy some more Ronson. And, of course, Mommy and Daddy are no help: they know it's just our cruel society victimizing their little shit."

Priscilla studied DeMarco as they drove past him. "Duly noted," she said.

Rizzo fumbled through his jacket pocket and produced a packet of Nicorette. "See, that's what I mean," he said as he began to wrestle with the packaging. "How the job's changed. Years ago, a kid like that, if he torched a cat, a sector car would grab him and break his fuckin' arm. After that, he'd either knock it off or go do it some-wheres out of the precinct. But not anymore. Those days are gone."

Priscilla smiled. "There *is* something to be said for the old-fashioned corrective interview, that's for sure," she said.

"Damn right," he mumbled, at last freeing the gum and popping it into his mouth.

"Joe," Priscilla said gently, "I never smoked a day in my life, but even I know you got to either chew the gum or smoke the weed. You can't do both. That nicotine is poison, brother. They spray it on crops to kill insects."

Rizzo chewed slowly. "Well," he said with a small smile. "Fuck it. Something's gotta kill ya. Might as well be chewin' gum."

CHAPTER TWO

THAT EVENING, PRISCILLA JACKSON GAZED across the table into the happy, animated face of Karen Krauss. Karen raised her glass of Chardonnay.

"To your promotion," she said. "We never really celebrated. Let's do it now."

Priscilla reached out, clinking her vodka gently to Karen's glass of wine.

"As my new partner would say," Priscilla said, "*salud*."

The restaurant, on Third Avenue in Manhattan, stood just two blocks from their newly rented brownstone apartment on East Thirty-ninth Street. Its main room was softly illuminated beneath a deco style ceiling, a massive oval wooden bar dominating the center of the dining area. Discreet servers hurried to and fro as the restaurant began to fill. It was the start of the long Columbus Day weekend.

Priscilla looked around. "Nice place," she said. "How are the prices?"

"Not bad, considering the location and style. Not to mention the food, which is terrific."

Priscilla sipped at her drink. "Sounds good," she said. "We should make it an early night, though. I'm off till Monday. Tomorrow we can pick up paint and rollers and stuff and get started painting the apartment. Hell, it's only four small rooms; by Sunday night we can have it mostly done."

Karen's smile broadened. "Well, we'll have to talk about that. But first, tell me about your day. How'd it go? Anything exciting?"

"Yeah," Priscilla said. "Lots. I took a tour of the precinct, met the squad boss. They call the guy 'The Swede,' and believe me, he's even whiter than you are. Then I got hit on by some asshole lover-boy first grade named Rossi. Had to straighten him out. Word should get around the house pretty fast that I'm one of *those*."

Karen chuckled. "You know, Cil, there is something to be said for subtlety."

"Yeah, right. Maybe at your law firm, with all the good little boys from Hah-vaard. But not at the Six-Two. I got the message across the way I had to. Like a brick through a plate-glass window."

Karen beckoned for a server. "Let's order," she said. "I'm starved."

When the waiter had left them, Priscilla continued. "The rest of the tour, Joe and I went over his caseload. He brought me up to speed. On Monday, in Bensonhurst, most people will be off from work. They take Columbus Day very seriously there. He says it'll be a good day to work the cases."

As they ate their first course of soup, Priscilla asked, "So what's up? You said we have to talk about the painting."

Karen's face brightened. "Well, I had lunch with my mom today. She's arranged for her decorator to come by our place tomorrow. He'll bounce some ideas off us and then he'll arrange everything: painting, papering, carpets, tile—whatever. And it's all on Mom and Dad. A gift to celebrate our moving in together."

Priscilla paused mid-motion, lowering her spoon into the cup before her. "Are you kidding?" she said, her voice flat. "We've talked about this. I may not be in the Krauss family income bracket, but I'm not a freakin' beggar."

Karen frowned. "It isn't charity, it's a gift, a gesture, from two very supportive and caring people. They think of you like a daughter, Cil, they love you. You know how it is for people in the life, not to mention interracial. Name someone you know with folks as cool as mine."

Priscilla sat back in her chair, sipping her vodka. She thought of her own mother, a troubled, alcoholic wreck of a woman who, upon learning her youngest daughter was gay, had nearly assaulted and then banished Priscilla from her life. They had not seen or spoken to one another since.

She smiled sadly and raised her hands, palms outward. "Okay," she said. "They are righteous. Who knows? Since they're cool with the gay thing, and cool with the black thing, maybe your mother can even get cool with the cop thing."

Karen reached for her wineglass. "And the decorator?" she asked.

Priscilla sighed. "Okay. We'll listen to what the little fag has to say."

Karen smiled and sipped her wine. "Good. That's settled." She leaned back over the table and added, "And don't say 'fag.'"

ON MONDAY afternoon, Columbus Day, traffic heading into Brooklyn was light. Priscilla arrived at the Six-Two twenty minutes early to start the night tour with Rizzo. She signed in, nodded greetings to the half dozen faces she recognized from Friday's introductions, then sat at her gunmetal gray desk in the corner of the squad room and began to fill out the Precinct Personnel Profile form required of all new transfers. While she carefully listed Karen's cell and work numbers under the emergency notification section, a shadow fell across the desk's surface. She raised her eyes to see Rizzo standing there smiling at her, a paper coffee cup in each hand.

"One sugar, splash of milk, right?" he asked.

Priscilla returned the smile and took the offered container. "Yeah, Joe, exactly. Mike never told me you were a mind reader."

"No mind reader. I saw you mix it at breakfast Friday, that's all."

"Well, thanks."

Rizzo sat on the corner of her desk, sipping his coffee. "Speaking of Mike, this here is his old desk. Probably still smells like that fancy cologne he used."

"Two years I smelled that," she said. "Gave me a goddamned headache."

"Well, you put up with shit for a good partner. Working with him was one of the best years I had on the job. Mike's a good guy."

"The best," Priscilla replied with a nod. "And we should get along okay, having Mike in common and all."

Rizzo shrugged and drank coffee. "Let's hope," he said. "He's a good-looking son of a bitch, too, so at least you still got that. With me, I mean."

"Not quite, Joe, not exactly," she said.

Rizzo feigned shock. "What?" he said. "My wife says I'm fuckin' gorgeous."

Priscilla turned back to her paperwork. "Yeah, well, straight women are like that. They've got to be a little delusional. Keeps 'em sane."

Rizzo stood. "Don't feel you gotta hold back . . . you just speak freely, you hear?"

"No problem, Partner. That's my style."

He turned to move away. "Give me a holler when you're ready. I'd like to get out on the street. We need to get to work on our cases. Especially that asshole over near New Utrecht High who's been wavin' his dick at schoolgirls down by the train entrance. I got a lead on 'im and we need to talk to some of the victims. I'll be at my desk."

"Okay, I only need a few minutes more."

"Take your time," he said, crossing the cramped squad room to his own cluttered desk near the window.

THREE MEN sat in a rear booth of Vinny's, a small corner pizzeria in Bensonhurst. All in their mid-twenties, they had spent the last few hours of Columbus Day drinking beer and shooting pool at the Park Ridge Bar and Grill, three blocks south of the pizzeria. Now, slightly intoxicated and hungry, they talked and laughed loudly as they devoured a thick-crusted Sicilian pie.

The street beyond the plate-glass window in front was dark. A cold October wind was blowing, the streets of the working-class neighborhood dark and deserted.

At ten minutes to nine, one of the group, Gary Tucci, slid out from the booth and rose to his feet.

"I gotta get going," he said. "I got to be in at six tomorrow. Take it easy, guys, I'll see you."

Tucci's two companions waved him good night, and he turned to leave. Walking along the narrow pathway between the service counter and a row of booths to his right, Tucci stumbled. Looking down, he realized he had tripped over the extended right leg of the pizzeria's only other patron, a brooding, dark-haired man of about forty.

"Sorry, guy," Tucci said. "Didn't see your foot."

The man's face darkened. "Maybe you oughta watch where the fuck you're walkin', asshole," he said.

Tucci paused and turned slightly toward the man. "Yeah?" he said. "And maybe *you* should keep your big feet outta the aisle."

The man glanced to the rear of the pizzeria, noting Tucci's companions, now turning in their booth toward the sound of voices.

"You a tough guy, with your two friends backin' you?" the man said, shifting in his seat, beginning to stand.

"Hey, fellas," the owner said from behind the counter. "Take it easy, it was just a little accident."

"Bullshit," the man in the booth said. "This prick kicked me. He saw my foot there, I don't see no Seein' Eye dog leadin' him outta here. He fuckin' kicked me."

Now, with considerable speed, the man cleared the booth and stood up, shoving Tucci hard, forcing him onto the countertop. Tucci, despite his own drinking, caught the odor of alcohol coming from the man. He also saw the blind rage burning in his eyes.

"Yo, chill out, guy," one of Tucci's companions said, standing as he spoke.

"Sit down, Coke," Tucci said. "I can handle this." He then turned his gaze to the man. "You got a problem here, buddy, come outside and let's do it," he said, his voice low and tight.

The man's face contorted with even greater rage. "Fuckin' punk," he said, throwing a looping right roundhouse at Tucci's head.

Leaning backward, Tucci raised a stiff left forearm to intercept the blow. Then, crouching slightly, he thrust forward, pumping a short, fast right uppercut. His balled fist caught the man squarely on the jaw, driving it upward, teeth smashing together and shattering with the impact. Pinkish, blood-tinged saliva sprayed about his upper lip and right cheek, and his legs buckled. Tucci bulled forward, shouldering the man backward, sprawling him into the bench seat of the booth.

"Stay down, asshole," Tucci hissed, "or I'll send you to the fuckin' hospital."

Andy Hermann, the second of Tucci's companions, approached, a broad smile on his face.

"Don't start shit with a Golden Glover, Jack," he said to the dazed, bloodied man, using his best Frank Sinatra inflection. Then he turned to Tucci. "C'mon, let's get out of here. Let's pick up the paper and go home."

Tucci, adrenaline pumping, considered it. Then the third young man, nicknamed Coke, grabbed him, pushing him toward the door. "C'mon, Gary," Coke said. "Walk."

Reluctantly, Tucci allowed himself to be shoved along. As the three reached the exit, the man in the booth pulled himself upright in his seat, his legs still too shaky to risk standing.

"I'm gonna kill you, motherfucker," he called. "Kill you!"

Tucci's face flushed with renewed anger. "Yeah? Well, when you decide to do it, you can find me at Ben's candy store, over near Seventy-first Street. That's where I hang out. Come kill me over there. I'll be waitin' for you."

With that, they left. After a moment, the man stood, his face red, blood trickling from his mouth.

Nunzio, the owner of the pizzeria, shrugged from behind the counter. "I tried to warn you, buddy. Nobody fucks with that kid. Nobody."

The man glared at Nunzio, then turned and reeled out the door, turning right and stumbling around the corner and down Seventieth Street.

The huge, white-faced clock on the pizzeria wall read eight fifty-six.

Ben's candy store, one block south of Vinny's, was an illuminated oasis on an otherwise darkened stretch of Thirteenth Avenue. The other stores, depending on their specialties, had either closed early for the traditional Italian-American Columbus Day observance or had been closed the entire day. The streets were empty, with only the occasional passing of a vehicle or a rumbling city bus. Periodically, a car would veer into the bus stop in front of Ben's and someone would jump out and run in for the late edition of the *Daily News,* a *Daily Racing Form,* cigarettes, or a container of milk.

Gary Tucci, Jimmy "Coke" Cocca, and Andy Hermann made their way along the darkened avenue. As they had done since childhood, Coke and Andy shared by association in Tucci's short, sweet, and devastating victory in a fight he had neither sought nor encouraged. Their youthful invincibility made them oblivious to the chilling wind, their laughter echoing through the concrete and glass, steel and asphalt canyon they knew so well.

It was easy enough, then, for the brooding man to surprise them, when, some brief moments later, they emerged from Ben's, newspapers in hand, still high on the night's adventure.

The man leapt from the shadows of the Majestic Gift and Lamp Shop, the storefront to the right of Ben's, a rifle grasped tightly in his hands.

It was Coke who reacted first. The sight of the angry man sent Coke back in time, back to the darkened, narrow streets of the slums of Baghdad, and back further still to his training days at the Marine base on Parris Island.

Coke sprang forward, grabbing the rifle barrel, twisting it violently downward and to his left.

"Gun!" he shouted, then again, "Gun!"

But it wasn't a trained, armed, and deadly Marine comrade who responded to his call, it was Gary Tucci, now frightened and confused, and driven not by training and experience but by instinct, terror, and an innate courage. Tucci stepped forward, also to Coke's left, and reached out for the man.

They were all stunned by the flash. It appeared to come out of nowhere, illuminating the darkened street and turning the scene into a surreal, sharply shadowed false daylight. Then came the sound. A deafening, ear-ringing release of energy and black powder exploding. Then, almost simultaneously, a lesser bang sounded from across the broad avenue as the darkened fluorescent bakery sign shattered under the ricocheting bullet.

The scene froze for an instant before Tucci collapsed, falling to the pavement like a puppet with severed strings. Then, like a resumed video recording, the scene began to play itself out once again.

Startled by the shot, Coke had let his hold on the weapon's barrel weaken, and the shooter pulled it from his grasp. All three men looked downward to the fallen Tucci. He looked up at them, one to the other, a calm, detached look on his face. Then they followed his dropping gaze.

Tucci's right foot lay shoeless, his black Nike having been blown from it, landing in the gutter twenty feet away. The dark gray athletic sock he wore was pushed inward into a gaping, black hole rimmed with white froth, where his instep had once been. As they watched, the hole suddenly welled with thick, rich-looking blood. It was the color of dark burgundy wine and pulsated in rhythm with his increasing heartbeat. Then came Tucci's scream, the gut-wrenching, ear-shattering howl of unbearable agony.

The sound shattered the brief stillness of the scene, once again seemingly freed from its eerie pause mode. The shooter, now trembling and panic-stricken, backed away. Andy Hermann dropped to his knees, reaching out to Tucci, watching the blood overflow and bubble out onto the dirty sidewalk. Jimmy Coke, rage now roaring in his brain, turned to the shooter.

The man backed farther away, his eyes wild, his finger jerking on the trigger of the rifle pointed at Coke's chest. The weapon, a bolt action Winchester .30–06, did not fire; the bolt had not been recharged.

The man then turned and ran diagonally across the avenue to the far sidewalk and back toward Seventieth Street. A moment later, a reanimated Coke took off after him, his mind whirling, his fingers twitching, searching for the reassuring feel of his Marine Corps M-16 1A automatic weapon.

Reaching the halfway point to Seventieth Street, the man, still running, pulled furiously on the bolt of the weapon, chambering a second round. He then spun to face his pursuer, raising the weapon.

Coke, now crashing back to the reality of the situation, suddenly confronted his danger. He threw himself to the left, behind a black Buick parked at the curb, waiting for the shot to sound.

But the shot never came. When, after a moment, he peered around the right quarter-panel of the Buick, he saw the man turning the corner of Seventieth Street, heading east toward Fourteenth Avenue. After another few seconds, a dark pickup truck roared out from Seventieth Street, turning right onto Thirteenth Avenue and disappearing into the night, its engine straining under full throttle.

Coke twisted around, pressing his back into the reassuring bulk of the Buick. Listening to his heart pound, his head fell forward, dangling on suddenly weakened neck muscles. As his body undertook the familiar, quaking reaction to the subsiding adrenaline rush, his eyes welled.

He sat there for a time, making no effort to stop the tears.

AT NINE-TWENTY p.m., Rizzo sat behind the wheel of the Impala jotting notes into his pad, Priscilla sitting beside him, the car parked before a large apartment house on Sixteenth Avenue. They had just come from the small apartment of one Bruce Jacoby. Rizzo had been developing Jacoby as the prime suspect in a series of indecent exposure incidents that took place near the local high school.

"So," Priscilla said. "You figure this guy for the perp?"

Rizzo responded without looking up. "Yeah. No doubt. That's why he lawyered up so fast." He finished his notes, then reached to start the engine. "When his lawyer comes into the squad room tomorrow, we'll settle this. Guy's guilty as sin."

At that moment, the Motorola beside Priscilla squawked to life.

"Dispatch, six-two one seven, copy?" a female voice sounded in singsong cadence.

"That's us," Rizzo said.

Priscilla raised the radio to her mouth. "Six-two one seven dispatch, copy, go."

"Six-two one seven, see the detective eye-eff-oh seven-one oh-six, say again, seven-one oh-six one-three avenue, copy?"

Priscilla reached across the seat and took Rizzo's notepad, bracing it against her leg and slipping a Bic from her pocket.

"Dispatch, one-seven to seven-one-oh-six, one-three avenue," she replied, jotting the address. "What's the job, copy?"

"One-seven, male white shot, nonfatal. See the detective, k?"

"Ten-four dispatch, one-seven out, k?"

"Ten-four."

Rizzo pulled the car away from the curb and headed for Thirteenth Avenue. "What was that location?" he asked.

"In front of Seventy-one-oh-six Thirteenth," Priscilla said. "See the detective."

"That's interesting," he said. "Why see the detective? Why not see the uniform or the citizen or whoever? If there's a bull there already, whadda they need with us? The call wasn't to aid investigation, it was a response to incident."

Priscilla shrugged. "Don't know, Partner, I'm new at this, remember?"

Approaching Seventy-first Street, Rizzo slowed the car and carefully negotiated the thin crowd of onlookers, police cars, and uniformed officers milling in and around the expanse of Thirteenth Avenue. Nearing the sidewalk area cordoned off with yellow crime scene tape, he double parked the Chevy and shut it down.

Rizzo and Jackson approached a short, squat man wearing a weathered overcoat, a blue and gold detective badge dangling upside down from the lapel.

"Hello, Anthony," Rizzo said to the man. "How you doing tonight?"

Detective Anthony Sastone smiled. "Fine, Joe. How about you?"

"Good. This here is my new partner, Priscilla Jackson. Cil, Anthony Sastone, Six-Eight squad. Our neighbor."

They shook, then Rizzo turned to the business at hand.

"Tell me," he said to Sastone.

"Male white, twenty-four, gets into a fight with the perp over at Vinny's on Seventieth Street. The vic wins. Perp says, 'I'm gonna kill you.' Our hero says, 'Well, I'll be on the corner, hanging out by the candy store. Come and kill me there.' Two minutes later, the perp shows up with a rifle. There's a struggle, gun goes off, blows half the guy's foot off. Look here, see? Round went right through his foot and into the sidewalk, ricochetin' across the street and blowing out the storefront fluorescent on the bakery. I took a look. Bullet may be lodged in the mortar between the bricks. Probably beat to hell, though. No ballistic value, other than maybe caliber."

Rizzo looked down at the sidewalk. A chunk of cement had been pulverized, leaving a gaping hole the size of a paddle ball, blood splattered all around it. Puddles of blood sat at the bottom of the hole and on the rough cement surrounding the area of impact.

Rizzo looked up to Sastone. "I got a question, Anthony," he said, his voice neutral.

"Shoot," Sastone answered, with a sly smile.

"Why do I care about this? I'm standing on the west side of the avenue. This is Six-Eight territory." He pointed over Priscilla's shoulder to the other side of Thirteenth. "That's the Six-Two over there. Feel free to cross over and dig that bullet out, *paesan*. I'm always willing to cooperate."

Sastone laughed. "Yeah, I figured there might be an issue. When I rolled up and got the story from the Six-Eight uniform, I got on the horn. My boss called your boss. You ever hear the term 'continuous stream,' Joe?"

Rizzo nodded and reached for his cigarettes. "Yes," he said, "yes, I have. It means if shit flows across the street and pools up, some lazy cop might want me to walk over and step in it."

Again Sastone laughed. "The bosses, Joe. They decided between them. Your shift commander agreed: the assault which resulted in the shooting was part of one criminal action, and that action started over there"—he reached around Rizzo and pointed one block north to Vinny's Pizzeria—"on the *east* side. The Six-Two side."

Rizzo lit a cigarette and turned to Priscilla. "Do me a favor," he said. "Call the house and check this out."

"Okay," she said, reaching for her cell and walking away to make the call.

"What," Sastone said in mock disbelief, "you don't believe me?"

Rizzo laughed. "Well, you know, Anthony, I been a cop over twenty-six years and not once in all that time has another cop ever lied to me. I'm figurin' the law of averages gotta catch up sometime. Maybe tonight's the night."

"Okay," Sastone said with a shrug. "Knock yourself out. But just so you know, the Six-Two sector is holding the two eyeballs over there. The vic got bussed to Lutheran Hospital. He lost a lot of blood, but he should be okay. His waltzin' days may be over, though."

Rizzo looked again at the bloody hole in the concrete. "That there hole didn't get punched by a twenty-two, that's for sure."

Sastone shook his head. "No. More like a thirty-oh-six, at least."

Rizzo scanned the scene. "Find any shell casing?"

"No. Time the sector got here, the place was crawlin' with citizens. Lotsa kids, too. Casing coulda got grabbed for a souvenir. If there even was a casing, that is. Only semiautomatics throw casings after a single shot, and I haven't ID'd the weapon yet."

"You talk to the witnesses?" Rizzo asked.

"Just a little. I figured this for a Six-Two case, Joe. Didn't want to contaminate the investigation for you."

Rizzo grunted and blew smoke at Sastone. "Very considerate of you," he said.

Priscilla returned to Rizzo's side.

"Boss says it's ours," she said, her face expressionless.

Rizzo shrugged. "Okay. Let's do it, then. Anthony, you get a description of the shooter?"

"Yeah," Sastone answered, pulling out his notepad and flipping it open. "Male white, about forty, six feet even, 'bout one-ninety. Brown hair, short. Wearing a plain dark jacket and camouflage fatigue pants with dark brown boots."

Rizzo frowned, reaching absentmindedly to rub at a slight eye twitch. "What kinda fatigues?" he asked.

"Military fatigues," Sastone said.

Rizzo shook his head and flipped the Chesterfield into the street. "No shit?" he said. "Military fatigues? I thought sure theyda been prom fatigues."

Sastone furrowed his brow. "What?" he asked.

"Were they brown and tan desert fatigues or green and black jungle fatigues?"

Sastone shrugged. "I don't know. What's the fuckin' difference? The guy had on fatigues. Me, I was in the Navy. We dressed like gentlemen."

"Okay, Anthony. Thanks. I'll take it from here. Leave the two Six-Eight sectors here. I can use the help, okay? Professional courtesy."

Sastone nodded. "No problem. Glad to help. You want my notes?"

Rizzo shook his head. "I'll make my own. See you 'round." He turned to Priscilla. "Let's go and talk to the two eyeballs. Call the house again, see if they can send some bodies over here. Watch where you step, there's blood behind you."

Rizzo crossed the street to the blue-and-white Six-Two radio car, idling softly, its light bar flashing white and red. He approached the uniform leaning against its front fender.

"Hey, Will," he said. "I need a minute with the witnesses."

The cop shrugged. "Go ahead, Joe. I got nowhere to go."

Rizzo climbed in behind the wheel, turning to face the two men in the rear seat. They appeared in their mid-twenties, casually dressed and nervous, a distinct odor of alcohol on their breath.

"I'm Detective Sergeant Rizzo," he said. "Who are you?"

"I'm Jimmy Cocca," one said.

"Andy Hermann," said the other.

"Tell me what happened. Start from the beginning, the pizza store or whenever this thing got started. One at a time."

Rizzo looked them over and decided on Cocca. "You start," he said, pointing at the man. "And you. Don't interrupt him. Let him tell me what he saw, then you can tell me what you saw. It might not be the same thing."

"Okay," Hermann said.

"And Jimmy. Don't get dramatic. Just stay calm and tell me, okay?"

"Okay," Jimmy answered.

Rizzo smiled, trying to relax the young man. "What do they call you, Jimmy?" he asked. "Your buddies, I mean."

The man smiled weakly. "Coke," he said. "They call me Jimmy Coke. But not causa the drug or nothin'. Because of my name, Cocca. So Jimmy Coke."

"Yeah," Rizzo said. "I figured. Okay, Coke. Tell me."

At that moment, Priscilla climbed into the passenger seat.

"Shift boss is sending another radio car. When Schoenfeld and Rossi finish up what they're doing, they'll come by and help."

"Cil, it'd be nice for you to sit in on this interview, but I need you on the street till Schoenfeld gets here. Get the uniforms organized. Canvass the crowd, see if anybody knows anything. Most of 'em probably live in the apartments above the storefronts. Maybe somebody was lookin' out the window and saw something. Get plate numbers on all the cars parked within a block of that pizza place. And notify CSU. I'd like somebody to dig that bullet outta the wall and take some shots of that hole in the sidewalk."

"Okay, Joe. I'm on it." Priscilla climbed from the car.

Rizzo then turned back to Coke. "Go ahead. Tell me."

When the man was done, Andy Hermann gave his version. It was the same as Coke's.

"So neither of you ever saw the shooter before Vinny's, right? He was a stranger to you both?"

"Yeah."

"Never saw the guy before."

Rizzo turned to Coke. "And the rifle was a bolt action?"

"Yes," Coke answered. "Absolutely."

Rizzo nodded. Priscilla returned then, climbing back into the passenger seat of the radio car.

"Nobody else coming forward," she reported. "CSU said either them or Borough Recovery will be here by midnight. Uniforms are working the license plates. Still no Schoenfeld or Rossi."

Rizzo turned back to the men in the rear seat. He addressed Coke. "We'll call you chasin' the guy heroic, Coke," he said. "But somebody else might call it a little dumb."

Coke shrugged, but remained silent.

Rizzo continued. "Where exactly was the guy when you saw him jack that fresh round into the chamber?"

Coke thought a moment before responding. "I ducked behind a parked black Buick. He was maybe three cars up from me."

Rizzo nodded. "Okay. You guys are almost done here. Tomorrow come down to the precinct. Bath and Bay Twenty-second Street. There'll be a steno to take your statements."

"Can we go see Gary at the hospital?" Hermann asked.

"Not tonight," Rizzo said. "We need to talk to him, that'll be enough for him. Let him get some rest. Visit tomorrow if he's still there. Who knows, they might discharge him tonight."

Cocca shook his head. "No way, man. I did two tours in Iraq, I seen shit like this. His foot is fucked; they got to operate on it." He glanced at Priscilla. "'Scuse the language," he said.

She smiled at him. "I think I heard the words before," she said easily.

"Wait here, guys," Rizzo said. "Let me talk to my partner a minute. Then the officers will drive you both home. Remember, tomorrow, the precinct. Come at twelve noon. Okay?"

They nodded. "Sure," Cocca said. "We'll be there."

Rizzo and Priscilla stepped out of the car. Rizzo led her out of earshot of the witnesses.

"Do me a favor, Cil. Get all their contact info. Take their addresses off their ID's or licenses or whatever, get their work locations and phones, home phones and cell numbers, okay?"

"Sure. What's next?"

"Well, I gotta fill you in on the details. We need to talk to the pizza guy and take a look around up there. Then we'll go to the hospital and talk to this Gary Tucci. We've got a good description of the shooter from Coke and Hermann, but Tucci may have more to add. Plus, who knows? By tomorrow, the guy could be dead from a staph bug he picks up in the ER. So we better go tonight. And I need Schoenfeld and Rossi to canvass Seventieth Street. I'll tell you why later. For now, just get that contact info. Then meet me up at that pizza joint. Tell all the uniforms to send Schoenfeld over to me when he shows up."

"Yassa, boss," Priscilla said, rolling her eyes at him.

Rizzo laughed. "Hey, that's why they call it 'detective third grade.' Get goin'."

She smiled and walked away.

Rizzo turned and headed toward the pizzeria, scanning the street as he went. When he reached the corner, he saw two Six-Eight uniforms jotting down license plate numbers of parked cars. He approached the nearest one and glanced at her name tag.

"Hey, O'Toole, how you doing?" Rizzo asked.

The cop looked up from her memo book, took in the gold shield on its silver chain dangling from Rizzo's neck.

"Peachy," she said with a smile. "And you, Sarge?"

Rizzo returned the smile. "Yeah," he said. "Me, too. Peachy. Listen, you got batteries in that flashlight on your belt? Do me a favor. Somewhere a couple a cars north of that black Buick over there, the shooter bolted the rifle to chamber a round. Take a guy or two with you and see if you can find a spent shell casing. If you do, leave it where it is and call me. I'll be in the pizza joint."

She flipped her memo book closed and reached behind her back, stuffing it into a rear pocket.

"Sure, Sarge, no problem." She turned and looked over her shoulder, calling to her partner. "Hey, Ricky, c'mere. I need you, baby."

Rizzo walked away, toward the pizzeria, thoughts of his daughter, Carol, entering his mind. The sight of Detectives Schoenfeld and Rossi rolling to a stop next to him in their black Impala turned his attention back to business.

"Hey, guys," he said through the open passenger window. "Thanks for coming up."

Detective Nick Rossi smiled, his pearly white teeth and deep blue eyes twinkling with the reflected neon of the nearby pizzeria.

"No problem, Joe," he said. "Just keep that mullenyom partner of yours on a leash. I don't think she likes me."

Rizzo laughed. "Now what broad wouldn't like you, Nick? With that shiny black hair and all."

Detective Morris Schoenfeld leaned over from the driver's seat. "Whaddya need, Joe?" he asked. "I think we got the picture here—fight inside there, loser gets a gun, shoots winner. I'd like to get started so we can wrap it by midnight, okay?"

Rizzo nodded. "Okay, short and sweet. Shooter had a vehicle on Seventieth Street, dark-colored pickup, no plate, no make. I need a house-to-house for witnesses. We got plenty of uniforms here, use them to help out. We need to get on it while people are still awake. It's bedtime soon. Okay?"

Rossi nodded. "Okay," he said. "What else?"

"CSU or Borough Evidence Recovery will be here by midnight. Make sure a blue-and-white sits on the scene till they show. I'm gonna talk to the pizza guy. I got two uniforms lookin' for a shell casing. If they find it, tell CSU I need photos, then bag it for prints. That oughta do it."

With that Priscilla walked up, Rossi's Friday come-on to her still fresh in her mind. She smiled at him, her face radiating beauty. "Hiya, lover boy," she said in a schoolgirl cadence. "How's it hangin' tonight, baby?"

Rizzo's and Schoenfeld's laughter was countered by Rossi's raspberry.

"Jesus Christ," he muttered, his head shaking.

Rizzo and Priscilla turned and headed into the pizza place, still laughing.

As they entered, the owner-operator of Vinny's Pizzeria greeted them from behind the counter.

With a glance at Priscilla, he swung his eyes to Rizzo and smiled broadly, eyeing the gold detective-sergeant badge.

"Hey, Sarge," he said. "I been waitin' for you guys to show; otherwise, I'da closed up by now."

Priscilla looked at the wall clock. "It isn't even ten-thirty yet," she said.

"She worked Manhattan, Nunzio," Rizzo said by way of explanation. "The Upper East Side, no less." Now he turned to Priscilla and continued. "This isn't like the city, Cil. Here, this time of year, the streets are empty. 'Cept for pockets of teenagers hangin' out here and there. And once the winter sets in and it gets dark by four-thirty, it's like a ghost town. These are workin' people live here, punching time clocks. They come home from work, eat dinner, do some chores, watch TV, then go to bed. Right, Nunzio?"

The man nodded. "Yep. That's about it. 'Cept, maybe in the spring and summertime. Then it's different."

The man waved a hand at Rizzo. "Go," he said. "Go sit down, Joe. I got some slices warming in the oven. On the house, no problem. Sit, I'll bring them over. What are ya drinking?"

"Sprite for me, thanks. Cil?"

She thought a moment. "You got bottled water?"

Nunzio nodded happily. "I got everything, Detective, whatever you want."

"The witness told me the perp was seated in a booth," Rizzo said to him. "Which one? Maybe we can lift some prints from it."

"Sorry, Joe," Nunzio said sheepishly. "I already wiped it clean. After the guy left, I was closin' down, cleaning up. So . . . I wiped it down with Lysol."

"Okay," Rizzo said. "I understand, no big deal." Then he and Priscilla moved to a rear booth in the empty dining area.

"So it looks like you know this guy Nunzio," Priscilla said.

Rizzo shrugged. "All the Six-Two cops know him. Six-Eight, too, since Thirteenth Avenue is the precinct dividin' line. He's a good guy, and he makes the best pizza around. I get takeout pies for me and Jen and the girls. I live about twelve blocks from here, in the Six-Eight."

Nunzio approached the table, a large plastic cup of soda for Rizzo and a bottle of Poland Spring for Priscilla. He placed the drinks on the Formica table and moved away quickly, returning with a round metal tray and four smoking slices of Sicilian pizza on paper plates. He took a seat next to Rizzo.

"So," he asked, his voice somber. "How's the kid that got shot?"

Rizzo reached to the tray and took a plate. "I don't know. Didn't sound fatal but it didn't sound too good, either. I hear he lost a lot of his foot. We'll see."

Nunzio compressed his lips and shook his head, anger touching at his eyes.

"Crazy son of a bitch who shot him, he ever comes in here again, I got somethin' for him, believe me. He likes to fuck with guns? I got somethin' for him."

Rizzo blew on the hot pizza and smiled. "Don't say nothin' stupid now, Nunz," he said.

The man bobbed his head. "I said what I hadda say. Let him show his face in here again. Let him."

"Ever see him before tonight, Nunzio?" Rizzo asked.

"Sure. Guy's been in here five, six times this year alone. Always the same, always all pissed off. Don't even enjoy my pie, just wolfs it down like a *gafone*. I swear you can smell the acid in this prick's stomach, he's wound so tight." Then he glanced sheepishly at Priscilla, his face beginning to redden. "I'm sorry, Priscilla, excuse my French."

Priscilla smiled, chewing her first bite. "Hmmm," she purred. "This is some good fuckin' pizza, Nunzio."

Nunzio's flush deepened, and he turned back to Rizzo. "But," he said, "I gotta tell you, Joe, I know squat about the guy. No name, nothin'. Tonight, he was loaded, like most times he's been in here. Shit, I could smell the booze on 'im from way over there, by the friggin' chopped garlic."

Rizzo smiled. "The three kids were a little fired up, too, wouldn't you say?" he asked.

Nunzio shook his head sharply. "Few beers, Joe, couple a beers. For the holiday. I know those kids. They grew up in here eatin' my pies. They're good kids. And Gary, the one got shot, he coulda been a middleweight contender. Fastest hands I ever seen. Semifinaled the Golden Gloves when he was seventeen, won the next year. Even the freakin' nig . . . black guys couldn't lay a glove on him."

He glanced again at Priscilla. She smiled tightly and twisted the cap off her water bottle. "How 'bout the spics, Nunzio?" she asked coldly. "They have any better luck?"

Again, Nunzio reddened, his eyes darting away from Priscilla's. Rizzo reached out a hand, patting him gently on the face. "I got an idea, Nunz," he said. "Knock off the narrative. I'll ask the questions, you give the answers. You know, like in the movies."

Nunzio nodded. "Okay," he said sheepishly. "That sounds like a good idea."

When they had finished with the man, Rizzo and Jackson left, meeting up with Officer O'Toole at the door.

"Just coming to get you, Sarge," she said. "We found that casing."

Rizzo lit up. "Show me," he said.

The brass casing lay in the gutter, nestled among cigarette butts and scraps of paper. Using O'Toole's flashlight, Rizzo bent to the casing and examined it.

"Thirty-oh-six," he said. "Like Sastone figured."

He stood and brushed grit from his pants leg. "Thanks, O'Toole, good work. Tape off the area. When forensics shows, let them get some pictures and bag the shell."

The cop, fair-skinned and twenty-something, smiled.

"You got it, boss," she said.

Later, following Rizzo's directions, Priscilla drove the Impala toward the Lutheran Medical Center.

"You may hear an occasional 'nigger' slip out here and there, Cil," he said. "Kinda comes with the local territory."

"Yeah," she said without anger, "I know. Territory keeps gettin' smaller, though. So that's a good thing."

"Yeah," Rizzo said absently. "Anyway, you got any thoughts on this case, Cil?"

She shrugged. "Shooter knows Vinny's, been there a few times before. Chances are he lives local somewhere. Nunzio didn't remember ever seeing the guy pull up in a vehicle, so maybe he lives in walking distance. The guy likes to booze it up, we oughta check out the local bars. See where he was drinking tonight. How many guys coulda been running around wearing fatigue pants on Columbus Day?"

Rizzo pursed his lips. "Pretty good," he said. "And those fatigues—ever since Bush the Elder sent Stormin' Norman and the boys and girls into Kuwait, the civilian fashion statement of choice has been brown-and-tan desert fatigues. The green-and-black jungle fatigues are from the old Vietnam days. But our shooter, according to the witnesses, he goes green and black."

"Maybe he's some bugged-out Viet vet," she said.

"Too young for that," Rizzo said. "Everybody who saw him pegs him about forty."

Priscilla shrugged. "So he's a military buff. Likes to dress the part, show what a hard-case dude he is."

"Not likely," Rizzo said.

Priscilla glanced at his profile as she drove.

"Why's that?" she asked.

"Well," Rizzo began, "it don't add up like that. Guy had on a winter Thinsulate civilian jacket over the fatigue pants, and he was wearing dark brown boots. A wannabe army guy in jungle gear would have on a military jacket and matching black combat boots. So it don't add up."

They drove in silence for a few moments.

"Too bad Nunzio didn't see him tear-ass away in that pickup," Priscilla said after a time.

Rizzo nodded, scanning his notes as he answered. "Yeah, well, everybody has to hit the head once in a while. Bad timing for us."

Priscilla turned her lips down. "I hope that cracker washed his fuckin' hands before he kneaded the pizza dough I just ate," she said distastefully.

"A-fuckin'-men," Rizzo said, laughing.

"IS IT my imagination," Rizzo asked Priscilla, "or was that nurse comin' on to you?"

Having been informed at the hospital that Gary Tucci was in surgery and could not be interviewed until Tuesday evening at the earliest, Rizzo and Priscilla returned to the Impala.

Priscilla unlocked the driver's side door and climbed in. "You mean that little redhead with the cleavage? Bet your ass, honey."

Rizzo shook his head. "Bad enough when I was workin' with Mike I was the invisible man. Now with you, too?"

Priscilla laughed as she started the engine. "Hey, Joe, I am *smokin'*. Ain't you noticed yet?"

"Yeah, I noticed. Are there even any straight women left, for Christ's sake?"

"Don't worry, Joe, there's plenty. More than enough to keep the species going."

Now it was Rizzo who laughed. "Well, ain't that a black lining to a silver cloud. But how'd she know? The nurse, I mean? You give her the secret handshake? Is it like that *Star Trek* guy with the fingers? What?"

"You get a vibe, sometimes. If you're interested, you put out a feeler. If you don't get ignored, you flirt a little. That's all that just happened, Joe, so don't start hyperventilatin' on me."

"Hey, it don't bother me," Rizzo said. "A nurse or two hit on me here and there. Back in the day."

Priscilla smiled broadly. "Is that right? So, you tellin' me that Florence Nightingale chick was straight? That what you sayin'?"

"Just look where you're going, wiseass. More than a few drunks out here tonight." He glanced at his Timex. "Let's go back to the scene, check in with Schoenfeld and Rossi. I wanna make sure that shell casing is photoed and bagged for prints. CSU'll do it for sure, but if it's Borough, who knows?"

They rode in silence, Rizzo deep in thought. After a while, he said absentmindedly, "That nurse, that redhead. She was pretty hot-looking."

Priscilla shrugged. "My trolling days are over. Me and Karen for-evah and evah."

"That's good, Cil."

"But I gotta tell you, it ain't gonna be easy. This cop gig is a babe magnet. It's what hooked Karen on me. At first, anyway. Now she gets all righteous and concerned and tells me to quit and hook up with one of her old man's business dudes, but, deep down, she really gets off on the cop thing."

Rizzo laughed. "I think Jen did, too, back when I was in the bag, all blue and shiny."

"See?" Priscilla said. "It's all the same shit. All the same."

"That reminds me," Rizzo said. "I got a speech I give all my new young partners. Seems like only yesterday I was givin' it to Mike."

Priscilla glanced at him quickly, negotiating a stop sign at the same time.

"Is it the 'You gotta have options' bullshit Mike told me about? Some crap you're always telling your kids?"

"No, not that one. And it's not crap: it's gospel."

"Okay. What then?"

"It's my other speech," Rizzo said. "I got three single young daughters. I need you to steer clear of them. And don't get your panties all twisted up," he interjected quickly when Priscilla's head snapped around and her eyes burned into his face. "Relax. It's got nothin' to do with you being gay. Or friggin' black, either. Although, I gotta say, either one would be enough to kill my mother."

Priscilla shook her anger away. "Are they gay?" she asked in tight tones. "Your girls?"

"Not that I'm aware of," he said.

Now color came to her face beneath the cafe-au-lait skin tone. "Then what the fuck, Joe? You think I got some magic dust I sprinkle on their asses to switch 'em over?"

He chuckled. "Whadda I know? But it don't matter—like I said, I tell all my partners the same thing. Ask Mike if you don't believe me. I just don't want any cop sons-in-law. Guy cops, lesbian cops, cops from outer space, it don't matter, no friggin' cops. Period."

Priscilla slapped lightly at the wheel of the Chevy.

"Another one! Another fuckin' cop bigot like Karen's mother."

Rizzo smiled and opened the glove compartment, digging out an unopened pack of cigarettes.

"So sue me," he said, tearing at the cellophane.

CHAPTER THREE

THE FOLLOWING MORNING, Rizzo sat at his kitchen table, poking absently at a bowl of cornflakes. He had a busy day ahead: lunch at one with his ex-partner Mike McQueen, then another four-to-twelve night tour with Priscilla. The witnesses to the shooting—Cocca, Hermann, and Nunzio—would give their sworn statements at noon to the police administrative aide and day tour detectives at the Six-Two. The alleged flasher, Bruce Jacoby, might or might not show up at four, with or without his lawyer, and Rizzo and Jackson still needed to get to Lutheran to interview the shooting victim, Gary Tucci, and to visit the local bars as Priscilla suggested. Rizzo also had to consider another neighborhood canvass for additional witnesses or someone who could I.D. the dark pickup truck in which the shooter had fled.

"Plus follow up on that shell casing," he muttered aloud.

"Talking to yourself, Daddy?" he heard.

Turning, he saw his middle daughter, Jessica, enter the kitchen, a small book bag in her hand. Like her mother, Jessica stood five feet eight inches tall, lean with dark brown eyes, and long, thick brown hair.

"Hey, honey," he said. "Home already?"

She shrugged and dropped the bag beside the table, bending to kiss Rizzo's forehead and sighing.

"They canceled my ten-fifteen. The professor was out soul searching, no doubt, and he couldn't make it. I only have the two classes on Tuesdays, so here I am." Twenty-one-year-old Jessica was in her senior year, commuting to and from her parents' Brooklyn home to Manhattan's Hunter College.

Rizzo used his foot to push a chair back from the table.

"My good luck," he said. "I get to see you a little." He thrust his jaw toward the chair. "Sit," he said. "You want coffee? I just made it."

Jessica dropped into the seat and smiled at her father. "Are you serious? It's almost eleven o'clock, Daddy, I'm already swimming in Starbucks."

"Yeah," he said. "Starbucks—aka Maxwell House, only four bucks a cup."

"I know, Daddy," she said, rolling her eyes.

"Actually," Rizzo said, growing serious, "it's good you're here. I really need to talk to you."

"Oh?" she asked. "'Bout what?"

"About your sister," he said.

Jessica wrinkled her brow. "Okay. Which sister?"

"Your kid sister, Carol. I need you to talk to her."

"You want me to give her the birds and the bees talk, Daddy?" she asked. "'Cause I hate to break it to you . . ."

Rizzo shook his head. "No—birds and bees I can handle myself," he said.

"Oh, really," she answered, laughing. "Since when?"

Rizzo looked puzzled as he replied. "Whaddya talkin' about? I raised three daughters, didn't I?"

"Yes, but none of us ever heard any s-e-x talk from you."

"Well, maybe. But I still handled it. I had your mother tell you."

Jessica's laughter returned. "And that's 'handling' it?" she asked.

"Sure," he said. "It worked, didn't it? You all know where the parts go, don't you?"

"Yes, Daddy," Jessica said, nodding solemnly. "Thank you."

"Okay," he said with a grin.

"So, what's up with Carol?" Jessica asked, leaning forward in her seat. "Is it still this police thing?"

Rizzo nodded. "Exactly. The test is comin' up very soon, and personnel just sent out a fax saying that expedited hiring will get

33

under way in record time. That means by this time next year, Carol could have graduated from the academy already."

"Oh," Jessica said, frowning. "Does Mom know about this? The last she and I spoke about it, Mom figured we were a year away from Carol even getting canvassed to be hired."

Rizzo answered, shaking his head. "I haven't told your mother yet, but it's bound to start showin' up in the papers and on the news. The department wants the word to get out, that's how desperate they're gettin'. That's why Carol's able to take the test in Suffolk County, at Stony Brook. When I came on, you wanted to be a cop, you took the test at a high school in one of the five boroughs. On a Saturday morning. Now, they're even givin' the damn test in Philadelphia. Imagine? They're wavin' the Big Apple at kids a hundred miles from here. That's how hard up they are for recruits."

Jessica shook her head slowly, but didn't speak.

"You gotta talk to her, Jess. Talk some sense into her. She's just a kid, a sweet, naïve kid. She thinks she's gonna stop the madness, save the citizens. It isn't like that, Jess. Maybe it never was, but it sure as hell isn't now."

"I know, Daddy. But Carol is determined. What right do I have? If she told me what to do with my life, I wouldn't like it very much."

"Forget rights," Rizzo said sharply. "She's your sister. You want her out bumpin' heads with skells and psychos while every latte-sucking liberal is standing behind her with a camera phone protecting the dirtbags from the oppressive fascist cops? You think that's gonna work out for her?"

Jessica saw the passion in her father's eyes, and it unsettled her. She blinked nervously.

"Take it easy, Dad," she said. "Don't have a heart attack."

Rizzo leaned even closer to Jessica.

"Talk to her, Jess," he said, regaining a softer tone. "For her own good. Talk to her. She may listen to you."

Rizzo sat back in his seat and began fumbling in his pocket for the Nicorette.

"I don't think your mother and I can do it alone," he said softly. "I think this might have us beat."

Jessica frowned. She saw something in her father's eyes. Something she had never seen there before: fear.

DETECTIVE SECOND Grade Mike McQueen strolled into Pete's Downtown Restaurant and took a seat at the bar. He turned to the young female bartender and ordered a straight-up Manhattan. It was twelve forty-five: Joe Rizzo would soon meet him for lunch at the popular Brooklyn restaurant.

At six feet even, with sharp blue eyes twinkling in a well-featured face, McQueen cut an impressive figure in his new charcoal suit. The suit had been specially tailored, showing no hint of the semiautomatic pistol belted to his right hip. He sipped his drink and waited, occasionally returning the admiring smile of the pretty young bartender.

McQueen was twenty-nine years old with nearly eight years in the NYPD. He had spent the preceding year as a rookie detective third grade, partnered with Joe Rizzo at the Sixty-second Precinct.

As he drank, waiting for Rizzo, a smile touched his lips. His recent transfer to headquarters at One Police Plaza had been the result of their brief partnership. With that transfer, he was now poised to advance his career in ways that, six months earlier, he wouldn't even have dared to imagine. And he owed it all to Joe Rizzo.

As McQueen pondered his good fortune, Joe Rizzo's Camry, westbound on Old Fulton Street, turned right onto Water Street. He nosed it into the curb and shut it down. Climbing from the car, he glanced at his Timex: twelve-fifty.

The neighborhood, situated between the Brooklyn and Manhattan bridges, was now known as DUMBO, an acronym for Down Under the Manhattan Bridge Overpass. The area was at the height of transformation from a forsaken nineteenth-century industrial area to a thriving, urban hub with hulking old factories, warehouses, and liveries being converted into high-priced condominium complexes with ground-floor eateries, specialty shops, and small, artsy businesses.

As Rizzo dug out a cigarette, a last smoke before lunch, and leaned against the Camry, a brutal memory came to him about this very location. As a young patrolman, he and his partner had once discovered the decaying body of a homeless woman, her throat violently slashed, in the shadow of the historic Fireboat Station House which, back then, stood abandoned and dilapidated at the foot of Old Fulton, the flat, calm waters of the East River stretched before it.

Rizzo gazed across the fifty yards separating him from the old building, now gaily festooned in white and red and housing an old-fashioned ice cream parlor, young professionals on their lunch hour entering and exiting, the bright October sunshine washing over the scene. To the right of the Fireboat House, with its cluttered parking lot, stood the River Café. Directly across from Pete's where Mike was waiting, the stone mass of the Brooklyn Eagle building where Walt Whitman had once been a reporter stood in majestic restoration—now the condominium home to scores of young, successful Brooklynites.

Rizzo shook his head in wonder.

"Things sure have changed," he muttered aloud, making a mental note to introduce his Manhattanite partner, Priscilla, to this corner of Brooklyn, so different from her old Bed-Sty neighborhood and her new working confines of Bensonhurst's Sixty-second Precinct.

He glanced again at his watch, tossing the cigarette away, and walking toward Pete's Restaurant.

Once seated with Mike McQueen in the rear of the main dining area, Rizzo smiled across the table.

"So, Mike," he said. "You look great. How are things across the river? You playin' nice with all the other Plaza boys and girls?"

"Yeah, so far, so good. Piece a cake. When I told my lieutenant I was heading over the bridge to meet you, he told me not to hurry back. It's pretty relaxed where they have me working."

Rizzo shook his head and sipped at the double-rocks Dewar's now before him. "I'd eat the gun if they ever tied me to a friggin' computer all day. Christ." His lips turned down. "You sure you're okay with it?"

"Better than okay," McQueen answered. "I run complete profiles on everything going on anywhere in the department. I cross-reference crime stats and major cases, looking for patterns or emerging problems. Sometimes I troll for predators, pedophiles, stuff like that, but mostly I'm nosing in on everything the department's up to. It's the place to be, Joe. At least for now. They already bumped me up to second grade. That would never have happened so fast if I was still at the Six-Two, no matter how many cases we cleared."

Rizzo nodded and reached for his menu, flipping it open. "That's true enough," he said.

"In my spare time, I scan through stuff, you know, looking for something I can capitalize on. Maybe something to help me catch somebody's eye, make myself look good. And who knows, someday maybe I can move over to Policy and Planning, where I kinda always wanted to be."

"What is it, three weeks, a month you're over there, and already you're jockeyin' for position? You learn fast, kid."

McQueen drained his drink. "Well," he said, "that's how it's done. And it might not be too hard, either. Some of the guys I've met over there aren't the brightest lights, if you know what I mean."

With a grin, Rizzo replied. "Yeah, well, don't sell them short, and watch your back. Remember, they were all smart enough to hook their way into the Plaza."

"Like me, eh, Joe?" McQueen asked.

As he watched Rizzo's eyes, McQueen ran the details through his mind: how he and Rizzo had tracked down the runaway daughter of a local Brooklyn political powerhouse, City Councilman William Daily. When closeted skeletons had turned up during the investigation, Rizzo had deftly utilized them to both his and McQueen's advantage.

But the skeletons had never been buried. Instead, they were still lurking, lurking as evidence in the form of a purloined Panasonic microcassette. Lurking in the basement of Joe Rizzo's Bay Ridge home.

The tape, McQueen thought. The damn tape that could alter the lives of everyone connected to it.

"Yeah," Rizzo replied, pulling McQueen from his thoughts. "Like you. But you belong over there, Mike. You're a sharp guy, and a good cop. Maybe they aren't."

"Thanks."

Rizzo shrugged. "Don't thank me, I didn't give you your brains. If they give you half a chance over there, you'll be runnin' your own squad in a few years."

"We'll see," McQueen said. "But hopefully I'm done with the streets. Almost eight years, that's enough, and I still may try for the Academy. Teaching. I think I might like that."

"I can see you there, Mike. You look the part."

McQueen smiled. "Well, looks are important. Very political at the Plaza. They're more a bunch of frustrated yuppies than they are cops."

"We learned a little somethin' about politics with that runaway Daily kid, now didn't we, Mikey?"

McQueen's face turned more somber. "Yeah, I guess we did."

They ordered their meals, then caught up on each other's lives. Rizzo filled him in on Priscilla Jackson's first few days at the Six-Two squad. McQueen laughed when Rizzo related her first encounter with the precinct Romeo, Nick Rossi.

"That's my Cil," Mike said.

Later, with McQueen sipping a cappuccino and Rizzo dark coffee, the older cop shifted in his seat and leaned slightly forward. When he spoke, it was in a soft, low voice.

"We need to talk, kid," he said.

The change in mood wasn't lost on McQueen. He placed his cup down on the white linen tablecloth and sat back in his seat.

"Yeah. I figured," he said, his blue eyes neutral.

Rizzo smiled sadly. "Yeah. I figured you figured."

McQueen waved for the waiter.

"Another straight-up Manhattan and Dewar's, rocks," he said. He turned back to Rizzo. "About the tape. Right?"

Rizzo nodded. "Yeah. About the tape. I know we agreed to sit on it. For six months. Keep Councilman Daily's dirty little secret for a while longer. In the meantime, we'd get you over to the Plaza, courtesy of Daily and his influence."

"Yes," McQueen said, "and get you six months of phantom overtime to pad your pension."

Rizzo nodded again. "Yeah, but most importantly, to buy us some time. Distance ourselves from it all, so maybe we'd get under the radar."

The waiter arrived and placed their drinks on the table. McQueen reached for his.

"How's that overtime thing working out?" he asked.

"Good," Rizzo replied, with a shrug. "It ain't exactly phantom, but that's okay. It's more legit this way. See, Daily set it up through a flunky of his at the Plaza. They call it Confidential Administrative Overtime. Daily's man processes the O.T. personally, and it gets billed through the Homeland Security federal funding. City Finance never feels it, and it doesn't show up on the yearly Six-Two overtime stats, so no red lights start flashin' over there."

Sipping his second drink, McQueen spoke around the rim of the glass.

"Do you have to actually do anything for it?" he asked.

Rizzo answered as he reached for his Scotch. "Yeah," he said. "There's a large Middle Eastern presence on the northeast side of Bay Ridge. I live on the southwest side of the Ridge, Dyker Heights. So, every so often, I drive by the northeast. Check things out. Talk to some old-timers, the remnants of the Irish and Scandinavians that used to dominate that section of the neighborhood. And I talk to some of the Asian newcomers once in a while. Then I write out a report on the local Muslim activity and fax it over to Anti-terror Intelligence. They file it away, and everybody's happy."

"So, okay," McQueen said.

Rizzo nodded. "Well, by my count, the six months for that tape we're holdin' comes up this February. Am I right?"

McQueen shrugged. "Yeah. February."

Rizzo put down his rock glass and leaned across the table. When he spoke, McQueen could smell the liquor on his breath.

"I need an extension, kid," he said softly.

Rizzo pretended not to notice the relief that flickered briefly in the young cop's eyes. He kept his own face neutral.

"Oh," was all McQueen managed.

"Yeah," Rizzo said. "An extension. These friggin' tuition loans won't go away just because I retire, and it'll be a couple a years before Marie is a doctor and can assume the loans Jen and me owe, never mind her own. Not to mention my other two girls."

"How much time, Joe?" McQueen asked casually.

Rizzo spread his hands and cocked his head to the side. "Not sure," he said. "A year, maybe—say, next October. Then with the administrative O.T., plus my regular O.T., I can get out with enough pension to carry the loans till the girls can take 'em off my hands. And by then, we'll be far enough away from it that maybe no one will connect us to it when it does go public."

McQueen smiled. "I understand. To tell you the truth, I could use a little more time myself. I need to make some contacts, some friends at the Plaza. That way, when we put that tape into the right hands, if the shit hits the fan and Daily does realize we screwed him, at least I'll have some allies. Some cover."

Rizzo nodded. "Sounds fair, Mike. After all, I'll probably be out, my pension in hand, outta their reach. You should have some cover, too. Insurance, sorta."

McQueen drank deeply, draining the glass. "Yeah," he said. "Insurance."

Later, leaving the restaurant after they'd eaten their lunch, Rizzo walked McQueen to his shiny black Mazda, which sat parked at an expired meter on Old Fulton Street. They shook hands.

"We'll get it done," Rizzo said solemnly. "Just a little later than we figured."

McQueen, two Manhattans sitting heavily on his eyelids, smiled sadly. "Yeah," he said, "we'll get it done."

PRISCILLA JACKSON took a seat on the heavy wooden chair beside Joe Rizzo's squad room desk. She tossed the legal-size papers onto the cluttered desk surface.

"Well, Joe," she said, "I read all three."

Rizzo glanced at the sworn statements of Jimmy Cocca, Andy Hermann, and Nunzio Nottadomo, taken earlier by Six-Two personnel.

"Good," he said. "Now you know as much as I do. Good statements, weren't they? Bobby Dee might not be the best bull on the squad, but he *is* the best statement taker. He gets all the info, short and sweet."

Priscilla nodded. "I'll remember that. Now what? Do we start on that bar canvass?"

Rizzo shook his head. "Not yet." He looked at the wall clock. "It's only twenty after four. If we do it, we should start callin' around to the bars later, about eight or so. More likely to catch the same bartender who worked last night."

"Makes sense. So, what now?"

Rizzo sat back in his seat. "Well," he said, "I figure we discuss it. The shooting, I mean. I got a theory."

"Yeah, Mike told me about those theories of yours. So let's hear it."

Nodding, Rizzo said, "Okay. By the way, Mike says 'hi.' Next time I'll bring you along, he'd love to see ya."

"Good deal, Joe. So, what's the theory?"

"Okay, get comfortable," Rizzo said. "You read the statements. Whadda we got? Incident starts in a well-known, popular local pizza joint, a place the shooter's frequented over the last year. So, let's assume he lives someplace close by. He wears jungle fatigues and drives a pickup truck. Schoenfeld and Rossi and the uniforms canvassed the residents of Seventieth Street, presumably where the truck was parked while the shooter ate his pizza then got his ass kicked by Tucci. Nobody they spoke to could say anyone livin' on the block owns a pickup. This ain't Texas, not too many noncommercial pickups around. And Cocca said the truck was clean, no writing or company logo on the door. Seventieth Street is all residential, mostly two-story, one- and two-family homes. Most families been living in those houses for generations. They all know one another. If there was a truck-driving, fatigue-wearin' lunatic livin' on the block, they'd all know about it. So, we can assume the shooter *doesn't* live on Seventieth Street."

Priscilla smiled. "All this ass-umin' could be risky," she said.

"Yeah, well, it usually is, but hear me out. So, Tucci smacks the shooter around. Shooter makes his threat, the young guys leave. Nunzio says the shooter leaves the pizzeria less than a minute after the kids. Nunzio goes in the back room, starts getting ready to close, cleans the booths and hits the head. Next he knows, the radio cars are lightin' up the avenue."

Rizzo paused, taking a Nicorette from his pocket. Priscilla watched impatiently as he fumbled with the packaging.

"Damn, Joe," she said harshly, "give it here."

She took the gum and stripped the backing, pushing the Nicorette partially through the foil and handing it back to him. "Now tell me the fuckin' theory before my first pension check gets here."

Rizzo pushed the gum into his mouth.

"Guy runs out of the store and around the corner. Then, about two minutes later, he's a block south at Seventy-first Street, waiting for Tucci to come out of Ben's candy store." Rizzo paused. "Question: Where'd he get the rifle from so fast? Assumin', as we are, that he don't live right there, right on Seventieth Street."

Priscilla shrugged. "The truck, I guess. He got it out of the truck."

Rizzo pointed at her. "Bingo. Where else? Now, answer this: Who's runnin' around Brooklyn in a pickup truck wearing jungle fatigues and packing a thirty-oh-six rifle?"

Priscilla smiled slowly. "A Great White Hunter," she said.

"Once again, bingo. A hunter. While you were readin' the statements, I went online. Hunting season just got under way upstate New York, parts a Jersey, Pennsylvania, and Connecticut. Deer, mostly. Some bear. This asshole is a hunter. That explains the brown boots. He's not a military nut, probably was wearin' Timberlands. And his heavy camouflage hunting jacket woulda been too hot for the drive back home from whatever-the-fuck woods he was in, so he slipped on a lightweight civvies Thinsulate. He was probably boozin' the whole three-day weekend, maybe even in the truck driving home. Probably struck out, Bambi outsmarted him and he's coming back empty-handed. Instead of going home and smackin' the old lady around, he maybe stops local for some more booze, then figures he'll grab a couple a slices of Nunzio's Sicilian. When Tucci steps on his friggin' foot, three days of macho bullshit erupts in the guy's squirrel brain. Then the kid TKO's him without breakin' a sweat, and it's just too much. The guy feels his dick shrinkin' by the minute, so he figures he'll grab his rifle and grow some of it back. See?"

"So we start checkin' out the gun shops, hunting clubs, whatever. Right?" Priscilla asked.

He nodded. "Exactly. Guy probably needs to show photo I.D. for his ammo buys. We could get lucky. There can't be more than a half-dozen hunting joints in the whole borough, only one or two in the precinct. And if the shooter is a Bensonhurst boy like we figure, he probably shops local. Most people around here do, the whole neighborhood is like a small town."

"Yeah," Priscilla said. "A town in the freakin' Ozarks. Ten years I worked a radio car, two in the South Bronx, eight more up and down Manhattan. I saw a lot of crazy shit, Joe, but this is the first street shooting I ever seen where a rifle was the weapon of choice."

"Yeah, well, that's what got me started. That and the camou-flaged jungle fatigues. We don't get many shootings in the Six-Two, but when we do, it's usually a mob hit. Head shots, up close and personal. And always with a handgun."

"So," Priscilla said. "I guess we drop the idea of checkin' the bars."

"For now," he answered. "It's still a good idea. But I think we'll put it on hold for a while. What we need is a sketch of this guy. I want to go see the boss, D'Antonio. The Swede. Have him call over to Borough, set up the police artist with the three eyeballs and the vic. Then we can hit the gun shops *and* the bars with a sketch of the guy in our hands. See where we get lucky first."

"Okay," Priscilla said, standing. "Let's go see the boss."

Rizzo smiled. "Not just yet, Cil," he said. "I think I see a lawyer, and he's coming this way."

She turned. A tall, disheveled-looking man with sandy brown hair, a worn blue suit, and wire-rimmed glasses was nearing Rizzo's desk, a uniformed officer beside him.

"Hey, Joe," the cop said. "This guy's a lawyer. Said he needs to talk to you."

"Okay, Randy, thanks." Rizzo stood and indicated the chair Priscilla had just vacated.

"Have a seat, Counselor," he said easily. "Forgive me for not shaking hands. Germs and all."

The man's lips turned down, but he sat.

"I'm Sergeant Rizzo. My partner here, Detective Jackson."

The man cleared his throat. "Dan Webster," he said. "I'm Bruce Jacoby's attorney."

Rizzo laughed. "Well, imagine that? Daniel Webster, eh? Any 'Devil and . . .' jokes you ain't heard yet?"

Webster smiled weakly. "Probably not," he said.

"Okay then," Rizzo said, sitting down again. "What can I do for you, Mr. Webster?"

"Well, Sergeant, my client is very upset. He says you and your partner, presumably her, came to his home last night. He says you threatened him. He also said—"

Rizzo held up a hand and silenced the man. "I don't really give a fuck what he said, Counselor, and neither does *she*. Let's get down to it: Jacoby has four prior arrests for public lewdness. He copped to three of 'em, one was dropped. That vic was twelve years old and her parents didn't want her playing in the sewer with all the shit bags down at the Criminal Courthouse. I got four positive I.D.'s from victims in this case. They picked your guy out from a photo array. One of the vics is a thirty-something-year-old teacher. Spends a lotta time partying at Club Med or wherever the fuck, and she gave us some details on your guy's schlong. Sorta like an expert opinion, you could say. Plus, I already spoke to Brucie's boss. Seems like every time a daylight incident took place, Brucie was either off or out sick that day."

Here Rizzo paused and looked up at Priscilla, winking at her discreetly.

"So," he continued, "if you came here to threaten me, Counselor, my boss is across the squad room in his office. Name's Vince D'Antonio. Lieutenant Vince D'Antonio. He'll be glad to listen to your complaint, give you the telephone number of Civilian Review, in case you don't have it memorized, and then he'll throw you the fuck outta here."

Rizzo leaned in closer to the man. "But," he said, his voice turning softer, "if you came here to talk, we can do that, too."

The lawyer, a few years older than Rizzo, smiled.

"It's oddly refreshing to do business with an old-timer, Sergeant," he said. "Most of the younger cops are so tentative and nervous, they almost appear paranoid."

Rizzo laughed. "So, okay. What's the deal?"

The lawyer shifted the briefcase he held on his lap and glanced at his wristwatch.

"Well," he said, "in view of what you've said, and assuming it's accurate . . ."

Rizzo nodded. "It's accurate. You can leave here with victim statements and copies of Brucie's work timesheets, if you want 'em."

Webster sighed. "Won't be necessary. Mr. Jacoby is willing to surrender to the District Attorney's Office. I just have one favor to ask."

"Tell me," Rizzo said.

"Mr. Jacoby is particularly close to his mother. This Saturday is her seventieth birthday. He'd like to be with her to celebrate. I'm asking for a surrender date after that. Say, next Monday."

"No," Rizzo said, shaking his head. "Fuck him and his mother's birthday. He wants a favor from *me*, he surrenders to *me*. Not the D.A. Me. Me and my partner. If you can't agree to that, me and Jackson here get in the car and go grab him right now. I don't need anybody's permission to lock up some shit-head."

Rizzo smiled and leaned back in his seat. "You know, Counselor, just between us old-timers."

Webster drummed his fingers on the briefcase, weighing the options.

"And if we agree, you'll give him till Monday?"

Rizzo leaned forward, close to the lawyer. "Hell yes, Counselor," he said. "I'll even send the old gal a friggin' birthday card."

LIEUTENANT VINCE D'Antonio looked across his desk to Jackson, then Rizzo.

"And you figure this shooting warrants a police artist, Joe?" he asked.

Rizzo nodded. "Absolutely. It'd be a shame to waste these witnesses

45

here. All four of 'em saw the guy in the pizza store, under those fluo-rescents, while everybody was still relatively calm. We can get a good composite from them. Then me and Cil show the sketch around the bars and gun shops. We're sure to get a hit."

Vince D'Antonio, the fifty-three-year-old commanding officer of the Six-Two detective squad, sat back in his chair and frowned. His fair skin, blue eyes, and blond hair had earned him the nickname "Swede."

"This might be a tough sell," D'Antonio said after a moment. "After all, this isn't a murderer or a rapist or child molester. Borough Command may nix it."

Rizzo shrugged. "Try, Vince. All I'm askin'. And remember, after Tucci got shot, the guy pointed the rifle at Cocca's chest and worked the trigger. It was a bolt-action rifle, not a semi, so it didn't fire. But we can still make an attempt murder out of it. That makes *two* counts attempted murder, criminal use of a firearm, assault one, and what-ever else the D.A. can find in the penal law."

"I read the DD-fives. I know the story." D'Antonio paused and rubbed at his eye. "I noticed you didn't talk to the victim yet, this Larry Tucci kid."

"Gary," Rizzo said. "Gary Tucci."

D'Antonio nodded. "Yeah. Gary. Whatever. Before we go to Bor-ough, shouldn't you at least talk to the kid?"

"We tried. But they had to dig bullet and cement fragments out of his foot, then try to put it back together. He was under the knife when we got to Lutheran." Rizzo looked at his watch. "Doc told me we could see the kid tonight. Why don't you think about the artist request, Vince. Me and Cil will talk to the kid. We'll find out when he's getting discharged. Then the artist can sit down with all four. One-shot deal. You get us that sketch, boss, we'll get you the shooter."

After a moment, D'Antonio nodded. "Okay. Talk to the kid first. In a couple a days, if we need to, maybe we can get it done."

Rizzo pushed his chair back and stood up. Jackson did the same. "Thanks. You know I never ask you for this kinda shit. But Borough is tough. I don't have anybody left I can call over there to cash in a favor."

"Well, that's good to hear," D'Antonio said. "At least there's one place in the department that doesn't owe you."

"Yeah," Rizzo answered. "Speakin' of which, Ronnie Torres called me about twenty minutes ago. He *does* owe me, so he pushed that shell casing to the head of the line. He took a partial print from it. Not enough to run for an I.D., but he lifted enough points to call a match if we print a suspect. You get us that sketch, we put a name to the face, lock him up and print him. Then we nail him with the witnesses *and* the print. Case closed."

D'Antonio nodded and reached for his pen. Turning back to his paperwork, he spoke once more.

"Talk to the victim, Joe. Then we'll see."

"Okay, boss, thanks," Rizzo said, turning to leave.

D'Antonio looked up at them. "By the way, how are you two getting along?"

"Great," Rizzo said. "No problem."

D'Antonio turned his eyes to Priscilla. "And you, Jackson?"

"Fine, Lieutenant. Just fine," she said.

"He treating you okay?" D'Antonio asked.

"Yeah, boss, he's glad to have me. I may not be as pretty as McQueen was, but I'm a hell of a lot smarter."

CHAPTER FOUR

"SO, GARY," RIZZO ASKED in the cramped confines of Gary Tucci's hospital room. "How you doing?"

It was nine-fifteen, just after the official end of visiting hours. Rizzo and Jackson, after making their introductions, had taken seats next to the large hospital bed. Tucci, pale and drained-looking, sat propped against three pillows, his wounded foot elevated and bandaged.

The young man tried to smile. "I've had better nights, Sarge," he said. "Lot better."

"I'll bet," Rizzo said. "Then again, you had worse, too. Like for instance, last night—when this guy shot you."

Tucci nodded, his lips tightly compressed.

Rizzo shifted in his seat, pulling out his notepad.

"Why don't you tell us what happened, Gary," Priscilla asked. "Start from the beginning at the pizza place."

"Yeah," Rizzo added, clicking his Parker. "Tell us."

The young man sighed and nodded again. After a moment, he began his narrative, adding nothing Rizzo and Priscilla hadn't heard from the other witnesses. When he was finished, his eyes were moist with the memory, but no tears escaped.

Rizzo shook his head. "Sorry, kid," he said, "but sometimes shit like this happens."

The words brought a pensive look to the man's face. "Yeah," Tucci said. "Shit does happen."

"Ever see this guy before Monday?" Priscilla asked.

"No. Never."

"Do you think you can I.D. him?"

"Absolutely." Here Tucci's expression hardened. "I got close enough to 'im to clean his clock pretty friggin' good. That uppercut was always my money punch."

Now Rizzo spoke. "Yeah," he said, "Nunzio was pretty impressed. Said you knocked the guy up on his toes."

Tucci nodded. "Damned right. And you know what? I pulled that punch. I didn't wanna knock the guy's jaw up into the base of his goddamned skull. I figured he was just an asshole with too many drinks in him. If I'da known he was gonna cripple me, I'da beat him to death."

Rizzo reached out and patted Tucci on his uninjured leg. "You handled it just right. You couldn't know the guy'd come gunnin' for you."

Tucci shook his head angrily. "He *told* me he'd kill me, said it right out loud. Son of a bitch, if I believed him, I woulda pounded his face into that pizza booth."

"Okay, Gary," Priscilla said gently. "Don't be getting all wound up, popping a stitch or spiking your pressure."

"Okay," Tucci said, "okay." Then he smiled. "At least I cracked the asshole's teeth for him. I can settle for that, I guess."

"Good for you," Priscilla said.

Rizzo rubbed an eye, soothing a slight tic. "Broke his teeth?" he asked. "How you know that?"

"I heard it," Tucci said. "When I connected with that short right uppercut and slammed his mouth shut. I've heard it before, in the ring. If a guy don't bite down right on his mouthpiece and he takes a hard hit, 'specially an uppercut, he can bust a tooth or two. This guy in the pizza place, he didn't have a mouthpiece. And from the sound, I'd say he cracked more than one tooth. I hope he loses 'em, the bastard."

Rizzo sat back and turned to Priscilla.

"The kid just saved us some shoe leather, Cil," he said. Then, turning back to Tucci, added, "We just may get this guy. Lock his ass up. He may have some rough nights ahead of him in stir on Riker's Island."

Rizzo stood. "We'll see," he said.

Later, riding down in the elevator, Rizzo turned to Priscilla.

"You know," he said, "I was so impressed with your bar idea and my hunter theory, I coulda missed this."

Priscilla nodded. "Yeah. Busted teeth. The guy had to get treated for that."

"Yeah," Rizzo responded. "And if our other idea 'bout him being local is correct, then dollars to doughnuts his family dentist is from the neighborhood, too. Hell, my guy practices about two blocks from where I live. Has his office right on the lower level of his house on Tenth Avenue."

"So we track him through the dentists, not the bars or hunting leads," Priscilla said.

"Yes," Rizzo said as they reached the lobby and left the elevator. "The bar and hunter stuff, that was all theoretical. The busted teeth, that's fact. We go with fact over theory every time."

As they neared the gray Impala, parked at the side of the ambulance entrance ramp, Rizzo shook his head.

"Now I gotta go back to Vince and tell him to hold off on that artist request. And him the guy pushin' us to see the vic before running off half cocked, like a couple a half-assed rookies."

Priscilla laughed, her face beaming. "Instead a just *one* half-assed rookie, eh, Joe?" she said.

"Yeah," Rizzo answered, pointedly glancing behind his partner. "But from where I'm standin', there ain't nothin' half-assed about you, honey."

Again Priscilla laughed. "Yeah," she said. "Karen mentions that once in a while. With the same dopey grin you got now."

WHEN PRISCILLA arrived at the Six-Two at four p.m. Wednesday, she found her partner at his desk, sipping coffee from a paper cup and leafing idly through a *Daily News*.

As she reached the desk, Rizzo greeted her. She sat down. "I thought I'd find you workin' the horn to all the dentists in the precinct," she said to him. "Isn't that the excuse you used to grab some early overtime? Takin' a little break, are we?"

"Nope," Rizzo said. "Done with that. I hit gold on the eleventh call. Guy over on Twenty-fourth Avenue." He looked down at the scribbled note sitting atop a messy pile of papers on his desk. "A Dr. William Davenport, DDS. I spoke to his receptionist or secretary or whatever they call themselves. She said they had to schedule an emergency appointment for nine a.m. Tuesday morning, two hours before their regular office hours. The call came in Monday night through the doc's service."

Priscilla smiled. "Let me guess: couple of broken teeth?"

Rizzo nodded. "Yep. Two cracked molars and a chipped incisor." He paused and sipped at his coffee. "Wanna hear the best part?"

Priscilla shifted in her seat, crossing her leg. "It gets better?" she asked.

"Yeah. Guy said he broke the teeth in a little accident he had. Seems he was out huntin' all weekend, and Monday night, guess what happened?"

"A bear smacked his dumb-ass head and busted his teeth?" Priscilla asked.

"Not exactly," Rizzo said. "Seems he tripped on something and banged his jaw. On the tailgate of his pickup truck."

"Well, well."

"Yeah. And right about then, the woman I was talkin' to started getting a little uptight. Thought she was fuckin' with doctor-patient stuff, so she put the doc on. His office hours end at five today. We got an appointment with him then." Rizzo peered at Priscilla's mouth. "You got any dental issues? Maybe we can get you a free cleaning or something."

She stood up. "I'll pass, Joe. Tell you what, I have to fill out the union forms so they can switch me over from the PBA. I need to get them to the delegate's in-box today. So how far is it to this guy's office?"

"Ten minutes. You got plenty of time. I'll be waitin' here."

JUST BEFORE five, Rizzo at the wheel, the two detectives drove toward the dental office of Dr. William Davenport.

"So how's the redecorating project going?" Rizzo asked.

"Okay, I guess. Don't ask what it's gonna cost. Me and Karen coulda done the whole deal, painted all four rooms in a couple of days. For two, three hundred bucks."

"Yeah, well, I'd be happy I was you," Rizzo said. "Get the in-laws to pick up the tab, avoid all that aggravation and mess. You oughta count your blessings."

"Yeah, I know. And they can afford it, that's for sure. But this is just an apartment, not a condo. Lot a money to spend on something we don't own."

Rizzo slowed for a light and glanced over at his partner.

"What kinda building?" he asked.

"Nice old brownstone. On East Thirty-ninth off Third Avenue. We're up on the second floor with one other tenant."

Rizzo nodded, watching the traffic light. "Sounds nice. But like I tell my kids, rent is money down the drain. You gotta own something, build up the equity. The old Italians around here, the old-timers from the other side, you give 'em a choice between twenty thousand shares of some stock and a quarter acre of land, they'll go with the land every time."

"Depending on the stock, real estate might be the way to go," Priscilla said. "But right now I'm not looking to buy. Karen will never leave Manhattan, she's too into it. And anything in the city is way out of my league, dollar-wise."

"Yeah, okay," Rizzo said. "But Karen's a high-priced lawyer making big bucks. Proportion it out and buy something soon. You won't regret it."

After a moment or two of silence, Priscilla replied. "I'd rather wait. We'll do one-year leases, then see," she said.

Rizzo grunted and eased the car forward as the light changed.

"Sounds like cold feet to me," he said. "You lookin' to keep the door half open, are you?"

She shook her head. "No. Not really. But there's no hurry with anything. We can chill for a while."

"Okay, Partner," Rizzo said. "But remember this, somethin' else I tell my girls. You *buy* together, better odds you *stay* together. Financial ties have saved more marriages than Dear Abby."

"I think Dear Abby is dead, Joe," Priscilla said.

"Well, then, Dear Whoever-the-fuck. You get my point. You tangle up your finances, it's more of a commitment. So if Karen burns the toast once too often, you can't just say, 'Fuck off, Sweetheart,' and head for the door. It's like *insurance,* Cil. Believe me."

"Well, Karen and I aren't married."

Rizzo shrugged. "Civil-unioned, married, whatever. Same shit."

Priscilla shook her head. "We ain't anything yet. Just together, that's all. I get my medical and pension through the job, she gets hers through the law firm. Don't be gettin' me overcommitted here."

Rizzo glanced at her as he wove through the traffic on Twenty-fourth Avenue.

"Didn't you recently tell me you were done trollin' around? When that redheaded nurse was droolin' over you?"

"Sure," she said with a small smile. "But you never know. That's all I'm saying—you never know."

"I get it, Cil. So, you're the *guy* in this couple, eh?"

"Yeah, right," she said. "Let me explain somethin'; there *ain't* no guy. That's sorta the point, Joe. We're both female. Don't be stereotyping my situation to fit your fantasies. Didn't Mike warn you about me, Partner?"

"You bet. He warned me I'd have your shoe up my ass the first week we worked together."

Priscilla laughed with Rizzo. "You're right on schedule, *paesan,*" she said, shaking her head gently. "Right on schedule."

He slowed the car and angled in toward the curb to an open parking space. "This is it," he said, glancing at the address on the building. Then, turning to his partner, added, "Just remember what I said. About the finances. Insurance, Cil. Doesn't hurt to have some insurance."

She released her shoulder harness and reached for the door handle. "Okay, Daddy," she said. "I got it. In a year or so, they may reach me on the sergeant's list. Sooner maybe, with all those retirements comin' up. Then maybe I can swing my end of the nut a little better. So, we'll see."

Rizzo shut down the Impala's engine and nodded.

"Good," he said. "Now let's go to work."

"TO BE perfectly honest, Sergeant Rizzo, he's never been one of my favorite patients."

Dr. Davenport, a silver-haired, stout man of about sixty, gazed across his broad, neat desk at Rizzo and Jackson.

"And I can't say I'm overly surprised to have police asking about him."

Rizzo slipped his notepad from the inner pocket of his jacket.

"Why is that, Doctor?" he asked. "He ever get rough in here?"

The dentist shook his head. "No, not really. But he's . . . unpleasant. A bit nasty with my staff. He usually seems in a bad mood, angry about something. So it's no real surprise that his injuries were sustained in an altercation and not a fall, as he told me."

Priscilla leaned in slightly.

"Can you describe him, sir?" she asked. "Height, weight, age, features?"

Davenport shrugged. "Certainly," he said. He then gave a description matching those given by the witnesses and victim.

The detectives exchanged glances, then Rizzo clicked his Parker.

"What was that name and address, Doc?" he asked.

Davenport stood. "His name is Carl Jurgens," he said. "I'll need to get his folder for the rest. My assistant was supposed to put it on my desk before she left, but I guess she forgot. Give me a moment."

"Sure," Rizzo said pleasantly. "Thanks."

When the dentist left the room, Rizzo leaned over to Priscilla. "Good help is hard to find," he said.

"Be thankful you don't have that problem," she answered.

When Davenport returned, Rizzo jotted down Jurgens's home address and phone number. Then he raised his eyes to the man.

"How's he pay you, Doc?" Rizzo asked. "Cash, check, insurance?"

He quickly scanned the folder's contents.

"Well, let me see . . . my staff usually handles billing." After a moment, he found it. "Here it is," he said. "Insurance. He pays a small yearly deductible, then we accept his insurance assignment as payment in full."

"Is the insurance through an employer?" Rizzo asked.

The dentist ran his finger across the paper before him. "Yes," he said, "it appears to be."

"Who's the employer?" Priscilla asked.

"Gordon's Sporting Equipment," Davenport answered, raising his eyes to Priscilla's. "The big outdoor supplies store."

Rizzo nodded. "National chain, I think," he said. Then, shifting in his seat, he asked, "Any follow-up visits scheduled, Doc? For Jurgens?"

Again the doctor scanned the file. "Yes. He needs to come in when his permanent crowns are ready. That should be in about two weeks. But I see we have him scheduled for Monday afternoon first."

"This coming Monday?" Priscilla asked.

"Yes," Davenport said, nodding. "That would be for the chipped incisor." He looked from one detective to the next. "I need to restore it with a bonded filling."

"What time is that appointment, Doctor?" Priscilla asked.

He frowned. "I'm really not comfortable with all of this, Detective," he said. "My assistant opened the door here by telling you about his injuries, and I've added a bit to that. I'd rather not be involved any further. If you're thinking about intercepting him when he comes for his follow-up care, I'd really rather you . . ."

Rizzo raised a hand in a calming gesture. "Don't worry, Doc," he said soothingly. "That's one way we could do it, but not the only way. We've got his address and employer, you don't need to be involved any further. When he shows up Monday, treat him the same way you normally would. I wouldn't mention any of this to him, and tell your staff not to, either."

Rizzo stood, indicating the interview was over. Jackson rose also.

"'Course," Rizzo said as he reached across the desk to shake hands, "don't be surprised if he misses that Monday appointment. He may have a more pressing engagement."

★ ★ ★

THE FOLLOWING afternoon, Thursday, at four o'clock, Joe Rizzo once again worked the phone in the Six-Two detective squad room. After some fifteen minutes, he replaced the black plastic receiver on its cradle and stood. He crossed the room and sat heavily in the chair beside Priscilla's desk.

"Just got off the phone with Gordon's Sporting Equipment," he told her. "Their corporate office over in Harrisburg, Pennsylvania. You ready for this? Our man Jurgens works in the Brooklyn store. Over on Bay and Shore Parkways, right here in the precinct. Gordon's is big on hunting stuff—rifles, tents, knives, clothes, stuff like that. They're one of only two places in the whole precinct. Imagine? We'da been showing that artist sketch around, maybe showin' it to Jurgens himself and askin' him if he ever saw the guy." Rizzo laughed. "Who figured the guy *worked* in a place like that?"

Priscilla shrugged, a smile touching her lips. "This job stopped surprisin' me a long time ago," she said.

"Yeah," he said. "Sometimes I forget how it is."

"Did you call over to the place?" she asked.

Rizzo shook his head. "Didn't have to. Friggin' Nazi at corporate was all anxious to show me what good citizens these hunter types are. He went into the company payroll file. Jurgens is scheduled to work till closing tonight, nine o'clock."

"You wanna make the pinch at the store?"

He nodded. "Yeah, I think. Guy seems to be a boozer, chances are the best time to catch him sober is at work. And he'll probably be less likely to give us a hard time if he isn't tanked up. Plus, he may be embarrassed in front of his coworkers and just deny it all and come along quietly." Rizzo paused for a moment. "Yeah. I think we grab him at work," he continued. "After we bring him in, we'll print him and have my buddy Torres compare the partial from the shell casing. That should be the clincher."

"Let's go, then," Priscilla said. "We take him now, I can run him through Central Booking and still get home by midnight."

"What makes you figure I'd stick you with the paperwork?" Rizzo asked lightly.

"Shit," said Priscilla, "I never seen an old pro take a collar on straight time. We pinch the guy at ten tonight, you'd be shoving me aside for the overtime. But not this early in the tour."

"I forget sometimes, Cil," Rizzo said, "you been on the job for a while."

She nodded. "Long enough, brother. Long enough."

"You run that DMV?" Rizzo asked.

"Yeah. Jurgens has a two-year-old black Ford F-one-fifty pickup registered to his home address on Stillwell Avenue."

"Good," Rizzo said. "Another nail in his coffin. You haven't been out in the field with that gold shield for a full week yet, and you cleared two cases. You're a friggin' star already."

"*We* cleared two cases, Joe. And I think it's you who's the star."

Rizzo laughed. "Yeah. I forget that, too, sometimes. C'mon, let's go grab this asshole. I got a feelin' he's about to lose his God-given right to bear arms."

Later, as Priscilla drove the Impala toward the large shopping center that housed Gordon's Sporting Equipment, Rizzo cleared his throat and shifted in his seat. Priscilla glanced over.

"What?" she asked.

"Well," Rizzo said, wrestling a piece of Nicorette from its packaging and putting it into his mouth. "This guy Jurgens. Chances are he'll come along nice, like a good boy, but, you never know. He could decide to get stupid. Real stupid." Rizzo looked at his partner's profile, his eyes hooded.

"You up for some shit, Cil?" he asked.

She blinked hard. "What?" she asked.

Rizzo shrugged. "Just the two of us. If he wants to rock and roll, we gotta get it done. I'm just sayin' . . ."

She shot him a hard look, her dark eyes blazing.

"Yeah, Goombah, I hear what you saying. You ever ask Mike that question?"

Again, Rizzo shrugged. "Not in so many words," he said mildly.

"Any of your *male* partners?" she demanded.

With a weary smile, Rizzo said, "Yeah, now that you mention it. One or two."

Priscilla swung the Impala to the side of the avenue, stopping sharply and slamming it into park. The car rocked against the inertia as she turned to Rizzo.

"On my worst day," she said, her eyes hard, "I can kick Mike's butt and yours, too. Don't worry 'bout it. Don't you ever worry 'bout it. And you can just kiss my black ass, Joe, for asking me that question."

"Okay, I hear you. Loud and clear." He leaned toward her and smiled. "You can't blame a guy for askin'."

She shook her head. "Damn," she said. "You are some piece of work." She slipped the car into gear and pulled away. "We can handle this dude, Joe," she said. "*I* can handle him myself. You just suck on that gum, brother, and chill out."

THE SHORE Shopping Plaza was a sprawling, L-shaped complex of stores, built on a landfill that extended into the waters of Lower New York Bay. To the north, the Verrazano Bridge arched over The Narrows, connecting the boroughs of Brooklyn and Staten Island. The mall housed a huge Pathmark supermarket, a Citibank boasting a drive-thru appendage, a half dozen specialty shops, and the anchor of the complex, Gordon's Sporting Equipment. The shopping plaza was only a short drive from the Sixty-second Precinct building.

As she drove across Shore Parkway and prepared to turn left into the complex's large outdoor parking lot, Priscilla sighed.

"I got some mixed feelings about this," she said.

"About what?" Rizzo asked.

"About picking up this jackass where he works. I know the guy's a fool and deserves a kick in the ass, but it's kinda cold, grabbing him in front of his coworkers."

"Better to cuff him in front of the wife and kiddies?" Rizzo asked. "There's no easy way to do this. Besides, he fucked up, he gets what he earned. End of story. When you were a uniform you made spontaneous collars, usually right at the scene. This is how detectives make arrests."

Priscilla shrugged. "I know," she said. "Just don't seem right, is all."

Rizzo grunted. "Let me explain about that, partner. There is no right. There is no wrong. There just *is*."

She angled the Impala toward Gordon's, accelerating across the sparsely occupied parking lot.

"Yeah," she said. "Mike told me about that. Said it was some of the nonsense your old man handed you when you were a kid."

Rizzo opened the glove compartment and reached for his pack of cigarettes.

"It was my grandfather," he said. "My old man died when I was nine, so me and my mother and sister moved in with my grandparents. Right here in Bensonhurst, over on Eighty-fourth Street and Seventeenth. Matter a fact, the high school where that guy Jacoby was wavin' his joint, New Utrecht High, that's my alma mater."

"Oh, yeah?" Priscilla asked, parking the Chevy twenty yards from Gordon's side entrance doors.

Rizzo nodded and undid his shoulder harness. "Yeah," he said. "I went from high school to the army for four years, then into the NYPD."

Priscilla put the car into park and shut it down. "I got my associates at Bronx Community, then went on the cops," she said.

They climbed out of the car, Rizzo spitting out Nicorette and lighting his Chesterfield. They both leaned against the Chevy as he smoked.

"So what made you pick the cops, Cil?" he asked. "With me, it was a family thing. My grandfather was a cop for most of his life. I grew up with it. It was all I ever wanted to do. I was even an M.P. when I was in the Army."

Priscilla nodded. "Lotsa guys come on the job like that. Me, I was brought up in a pretty fucked-up environment. My mother was wild, drunk, always runnin' with men." She turned to Rizzo and smiled sadly. "But I knew this old black beat cop when I was real young. His name was Ted and he always treated me special. Sometimes I would pretend he was my father, bein' how I never actually knew my real one." She shrugged. "So I guess, in a way, we got the same reason, kinda a family thing."

"Yeah, kinda," Rizzo said. "But, tell you the truth, if I was a kid now, twenty, twenty-one, I'd never wanna come on this job. It's apples to oranges from when I started." He looked out over the flat waters of the bay, nestled under the darkened sky and dragged deeply on the cigarette. "Apples to oranges," he said again, a wistful note in his voice, an unfamiliar tone to Priscilla's ear.

She nodded. "Lots of old-timers feel that way. Down on the job, sayin' it's changed, too political, can't trust nobody, all that. But, you know what, Joe? It's the times that've changed. Some for the good, most for the bad. But the job has always been good for me. Gave me order, structure. Somethin' to be proud of. I know it can eat people up and spit 'em out—I've seen plenty a that—but if you tough it out, it's meaningful. It's *real*, Joe. *Real*."

Now Rizzo, the wise-guy edge back in his tone when he spoke, patted her arm.

"Yeah," he said, tossing the cigarette away. "Real. Just keep in mind what my grandfather said. What *I* say about no right, no wrong. That ain't *nonsense*, like you called it. That's *wisdom*, kiddo. Wisdom." He glanced at his watch.

"Now," he said, his eyes twinkling under the artificial lights of the parking lot. "Lets us go do something *meaningful*. Somethin' *real*. Let's go lock up this shit-bag."

RIZZO LEANED back casually, resting his shoulders against the stacked boxes behind him. He, Priscilla, the store manager, and a sullen Carl Jurgens were gathered in the stockroom at the rear of Gordon's Sporting Equipment. After standing in awkward silence for a moment, the manager cleared his throat.

"Well," he said, glancing from one to another. "I'll leave you here, then?" The man, tall and thin, in his mid-thirties, smiled at Rizzo. "If this is okay with you, that is. As I said, if you want more privacy, my office is . . ."

Rizzo held up a hand. "This is fine," he said. "Thanks."

"Okay, then," he said, and left the room quickly, closing the door behind him.

Rizzo folded his arms across his chest and looked at Jurgens.

"So, Carl," he said in a pleasant conversational tone. "Got any idea why we dropped by to see you?"

The man flushed slightly and avoided eye contact. "No," he said flatly. "I don't."

Priscilla, to the man's right, said, "Why don't you tell us where you were on Monday night? Around nine o'clock."

The man glanced nervously at her, then swung his eyes to Rizzo.

"Sounds like a reasonable question, Carl," Rizzo said. "Why don't you answer her?"

Jurgens looked back at Priscilla, a sheen of perspiration glistening on his forehead. He cleared his throat before answering. "Monday? Monday night?" he asked.

Priscilla nodded. "Yeah. Monday night. Columbus Day. 'Bout nine o'clock."

Jurgens nodded. "Yeah, okay. Monday, Monday night at nine . . . I was home. With my wife."

Rizzo eased away from the boxes, unfolding his arms. "Is that right, Carl? Home with the wife?"

"Yeah," he said, his voice gaining strength. "You can ask her. She'll tell you."

Rizzo nodded. "I bet she will, Carl. I bet she will. But you know, your wife might not be gettin' the whole picture. She may not know that legally, the only right she has is she can't be forced to testify against you. But she *can* be charged as an accessory after the fact if she lies to cover for you."

Jurgens's flush deepened. "Accessory to what?" he said. "Cover for what?"

Rizzo glanced at Priscilla. She looked quickly to Jurgens, saw the anger stirring. Discreetly, she slipped her cuffs from where they were tucked in her belt at the small of her back.

Rizzo stepped in closer to Jurgens. "Turn around," he said, his voice deep and threatening. "You're under arrest."

Priscilla moved quickly, cuffing first Jurgens's right hand, then twisting it to meet his left wrist. She snapped on the second cuff, deftly adjusting its grip. Rizzo ran his hands rapidly over Jurgens's body, keeping his own left leg angled inward to protect his groin.

Jurgens blinked in disbelief, straining against the Smith & Wesson handcuffs.

"Under arrest? What the fuck for?" he stammered.

Rizzo reached a hand into Jurgens's front pants pocket, extracting a six-inch folding knife with a scarred bone handle.

"Two counts of attempted murder, second degree, two counts criminal use of a firearm, two felony counts assault, one misdemeanor count." Now Rizzo gave a slight smile. "And whatever else the college boy A.D.A. can find in his penal code Cliff notes."

Jurgens compressed his lips. "I want a fuckin' lawyer," he said. "A lawyer!"

Priscilla took the knife from Rizzo. "Okay, Carl," she said. "We heard you."

"What's that?" Rizzo asked Jurgens, indicating the knife.

The man's eyes darted to the weapon. "That's my pocket knife," he said. "I'm a sportsman."

Rizzo nodded his head. "Yeah, Carl," he said, taking the man by the arm and turning toward the door. "We already figured that out."

As they walked him out, Priscilla began Jurgens's Miranda warning. "You have the right . . ."

Chapter Five

IT WAS ASTONISHING, REALLY. After all the fear, apprehension, and doubt, all the painful reflection.

The man grunted with satisfaction. Killing, as it had turned out, came easily to him. It was the simple enactment of a well-conceived plan, oddly not unlike any other plan, financial or professional, for instance, one faced as one's life progressed.

He looked down at the lifeless mass collapsed at his feet. How strange, he thought, that he had never before realized his capacity.

Imagine, to have lived a lifetime within the confines of his own consciousness and not have been aware of such a rich and useful resource—the ability to kill without remorse, without misguided sympathy, without the inconvenience of weakness or moral dilemma.

The man's satisfaction deepened, and he sighed. It was a relief, really. Now he knew, knew without question, that he was capable of doing it, and what's more, doing it so very easily.

Thank the devil, he thought, for there remained one more murder to commit.

One more act of self-preservation.

He turned to leave the small, sad basement apartment.

As he stepped out onto the rain-swept, darkened streets of Brooklyn, he scanned his surroundings.

His next murder, his next performance, would be in a far more splendid setting. One so more fitting for a man of his position.

★　★　★

JOE RIZZO sat bolt upright in bed, perspiration covering his body, the ghostly musty odor of the old Plymouth radio car distinct and sour in his nostrils, a guttural yelp escaping his throat.

He glanced quickly around the darkened room, saw the red digital alarm on the night table: 6:12 a.m.

His heart racing, Rizzo turned in the darkness toward Jennifer. His sudden, violent movement had awoken her, and he saw her reaching for the bedside lamp to switch it on.

"Joe?" she said. "Joe? Are you okay?"

Rizzo, breathing deeply, willing his heartbeat to slow, extended a gentle hand to his wife.

"Yeah," he said, more breathlessly than he would have liked. "Yeah, hon, fine. Just a dream. Shut the light, Jen, go back to sleep."

Jennifer sat up, glancing at the clock. "It's okay," she said, studying the near feral, yet bewildered look in his eyes. "I have to get up soon anyway." She put her hand on his shoulder. "Are you sure you're okay?" she asked again, gently.

Rizzo ran a hand through his hair and managed a smile. He tossed the bedcovers back, away from his body, allowing the cool air of the room to touch his damp skin.

"Yeah," he said. "Just a friggin' dream, that's all."

Jennifer's dark eyes reflected warmly in the bedside lighting.

"A *dream*?" she said. "Looks more like a nightmare to me." Now she squinted, peering at him more closely.

"Was it *that* dream, Joe?" she asked, her tone neutral.

Rizzo nodded, using his T-shirt sleeve to clear sweat from his eyes.

"Yeah," he said. Then after a moment, he shook his head in disbelief. "Can you imagine this? With all I've seen over the years? The dead babies, the dozens of murders, the burned corpses, the shooting vics, every goddamned thing. All of that, never a nightmare. But that one kid, that one poor kid, still haunting me after all these years." He shook his head again. "It just doesn't make sense."

Jennifer shifted her body, facing him more directly.

"Well," she said, rubbing gently at the knot of muscle in his powerful shoulder. "Like I've said before, you were just a kid yourself.

Probably the same age she was. And you had just started on the force. An experience like that can stay with you."

Rizzo reached to his night table for a Nicorette packet. "Yeah," he said, tearing at the cellophane. "But still. Twenty-seven years later, almost. Enough already."

Jennifer nodded, unsure of what else to say. "Well, it's over now. Try to relax."

Later, as he lay in bed listening to Jennifer's shower hiss from the master bath, he replayed that long-ago day in his mind for the thousandth time.

It had been his very first morning tour, in the old Seventy-fifth Precinct, on the Brooklyn-Queens border. It was a Sunday morning, just past seven a.m., less than an hour remaining on the tour. His training officer, a twenty-year veteran who had harbored no ambition beyond a sector car patrol, had parked the Plymouth on a wooded, deserted stretch of service road lying north of the Belt Parkway. The cop, Sonny Carusso, sat asleep behind the wheel. "Cooping," the old-timers had called it back in those days.

Rizzo had watched the skies over Jamaica Bay dawn with a new April morning and now sat struggling with the Sunday *News* crossword. Then suddenly, the old Motorola shortwave, hanging in silence from its bracket on the under dash of the Plymouth, crackled to life.

Magically, at the sound of the dispatch, Carusso's eyes opened. With hooded lids, he glanced first at the radio, then to Rizzo.

"That's us, kid," he said, glancing at his wristwatch. "Bad fuckin' timin' to be pickin' up a call."

Rizzo reached out and took the hand mike, keying it and sending a terse "ten-four" back to dispatch.

Carusso sat up in his seat and slipped the car into gear, wiping the sleep from his eyes with his left hand.

"Write the time on the recorder sheet," he told Rizzo. "Oh-seven oh-six. And the job location."

Carusso accelerated harshly, the valve train in the battered Plymouth V-8 rattling with the sudden strain. He raced eastbound along the service road, the car's red dome light swirling, then slowed sharply, swinging a harsh U-turn and hurling the car onto the westbound entrance ramp of the Belt Parkway.

They reached the scene in moments. Rizzo noted the half dozen autos randomly scattered on the highway, blocking two of its three westbound lanes. Carusso wove the radio car deftly through the crowd of citizens who stood in the roadway, touching the horn rim and sporadically sounding short "wup-wup" siren bursts.

A body lay facedown on the concrete of the highway, straddling the entrance merge and right-hand traffic lanes.

Rizzo hurried to the body, that of a young woman—blond, naked, her body raked with bloody scrape marks. The back of her skull glistened with gray-red slime, the bone crushed, blood and exposed brain matter pulsating with each of her rapid heartbeats, welling from the skull and flowing in meandering rivulets across the pale skin of her neck and back.

Rizzo bent to one knee, his throat constricting, his own heart rate rapidly increasing. He tentatively reached out a hand, unable to bring himself to touch the naked flesh.

"It wasn't my fault!" he heard someone say, and Rizzo turned to look over his shoulder. A man, about thirty, tall, hair disheveled by the wind blowing across the highway, was imploring Carusso. "She ran out right in front of me, right out of the bushes, right in front of my car. I swerved, I tried to miss her, but . . . but . . . I couldn't."

Carusso took the man by the arm, leading him toward the shoulder of the roadway.

"Joe," he said as he walked, "get on the horn . . . see what's holdin' the ambulance. Hurry up."

Rizzo stood on weakened legs, turning and running back to the radio car. Frantically, he radioed for expedited medical backup. Then he went back to the girl, again kneeling at her side.

During his four years of service as an Army M.P., Rizzo had seen some ugly things, things he preferred not to think about. But never had he seen anything like this. As he looked down at the woman, the girl, an eerie, dry hollow rattle suddenly sounded from deep within her chest cavity. Simultaneously, the pulsating blood from the head wound went oddly still. It began to pool within the skull, filling the depth of the depression and again spilling slowly onto the already bloodstained pavement.

Rizzo glanced up over his shoulder at Carusso, now standing above and behind him. "She just died," he heard the older cop say. "It's over." Rizzo stood slowly, his hands trembling, his breath coming in short, shallow gasps.

Carusso took him by the arm.

"Hey, kid," he said softly. "Get hold of yourself. Stiffen up. Go see if there's anything in the trunk. We gotta cover her up a little, give her some dignity. She don't need to have her ass out here on display. Go ahead. Go find somethin'."

Later, Rizzo examined the abandoned car hidden in the bushes off the side of the highway. It was an old Dodge, the engine still hot, ticking in the April morning air with an eerie cadence.

The woman had been stripped naked, sexually assaulted, and savagely beaten in her own car. The medical examiner would later determine there had been at least two assailants involved. At some point, the girl had broken free, terrified and panicked, running blindly from the car and into the path of oncoming highway traffic. There she had been struck with violent force and dragged under a car, then ultimately thrown free from its undercarriage. The terrified driver, hearing her body thump and thrash beneath the floorboard, swerved and skidded off the roadway onto the grass shoulder.

The responding detectives examined the Dodge, but it had yielded no usable clues. The case remained open, no arrest had ever been made.

Now, nearly twenty-seven years later, Joe Rizzo lay on his bed staring at the ceiling.

The dream came periodically. Often, at first, then once or twice a year. Lately, he had gone nearly two years without having it, and Rizzo thought he knew what had triggered it this time.

He swung his legs off the bed and sighed, sitting up and rubbing at his face.

The dream was always the same. They were alone on the highway. Just Rizzo and the body. No vehicles, no Carusso, no citizens. The cold wind blew over the desolate scene, chilling him.

The girl, scarred, battered, bloody, and naked against the dirty, cold concrete of the roadway, gave her death rattle. The pulsating blood went still, tranquil, inanimate.

Rizzo held a soiled blanket. Gently, he covered the girl's naked body and face. As he stood on the empty highway, the wind rushing in his ears, gazing down at the covered corpse, his eyes began to tear.

Then, slowly, the blanket began to stir. The young woman pulled the blanket from her face with a bloodied, trembling hand. Rizzo stepped back suddenly, enveloped in a fear that overwhelmed his grief. He stared at the pretty young face, blond hair wisping lightly in the breeze against the skin, the eyes now wide open. Blue, sharp, piercing. The pale lips parted, and in a throaty, wet voice, the young woman pleaded to him. "Help me," she said.

Terrified, he backed farther away, his bowels going loose with fear.

"Help me," she whispered, desperation and chilling terror in her eyes. "You're a cop. Help me. Please."

Then he would awaken, violently sweating, arms flailing, panic-stricken. Time after time.

Rizzo sighed. "And that," he said aloud, "is the reality of it."

"The reality of what?" he heard suddenly. Startled, he turned quickly. Jennifer, rubbing at her hair with a fluffy towel, stood naked in the bathroom doorway.

"The reality of being a cop," he said to her. Rizzo shook his head sadly. "That's what Carol doesn't get. What she doesn't understand."

Jennifer crossed the room, sitting beside him on the bed.

"Is this about that damn nightmare of yours?" she asked.

He nodded. "Yeah. That's what triggered it this time, this business with Carol going on the cops. She figures she'll be a big hero, Charlie's friggin' Angel, riding to the rescue in her blue-and-white. Then she'll spend the next twenty years learning the truth. How you wind up kneeling on the road watchin' some kid die, with some old cop tellin' you to note the time. For the incident report. Note the time and go get a goddamned blanket."

Jennifer laid a hand on his shoulder but remained silent. Rizzo glanced at her face, saw the tension in her jaw.

Forcing a smile to his lips, he leaned over and gently kissed her cheek, laying a soft hand on her thigh.

"We'll handle it, Jen," he said. "Believe me, we'll handle it."

She nodded, still silent, grim-faced.

He nuzzled her ear. "We need to have a date soon, hon," he said, lightening his tone, willing his body to relax. "Okay?" he asked.

"A date?" she said, a small smile forming. "You mean, like when we were in high school?"

Rizzo allowed his own smile to broaden. "Well," he said, "considering you're sitting next to me naked on the bed, I figure more of a college-type date. Remember?"

Jennifer brushed his hand from her thigh and stood. She removed the towel from her head, shaking her dark hair free.

"Yes, of course I remember. But relax, sailor, let's not start 'dating' just now. I've got to get to work."

"Well, then, get that nice-lookin' ass out of my face or you may be late for homeroom."

Jennifer laughed, her tension nearly gone, and spun from his exaggerated efforts to grab her, disappearing back into the bathroom and slamming the door behind her.

Later, as they sipped coffee at the kitchen table, Rizzo now in his bathrobe, Jennifer dressed and ready for work, he saw the tension return to her face.

"Can we really do it, Joe?" she asked. "Can we really handle this with Carol?"

He smiled, trying to convey a confidence he didn't feel.

"Sure we can," he said. "This expedited hiring they announced, that shook me a little, I admit. I figured we had more time. But . . . I got a plan."

Jennifer glanced at the wall clock. "I have a few minutes. Tell me. What's your plan?"

He shrugged. "Well, it's nothing new. What we've always done with the girls. All three of 'em. The truth. My plan is the simple, friggin' truth."

She leaned in over the table, closer to him. "Meaning what?" she asked.

"The Daily thing, for one," Rizzo said. "That whole mess me and Mike stumbled into. The tape I got stashed in the basement. The whole fuckin' mess. And that other business, the internal affairs thing that drunk Morelli got me jammed up with. That whole rotten ball of crap. I'm gonna tell Carol about it. All of it. How I.A.D. was squeezin' me to rat out Morelli; how I played Councilman Daily to use his juice to squash it. I'm gonna tell her how me and Mike are sittin' on that tape—withholding evidence, riskin' an accessory charge, all because we couldn't trust anybody, couldn't go to the bosses with any confidence. And let's face it, to grease our own wheels, too. To get Mike to the Plaza, get Cil her gold shield, get me some pensionable overtime. I'm gonna tell her that to fight them, to do what *she* would consider the 'right' thing, we had to *become* them, no great difference between us. Not in Carol's world, anyway. I'm gonna lay it all out for her. Make her see that her daddy's not some knight on a white horse. No, Daddy's just a street fighter, fighting both sides of every battle. And in the real world, *that's* what makes a good cop. The fire to fight the fire and still survive. It's not right, it's not wrong. It just *is*."

Now Rizzo paused, allowing himself to calm down. "The fire to fight the fire," he repeated. "That and the blanket. Always the blanket."

He sighed. "To cover up the bodies," he said softly, nodding. "To cover up the fuckin' bodies."

LATER THAT morning, Rizzo sat sipping coffee and looking into the bright, animated eyes of his youngest daughter, Carol.

"Nice place," he said, eyeing their surroundings. "I always liked it here."

"Yes," Carol answered, reaching for her own container of coffee. "It is pretty cool."

The Student Activities Center sat squarely in the middle of the Academic Mall on the sprawling Long Island campus of Stony Brook State University.

Now Carol smiled across the small round table at her father, her light brown eyes twinkling under the fluorescent lighting.

"So," she said casually. "To what do I owe the honor of this unexpected visit from my father."

Rizzo nodded slightly. "Fair question, I guess," he said.

She put her coffee down and twisted her lips as she spoke. "Bet I can guess," she said.

Rizzo laughed. "Yeah, I bet you can." Then, after a small pause, his face grew somber. Leaning inward on the table, he interlocked his fingers, laying his hands atop the table's cool surface.

"The test," he said. "Next week."

Carol sighed. "What about it, Daddy?" she asked, her voice firm.

"Would you have been right?" he asked. "If you had guessed, I mean?"

Carol, without amusement, nodded. She waited for him to continue.

After another pause, he did. "There's no reason for you to take it, hon," he said. "Why sit through a couple a hours of a police entrance exam for a job you're not gonna take anyway?"

Carol shook her short brown hair. "Except I am going to take it," she answered, her tone clipped. "As soon as I clear the medical and physical and psychological." She paused, holding her father's cool gaze. "I am going to take it," she repeated. "It's what I want."

Rizzo shook his head, the carefully rehearsed and chosen words of his argument fading to a slight, panicky anger.

"It's a bad idea," he said.

"Is it?" Carol said, more forcefully than she had intended. "For who? Me . . . or you?"

Rizzo's anger rose. "For you," he said, his voice cold.

Carol shook her head sadly. "Really? Are all cops bad liars, Dad, or just you?"

Rizzo grunted with bitterness. "The best liars in the world are cops, Carol," he said. "That's one of the first things you learn when you go on this job. How to lie." He shrugged. "If I had a dollar for every time I testified without perjurin' myself, I couldn't pay for these two coffees."

She gave a humorless laugh. "Okay, Dad, exaggerate. Anything to help you make your point."

He shook his head. "I don't have to exaggerate to make my point. The truth is more than good enough. All I'm saying is being a cop isn't a good career for a young girl, a young person. It's not the kinda life you want to lead, Carol, it's—"

His daughter cut him off, her own anger now tugging at her facial muscles. "Just what makes you think you know what kind of a life I want to lead?" she said. "Wasn't it you, you and Mom, who lectured us every damn day about how we could be this, we could be that, anything a boy could do, we could do? Wasn't that you? Now, all of a sudden—"

Rizzo interrupted. "This has nothin' to do with that," he said, more harshly than he had intended. "Yeah, you could be a cop, just as good a cop as any son of mine coulda been. But you know what? If you were my son, I'd be tellin' you the same thing. Yeah, you can be a good cop, you can be a good ax murderer, too. But that don't mean you should be one, just 'cause you can be."

"But Daddy . . ."

Rizzo shook his head so sharply, the movement transferred to the tiny table, shaking their coffee containers. "The job isn't what you think it is," he said. "Maybe it never was, but it sure as hell isn't these days. You wanna be some kinda hero, you wanna change the world, saves lives? Become a schoolteacher, like your mother. You think I ever prevented a crime? You think I ever made a friggin' difference? Maybe once, twice in twenty-seven years. The resta the time, I was too late—the woman was already raped, the baby already thrown out the window, the pizza delivery guy already shot to death for the twenty bucks he was carryin'. It's always already done, Carol, you don't stop it from happening."

Now it was Carol who shook her head sharply. "That's total B.S., and you know it. You're only saying that to make a point. All those arrests you made over the years, hundreds, maybe a thousand. You have no way of knowing how many crimes, how much grief and suffering you prevented, how many lives you saved by putting all those criminals behind bars. You know it's true, Daddy, you know—"

"It sucks the life outta you," he said, his anger now clashing with a sudden onset of depression welling in his chest. "It eats at you, a little bit at a time, till one day you wake up and you ain't there anymore. Somebody else is. Somebody you partnered with years ago, when you were a rookie, some old cop long retired, or dead. And now he's back, wearin' your clothes, livin' your life." Rizzo's eyes implored her. "Believe me, honey. It sucks the life outta you. It puts out your fire. Like a slow, constant trickle of water, drop by drop, bit by bit, till the fire is all gone."

Carol, so self-assured just moments before, now sat studying her father's face, her resolve wavering with the sight of him so upset.

"All right, Daddy," she said, her tone now soft. "I realize it can be a difficult life. But anything worthwhile is difficult." She smiled. "Another one of the things you taught me."

"Don't make me fight my own words, Carol," he said. "Please."

"You're not," she said, leaning closer to him, laying a hand on his arm. "You're fighting the truth. Those words you spoke years ago. That's what they were, the truth."

He sighed and ran a hand through his hair, digging spurs of determination into his consciousness even as he frantically fought to recall the words of his measured, rehearsed argument.

"Do you want your fire extinguished?" he asked helplessly. "Do you think lockin' up a few skells will make it all worthwhile?"

Carol's smile faded, her own determination taking hold again.

"Dad," she said. "You're just not being honest with yourself. Don't forget I grew up watching you. I saw, I heard. I remember when you'd be working a case, dozens of times, important, meaningful cases. I remember seeing you all psyched up and full of energy, tearing into your work. That seemed like fire to me. Real fire."

Rizzo looked into her eyes and saw the inevitability of her determination. Even as a strange, almost disjointed pride welled within him, his anger, more insistent, more pugnacious, rushed back into his head. He stood suddenly, pulling his arm out from under her still present hand. He looked down at his daughter as visions of childhood transgressions, less than perfect report cards, and sibling squabbles flashed before his eyes, all of them dwarfed and dropped on the trash heap of insignificance by this sudden adult situation.

"Forget the goddamned cops, Carol," he said harshly. "You're not takin' that test and you're not taking the job. End of story."

She shook her head. "I refuse to discuss this anymore," she said with near equal toughness. "How dare you issue fiats! If we're going to continue to argue about this, I'll just not come home. I'll stay at the dorm through the holidays."

Rizzo nodded, turning to move away. "Yeah," he said. "You do that. Sleep in an empty dorm room for the holidays. It'll be good practice for you—for sleeping in a radio car at three a.m. on Christmas morning, next to some fat, smelly old cop, or sleeping on the floor of central booking waitin' for some idiot A.D.A. to show up and process your complaint. Sleepin' in some stinkin', piss-stained precinct holding cell 'cause of some round-the-clock emergency, or outside some shit hole tenement where somebody just found a dead junkie after two months. Sleeping with cigarette filters stuck up your nose to dull the stench, markin' the hours till some third-world medical examiner shows up and announces, yeah, the guy is officially dead." Rizzo nodded. "Yeah, Carol, I did every one of those things, more times than I can remember."

He dug his car keys from his pants pocket, his face flushed. "Then I'd come home and tell you and your sisters a 'Ben the Bear' story. Some of the guys just went to the precinct bar, got drunk, and wound up screwing some bimbo who was out trollin' for cops."

He turned and began to walk away, his eyes searching for the exit.

"We'll see what works for you," he said over his shoulder, picking up his pace and leaving her sitting there alone.

CHAPTER SIX

November

MONDAY, NOVEMBER 3, DAWNED cold and dreary, a misty rain moving through Brooklyn on a light westerly wind. The front pages of the tabloids screamed bold, black headlines. The *New York Times,* normally crime free on page one, featured the story prominently.

Avery Mallard, native New Yorker and Pulitzer Prize–winning playwright, had been found murdered in his Manhattan home, his body sprawled before a showcase filled with Tony awards, New York Drama Critics Circle awards, two Emmys, the Pulitzer itself, and more than a dozen lesser prizes.

Joe Rizzo sat in the front passenger seat of the Impala reading the *Daily News*'s version of the murder. Priscilla Jackson wove the car through the now familiar streets of the Sixty-second Precinct, her right hand lightly on the wheel, her left resting on her thigh.

"Shame about this guy," Rizzo said, closing the paper and tossing it carefully onto the backseat. "He was only sixty-one. Paper says his best years were behind him, though."

Priscilla shrugged. "Yeah, maybe. But his new play, *An Atlanta Landscape,* they say it's a shoo-in for the big awards."

"Yeah, I read about that," Rizzo said. "Bunch of bleedin' heart bullshit. For sure it'll get all the attention."

"Yeah, well, not everything can be '*Animal House* Meets *The Odd Couple*,' Joe," Priscilla said. "Some works actually got somethin' to say, Partner. Matter of fact, Karen and I saw that play about a month ago. It was terrific."

Rizzo arched his brow. "Well, ain't you the literary one. All those misspent years workin' Manhattan got your head turned around."

Priscilla shrugged. "No, not really. Actually," she said in a neutral tones, "I do a little writing myself."

Rizzo turned to her. "No kiddin'? Like what? Plays like this guy Mallard?"

"No, not exactly," she said. "And for your info, *nobody* writes plays like this dude. He was the master, had a lifetime run of great works including this new one. No, me, I just write some short stories. And I've been foolin' with a novel. Karen even talked me into taking a class at the Ninety-second Street Y. I go on Tuesday nights when we're not working."

Rizzo nodded. "Well, imagine that: a regular Josephine Wambaugh I'm workin' with."

"Not quite, brother, not quite," she said, "but I'm tryin'."

"Good for you, Cil. I wish you luck with it."

She frowned, turning her attention fully back to driving.

"Between me and you," she said, "this is some very private shit. I only told Mike about it a week ago. With you and Karen, that's just three people who know. I wouldn't want it getting around the precinct."

"I'll bet," Rizzo said with a laugh. "Don't worry. Far as I'm concerned, you can barely read, let alone write. Just like the rest of us dumb-ass cops. My lips are sealed."

She nodded. "Good. I just told you in case it ever comes up. With Mike, maybe, or if you ever meet Karen. Wouldn't want any awkward moments."

"No, Cil. We wouldn't want any awkward moments while I'm sippin' sherry with you and your girlfriend. Heaven forbid."

"Good," Priscilla said. "Now, what was that address? This is Sixty-seventh Street."

Rizzo glanced at his notepad. "Fourteen-forty."

They scanned the addresses of the neat, attached row houses that lined the street, then Priscilla swung the Chevy to the curb and parked.

As they undid their shoulder harnesses, Rizzo glanced around.

"I knew this block sounded familiar," he said. "My daughter Carol had a friend from Catholic school lived here somewhere. Years ago when she was in grammar school."

Priscilla reached across to the glove compartment and removed her notepad. Then, sitting upright, she used the rearview mirror to smooth her hair.

"Yeah?" she said. Then, with a slight glance to Rizzo, she asked, "How's that goin', by the way? That situation with Carol and the cops? You talk to her yet?"

Rizzo nodded grimly. "Oh, I spoke to her, all right."

Priscilla saw the tense creases at his eye.

"And?" she asked again, swinging her eyes away from him. "How'd it go?"

He told her of his Stony Brook meeting with his daughter. When he had finished, Priscilla shook her head, her lips twisted.

"Jesus, Joe," she said. "You couldn't have fucked that up any more if you were tryin'." She shook her head once more.

Rizzo glanced over from the Impala's passenger seat, his jaw working a piece of Nicorette. "You sound like my goddamned wife. I can use a little support here, for Christ sake."

"Yeah, well, what you call support, I call a hand job," Priscilla replied. "I'm telling you, you gotta fix this. And fix it fast."

Rizzo shook his head. "Bullshit," he said.

Priscilla answered with a snort. "No, Joe," she said. "No bullshit."

"You know what she told me once?" Rizzo began. "One of her criminology professors—can you imagine what this asshole is like?—tells the class that all across America, at different times over the years, cities started to get tired of their own existence. The buildings got grimy, the trains and buses started wearin' out, the roads and bridges got beat up and were falling apart. And, of course, the crime got worse and worse. He told them how it happened in New York years ago, Los Angeles, Chicago, Detroit, Philadelphia. And you know what he tells them saved those cities?"

"I got a feelin' I can guess, Partner," said Priscilla. "But go ahead, knock yourself out, tell me."

"Cops," Rizzo said, turning to face her. "Friggin' cops turned it around. And you know how?"

Priscilla shook her head. "No. But let me ask you something. What's the name of the course this guy teaches?"

Despite his lingering anger, Rizzo smiled. "Community Policing," he said.

"Well, then," Priscilla said, "I'm gonna guess the cops saved the world, one city at a time, by community policing."

Now, despite himself, Rizzo laughed. "Bingo," he said. "He used the old, 'Stop the small stuff—the graffiti, the noise, the litter, the friggin' jaywalkin', and before you know it, all the major shit's gone.'"

"Did the guy happen to mention the influx of mocha-sucking yuppies movin' in that actually saved those cities?" she asked.

"No, I think he left that part out."

"Figures," Priscilla said.

"That's exactly what I'm talkin' about, what I'm tryin' to make Carol understand." Rizzo went on, frustration building in his tone. "All this make-believe bullshit that surrounds the job, the half-assed ideas everybody gets from television, movies, all that shit."

"Take a breath, Joe," Priscilla said calmly. "Step back from it a little bit, okay? It ain't the end of the world if Carol comes on the job. Look, it's been good for you, good for me, it can work out for her, too. And if it doesn't, she quits. But you gotta let her find out for herself if—"

Rizzo shook his head angrily.

"No way," he said. "No friggin' way my daughter becomes a cop."

Now anger stirred in Priscilla, her tone growing sharp. "For Christ sake, listen to yourself. You see me sittin' right here next to you, and you're ranting about your daughter comin' on the job like she's catchin' the fuckin' clap. What are you sayin', Partner? Bein' a cop is good enough for somebody like me, but not good enough for your freakin' little princess?"

Rizzo glanced briefly at her, saw the hurt and anger in her eyes. He turned his gaze back to the street, shaking his head slowly, his voice softening.

"No, Cil, relax, please," he said. "That's not what I'm sayin'. Just with you and me, it was different. I grew up in a tough neighborhood in Bensonhurst, hanging out on street corners, getting into all sorts of shit. Hell, half my friends got themselves arrested, two of 'em shot to death. One guy I went to high school with is doin' double life sentences in Attica. And you, you grew up in the South Bronx, no father, a fucked-up mother. By the time you were twelve, you knew the score better than Carol does now, and she's almost twenty. It's different with you, Cil. You're street smart, tough. You don't wear your heart on your sleeve, you don't have unrealistic expectations about the average guy on the street. Carol's just too soft, too trusting. And it's probably my fault, me and Jen's, maybe we pampered the girls too much, sheltered them. If she becomes a cop, she'll pay the price for that, pay the price for my mistakes." He sighed. "Come on," he said gently. "You know the deal, you've seen it. These kids comin' on the job from Long Island, upstate New York, wherever. They ain't got a clue. The streets eat 'em alive. All that Sesame Street bullshit they grew up with, 'Teach the World to Sing' crap, they actually believed all that. They come on the job and that's when they see the real deal, what human nature's really like. Hell, you knock out the electricity, cut the food supply for one friggin' day, all of a sudden it's the third century. The fuckin' Huns versus the Vikings, and everybody loses."

Priscilla remained silent. Rizzo turned to face her. "Civilization is just a facade. You know it. I know it. Every cop knows it. But Carol, she don't know it. She was never on the streets. She may as well have grown up in fuckin' Mayberry with Aunt Bea bakin' her pies."

"Okay, Joe," she conceded, "I see where you're coming from. But consider this: you only know Carol as her father, and see her only from that limited viewpoint. She may be tougher and a little more realistic than you figure. If this is something she really wants to do, you got to figure she's thought it through. Carol's lookin' for your support. She *needs* your support. But, believe me, if she don't get it, she'll adjust. She wants to be a cop, she'll be one." Priscilla sighed. "I know what it's like not having a parent's support." She paused before continuing. "And I've seen the other side, too. With Karen. Her parents were always there for her. No matter what. With the gay thing, with the 'I wanna be a lawyer' thing." She smiled, her eyes twinkling. "Hell, even with the big thing—the black cop girlfriend thing." She shook

79

her head. "You don't have to like it, Joe. You don't have to encourage it or pretend to be happy about it. And you can still make your case against it, clear and calm, without beatin' on what's probably your big old hairy Italian chest. You can discuss it with her. You know, like two adults. Then you gotta let her decide. And when she does, you smile at her, you wish her luck, and you back her up the whole way." Priscilla's expression turned sad, and the twinkle drained from her eyes.

"That's what a father does, Joe," she said. "From what I've been told."

Rizzo looked at her with a sad smile.

"Yeah, that's what I hear, too."

They sat in silence. After a few moments, Rizzo spoke again.

"I was just gonna tell her what it's like. Tell her about the dead kid on the highway, about the I.A.D. jam-up I got myself into, about the shit me and Mike got tangled up with, about the political flunky bosses." He sighed, running a hand through his hair, his eye twitching nervously.

"I was gonna tell her all about it," he repeated. "Instead, I completely lost it. Went right into a tirade, just like my grandfather used to do when he came home from the job too full of bourbon." Rizzo shook his head. "If I know Carol, even if she changes her mind and decides she'd rather become a friggin' nun, she'll still go on the cops. Just to show me I can't push her around."

Priscilla hesitated a moment, then laughed, slapping backhandedly at Rizzo's left arm.

"There you go, Partner," she said. "You're startin' to look on the bright side of this thing already."

Rizzo turned to her, a puzzled look in his eyes.

"Hell," she said. "At least she didn't say she wants to become a nun. Now *that* would call for a fuckin' tirade."

Rizzo laughed grudgingly. "Yeah," he said, "really."

She turned to face him fully.

"You know, Joe, it ain't the end of the world if she goes on the job. There's worse shit parents got to deal with."

"Yeah. I'm aware of that," Rizzo said. "But we're talkin' about *my* daughter, *my* little girl. Not some hypothetical kid somewhere. *My* little girl."

Priscilla sighed. "I know, I know."

Rizzo's face animated, his cheeks flushing slightly. "No," he said firmly. "You *don't* know. You don't have kids." A pensive look came to his eyes.

"When my girls were little," he said, "I'd tell them stories. Bedtime stories. When I was home to do it, that is. Carol was always the toughest. See, I'd make up the stories. I'd give them a choice: Ben the bear, Flipper the dolphin, or Lassie. Marie usually went for Lassie. Jessica bounced from one to the other. But Carol, she was tough. She'd pick combos—Ben and Lassie, Flipper and Ben—like that." He raised his eyes back to Priscilla's, pulling himself back into the car from those faraway nights. He smiled sadly. "You got any friggin' idea how hard it is to make up a story with a goddamned fish combination? A fish and a bear? Or a collie?

"I'd have 'em all go waterskiing. On a river. Flipper pulling the other guys." He laughed. "One time Carol asked me, 'Where'd they get the skis, Daddy?'"

Amused, Priscilla asked, "I'm a little curious myself. Where *did* they get the skis?"

"Where else?" Rizzo asked. "Santa Claus."

That brought a laugh from her. "Of course."

He shook his head at the memory. "What *I* always wondered was, how'd they make the arrangements? To meet, I mean. What'd they do, e-mail each other?"

Priscilla opened the driver's door and swung a long leg out of the car.

As he opened his door, Rizzo turned to her again.

"She can't do this, Cil," he said in a low voice. "It's not right for her. It'll hurt her." Again his head shook. "She's still my little girl."

Priscilla pressed her lips, uncomfortable with Rizzo's obvious pain.

"Yeah," she said kindly. "She'll always be your little girl, I guess." Now her own mood turned sad, and she made a conscious effort to push it away. "I wish I had been somebody's little girl. Damn, I wish

I had. Wish I *was*. But, you know what? I handled it. I still handle it. Because I'm an adult now, Joe. Not a little girl. A woman."

Priscilla climbed from the car, leaning back in to address him one more time.

"And so is Carol. Whatever happens, however this plays out, she'll handle it. Like a full-grown woman."

Rizzo remained silent.

"Now," Priscilla said, her voice businesslike, "let's go do our job. Let's go get *real*." Then she added one last thing. "And by the way, Joe. Just in case it should ever come up. A dolphin is a *mammal*, not a fuckin' *fish*."

THE TWO detectives sat in high-backed upholstered chairs in the neat, sparsely decorated living room. Across from them on a plain black sofa, three civilians sat facing them.

"I have a question," Rizzo said. "About the names."

Twenty-nine-year-old Cornelia Hom nodded.

"I'm sure you do, Sergeant," she said.

Rizzo continued. "I have your grandmother's name as Hom Bik and your grandfather's as Hom Feng. Is that correct?"

"Yes," Cornelia answered. "Hom is the surname. Chinese names are the reverse of English—surname first, given name second."

Priscilla said, "So it's Mr. and Mrs. Hom. Is that right?"

"Yes," Cornelia said. "And, as I told you, they both understand English and speak some. They're just more comfortable with me here, which is why I took off from work today."

"Where is that, Ms. Hom?" Rizzo asked.

"Morgan Chase," she replied. "On Broad and Wall Streets."

"Okay," Rizzo said, jotting it down. "Before we leave, I'd like all your numbers—home, business, cell. In case we need to contact you."

Cornelia nodded. "Of course," she said.

Rizzo looked at the elderly couple to Cornelia's right. "You folks were robbed four nights ago," he said. "I apologize for the delay in getting here. The case was originally assigned to the day tour the morning following the crime. The detectives who caught it have been in court since then, testifying on other cases, or were on regular days off. This morning, my boss reassigned the case to us. I checked the file. The first detectives assigned had done some preliminaries. This is the third mugging in the precinct in the last month. All elderly victims, always at night."

Rizzo turned his attention back to Cornelia Hom.

"That's unusual for this particular neighborhood. We don't have a lot of street robberies in this sector of the precinct. The assigned detectives were looking at the other two cases, looking for a link. So, our visit here today isn't the first police action taken. But, again, I apologize for the delay in getting out here."

Cornelia Hom nodded. "Thank you, Sergeant."

"The other two victims were Italian-American, so the common links were age, method, and time of assault," Rizzo said. "So if they are linked, we're not looking at a bias crime."

"And the muggers?" Cornelia asked.

"Mugger," he corrected. "Looks to be a lone operator." Now Rizzo turned back to the elderly couple. "And just as you reported in your case, the perpetrator in the other two cases is also described as being Caucasian."

Cornelia Hom nodded again. Both elderly victims smiled at Rizzo, then Priscilla, but remained silent.

"All right then, Sergeant," Cornelia said. "Would you like to question my grandparents?"

Rizzo picked up his pen. "Yes," he said. "If there's a problem with language, I assume you can help out?"

She smiled. "I speak fluent Chinese in four dialects. I also speak Japanese, Korean, Vietnamese, and some Thai. At Morgan Chase, I'm the Eastern accounts liaison officer."

"Okay," Rizzo said, then turned to the victims.

"I was glad to hear you weren't seriously injured," he said. "Just pushed around a bit and, of course, badly frightened. You were seen at the emergency room and released, correct?"

"Yes," Hom Feng said with a short nod of his head.

"Good," Rizzo replied, smiling into the dark, friendly eyes, wide set in the old man's weathered face.

"So," he continued, "according to the Aided Report the uniformed officers filed, the incident took place on the corner of Seventy-first Street and Fifteenth Avenue, correct?"

Hom Fen frowned. "No," he said with the same short nod. "Seventy-second."

Rizzo rubbed at his eye, looking again to his notes.

"The cops who responded said Seventy-first in the report," he said. "Is that wrong?"

Cornelia Hom leaned forward. "Is it of some importance, Sergeant?" she asked.

Rizzo nodded. "It could be. This happened at about nine-thirty at night, correct?"

Cornelia glanced to her grandfather.

"Yes," he said.

"But Seventy-second Street, not Seventy-first?" Rizzo asked.

"Yes," Hom Feng repeated.

Rizzo glanced to Cornelia, a question in his eyes.

She smiled at him. "Yes, Sergeant. They *are* old. But they are both sharper than I am. *I* may not know what corner I'm on, but I assure you, they do." She turned slightly in her seat, facing her grandparents.

"May I?" she asked with a glance to Rizzo.

He sat back in his seat. "I wish you would."

She spoke in rapid and precise lyrical Cantonese, eliciting a smile of pride on both elderly faces. It was her grandmother, Hom Bik, who responded. Her voice was strong and clear, also lyrical in her native tongue.

Cornelia turned to Rizzo. "They are certain, Sergeant. The attack took place on Seventy-second and Fifteenth, the northeast corner to be exact. Afterward, they walked over to the next street, Seventy-first, because there was a store open there, a late-night grocery. That's where the police were called from. Neither of them has a cell phone."

"Yeah. I figured. My mother is seventy-eight and she just agreed to get cable TV," Rizzo said.

Cornelia smiled. "Generational traits transcend cultures, I guess."

"Seems like it." Rizzo cleared his throat, turning again to Hom Feng and his wife. "So," he said, "you were attacked right on the corner, right in front of the schoolyard? The P.S. one-twelve school-yard on the corner?"

"Yes," said Hom Feng. "Schoolyard."

Rizzo turned to Priscilla. "You may be my lucky charm, Detective Jackson," he said with a wink. "Why don't you ask the rest of the questions? I'll take some notes."

He turned back to the Homs. "This might take awhile," he said.

"Time well spent, I think. Time well spent," Rizzo added.

LATER, SITTING in the Impala in front of the Hom residence, Priscilla recorded and expanded her notes while the minute details of the interview were still fresh in her mind.

Rizzo turned to her.

"Like I told them," he said, "muggings around here are rare. Only time we see one is when some asshole junkie gets so strung out, he forgets to be afraid and grabs some old lady's purse."

"Afraid? Afraid of what?" she asked, without looking up from her pad.

"Afraid of Louie Quattropa. Remember your first day in the precinct? We drove around and I pointed out the Starlight Lounge? That's Quattropa's base of operations. He's the Brooklyn mob boss, commands the old Columbo gang. Louie takes a hard line with local street crime, especially since it don't put any money in his pocket. He thinks he's building goodwill in the neighborhood by enforcing the laws he deems worthy of enforcin'."

She looked up from her writing. "Enforcing how?" she asked.

"Oh, kinda like Genghis fuckin' Khan enforced the law. With a heavy hand." Rizzo dug out a piece of Nicorette. "If you're gonna work the precinct, you oughta know its history," he said. "You know, like when you were assigned the Upper East Side and you knew where all the 'Jackie-O slept here' signs were located. Like that."

"Okay, Joe. Educate me."

"Well, years ago some asshole decided to rob the famous jeweled crown that was on display in the local parish, Regina Pacis. Quattropa wasn't the boss of all bosses then, just the Bay Ridge–Bensonhurst capo. About a month later, the crown comes back to the church by parcel post. Then the cops in the Seven-Six find a local b and e man with his hands chopped off, two slugs in the back of his skull, and a crucifix nailed to his forehead. Theory is, the guy's the one who stole the crown, and he had pissed off Quattropa."

Priscilla turned back to her notes. "Oh," she said. "So it went like that."

"Yeah. It went like that. It *always* goes like that when you mix righteous indignation with a murderous, megalomaniacal personality."

"Megalo-fuckin'-maniacal?" Priscilla said. "You takin' vocabulary lessons?"

"Maybe it's *me* should be the friggin' writer," he said.

Shaking her head and smiling, she agreed.

He resumed his tale. "Last time we figure Quattropa stepped in was 'bout four, five years ago. When this crazy kid from Sixty-fifth Street wound up frozen solid, a kid all the cops knew, Perry Pino. Took two days to thaw him out."

Priscilla looked up, her eyes wide. "Now *that* story you gotta tell me, Joe."

"Yeah," he said with a chuckle, "all the boys and girls like that one. See, down one of these blocks, I forget which one, there's a free-standin' ice pavilion. About twenty-five feet long, ten feet high, with steps leadin' up to a platform in front of it. You put your money in the slot, and the thing dispenses giant bags of ice. Ten, twenty pounds, whatever you want. Lotsa local businesses use it—restaurants, fish markets, like that. So, one day, this old lady from the neighborhood, she goes to the pavilion to get some ice. She's throwing a birthday party for her grandson and she's making home-made ice cream, havin' a backyard cookout, real Norman Rockwell shit, Brooklyn style. Well, seems like our boy, Perry, was in need of a few bucks. Gas money, maybe, for his shiny hot-rod Camaro. So he decides to mug the old gal. Trouble was, somebody saw him do it, somebody close to Quattropa."

"Sounds like trouble in River City," said Priscilla.

Rizzo nodded. "Big time. So, about a week later, the owner of the pavilion comes to restock his ice machine. He goes around back, finds the door broken into. And when he opens the freezer, guess what? There lies Perry, duct-taped hand and foot, gagged, beat up a little. And frozen solid. They fuckin' put him in there alive." He shook his head. "When I was a kid, I couldn't even watch my grand-father cook live crabs. He'd throw the poor bastards into the boilin' water, then talk to them in Italian and whack them off the rim of the pot with a wooden spoon when they tried to climb out."

With another head shake, he added, "But Quattropa and the boys, they got no problem tossin' some dumb-ass teenager into the deep freeze."

After a moment, Priscilla spoke up. "Now I can see why the Six-Two street crime stays manageable."

He laughed. "Yeah, and there are other examples. 'Course, none a those incidents could ever be traced back to Louie. But everybody knew. Cops, citizens, skells, everybody."

Priscilla finished up her notes and started the car.

"Well," she said cheerfully, "that was fun. What now, boss?"

Rizzo glanced at his watch. "Let's go back to the house," he said. "Drop yourself off. Then I'll take the car and head downtown. I have to be in court this afternoon on one of me and Mike's old cases."

Priscilla pulled the Impala out into the street, heading for the precinct. "Okay," she said. "I'll catch us up on paperwork and work the phones on some of our cases."

Rizzo nodded. "Good idea. Talk to Vince, too. Get him to switch us to four-to-midnight tomorrow."

"Why?" she asked. "We're scheduled eight-to-four tomorrow."

"Yeah, well, remember inside the Hom house I said you were my lucky charm?"

"Yeah. What's up with that?"

"Well, we just might be catchin' a break on this mugging. But we need to do the leg work at night. I'll explain it all tomorrow. Just get Swede to switch our tours."

"That's a problem for me, Joe," she said.

He looked at her. "Oh? Why's that?"

She shrugged. "Tomorrow's Tuesday. I got my writing class at the Y. Six-thirty to nine. I was expecting a day tour, not a night tour."

Rizzo raised his brows. "Well, excuse me," he said. "I forgot about that. Okay, then, Wednesday. Have Swede switch us on Wednesday."

"Okay, I appreciate it, Joe."

"Hey, it's the least I can do," he said. "After all, who else can I find to write my memoirs?"

He lowered the passenger window and spit his chewed-up Nicorette into the street.

"I sure as hell couldn't do it myself," he said.

CHAPTER SEVEN

WEDNESDAY AFTERNOON, RIZZO SAT at his desk in the Six-Two squad room, frowning down at a copy of the *Daily News*.

He sighed and reached for his coffee. It was three forty-five, and Priscilla would be arriving shortly for their rescheduled four-to-midnight.

He looked back to the newspaper. Statewide election coverage from the day before was featured. The local results were much less prominent, but had hit Rizzo's eye like a laser.

Councilman William Daily of Bay Ridge, running on his usual platform of family values, law and order, and good government, had easily won reelection over the local attorney who had run a barely active and knowingly hopeless campaign against him.

Rizzo sipped slowly at his coffee, the frown tugging at his facial muscles. He carefully studied the photo that accompanied the article.

Daily, standing triumphantly between his wife and oldest daughter, was smiling broadly, his right arm raised above his head, his left outstretched and pointing, presumably at the adoring crowd of unseen supporters before him.

The photo showed no sign of his younger daughter, Rosanne. Rizzo scanned the text of the story a second time, again noting the absence of even a passing mention of the younger girl.

He opened the bottom drawer of his desk, rummaging through the papers and notebooks randomly contained within. He took hold of a worn, brown notepad, flipped it open and then, satisfied, lifted it to the desk surface. He thumbed through the pages until he found the entry he sought and reached to the black phone on his desk.

"This is Detective Sergeant Joe Rizzo, NYPD," he said to the crisp-voiced female who answered. "I'd like a word with Dr. Rogers, please. If he's available."

"One moment, sir, I'll check," the woman said.

Soon the familiar voice of Dr. Raymond Rogers came through the line.

"Hello, Sergeant Rizzo," the psychiatrist said. "What can I do for you today?"

"Well, I was just reading the paper, Doc, and I see our friend, Bill Daily, was reelected yesterday. They even ran a family portrait in the local section. So I thought I'd give you a call, see how Rosanne was doing. The article about Daily didn't mention her."

Rizzo heard the doctor sigh. "No," he said, "I imagine it wouldn't." But when the psychiatrist continued, a new, satisfied tone had entered his voice. "As for Rosanne, she's doing well, Sergeant. Very well, in fact, although we're still early in the game. Her detox seems successful and the psychotropics, particularly the newer ones, have been quite effective. She's at a facility in Westchester County, one that specializes in teens and young adults. I visit her often, almost weekly. And Father Charles sees her every few days. He's been marvelous, actually. Extremely helpful."

Rizzo nodded. "Good," he said. "That sounds great. I'm glad I called."

"Well, I am, too, Sergeant," Rogers said. "After all, if it hadn't been for you and your partner, Detective McQueen, God only knows where the poor girl would be today."

"Yeah, Doc," Rizzo said with some bitterness, "a couple a real heroes."

"Yes, indeed," Rogers replied, not noticing or perhaps choosing to ignore the irony in Rizzo's tone: Rizzo couldn't decide which.

They made some small talk then bid each other good-bye. Rizzo hung up and sat back in his seat. He noticed Priscilla approaching, and chased Rosanne and her father from his thoughts.

"Hello, Cil," he said as she took a seat beside his desk. "Ready to do some leg work?"

"Sure thing," she said. "Always ready."

"Good." Reaching across the desk, he removed a manila file from his pile of papers and flipped it open. "I've been reading the precinct jacket on those other two robberies. Same pattern as the Hom situation: lone mugger, comes up from behind, grabs the elderly vic around the throat, makes his threats, takes the wallet in the first case, purse in the second, then shoves the vics forward hard enough for them to fall to the ground. By the time they recover, perp is gone, runnin' away. Best description we got here is from the Homs. It's the only case with two victims. Guess our perp figured all white boys look alike to old Chinese, so he wasn't too worried about taking on two vics at once."

Priscilla took the file from Rizzo's hand, scanning it. "If the Hom description is the best we have, we ain't got squat," she said, raising her eyes to Rizzo's. "All they say is male white, average height, nothing about build, hair/eye color, possibly a teenager. No help at all."

Rizzo nodded. "Yeah, I know that, but like I said, you may be my lucky charm."

"Yeah," said Priscilla, "you told me that twice already. What's your point?"

"Well, we caught a real break with that street corner, Seventy-second and Fifteenth. The northeast corner. We may have somethin' there."

Priscilla closed the precinct file, flipping it casually onto the messy desktop. "And what would that be?" she asked.

Rizzo sat back in his seat. "Frankie Fits," he said.

"Frankie Fits?" Priscilla asked. "Who the fuck is Frankie Fits?"

Rizzo glanced up at the wall clock, then back to Priscilla. "Neighborhood celebrity, Cil. Like that kid Joey DeMarco I pointed out your first day in the precinct."

She furrowed her brow. "That cat killer asshole?"

Rizzo nodded. "Yeah. He's a celebrity, too. But Frankie, he's harmless, not like DeMarco. See, he's mentally challenged, what the kids in the neighborhood call, 'all fucked up.' I'm not sure what his exact condition is, but he's had some neurosurgery in the past. Few years ago, he was walkin' around with a U-shaped scar on the side of his shaved head. Looked like he was wearin' a Colts football helmet."

"And he can help us how?" she questioned.

"Well, old Frankie, on top of his other problems, is epileptic. He has seizures periodically, especially when he gets stressed out. Some a the local kids like to tease him, get him riled up, bring on a seizure. The kids call the seizures 'fits,' so he's 'Frankie Fits.'"

Priscilla shook her head. "Little pricks," she said.

"Yeah," Rizzo said. "Brooklyn streets aren't known for their genteel ambiance. Anyway, Frankie must be pushin' thirty by now. Lives with his mother in a basement apartment near Our Lady of Guadalupe. He helps out around the rectory, cleans up, shit like that."

"Guadalupe? The church on Fifteenth Avenue?" Priscilla asked.

"Yep, that's it. On the *southeast* corner of Seventy-second Street. Right across Seventy-second is Public School one-twelve. On that northeast corner is the schoolyard where Frankie Fits spends most nights, sitting alone in the dark on the high steps that lead to the janitor's office."

"Are you kiddin' me, Joe?" Priscilla asked.

"No, really. A few years back, Frankie started hanging around the schoolyard when the kids were on recess. Some of the mothers freaked out, afraid Frankie might hurt one of their little darlings. They complained to the Six-Two cop assigned as school safety officer."

"What came of it?" Priscilla asked.

"The cop worked it out. He told Frankie if he stayed clear of the school during the day, he could be the night watchman. Like an assistant to the cop, you know, keep an eye on things. And Frankie went for it. Guess he figured he was helping out the little kids, protecting the school, whatever."

"So you figure he was there on the night the Homs got robbed?" Priscilla asked.

Rizzo nodded. "Yeah, that's what I figure. Frankie's there most nights, even in the worst winter weather. Sits on those steps till midnight, then goes home."

"That is some pitiful shit, Joe."

"Yeah, well, to us, sure. But to Frankie, it gives him a sense of purpose, a sense of worth. Like his church work does. And the guy's got the character to stick to it."

Priscilla stood. "So, let's go talk to him," she said. "If the perp is some neighborhood asshole, maybe Frankie can make him for us."

"Yeah," Rizzo said. "Maybe. Only thing is, all the local kids know Frankie sits up there at night, in the dark, on the steps, looking down at that corner."

She frowned. "So you figure it's a newbie or a transient?"

"Could be," Rizzo said. "Or maybe just somebody figures Frankie is too stupid for it to matter. Or the perp could be somebody Frankie'd be too scared to rat on." He shrugged. "We'll see. But it's too early now. Frankie doesn't get there till after he has dinner, and I'd rather not go to his home and rattle his old lady. I've got some paperwork to do and calls to make. Relax awhile, we'll head out a little later."

Priscilla nodded. "Okay. I've got some DD-fives to catch up on. Let me know when you're ready."

After she walked away, Rizzo turned back to his desk. The folded *Daily News* caught his eye. He picked it up and again scanned the photograph and report of Councilman William Daily's impressive election victory.

Things would have been different, Rizzo thought. Things *should* have been different. Had the microcassette hidden away in the Rizzo basement followed its rightful course after he and McQueen had first found it, the newspapers would be singing a different song about William Daily right now.

Rizzo tossed the paper angrily into the wastebasket at his feet.

"Fuck it," he said in a barely audible hiss. "His time'll come. It'll come."

Reaching for his paperwork, Rizzo tried to ignore the voice nagging at him, a soft, questioning voice.

"Fuck it," he said again. He turned to his work.

FRANKIE CORVONA was twenty-eight years old. The youngest of three siblings, he had been what the neighborhood women referred to as a "change of life baby," born unplanned to a forty-four-year-old

mother. Complications at birth involving a strangling umbilical cord had deprived Frankie's new brain of oxygen, causing irreversible damage. In addition to his severely reduced intellectual capacities, he had also been rendered epileptic. Later, additional problems arising from cranial pressures had further tormented him, resulting in a series of operations. The operations had preserved his life but further damaged his already ravished brain.

Frankie lived with his mother, drawing a disability stipend from Social Security. His father, long deceased, had left a modest pension behind. Frankie's two older siblings were only sporadically involved, bringing gifts of money for birthdays and holidays.

Rizzo pulled the Chevy to the curb on the north side of Seventy-second Street and shut down the motor. He peered into the darkness of the Public School 112 schoolyard.

"I can't see if he's there," he said.

Priscilla shrugged. "It's so fuckin' dark, I can barely see the steps." She opened the car door. "Let's go see," she said.

The two detectives crossed the sidewalk and climbed the three worn concrete steps leading to the schoolyard. Stepping through the open gateway of the six-foot iron fence that surrounded the yard, they paused, allowing their eyes to adjust to the blanketing darkness. The moonless night was cold and damp, illumination cast only from the corner streetlight where Seventy-second Street intersected with Fifteenth Avenue. Rizzo noted that the corner itself was well lit, the streetlight giving off a warm, blue-white glow.

They crossed the yard to the steep, narrow high steps nestled against the side of the ancient school building. In the cold darkness enveloping the steps, nearly halfway up, they saw the huddled mass of Frankie Corvona.

As they reached the base of the staircase, they paused, Rizzo placing a foot onto the second step and leaning forward, his right elbow laid casually across his knee.

"Frankie?" he said, his voice friendly and soft. "Is that you up there?"

In the darkness, they could barely make out the pale, round, full

face of the man. His large, wide-set eyes flitted from one cop to the other.

"It's Frankie," the man said in response. "Frankie."

"Well, I figured you'd be here, Frankie, keeping an eye on the place for us," Rizzo said. Then he turned to Priscilla. "See, what'd I tell you? We can always count on Frankie."

Turning his gaze back to the young man, he said, "I'm Joe. I'm a policeman. A detective. And this is my partner, Cil. She's a detective, too. We work for the Sixty-second Precinct. Sort of like you do, Frankie."

A small smile came to the man's lips. "I watch the school at night," he said, pride in his voice. "I watch the school."

"Joe told me about that, Frankie," Priscilla said. "And he told me you do a real good job, too."

Frankie turned his eyes to her. "You're black," he said.

"Yes, Frankie. I am."

He appeared to think about that for a moment.

"Dr. Towner is black," he said.

"Who's Dr. Towner?" Priscilla asked.

Frankie's face brightened. "He's my friend, he gives me medicine so I don't spin around too much."

Priscilla nodded. "That's good, Frankie. Real good."

Rizzo straightened up. "Frankie," he said, "you mind if we come up there? We'd like to talk to you a little."

Now Frankie's face clouded, his smile faded, his eyes darted nervously.

"I didn't go around the children," he said, a childlike defiance in his tone. "I didn't."

Rizzo nodded. "I know that, Frankie. It's not about that. It's something else. Something important that we need you to help us with." Rizzo leaned forward, glancing around, lowering his voice.

"It's *police* business, Frankie," he said. "We need your help with some *police* business."

Once again, the face brightened. "Oh," he said. "Oh."

"Can we come up?" Rizzo asked again.

"Sure," Frankie said, sliding across the step, leaning his left side against the school wall, making room.

They climbed the fifteen steps, and Rizzo sat down next to him, Priscilla one step above.

"Can I see your badge?" Frankie asked Rizzo.

"Sure," Rizzo said, reaching into his left pants pocket. He flipped the case open, the gold detective sergeant shield catching the faint light and twinkling against the worn black leather.

Frankie raised his eyes from the badge to Rizzo's face.

"Can I hold it?"

Rizzo extended the badge, pressing it into Frankie's hand.

"As a matter of fact," Rizzo said, "you *should* hold it. After all, this is official police business you're helping us with. Like a deputy, sort of."

Priscilla watched as Frankie raised the badge tentatively to his eye level, studying it, his face glowing with happiness. She pursed her lips and shook her head slightly, saddened. She glanced at Rizzo, but his face, neutral, remained on Frankie.

Frankie lowered the badge, holding it tightly in both hands.

"I went to Shea Stadium once," he said, some pleasurable memory swirling to the forefront of his thoughts. "When it used to be there."

"You root for the Mets, Frankie?" Rizzo asked.

Now Frankie appeared confused. "Mets?" he said, frowning. "I think so." After a pause, his smile returned. "Mets," he repeated. "They play baseball."

Rizzo nodded, glancing at Priscilla. She gave a small shrug in acknowledgment of the look, but remained silent.

Aware that stress could trigger a seizure in the man-child, Rizzo very gradually moved the conversation to the business at hand.

"So, Frankie, were you here last Thursday?" he asked. "Last Thursday night, around nine-thirty?"

Frankie frowned, dropping his eyes to the badge he held, running his finger across the embossed surface.

"I don't know," he said flatly.

Priscilla leaned forward, laying a gentle hand on Frankie's right shoulder.

"Do you know what day today is, Frankie?" she asked.

He raised his eyes from the badge to meet hers. He looked confused.

"It isn't day," he said with an assertive shake of his head. "It's night."

Priscilla nodded. "Yes, Frankie, of course. You're right. It is night. Do you know what *night* this is?"

His lips turned down, and he dropped his eyes from her. For a moment, shame sat heavily on his shoulders, but then, suddenly, he brightened. He laid Rizzo's badge carefully on his lap, then rummaged through his pants pockets.

Pulling out a chainless pocket watch, he smiled up at Priscilla and pointed to its large, round white face, the Roman numerals contrasting in bold black relief.

"When this hand is here," he said, pointing carefully to the crystal, "and this hand is here, I go home."

Priscilla glanced at Rizzo. Turning to Frankie, she smiled kindly and patted his shoulder.

"Good, Frankie," she said. "That's very good."

Frankie smiled proudly and returned the watch to his pocket, again taking Rizzo's badge in his hands.

Rizzo ran a hand through his thinning brown hair. "Okay, Frankie," he said gently. "Let me ask you this: Did anything happen over there? Over by that corner there?" Rizzo pointed a casual thumb over his shoulder, indicating the intersection. "Did anything bad happen over there that you can remember?"

Tension began to enter the man's eyes. Frankie glanced over his shoulder to Priscilla. She smiled and gently squeezed his arm.

"It's okay, Frankie," she said. "You can tell us."

He swallowed hard, glancing once more at Rizzo's badge, gripping it more tightly, then began to rock gently back and forth, his breathing becoming shallow.

"I didn't do it," he said softly.

Rizzo nodded, leaning closer.

"Of course you didn't, Frankie," he said. "But . . . did you see it?"

Frankie looked quickly from one detective to the other, then back to Rizzo's badge, then, lastly, into Priscilla's face.

"One of the bad kids," he said to her. "One of the gang kids. He pushed the people from China. They fell down. He ran away. I think . . . I think . . . he took their money. Their money for food."

"What's his name, Frankie?" Rizzo asked gently.

Frankie's face saddened. "I don't know. I don't know all their names."

"Whose names, Frankie?" Rizzo pressed.

"The bad kids," Frankie said softly. "The Rebels."

He again looked from one cop to the other. Slowly, a smile came back to his lips.

"You use money to buy food," he said, proud of this wonderous knowledge. "You use money to buy food."

RIZZO SLAMMED the car door closed and slipped the key into the ignition.

"Most people," he said, twisting the key and bringing the engine to life, "get made heroes by death. Not some great thing they do. Just by death."

Priscilla tugged at her shoulder harness, searching for the buckle in the darkness of the interior.

"What?" she said.

Rizzo shrugged, scanning the sideview mirror for traffic.

"We all know we're gonna die eventually, Cil, but we still get up every day, go to work, play with the kids, brush our teeth, pay our taxes, all that shit. Even though we know we're gonna die. That's what makes us heroes, knowing that death is waitin' for us."

He turned to Priscilla. "But Frankie, he probably don't even know. Doesn't *really* know he's gonna die. But that kid, he's a hero anyway. Even outside his own little fucked up universe, he's a real fuckin' hero."

Priscilla smiled. "Joe, that don't even make sense, but, I gotta tell ya, I know exactly what you mean."

Rizzo nodded, turning his attention back to driving, easing the Impala from the curb.

"You ever have some kid ask to see your badge, hold your *badge,* and then not ask to see your gun in the next breath? Ever?" He shook his head sadly. "That kid Frankie never even thought to ask about the gun. It don't interest him." Again Rizzo shook his head. "Maybe all of us shoulda got less fuckin' oxygen at birth. Maybe we'd all be too stupid to find shit to fight wars over. Too stupid to kill each other."

"You may be right," Priscilla said. "Better fuckin' world it woulda been, that's for sure. We coulda been just a bunch of two-legged deer, or a bunch of catchers in the rye, just like Frankie is."

Rizzo looked puzzled. "'Catcher in the rye'? Like the book?"

"Somethin' like that," Priscilla said, turning and gazing through the window to the slowly passing, darkened streets.

"I don't get it," Rizzo said. "What, did you talk about that book last night at your class? What's it got to do with Frankie?"

Priscilla turned back to face him. "Don't get me started on last night, Partner. Don't get me started."

Rizzo swung his eyes back to the road, smiling. "Sore subject? What happened, dog eat your homework?"

Priscilla hesitated, and after a moment Rizzo glanced her way.

"Was it that bad? You gonna clam up on me about it?" he asked.

She shook her head. "The guy who teaches the class, his name is Thom Carlyle. Ever hear of him? Wrote a bunch of novels all the critics loved but nobody bought. Not that he gives a shit, his family is old money. Anyway, he comes up to me after class, tells me how good my stuff is, how impressed he is. Wants me to come to his place Saturday night for a party he's throwing. Lots of writers, agents, editors, people like that. He wants to introduce me to his literary agent. He thinks she can help me."

"Well," Rizzo said, "I can see why you're so pissed off. Imagine the nerve of the son of a bitch, tryin' to help you out like that."

"That's not the issue, Joe. He leads into this invite by tellin' me how he originally didn't even want to accept me into his fuckin' class at all. Says my entry submission was weak—how'd he put it?—'Rankly amateurish.'"

"But he took you in anyway."

99

"Oh, yeah, he took me. Right after he got a phone call. Seems like Karen's old man knows a board member at the Y, so the wheels got greased for me and my weak entry submission."

Rizzo widened his eyes in mock surprise. "I'm fuckin' shocked. You mean, shit like that really happens? Wheels get greased? There goes my last shred of faith, right out the fuckin' window."

"I don't wanna discuss it," Priscilla snapped. "Shouldn'ta brought it up. Leave it at this, it just pisses me off, okay? Karen shoulda known better than to go to her old man behind my back. What am I, the little black poster child? The charity of the fuckin' week? What?"

Rizzo shrugged as he drove. "Maybe you're just family, Cil. Maybe the guy's doin' what he'd do for his daughter. What *I'd* do for *my* daughter."

"Well, I ain't his fuckin' daughter."

"Daughter-in-law, then." Rizzo turned briefly to her and winked. "Son-in-law, whatever the fuck. Relax. Welcome to the world. Besides, this guy, this teacher, now he's singin' a different tune, right? Now he figures you got the goods. You want my advice?"

"No. Not really."

"My advice," Rizzo went on, ignoring her, "is to go to that party. Kiss some ass, or maybe get your own ass kissed. This could be the break you need if you're serious about this writing stuff."

She sat silently for a moment. "I'm serious, Joe. *Real* serious."

"Okay, then. End of discussion. Go do what you gotta do. And thank Karen's old man. The guy did just what he shoulda done."

After a few moments of silence, Priscilla spoke up, her tone leaving Rizzo no doubt: the discussion was over.

"What now? About this Hom case, I mean."

He shrugged. "Well, we'll follow Frankie's lead to The Rebels. But we're going to have to develop this independent of him. Even if we could get the D.A. to use Frankie as an eyewitness, which, by the way, we could never do, can you imagine him on the stand? The newest, greenest Legal Aide lawyer could tear him apart, probably make him seize out right in the witness box." Rizzo shook his head. "No, Frankie's done his part. He's out of it from now on. We gotta work it from some other angle. An angle that plays out with the perp copping."

"No argument here, Partner," Priscilla said. "We'll just leave Frankie in his happy place."

"With the half-assed descriptions we got from all the vics, we couldn't even do a valid photo array. And if we tried a mug scan with no description on record, the defense would scream fishing expedition, demand a pretrial Wade hearing, and maybe get any I.D. precluded. Then we'd have nothin'. But now, with Frankie's info, now maybe we can figure a way to go. We'll see. Let's get back to the precinct."

The "bad kids" that Frankie had referred to were members of a local street gang known as The Rebels. They were one of two such gangs housed in the Six-Two, the other being The Bath Beach Boys. The Rebels were the younger of the two gangs, serving as a training ground for eventual admission into the older and more professionally criminal Bath Beach Boys. The Bath Beach Boys, in turn, then served as an apprenticeship for further criminal progression to the Brooklyn organized crime mob currently headed by Louie "The Chink" Quattropa.

The Rebels were generally aged fourteen or so to eighteen or nineteen. If by age twenty or twenty-one a member had failed to move up to The Bath Beach Boys, his organized-gang days were considered over, and most such failures moved on to relatively mundane lives of semirespectability or descended into drug addition. Some entered loner lives of crime, usually resulting in their premature death or long, repeated periods of incarceration.

During his many years in the precinct, Rizzo had dealt with both groups, as well as several neighboring street gangs from the Sixty-eighth, Sixty-sixth, Sixty-first, and Sixtieth Precincts.

Rizzo parked the Impala on Benson Avenue, and he and Priscilla walked a short block to the precinct. They went to the rear of the first floor and entered a small office marked "Community Policing."

Rizzo made the introductions.

"Priscilla Jackson, meet Sergeant Janice Calder, our community policing officer. We've apparently caught her on a very rare night tour. What's up with that, Jan? Have a fight with the old man?"

The uniformed sergeant, a twenty-year veteran and an acquaintance of Rizzo's, smiled. "No," she said. "My daughter is home from college for a few days, so I switched to four-to-midnights this week to spend some time with her. Her friends keep her busy at night."

Rizzo nodded, turning again to Priscilla. "Janice here makes sure the good people of the Six-Two are informed, educated, and aware. That way, they can all get to die in bed, unmugged, unraped, unshot, and unmolested. She also helps the precinct cops do a better job servin' the needs of the citizens, not to mention fixing an occasional parking ticket that might inconvenience some community board member or well-connected brother-in-law."

Calder laughed, reaching to shake Priscilla's hand. "Now, Joe here knows damn well I'd never do such a thing," she said. "Welcome to the precinct, Priscilla."

The two women made small talk, searching for friends in the department they might have had in common.

Then Rizzo got to the point.

"Is Tony in, Jan?" he asked, referring to her office mate and the precinct youth officer, Tony Olivero.

She shook her head. "No, he's off till Saturday. Does a day tour when he comes back in."

Rizzo nodded. "I need to go through his stuff. The Rebel photo book, specifically."

"No problem," Calder said with a shrug. "Help yourself."

Rizzo moved to Olivero's desk.

"What'd the little darlins do this time?" Calder asked, returning to her own desk and sitting down.

"We figure one of 'em for three street robberies," he answered.

Calder's eyes widened. "No shit? Those three the last month or so?"

Rizzo nodded, slipping a five-by-eight-inch photo album from the lower drawer of Olivero's desk. "Those are the ones."

She frowned. "Sounds wrong to me, Joe. The Rebels might be dumb, but they ain't stupid. The Chink finds out they're robbin' the locals, he may whack a Rebel ass or two."

"Yeah, it struck me as odd, too," Rizzo said. "But maybe one of the Indians is off the reservation. If Louie Quattropa don't scare this kid, we may have a newbie psycho on our hands."

"Well, I wouldn't worry about it," Calder said. "If he's pissin' off Quattropa, he's gettin' the short-stay rate."

"Yeah, probably," Rizzo agreed, standing up. "I'm gonna borrow Tony's picture file. Tell him for me if I don't get it back to his drawer by Saturday." He turned to leave.

"No problem, Joe, take care." She turned to Priscilla. "Good to meetcha. Don't bend over in front of this guy, Priscilla," she said, nodding her head toward Rizzo. "I never did trust him much."

Priscilla laughed. "Guess you haven't heard yet. I don't bend over for *any* man."

"Well, good for you, honey," Calder said. "I gotta admit, I have a few times and it usually wasn't worth the effort."

Rizzo shook his head. "Let me the fuck outta here," he said, heading for the door, the women's laughter ringing in his ears.

CHAPTER EIGHT

ON THURSDAY MORNING, Rizzo and Jackson made their visits to Bik and Feng Hom and the other two elderly victims of the recent street robberies. Each victim carefully leafed through the photo album Rizzo had borrowed from Olivero's desk. It contained full-color photographs of the eighteen members of The Rebels who held criminal records. None of the photos was identified as the assailant in the cases at hand.

Later, Rizzo sat behind the wheel of the Impala parked in front of the last house they had visited and sighed.

"Well," he said, "maybe Frankie was wrong."

Priscilla frowned. "Or maybe the perp is a newbie like we figured and not in the book yet. That would explain why he didn't know Frankie was probably sitting there in the dark, looking out over the corner. Or maybe he's clean, no record yet, so no picture. Or maybe these old vics just can't make the guy. They sure as hell couldn't describe him very well."

"They probably couldn't describe a teenage Frank Sinatra too well, either," Rizzo said. "But they'd still be able to pick his picture out of a mug book."

"Joe," she said, shaking her head gently, "why is it that every time you refer to anyone I've heard of, they're *dead*?"

"I don't know," he answered. "Guess I ain't that impressed with anybody you ever heard of who's still alive."

Rizzo started the engine, adjusting himself in the seat. "Let's go to work on our other cases, give this one a rest. Tonight, after dinner, I'll run down to the high steps on my own time, show Frankie this book of assholes, see if he can make one. If not, we can still go to plan B, even without a positive I.D."

"And what is plan B?" Priscilla asked.

Rizzo smiled, pulling the Impala out into the street.

"Tell you when I tell you," he said. "Let's see what Frankie's got to say first."

She shrugged. "Okay, boss," she said. "Whatever."

They spent the balance of the tour crisscrossing the precinct and its surrounding neighborhoods, methodically working some of the dozen open cases they carried. Later, at the precinct, they wrapped up with a paper trail of the day's activity.

At three-fifty p.m., her relief detective present in the squad room, Priscilla waved good-bye to Rizzo.

"See you Sunday morning, Joe," she said, referring to their next scheduled tour. "Enjoy the swing days."

"You too, kiddo. If I get lucky with Frankie later tonight, you want me to call you? Or should I save it for Sunday?"

"Call," she said. "We'll be home tonight. No plans."

Later, a little after nine o'clock, Rizzo left the schoolyard, photo album in hand, and returned to his Camry. Frankie, like the victims, had not been able to I.D. a suspect.

Rizzo glanced at the face of his Timex. He sighed. No use putting it off any longer, he was already out, it wasn't that late, it was as good a time as any. He started the car and headed for his last stop of the night.

In the sparse weeknight traffic, it didn't take long to reach the battered, litter-strewn block in the Red Hook section of Brooklyn. Rizzo parked under a streetlight, tossing the NYPD vehicle identification card onto the dash, hoping it'd be garlic to any vampires roaming the darkened, cold streets, searching for a car to boost.

He crossed diagonally to a dimly illuminated storefront, its painted windows opaque. From above the door, a bloodied and pained Christ gazed down at him from a two-foot-long wooden crucifix. The words "Non-Combat Zone," in military-style stenciling, were emblazoned with dark red lettering on the plain gray metal door. Rizzo reached out a hand and pressed the doorbell.

Father Attilio Jovino, although considerably older than Joe Rizzo, still cut an impressive figure. He had come into the priesthood only after a bloody and violent tour of duty in the jungles of Vietnam, and he still carried the hard-edged, flinty-eyed look of a U.S. Army Ranger.

Now, sitting at the desk in his office in the rear of the youth sanctuary he had founded more than fifteen years earlier, Jovino smiled across to his visitor.

"So, Joe," he said, intertwining his fingers and leaning forward across the desk. "I always look forward to your visits. And even more so since I usually get to share a cigarette with you."

Rizzo reached into his coat pocket, extracting a crumpled pack. "Yeah, well, there's a story there, Tillio, but that's for another visit."

Jovino shrugged as he dug out an ashtray from his desk drawer. "As you wish, my son."

They smoked in silence for a few moments, Rizzo's eyes occasionally rising to the huge crucifix hanging on the wall behind Jovino's desk.

"Is it Jesus making you uncomfortable," the priest asked, "or is there something on your mind?"

"Yeah, well, a little a both, I guess," Rizzo conceded. "I stopped by 'cause I needed to talk to you."

Jovino nodded and sat back in his seat. "I'm listening," he said, letting smoke trickle from his lips. "And we're alone here."

"Yeah, well, relax, Til," Rizzo said. "I ain't confessin' nothin' here."

Jovino smiled. "All right," he said. A moment passed, Jovino drawing on his cigarette. Then, again leaning forward, he asked in a soft voice, "But, if you were, would it perhaps have something to do with that twelve-thousand-dollar cash donation you recently bestowed upon my sanctuary? You know, you never did satisfy my curiosity about that."

"Well, that's okay, Father," Rizzo said with a shrug. "All you need to know is the money was clean. Clean as any money can be, anyhow. I hope it's being put to good use."

Jovino nodded. "Twelve grand saves more than one life around here. Considerably more. These runaway kids don't need all that much. Food, a little doctoring, kindness. Concern. And a good deal of faith and hope." He paused here and smiled warmly at Rizzo. "Wherever that money originated, it was delivered to these kids by Christ. That's good enough for me."

Rizzo took in a deep breath. "Yeah," he said, expelling slowly. "Christ."

Again Jovino nodded. "Christ appears in many forms. Sometimes even in the guise of a Brooklyn cop. A cop, I should add, who looks tired, seems uncharacteristically unsure of himself. What's the problem, Joe? You can tell me."

Rizzo tried to lighten his tone. "Not exactly a problem. Just a . . . a situation, that's all."

Jovino sat back in his seat. "Ah, yes," he said, "a situation. Of course. I experienced a few situations myself before I came to the priesthood. One involved the lovely young sister of my best friend. Another a small incident of mayhem in the highlands outside of Hue. I can assure you, my friend, I know something of 'situations.'"

Rizzo shook his head, dropping his eyes to the red tip of his burning Chesterfield. "It ain't quite that dramatic, Father." He raised his eyes slowly to meet Jovino's.

The priest spread his arms. "So, tell me, then."

Rizzo cleared his throat. "Remember back in August, when I stopped in? After me and Mike had found the Daily kid? I told you that I might be comin' across something, something very detrimental to Councilman William Daily?"

Jovino nodded. "Yes. Of course I remember. I agreed to deliver this hypothetical 'something' to the authorities, the federal authorities, as I recall, under the guise of its having appeared here at the shelter, presumably left by one of the runaways. It would have been problematic for you to go to the authorities without jeopardizing yourselves—you and Mike, that is."

Rizzo nodded. "Correct."

Jovino continued. "And then, shortly thereafter, you reappeared at my door, twelve thousand dollars in hand. You know, last year the

Brooklyn Chamber of Commerce donated five thousand to the Non-Combat Zone, Verizon Corporation eight thousand. So you, sir, are now my biggest single supporter."

Rizzo grinned. "Good for me."

"Yes," Jovino said with a nod. "Good for you indeed." The priest paused, taking a last drag on his cigarette, then very deliberately crushing it out in the ashtray.

"It was at that point that I assumed this material, this incriminating material concerning Councilman Daily, had at last made its way into your possession." He paused once more. "And yet, no such material has been presented to me to date."

He reached across the desk, shaking a second cigarette loose from Rizzo's pack. Lighting it, he raised his eyes through the smoke to Rizzo's.

"I wondered about that, Joe. I must say, I *still* wonder about that."

Rizzo nodded. "Yeah. I figured. Well, you can stop wonderin'. I have the material you're referrin' to. In fact, I've had it all along." He leaned forward and stubbed out his own cigarette. "That's why I'm here now. See, Daily just got himself reelected, and if a certain tape had already gone to the feds, that never woulda happened. I know that's my responsibility, my fault. And I can live with it. I just need *you* to know that it ain't over yet. I just need some more time. For a couple a different reasons. Just a little more time."

Jovino responded. "Well, originally, you had said something about six months or so. Of course, my understanding at the time was that you didn't yet have this . . . 'material.' Now I'm learning that isn't exactly so. I'm learning that I've been misled."

Their gazes locked. Rizzo noted a hardness begin to form in the priest's eyes.

"Is there anything else I need to know, Joe?" he asked in a low, flat tone. "Because if there is, now would be the time to tell me. Not next week, not next month, not six months from now. Now."

Jovino let out a sigh, releasing some of the tension that had come to his body.

"Now, Joe," he repeated softly.

"There's nothin' else," Rizzo said wearily. "I've been sitting on some evidence. The twelve grand, that was just something fell into my hands along the way. It has no rightful owner; it's better off where it is, helpin' these kids of yours."

Jovino pursed his lips.

"Is 'falling into your hands' similar to something 'falling off a truck,' Joe?"

"Not exactly," Rizzo said. "I swear to you, that cash was orphaned. Totally. Like I said, no rightful owner. It was as much mine as anyone's." He shrugged. "And I chose to give it to you. End of story."

Jovino leaned forward, frowning. "Except for this tape you continue to sit on. You know that I share no warm regard for Councilman Daily, but, personal feelings aside, there is a right and there is a wrong. You need to make a decision, Joe."

They held each other's eyes.

"What's it to be, Joe?" the priest asked softly. "Right . . . or wrong?"

AT SEVEN fifty-five Sunday morning, Rizzo sat down heavily in the chair behind his desk. He looked up at Detective Alphonse Borrelli, then back down to the slip of paper in his hand.

Raising his eyes back to Borrelli, Rizzo sighed. "When'd the call come in, Al?"

"'Bout five-thirty, six this morning," Borrelli answered. "The guy was a pushy prick. He told me he had your cell number and he'd call you at home. I told him to hold off, you'd be in soon enough. He finally admitted whatever he wanted could keep till eight."

"Thanks, Al. You might as well take off, I'm here and Jackson'll be in any minute. Matter a fact, there she is now. Take off. And thanks again."

The man shrugged, turning to leave. "No problem. Take it easy."

Priscilla approached Rizzo's desk, nodding at Borrelli as they passed each other.

"Mornin'," she said to Rizzo. "I'm gonna sign in, then grab some breakfast. The Roach Coach just pulled up in front. You want anything?"

He shook his head. "No thanks, Cil."

Rizzo dropped his eyes once again to the yellow notepaper in his hand. Sighing, he reached for his cell and punched in the Manhattan phone number. The call was answered on the second ring.

"This is Joe Rizzo," he said into the mouthpiece. "I'm returning Papa Man's call."

"Yeah, okay, hold on," a gruff male voice replied.

As he waited, Rizzo visualized Papa Man—large and burly, near sixty years old with black, unkempt grizzled hair and a tough, yet not unpleasant, face. He was the acknowledged leader of the New York City chapter of the Hell's Angels.

After a moment, another male voice came through the line, with a deeper and more resonant tone.

"Sergeant Rizzo, how good of you to get back to me so promptly."

Rizzo let air escape through his lips. "What's the problem, Papa Man?"

The man chuckled. "I hope I'm not interrupting your Sunday breakfast with the wife and kiddies at Friendly's, Sergeant."

Rizzo let a moment elapse. "What's the problem, Papa Man?" he repeated.

"Yes, of course, Sergeant Rizzo. Enough small talk between old friends. Let's get down to business. May I speak freely?"

"I'm on my cell," Rizzo answered. "Last I knew, nobody was listening in."

"Fair enough. As you may remember, I did you a small service a few months back. And, as I understand it, you parlayed that favor into a successful bit of police work."

"I remember," Rizzo said.

"Do you remember all the details, Sergeant? The fine print, if you will?"

"I remember."

Papa Man sounded pleased. "Good, Joe. Very good. I'll get to the point. One of my riders spent Saturday night partying in Brooklyn with an ex-wife or girlfriend or whatever. This particular rider isn't known for his moderation, and there are now allegations of DWI, criminal possession of a controlled substance, and resisting arrest being made against him. More seriously, assault on an officer. He called me earlier from Central Booking and asked for my assistance. I think what he had in mind was an attorney, but I thought, 'Hey, what about my old Brooklyn friend, Sergeant Rizzo? I bet he can help.' Was I right, Joe? Can you help?"

Rizzo let the man hear his sigh. "I believe our deal was, if one of your guys got jammed up over here, I'd take a look at it and see what I could do. That your memory, too?"

"Yes. Exactly. So, you'll take a look?"

Rizzo glanced at the wall clock. "What time they lock the guy up?"

"I think it was about three-thirty, four this morning."

"Which precinct?"

"The Nine-Four, over in Greenpoint."

"What's the guy's name?"

"We call him Zumba. He was born James Palmer."

"The arresting is probably doing the paperwork at Central Booking right now. I can get down there in about twenty minutes. I'll see what I can do."

"Thank you, Sergeant. It's good to know you're a man of honor who keeps his word."

"You know how this shit works, Papa," Rizzo said. "I owe you. Period. Honor and words got nothin' to do with any a this."

Rizzo could visualize the wolflike grin of the man. "Well, whatever, Joe. Just do what you can. Zumba can't stand a fall on an assaulting-a-cop charge. It'd ruin any chance he may still have for the Citizen of the Year award, you know?"

"Yeah, Papa. I can imagine. But remember, our deal was everybody has to be happy, not just you and this asshole. The arresting has to say okay to it. And if it's already reached the A.D.A., he has to go for it, too. It could be a tough sell."

"Well, from my experience with Brooklyn, Central Booking is a busy little place on Sunday morning. I doubt this minor a matter has come to the district attorney's attention yet. It's just a cop, just a uniform involved. See what you can do."

"I'll let you know how it goes," Rizzo said, then closed the phone, breaking the connection. He stood slowly, slipping on his overcoat and picking up the Impala keys.

Downstairs he intercepted Priscilla, coffee and egg sandwich in her hands. He filled her in quickly.

"Your old friend called," he told her. "Papa Man."

"Damn," she said. "What does the boss of the Hell's Angels want with you on a Sunday freakin' morning?"

Rizzo twisted his lips. "Whaddya think he wants?"

Memory dawned in her eyes. "Oh, he's cashin' that ticket from the meeting you, me, and Mike had with him last summer?"

"Bingo," Rizzo said touching a finger lightly to the tip of her nose. "I gotta run downtown to Central Booking. You stay here, hold the fort. It's just you and me this tour. If a job does come in, stall it. If you absolutely gotta roll on it, take a uniform along. I'll meet you at the job if you ain't in the squad room when I get back."

"Okay, Joe. How long you figure you'll be?"

Rizzo shrugged. "Twenty minutes there, twenty back, twenty to sell the cop my story. Figure an hour, hour ten. Like that."

Priscilla smiled at him coyly. "Sure you don't want me along? I can shake some ass, bat my eyes, grease the cop a little for you."

"No, you stay here where we both should be. Hell, maybe I'll get lucky and it's a straight female cop and I can shake my own ass."

"Okay," she said. "Just try not to throw your back out, Pops."

Rizzo shook his head and moved past Priscilla to the door.

The Sunday-morning traffic was almost nonexistent. As Rizzo drove toward the heart of Brooklyn, the downtown area, he considered the job at hand.

Throughout his career, Rizzo had carefully and consistently established a deep well of gratitude and obligation among his fellow officers for favors he had rendered. He had done the same with the various citizens who peopled the shadowy world of day-to-day police business. As a result, he could reach out almost at will to virtually any area within the department and collect his payback in the form of expedited service, specialized assistance, or influential intervention on his behalf—all repaid debts for accommodations he had once provided. Rizzo could reach just as deeply into the dark netherworld to mobsters and street criminals for similar help. It had been essential for his success.

Now, as he sped along the Gowanus Expressway, he reflected on how, more and more, he found himself on the other end of this cynical, yet pragmatic, arrangement, rendering the payback, as was now the case. As retirements, transfers, and other attritions chipped at those in the department who owed him, and changing demographics altered the Six-Two, the pool of those Rizzo was indebted to seemed to grow proportionately.

It was not, he realized, a healthy state of affairs.

Just one more reason to retire, he thought. The more payback he rendered, and the less he received, the better the likelihood that someday it would all blow up in his face. Yet it remained an unavoidable function of the job, a one-hand-washing-the-other way of life for him. It was a minefield becoming more difficult and dangerous to navigate.

Rizzo swung the Impala off the expressway and onto Atlantic Avenue. He made a mental note to discuss this morning's mission in more detail with Priscilla later in the day. Though he was almost certain she understood the nature of the game, he couldn't make assumptions. This morning's job was the perfect example. The last thing Rizzo wanted was to lend assistance of a murky legal nature to a Hell's Angel. Yet he was bound by the agreement he had entered into with Papa Man some months before. It was not, as Papa had misstated, a matter of honor. Not at all. It was simply a function of police business. Had he reneged, he would never again be able to reach out to the Angels should the need arise.

And if he reneged often enough on his promises, word would eventually permeate the subculture of the streets, and Rizzo would no longer be trusted, no longer be able to gather the scraps of information, cooperation, and accommodations necessary to the successful plying of his trade.

That's what he needed to impress upon Priscilla. As a detective, she should never enter into an agreement she was not fully prepared to follow through on, regardless of how distasteful or questionable in nature. The time for high-minded scruples was *before* the deal was struck, not afterward.

As he drove slowly along State Street, searching for a place to park in the area reserved for police and court officers, correction and probation personnel, he mulled it over.

Yes, he would explain it to Priscilla, in case she hadn't mastered it all during her ten years in uniform. She needed to know, and it was his responsibility to make sure she did.

But what about Carol? Would he someday have to explain it all to her? Would that responsibility fall to him as well, or to some other cop, someone unknown to him. The street education of his youngest child entrusted to a stranger?

Rizzo parked the car and climbed out, slamming the door behind him.

No way, he thought. No way would he let that happen.

He turned and crossed State Street, heading for the secured police entrance at the rear of the Brooklyn Criminal Courthouse. He shook his mind clear of thoughts of Carol and turned once more to the task at hand.

OFFICER FREDDY Clarton was a twenty-four-year veteran, currently assigned to the Ninety-fourth Precinct patrol unit, covering the old blue-collar Brooklyn neighborhood of Greenpoint. In three months' time, he would retire to the small North Carolina town where his grandparents and their parents had been born. Contained within the inner plastic sleeve of his uniform cap, he carried a small single sheet calendar. As each tour ended, he carefully placed a neat, red X over the date.

"Eighty-one more days," he said, as he sat sipping coffee with Rizzo on a small bench outside the holding pen area of Central Booking, located in the basement of the courthouse.

"That's great, Freddy," Rizzo said. "I got about a year to go myself."

Clarton shook his head. "Too goddamned long, Sarge, too goddamned long."

"It's the hand I got dealt," Rizzo answered with a shrug.

Clarton sipped his coffee, his eyes peering over the cup's edge to Rizzo.

"So, Sarge," he said. "You wanna get down to business?"

Rizzo had been glad to find that the arresting officer was an old vet and not some nervous rookie afraid of his own shadow. Now his appreciation for the black cop's seniority turned to an even more comforting respect for Clarton's street smarts and directness.

"Yeah, Freddy, I do," he said. "And just call me Joe."

The cop laughed. "Oh, Lord, this must be a good one, we gettin' all buddy-buddy here. What you need, Joe?"

Rizzo leaned closer to the man. "I read the arrest report and the rap sheet, Freddy. I know this guy Zumba is an asshole. And he ain't a friend of mine."

"Okay," the cop said with a nod.

"So," Rizzo continued. "This is the story. I owe a favor to the boss of the Angels. Over in Manhattan. The guy helped me with a runaway kid case, and it worked out good. This is his payback."

"What is?" Clarton asked, his eyes narrowing.

Rizzo took a deep breath and let it out slowly. "Okay, you got this guy on a DWI, possession, assault-two, and resisting. I need you to shit-can the assault charge. It's a D-felony. Drop it to obstructing governmental administration, an A-misdemeanor."

The cop frowned. "This shit is a pain in my ass. Only reason I'm even here is 'cause they got me workin' with some kid thinks he's gonna clean up Dodge City. This whole collar was his doin', then he tells me he can't book the guy 'cause he's gotta baptize his sister's kid this morning. Imagine that? When we first saw Zumba weavin' his bike and pulled him over, I told the kid to ignore it, let the guy go, but no, the kid is all righteous, can't let a drunk go with just a warning. See, the skell was only 'bout five blocks from his apartment. Shit, worst coulda happened was he wrecked and broke his own sorry neck. Damn fool out ridin' a motorcycle on a cold night in November, served him right if he went down. But no, my partner wants us to lock the guy up."

Rizzo smiled. "Kids," he said simply.

Clarton nodded. "Yeah. Younger every day, seems like. Anyway, so then the Angel mouths off a little, next thing I know, the kid slaps him and the guy goes ape-shit, so we got to tune his ass up. Then we toss 'im and find the dope. Now you come askin' me to drop the assault count. That really hangs me out if the guy starts bitchin' 'bout the lump I put on his head. I need that assault charge to cover my own ass, Joe."

Rizzo nodded. "Yeah, well, I understand. But I'll talk to the man in Manhattan. There won't be any bitchin' about you smackin' this shit-head around. The resisting charge still stands, and with an added obstruction, that more than covers your use of force."

Clarton considered it. "Well," he said after a moment. "I guess it's not like we broke his fuckin' head or anything."

"Exactly," said Rizzo. "What weight did the CPCS come in at?"

Clarton shrugged. "Haven't heard yet," he said. "It was just a taste, a little coke. What he had left over from his party-hardy night."

"Probably his wake up," Rizzo said.

Clarton ran a hand through his hair and sighed. "I hate to get into this kinda shit so late in the game. I don't wanna be spendin' my last few months with some I.A.D. or Civilian Review prick breakin' my balls."

"No way," Rizzo said emphatically. "You drop that assault-two, you'll never hear nothin' from this guy again. He tries to fuck this deal up, I go to his boss. Zumba gets thrown in the fuckin' river. Believe me, it won't be a problem. Let him pay his fines for the dope and DWI and take an A.C.D. or time-served on the two misdemeanors. Everybody'll be happy."

Clarton nodded. "What do I get out of this, Joe? Your undyin' gratitude?"

Rizzo laughed. "Yeah, exactly. Although, I gotta tell ya, my good-lookin' partner did offer to come along and shake her ass for you, but I told her no."

"I been awake for twenty-five hours straight," Clarton said. "I'm too tired for any ass shakin'." Now he shook his head, his small smile slowly fading. "Damn," he said. "Me workin' with a gung ho kid and you with a freakin' female. They're tryin' to kill us, kill off all the old men."

Rizzo stood, extending his hand. "Well, not much time left for them to finish the job, Freddy. We're both almost out the door."

They shook hands, Clarton standing to face him.

"Yeah," he said. "I guess." Then after a pause, added, "I'll re-write the report, shit-can the assault. When the A.D.A sees it and writes up the complaint, it won't be there."

Now, still holding on to Rizzo's hand, he leaned inward, his firm grasp pulling Rizzo slightly forward.

"But if this Zumba character ever comes up complaining about the slappin' I gave him, he *better* go in the fuckin' river."

He paused, his eyes hardening a little. "Or I got to come looking for you, Joe. Then *you* got to make it right."

Rizzo nodded. "I hear you."

CHAPTER NINE

AT TWELVE NOON, Rizzo sat at his squad room desk, a roast beef hero in front of him. Priscilla sat next to the desk, her lunch sitting on the pull-out writing board above the side drawer.

"So," Rizzo said, chewing as he spoke. "How'd it go at the party last night? Anything come of it?"

"Yeah, actually, something did," Priscilla said. "I met Carlyle's agent, a woman named Robin Miller. She's pretty well known in the publishing world."

"What'd she have to say?"

Rizzo saw animation come into Priscilla's eyes as she answered. "Carlyle had given her some of my stuff. A couple a my short stories and the first few chapters of a book I've been fooling around with. Miller liked it. She said she had some ideas she thought I should hear. Then she gave me her card and told me to call her on Monday. I gotta tell you, Joe, as much as I didn't want to go to that party, I'm glad as hell I did."

"Good," Rizzo said. "Sounds good. You may be on your way, kiddo."

"Funny, though. For a party, it was kinda somber. Seems like everyone there knew that guy Mallard, the playwright that got murdered. Once they found out I was a cop, everybody was asking me questions. They figured I had some inside info on who the killer might be."

"Did you tell them it's not the only case in town?" Rizzo asked.

"Yeah, in a way. But they were pretty shook up about it and wouldn't let it go. The guy was like a god to them."

Rizzo pursed his lips. "I'll bet if the cops ever do collar the guy that killed Mallard, all your new pals' liberal bullshit pity for the bad guy will go right out the fuckin' window. This is different, seein' as how it was one of *them* got killed. If it was just some dumb-ass street cop, they'd be out raisin' defense money for the perp."

"Relax, Joe. Don't go there."

He nodded. "Yeah. Well, I'm glad you made a connection. That's gotta help. But now, let's talk some business."

"Okay, boss, I'm listening."

"Here's the deal," Rizzo said. "After we eat, we take a ride over to Seventeenth Avenue, to the Rebels' hangout. We talk to the leader, kid named Costanzo Intrafiore. He's about nineteen, and word is he'll be movin' up the ladder to the Bath Beach Boys soon. Next stop after that is soldiering for one of Louie Quattropa's captains. See, Zee-Boy—that's what they call Costanzo—he's a real hard case. Genuine tough guy, not like some of the other Rebels. They're posers, some of 'em, two-bit punks playin' gangster. But Zee-Boy, he's the real deal."

Priscilla sipped at her bottled water. "You know the kid?" she asked. "Personally?"

"Oh, yeah, I know him okay. Matter a fact, we got sort of a special bond. See, he thinks I killed his uncle, and I think he's an asshole. 'Bout twenty years ago, Zee-Boy's uncle was runnin' The Rebels. Guy's name was Enzo. He was a hard case, too. If he'da lived, he woulda been a mob boss by now, maybe even Quattropa's right hand. Guy had a lot of potential."

Priscilla smiled. "I take it he died young. Did he leave a good-looking corpse?"

Rizzo shook his head. "Matter a fact, no. Actually, one of the ugli-est I ever seen. See, I was workin' patrol back then, in the Seven-Six. One night, about five, five-thirty in the mornin', we get a radio call. Blue Caddy, plate so and so, just stolen, vicinity Blippety-blip Street. Well, guess what? I'm at the wheel, sittin' at a red light on Court Street, and the friggin' Caddy comes up President and turns onto Court, right in front of us."

"It's good to get lucky sometimes," Priscilla said.

"Yeah. So I hit the lights and go after him. Guy speeds up, he's gonna run. So we chase. Fuckin' guy is doing damn near ninety, right on Court Street. I figure he's gonna blow a light, broadside some citizen comin' home from his night shift, and kill the poor schmuck. So I shut the lights, back off, break pursuit. My partner's calling in the location and direction of the Caddy, all by the book."

Rizzo took the last bite of his sandwich and began crumbling the wrapper as he went on. "So the Caddy never slows down, I never seen his brake lights come on, not even flicker. By now, he's doing about a hundred, at least. A garbage truck comes up a side street, catches the green light at the corner and makes a right turn, goin' maybe ten, fifteen miles an hour, right in front of the Caddy. The car smashes right into the truck. Sounds like a fuckin' bomb goin' off. The hood of the Caddy goes under the back of the truck, and the garbage hopper tears the whole top off the Caddy, along with Enzo's fuckin' head. Paramedics found what was left of it under a Pontiac parked forty feet from the impact area."

Priscilla winced. "Ick," she said.

"Yeah," Rizzo said, "ick. Well, that was the end of Uncle Enzo. Gave himself a death sentence for grand theft auto, the asshole."

"So, Zee-Boy wasn't even born yet, but he figures the whole thing was your fault. Right?"

Rizzo laughed. "Exactly. So we gotta figure a little friction when we go see him."

"Fuck him if he can't see the humor in any of this," she said with a shrug. "And when we do see him, is that when we go to the plan B that you mentioned the other day?"

He nodded. "See, with Zee-Boy ready to move up the junior mafia food chain, I'm bettin' he don't want any agita from The Chink."

Priscilla frowned. "The Chink? Quattropa?"

"Yeah. Unfortunate nickname in this particular case, ain't it? Can you hear Cornelia Hom if we let it slip in front of her?"

"Yeah, maybe we call him Mr. Quattropa when we're around her."

"Yeah, maybe," Rizzo agreed. "Anyway, if Zee-Boy does have

some loose cannon robbin' old ladies on Quattropa's turf, we can maybe squeeze the kid to self-police. Remember the old man's attitude about local street crime."

Priscilla shook her head in disbelief. "This teenage gang shit is weird. I thought the only ones left were in the ghetto. Never realized there were any working-class white-boy gangs runnin' around."

"Yeah, well, it's still the old days around here, Cil, in a lotta ways. Next door, the Six-Eight has two of their own gangs—The Monarchs and The Midgets. They mostly steal cars and sell 'em to the chop shops for the parts. Matter a fact, some kids register their family cars with the gangs. They drive over, show the car, ask for a bye. That way, maybe it won't get stolen."

"Unbelievable," she said. "Nineteen-fifties stuff."

Rizzo nodded. "Yeah. But there's some signs of modernization. When I was a kid, the girls were just gang mascots, trophies. Now, The Monarchs got a separate female division and The Midgets actually integrate the girls. 'Cause of all this women's lib bullshit they grew up with, I guess."

"See, Joe, there you go," Priscilla said. "You run hot and cold with this. You talk about your girls like equals, you raise 'em to be what they wanna be, then you say something like you just said. And freak out about Carol wanting to come on the job. You don't make sense, Partner. Is it real or is it bullshit? Make up your freakin' mind."

"Take it easy," he said. "Don't get nuts. I'm just sayin'—"

She held up her hand. "Yeah, yeah, I know what you're sayin'. What I'm wonderin' is do *you* know what the fuck you're sayin'?"

"Well, between my three girls, my wife, and now you, I guess I'll get straightened out eventually."

She nodded. "Yeah. Now let's go see Zee-Boy. I gotta admit, I'm a little curious, Joe. A little curious."

The Rebels' headquarters was located on a mixed commercial-residential block of Seventeenth Avenue. For decades the storefront had housed a family-operated tailor shop that had closed following the death of its elderly proprietors, Salvatore and Letizia Tommasino.

"I used to bring my family's clothes here when I was a kid," Rizzo told Priscilla as they pulled up in the Impala. "My grandparents' house was four blocks from here," he added with a small shake of his head. "Old man Tommasino musta flipped over in his grave when these jerk-offs rented the place for their hangout."

"Well," Priscilla said, "time marches on. Things change."

Rizzo grunted and unsnapped his shoulder harness. "Yeah," he said bitterly. "But just once, one fuckin' time, I'd like ta see somethin' change for the better. One fuckin' time."

Priscilla swung her door open. "Open your eyes a little more, Partner," she said over her shoulder. "Plenty of good stuff happens. You just gotta look for it."

"Yeah, Cil, sure. Wait'll you meet these fuckin' characters, see how la-di-da you're feelin' then."

They strode to the front door, solid metal with a small frosted window at eye level. Rizzo rapped hard on the door, then twisted the knob and walked in, Priscilla following.

The front room, which had once housed the store's counter and cash register, now contained a small television, scattered chairs, and a wooden rack holding a radio and various pieces of sporting equipment. There was no one in the room, and Rizzo turned his eyes to the right. A doorway covered with a heavy dark red curtain led to the larger rear room where dry cleaning and tailoring had once been done. From past visits, Rizzo knew the back room was now divided into three smaller rooms used for various purposes by The Rebels.

After a moment, the curtain stirred. A slight, pale teenager peered out from behind it, a frown on his lips.

"Who're you?" he asked.

Rizzo slipped the shield from his pants pocket, flashing it briefly. "Zee-Boy around?" he asked.

The boy shrugged. "I dunno," he said, his eyes falling from Rizzo's.

"Go find him, kid. Tell him Rizzo's here."

After a moment's pause, the teen shrugged once again. "Okay," he said, releasing the curtain and disappearing behind it.

Rizzo turned to Priscilla. "Let's make ourselves at home," he said, crossing to a worn, upholstered chair near the television and dropping himself into it. She followed, but remained standing, her back to the painted storefront window behind her.

After a moment, Costanzo Intrafiore, Zee-Boy to the locals, strode into the room. He stood five feet seven, stocky, his dark hair buzz-cut short, his black eyes small and hard. He smiled a cold greeting at Rizzo, glancing only briefly at Jackson.

"Hey, Joe," he said, a sneer on his lips. "Come to kill another Rebel?"

"Not today, kid," Rizzo said. "Some other time maybe."

"Whaddya want then?" Intrafiore said.

"Business, Zee-Boy. I wanna talk business." Now Rizzo glanced to Priscilla, then back to Zee-Boy. "*We* wanna talk business."

The youth looked to Priscilla, his eyes flat, then back to Rizzo.

"I didn't order no fuckin' pancakes, Joe, and watermelon ain't in season, so who the fuck is she?"

"I'm gonna do you a big favor, Zee-Boy," Rizzo said conversationally. "Later I'm gonna explain to my new partner here how your mother didn't raise you right, and maybe Detective Jackson will forgive you for that little remark." Rizzo leaned slightly forward in his seat. "Then again, maybe she won't."

Zee-Boy looked again to Priscilla, meeting her cool gaze with indifference. He turned back to Rizzo.

"Whatever you want here, Joe, we can do it without mothers," he said.

Rizzo cleared his throat. "Okay, let's start over. Zee-Boy, I'd like you to meet Detective Priscilla Jackson. Detective Jackson, Zee-Boy Intrafiore. He's the boss here."

Their eyes met, Priscilla crossing her arms against her chest. She nodded to Zee-Boy. He nodded back, then turned his eyes again to Rizzo.

"Whaddya want?" he asked again.

Rizzo shrugged. "Some of your time, that's all. Just a little of your time."

The youth seemed to consider it. Rizzo noted a slight nervous tic at the nineteen-year-old's right eye. After a moment, Zee-Boy responded.

"Okay. In the back."

They followed him through the red curtain and into the largest of the three rear rooms. Five Rebels sat sprawled on couches, easy chairs, and a battered aluminum beach lounger, watching the New York Giants pregame show on a large, flat-screen plasma TV. They looked up with hooded eyes as Intrafiore and the two detectives entered.

Zee-Boy glanced at the TV, then jerked a thumb over his right shoulder. "Out front, guys," he said. One of the youths, a pimply faced, lanky kid with long brown hair and a blue and red crucifix tattooed on his forearm, protested.

"TV out there sucks, Zee. Game's gonna start in five minutes."

Intrafiore seemed not to hear. "Come on," he said to Rizzo and Jackson. "In my room."

As they crossed deeper into the main room, heading for the door at the side, Intrafiore looked to the five Rebels.

"I said out front," he said softly. A moment passed, and with exaggerated body language indicating inconvenience and wounded pride, the five stood slowly and filed through the curtain. Intrafiore paused, allowing them to leave, then picked up the remote control, raising the volume of the television.

"Come on," he said, entering the small private room he had referred to as his.

The room contained a narrow single bed, unmade, against one wall, yet another television sitting on a battered wooden table, an audio center, and a small Formica table. Around the table, four folding chairs were randomly scattered. A large, silent air conditioner was poised in one half of the double window on the rear wall. The blinds were tightly drawn.

After arranging themselves around the table, Intrafiore sat back, tilting his chair onto its rear legs, hooking his thumbs into the thick, black leather belt at his waist. He looked across at them, his eyes mere slits, and Priscilla felt her stomach hollow under the gaze.

"What?" he asked.

Rizzo leaned across the table, his hands folded before him.

"Three street robberies," he said. "And countin'."

Intrafiore shrugged. "So?"

"So this," Rizzo said pointedly. "I got a citizen makes the perp as a Rebel. And I need to lock him up."

"So lock 'im up, then," Intrafiore said. "You don't have to waste my time. Lock 'im up."

Rizzo shook his head. "Not so simple. See, this citizen I got is scared. Doesn't wanna piss you and the other Dead End Kids off. So, you can see my dilemma."

"Yeah, I can see it," Zee-Boy said. "You got shit. So why don't you come back when you're holdin' some cards."

Rizzo glanced at Priscilla before turning back to Intrafiore.

"Oh, I got the cards, Zee-Boy." He pressed forward harder against the table. "I got the ace a fuckin' spades."

Intrafiore looked from one detective to the other, then settled his gaze on Rizzo. "What's that?" he asked softly. "You gonna sew some balls on your witness, get 'im to citizen up for the good of the community?"

Rizzo sat back, reaching for his near empty cigarette pack. He offered one to Intrafiore, was declined, and lit his own. Then, blowing smoke at the tabletop, he raised his eyes back to meet the hostile stare.

"No," he said. "No. What I was figurin' was, why bust my ass with this? I got other things to do. More important things. See, I figure I can get a little help on this one."

Intrafiore smiled brazenly. "Yeah, from who? The African queen over here?"

"No, Zee-Boy. Not this time." Rizzo dragged again on the cigarette, then casually tapped ashes onto the old, worn linoleum floor, noting the slight flicker of anger in Intrafiore's eyes.

"The Chink, kid. We all know how the old man feels about the neighborhood. If it ain't him doin' the stealin', he's a very righteous guy. So I'm thinking I go direct to him with the situation. I tell him, 'Hey, Louie, you know those two old Italians got robbed? And the old Chinese couple? Guess who did that shit, Louie, right under your nose. It was Zee-Boy Intrafiore and his band a retards.'" Rizzo nodded slowly. "Yeah, then I say somethin' like, 'Imagine that, Louie? A wise-ass kid like Zee-Boy havin' no respect for the neighborhood. Havin' no respect for *you*. And me without enough evidence to make an arrest stick.'" Rizzo locked eyes with Intrafiore.

"Best you can hope for is a busted head, Zee-Boy. And no graduation day. Not one of The Chink's captains'll ever put you to work knowin' the old man has a hard-on for you. You'll be boostin' car radios and runnin' numbers for The Bath Beach Boys till your Social Security kicks in."

Rizzo sat back, drawing deeply on his cigarette. "Unless, of course, somehow Louie was to get the impression it was *you* personally robbed them old bastards. Then I don't figure you for any Social Security payments." He turned to Priscilla. "How many quarters you need before you can collect Social Security, Cil?" he asked.

Priscilla smiled sweetly, her eyes on Intrafiore. "Forty," she said. "Ten years."

Rizzo nodded. "Yeah, like I thought." He turned back to Intrafiore. "Whaddya think, Zee?" he asked. "You figure you can dodge The Chink for forty quarters?"

Intrafiore hesitated for a moment, his face impassive, before spitting out, "You got shit, Rizzo. You're bluffin'. Whaddya tryin' to impress Oprah here, show her what a tough guy you are, maybe grab some black ass on a night shift sometime?"

"Now Zee-Boy," Rizzo said calmly, "you know me better than that." He paused, dropping his cigarette to the floor and crushing it out slowly under his shoe. Then he raised his eyes back to the Rebel leader. "You wanna try me out, asshole? Go ahead. Try me out."

Intrafiore tapped a finger on the tabletop, looking from one cop to the other before responding.

"Why would I let one of my guys pull local robberies? You think I'm that stupid? You think Chink'll figure me for that stupid?"

"I don't know," Rizzo said with a shrug, "and I don't give a fuck, either. I do know the perp is a Rebel, and I know *you* know he's a Rebel. So, real soon Quattropa's gonna know, too. Then my problem goes away." He paused. "End of fuckin' story. It's hardball time, kid. If I wanted to, I could pick up a little coke somewheres, H maybe, grab you on the street some night, lock you up for possession. That violates your probation, and you go upstate. Your Youthful Offender days are over. Welcome to the big leagues. I can fuck you ten different ways and not break a sweat. But I'm givin' you a chance here. I'm tryin' to be nice. Tryin' to do the right thing and give you a chance to help out with this. But you're wearin' my patience a little here."

Intrafiore snorted. "Fuck you," he said.

Now Priscilla stood slowly, placing her hands down on the tabletop, leaning in toward Zee-Boy's face. "You be nice to Sergeant Rizzo now, or I just might have to put my big black foot up your little white ass."

"See, Zee-Boy," Rizzo said. "You just piss people off. You better learn it ain't done like that in the big leagues."

Priscilla smiled at Intrafiore, an evil glint in her dark eyes. Slowly, she sat back down. Intrafiore swung indifferent eyes from her and back to Rizzo. After a slight pause, he spoke in a soft, almost pensive tone.

"So, how's it done, Joe?" he asked simply.

Rizzo nodded. "Now that's more like it. You give me a name. I get the vics to eyeball the guy. If they make him, end of story. If they can't, you squeeze the guy's balls till he cops. I already showed the Rebel face book around. The perp ain't one of your made guys. This kid has no record, he's new. He can stand a fall. I got a pretty strong feelin' you know exactly who he is, some new psycho even you're having trouble controllin'. Now's your chance to smack him down before he starts recruitin' against you, and save your own neck with Chink at the same time. You gotta figure Louie's already looking at these street robberies, already gettin' his Sicilian balls twisted. You give up the kid, I arrange it so Louie Quattropa will never know the perp is one of your guys. Then we all live happily ever after here in Never-Never Land."

He smiled at Intrafiore. "That's how it's done."

The young man pushed a hand across his buzz cut, looking again from one detective to the other.

"So you want me to hand you one of my guys? Like some pussy lawyer cuttin' a deal? That's what you want?"

"'Want' has nothin' to do with this," Rizzo said with a shrug.

" 'Want' is for kids. This ain't kid stuff, Zee-Boy. You make this deal or you got Quattropa or me or maybe both of us on your ass. However it plays, this kid you got off the reservation, he's goin' down. Either to me or Chink. Difference is, if it's Quattropa, you're goin' down with him. I'll make sure that's how it plays."

Both detectives stood.

"Think about it," Rizzo said, fishing a card from his pocket and dropping it onto the table. "Call me with the kid's name. My arrest report will never mention the Rebels. I guarantee it. Consider it a favor I'm doin' you."

As he turned to leave, Rizzo faced Intrafiore one last time.

"You got till Tuesday," he said, his eyes hard, his tone flat.

The two detectives showed themselves out. Intrafiore sat in silence for a moment, then sighed, picking up Rizzo's card.

He leaned back in his seat, slipping the card into the front pocket of his tight black jeans.

"Shit," he said softly.

"SO," PRISCILLA said as she drove the Impala slowly back toward the precinct house. "You think he'll go for it?"

Rizzo shrugged. "I don't know, I'm not feelin' real optimistic. I think maybe my history with the kid could work against us. Maybe I shoulda let the precinct youth officer, Olivero, handle this, or maybe Ginsberg and his partner."

"Who?" Priscilla asked.

"Mark Ginsberg and his partner, George Parker, the detectives who caught the first two robberies."

"Well, it makes sense for the kid to go for it," Priscilla said. "After all, if he's looking to move up to the mob, he can't be pissin' off the goombahs. Especially Quattropa. It makes definite sense for Zee-Boy to give up the perp."

Rizzo nodded. "Yeah, I know. But Zee-Boy is still just a kid. Kids do stupid shit. And he's more than a little crazy, maybe crazy enough to *want* to thumb his nose at The Chink."

Priscilla frowned and shook her head. "Crazy is one thing, stupid is somethin' else. Why would he take a chance like that?"

"Couple a reasons," Rizzo speculated. "One is, maybe he really *isn't* afraid of Quattropa. He sure as hell should be, but that don't mean he is. Also, from word I hear, one of Louie's captains, guy named Mike Spano, is maybe plannin' a move."

"Against Quattropa?" Priscilla asked.

"Yeah. I heard about it from a friend a mine works over at OCCB. He figured I might be able to use the info, since Spano operates outta Brooklyn. They call the guy 'Mikey the Hammer.' Made his rep as a button man."

"Has word reached the street yet?" Priscilla asked.

Rizzo shook his head. "Not that I know of. If it had, Spano would be dead by now. No, I don't think it's common knowledge yet, but if it's true, *somebody* besides OCCB has to know about it. And if somebody knows about it, Zee-Boy may know about it. He's got a relative or two in with the mob boys. So maybe he figures he disses The Chink and then, when the dust settles, he already looks good to Spano, and now Spano's the new boss."

Priscilla shook her head slowly. "That would be pretty ballsy for a nineteen-year-old."

"All the great ones were just ballsy kids once. From Capone to Galante to Castellano and Gotti and Quattropa. You can never be sure which one'll break out young."

"Well," she said. "We'll see. My money says Zee-Boy caves. Why jeopardize his future for some new kid on the block?"

Rizzo nodded. "You're probably right. I just hope he doesn't go direct to Quattropa and give up the perp. He may figure that'll score him some points with the old prick, but he's too young to see that if Quattropa does decide to act against the perp, Zee-Boy himself becomes a liability. He'd know too much about The Chink's private business. Louie would have to whack him, too, just to protect himself. Zee-Boy would be making a real mistake goin' that route. But, tell you the truth, I'm okay with chancing it. No great loss if two assholes turn up dead." Rizzo paused. "We'll see how it plays out. That's why I only gave him two days. I don't want him overthinkin' this."

After a moment or two, Priscilla swung her eyes to Rizzo as she slowed for a traffic light.

"What about that drug plant, Joe?" she asked, her tone neutral. "Would you really do that? Drop some dope on the kid and squeeze him?"

"Well, I figured you'd ask about that," Rizzo said. "Truth is I'da never said it in front of a new partner, 'cept I know you got a history with Mike. I figured I could trust you on it."

She nodded. "Okay. A threat's one thing. What I'm askin' is would you actually do it?"

"I don't like this street shit in my precinct, Cil," Rizzo said, the strength of his feeling showing in his eyes. "I don't like it any more than The Chink does. And this case, with the Homs, has really pissed me off. The neighborhood ain't been real receptive to these Asians movin' in the last few years. There've been some incidents. It's embarrassin' to me, and to most of the people with roots around here. So I'd like to nail this mugger. For a few different reasons."

Priscilla smiled. "I don't know what you just answered, Joe, but it wasn't the fuckin' question I asked you."

Rizzo pointed through the windshield. "The light turned green," he said.

She glanced up, then eased the car forward.

"Oh," she said, shaking her head. "Never mind."

"Like I told the kid," Rizzo said, searching his pockets for the packet of Nicorette, "this is the big leagues."

CHAPTER TEN

JOE RIZZO SAT AT HIS DESK in the Six-Two squad room, his eyes falling to the calendar. November 10: seventeen days until Thanksgiving. Carol would be home from college on the twenty-third, so he had less than two weeks to mend fences and perfect his argument, to once again try to dissuade his youngest daughter from planning a career with the NYPD.

He sighed. A major drawback of having partnered so successfully with Jennifer to raise three strong-willed, self-assured daughters now confronted Rizzo. He would attempt to push one of them along a path she herself did not wish to take. Even though it was a path that Rizzo knew to be an infinitely better one for her.

As he noticed Priscilla enter the squad room, it occurred to him that in many ways, Priscilla, allowing for cultural and environmental differences, closely mirrored his daughters. She wasn't much older than Marie, his oldest, and she was just as confident and focused as his girls. Rizzo was not unaware of the ironic pride he took in watching his new partner navigate the unforgiving ways of the job. Priscilla seemed to confirm, in a bizarre sort of way, the hopes he harbored for his daughters, hopes unshackled or defined by traditional gender roles and antiquated societal prejudices.

But Rizzo believed the matter at hand to be entirely different. This was his Carol, sweet, innocent Carol, sheltered in so many ways from the harsh realities of the world in general, and certainly from the murky, often morally ambivalent world of police work.

With another sigh, Rizzo reached for a case folder on his desk, flipping it open, preparing to make his morning phone calls. For now, he would ease Carol from his thoughts.

He still had twelve days. Time enough, he thought. Time enough.

Later on that morning, Rizzo headed to Priscilla's desk to discuss a case involving a series of forged medical prescriptions which had been turning up in local pharmacies. A female suspect, utilizing stolen prescription pads, was obtaining narcotics, presumably for resale on the streets. But before he could begin, Rizzo looked up to see detective squad commander Vince D'Antonio beckoning from the door of his office.

"Joe," D'Antonio called out, "can I see you in my office, please? You, too, Priscilla." The lieutenant turned back to his office, leaving the door open behind him.

"Looks like the principal wants us," Rizzo said. "Get your excuses ready."

Priscilla stood, pushing her chair back and shaking out her short hair. "Excuses for what? I'm clean, Partner. *You're* probably the one needs excuses."

Once inside, the door closed behind them, Rizzo and Jackson took seats in front of D'Antonio's desk. The lieutenant looked across at them, his deep blue eyes twinkling under the harsh fluorescent lighting. "Ready for me to ruin your day?"

Rizzo grunted. "Hey, Vince, isn't that what they pay you for?" he said.

D'Antonio nodded, looking from one detective to the other. "I guess so."

"What's up, boss?" Priscilla asked.

D'Antonio's expression grew somber. "We got a murder to look at, guys. Over on Bay Twentieth Street."

"What kinda murder, Vince?" Rizzo asked.

D'Antonio sighed. "The kinda murder Brooklyn South is gonna take a pass on. I just got off the phone with Jimmy Santori, the boss over there. All his guys have full dance cards, so he's delegating this to precinct level." He shrugged. "I can't bitch too much, either.

This'll be our first homicide investigation in over two years. I think you handled that one, too, Joe."

Rizzo nodded. "Yeah. Me and Morelli."

"Yes," D'Antonio said, his tone neutral, "Morelli."

Rizzo shifted in his seat. "What's the story on this one, Vince?"

"Well," D'Antonio replied, sitting back in his chair. "From what I've been told, male white, forty-seven, killed in his apartment. Name was Robert Lauria. Looks like a forced entry. Probably happened over a week ago. Last night, the landlord smelled the dead body and called it in."

"Gunshot?" Rizzo asked.

D'Antonio shook his head. "Strangled. Guy's neck was badly lacerated, a lot of bleeding. Whatever was used to kill him, it was thin, like a wire or cord."

"You really wanna give me a case that's already a week cold, Vince?" Rizzo asked. "I think Rossi would be better suited for wasting time on this."

"Joe, this is a *homicide,* not some divorcee got her IUD stolen. Leave Rossi out of it. It's you and Cil on this."

"The price of greatness," Rizzo commented to his partner. "No good deed goes unpunished."

"Hell," she said. "Homicide sounds good to me. The *real* big leagues."

"Yeah, right." Rizzo turned to D'Antonio. "Shall we get over there now?"

D'Antonio nodded. "Yes. I'm gonna ride on it, too. Just to make sure the Brooklyn South prima donnas at the scene show you both a little respect. Let's go."

RIZZO SWUNG the gray Impala to the curb, blocking a fire hydrant. D'Antonio, driving his dark blue Impala, pulled in behind. Three blue-and-white radio cars stood randomly scattered in front of the detached, two-story brick home where the murder had taken place. Another police department vehicle sat parked in the driveway of the house, its front bumper nosed against the plain wooden door of the detached garage.

Rizzo, Jackson, and D'Antonio left their vehicles and climbed the porch steps. The front door stood open, guarded by a uniformed Six-Two patrol officer. The entrance to the basement apartment to the right of the front porch and down six steep, concrete steps was cordoned off with bright yellow police tape, the area secure, awaiting the arrival of the forensics team. They entered the house.

A second uniformed officer led the three Six-Two detectives to an interior staircase to the basement floor. Once there, they met with the detective from Brooklyn South Homicide.

After introductions, Rizzo got straight to the point.

"Tell me," Rizzo said.

Detective Sergeant Art Rosen glanced to his notepad, then began his narrative.

"Body was found by the patrol supervisor. The basement apartment has two entryways: the street-side front door outside—the one sealed off with the tape—leads directly into the victim's kitchen. Then there's the staircase you just came down. This door"—he tilted his head to his left—"leads into the bedroom of the vic's apartment and it was deadbolt locked from the inside. Landlord only comes down the basement to get to the burner room, storage area, stuff like that. Last night, 'bout eleven, he came down here to check the oil level in the tank. He smells something, same thing you're smellin' now. So he knocks on the apartment door. No answer. Then it occurs to the landlord he hasn't seen or heard his tenant in a while. The guy paid his rent in cash on October twenty-eighth, thirteen days ago. That's the last time he was seen by the landlord or the landlord's wife."

"How many people live in the building?" Rizzo asked.

Rosen checked his notes. "Three, counting the vic. The two owners and the vic."

Rizzo nodded. "Okay, go on."

"Well, the landlord smells this, puts two and two together, calls the cops. Radio car rolls up at 2320 hours, checks things out, then calls for a supervisor. Six-Two sergeant rolls up 2350. He gets a master from the landlord, they go in through the kitchen entrance on Bay Twentieth. Body is on the kitchen floor. I been here since 0040."

He frowned. "Fuckin' stink worked into my nose hairs. I gotta wash it out soon as I leave."

"Well," D'Antonio said, "according to your boss, it's our stink now."

Rosen nodded. "Yeah, we're booked solid, Lieutenant, and I'm takin' some time off. My son's bar mitzvah's coming up next week."

"The M.E. here yet?" Rizzo asked.

"Yeah, he's been with the body over an hour. Want the preliminaries?"

Rizzo shrugged. "Sure."

Rosen read from his notes. "Body in the flaccid stage, maxed out fixed lividity. Advance putrefaction, larval stage finalized, pupae present, no adult flies emerging yet. Ballpark time of death less than twelve days ago, probably eight to ten. From the landlord, we know the guy was breathin' on October twenty-eighth, so it checks out with the physical markers."

Rizzo nodded. "Okay, thanks."

"I'm gonna go out to the car, finish up these notes, then I'm going back to Brooklyn South." Rosen turned to D'Antonio. "You got a card, boss?"

D'Antonio pulled a card from his pocket, handed it to Rosen and said, "Fax me all the notes. And your personal contact info in case we need to talk to you. You got a partner here?"

Rosen shook his head. "No, just me. Like I said, we're stretched thin."

"I thought homicides were down," Priscilla said to Rosen. "Citywide in general, but I heard Brooklyn in particular."

Rosen nodded. "Way down. So what happens? The brass cuts the overtime, doesn't replace the attrition, and expands our caseload to include attempts, not just done murders. Go figure. We're busier now than when the borough was doin' four hundred a year."

Rosen shook hands all around, then turned and climbed the stairs to the ground floor and relief from the permeating smell of death wafting into the basement from the rear door of the apartment. Rizzo turned to Priscilla.

"Point of information, Cil," he said. "From what Rosen just told us, we know the body cycled completely through rigor mortis, going to flaccid with fixed lividity indicating the body's been in one position since death. Lividity is maxed out, that only takes about twelve hours. It's the advanced maggot activity that puts the approximate date of the murder around ten, twelve days ago."

Priscilla nodded. "Will the M.E. be able to narrow that any?"

Rizzo shrugged. "Doubtful. He'll do the autopsy for cause of death, but exact date will be tough. It ain't a precise science, like on that television bullshit everybody watches. Maggots showing as early pupae make death around ten days, dependin' on other environmental factors."

"Well," Priscilla said, her voice businesslike. "Shall we go take a look?"

Rizzo pulled two pairs of latex gloves from the pocket of his outer coat. D'Antonio produced his own. "I guess so, kiddo. Here, put these on."

The three Six-Two cops went into the bedroom, then carefully crossed the room and entered a small foyer. From that vantage point, they could see directly into the kitchen. The body was covered, the medical examiner standing above it, a blue surgical mask covering the lower half of his ebony face. He was writing on a legal-size yellow pad, his brow furrowed.

"Hey, Doc," Rizzo said cheerfully. "How you doin' this morning?"

The man looked up from his notes, turning his eyes to the three detectives.

"As well as can be expected," he said, a West Indies accent tugging at his tones. "And a damn sight better than this poor bastard." With a dip of his head, he indicated the corpse.

"Was it definitely strangulation, Doc?" D'Antonio asked.

The man nodded, again turning to his pad and continuing his notemaking. "Most probably from behind, and with a garrote capable of deep cutting. The neck is badly lacerated. There was considerable bleeding while the heart was beating. Even afterward, some leakage continued." He glanced from above the mask to Priscilla, then to Rizzo.

" 'Tis quite a sight," he said.

Rizzo stepped forward and pulled back the blue plastic morgue sheet covering the victim, dropping it away from the corpse.

The body lay facedown, its head twisted to the right, the profile swollen, eyes and tongue protruding. Decomposition fluids had drained from the nose and mouth, the skin of the distorted, bloated face was marbled in a greenish-black weblike pattern, a few plump maggots moving slowly across the surface.

Rizzo bent to the body, peering carefully at the open right eye, which stared in sightless horror at the base of the kitchen sink. The cornea appeared darkly clouded and opaque. Rizzo stood, turning to the examiner.

"Date of murder may turn out to be important here, Doc." He added casually, "You notice that eye?"

Behind the man's mask, it was evident he was smiling. "Relax, Detective," he said. "I may just be a simple coconut island doctor, but I do know dead bodies. I assure you I will check the potassium levels in both eyes. Though it may not help much, other than to bolster my preliminary estimate of ten days."

"No offense, Doc," Rizzo said. "I'm just askin', that's all."

The man nodded. "Yes, of course," he said, glancing toward Priscilla. "I understand, and I'm sure your young colleague also understands your presumed need to ask." He clicked his pen closed, returning it to the breast pocket of his blue Windbreaker. "And now," he said, "I am finished here. When *you* are finished, release the body and I will next see it at the morgue. My initial report will be ready in a few days."

"And the autopsy?" D'Antonio asked.

The man shrugged. "I cannot say. As soon as possible. I will have some lab results by Wednesday or Thursday that may or may not help with the date of death. But the autopsy, I cannot say."

After they exchanged cards, the doctor left, passing a young Hispanic female morgue attendant, who stuck her head into the kitchen from the foyer.

"I'm here with the meat wagon, guys," she said. "I'll be outside, let me know when you're done."

137

Priscilla turned to her. "Okay," she said with a nod.

"She's got a long wait," Rizzo said. "Crime Scene ain't even here yet. We need photos, measurements, prints—all that shit." He ran a hand through his hair and turned to D'Antonio. "Vince, you sure you can't sell this back to Brooklyn South? Me and Cil are close to clearing a few of our cases. This homicide is gonna jam us up, time-wise. My stats are already down from workin' without a steady partner. This is gonna kill me."

"Sorry, Joe. Already tried. I don't like this any more than you do, these homicide hotshots takin' a fast look, seeing this is just some schnook nobody's gonna be writin' headlines about, and dumpin' it on us. But it's their call. You know that."

"Yeah," Rizzo said. "I know that."

"Aren't you on good terms with the boss over at Brooklyn South? Isn't he always tryin' to steal you outta the Six-Two?"

Rizzo understood. "Yeah, I know Santori, and no, I ain't reachin' out. Sometimes I feel like I owe more people than owe me, and I'm not addin' any more to the list. If you can't square it, fuck it, we'll just do it." He turned to Priscilla, who was now looking down at the putrid corpse. "Right, Cil?" he said.

Priscilla raised her eyes to meet his. "Right, we'll just do it." She turned back to the corpse. "Guy's wearin' pajama bottoms and a T-shirt, no shoes or socks." She pointed at the countertop next to the stove. "Teapot and a box of Lipton. Looks like it was either morning or maybe late night. Guy was just gonna have some tea."

She lowered her eyes once again to the corpse.

"Didn't work out too good for the poor bastard, did it?"

CHAPTER ELEVEN

SERGEANT BRIAN MALLOY WAS A FIFTEEN-YEAR veteran assigned as a supervisor of patrol at the Sixty-second Precinct. He and Rizzo were well known to each other.

Malloy, Rizzo, Jackson, and D'Antonio stood in a tight semicircle at the rear of the apartment in the small, ransacked bedroom. The room's two casement windows on the back wall were separated by a long, worn dresser. The four cops stood in front of the window closest to the single bed. Broken glass from a shattered pane lay at their feet.

"So, Brian," Rizzo said. "This is where you figure the perp came in?"

Malloy nodded. "Looks like it. When my patrol guys called and told me about the smell, I came here expectin' to find some old man dead in bed. I got the key to the front door from the landlord and let myself in. We found the body where it is now. We looked around, saw this broken window. Looks like somebody broke in, came across the victim, and wound up strangling him in the kitchen. You can see the bedroom was ransacked. Probably some fucked-up junkie lookin' for a quick score and not thinkin' too clear."

Rizzo nodded absently. "Yeah, more than likely." He looked around the room, his eyes falling on the nightstand beside the bed. A thick, gold wristwatch embossed with diamonds circling the crystal, lay there. It appeared heavy and very old, the numerals on its face in the floral, antiquated style of an earlier era.

"That's funny," he said, walking over to it. "This watch is right here out in the open, and the perp didn't grab it. Looks like an antique, from back in the forties maybe. And it looks expensive."

Priscilla, now next to him, bent to the watch and examined it under the bright sunlight streaming in from the window.

"It's expensive, all right," she said. "Karen's grandfather has one very similar to this. The guy's about ninety, he got the watch when he was a fighter pilot. This is a Breitling, it's Swiss made. He says it's worth about ten, twelve grand now."

"Well, it sure looks better'n my forty-dollar Timex," Rizzo said, rubbing at a slight twitch in his eye. "So our junkie genius missed his big score, eh? Too busy lookin' through the sock drawers?"

Priscilla looked at him. "Maybe."

He stepped back from the table. "We'll let CSU photograph the watch," he said, moving back to the window.

He bent to the broken pane once again, peering out into the backyard. "Let me ask you something, Brian. When you came in the front door, were both locks engaged?"

Malloy shook his head. "No, just the lock in the doorknob. At the time, I didn't think much of it, but later, after we found the victim, I started thinking about it. The guy had a two-hundred-dollar Schlage deadbolt on that door, but the cheap Kwikset knob lock was the only one he locked."

"Yeah," Rizzo said. "You'd figure he'd have the deadbolt thrown." He scanned the backyard, then straightened up, facing Malloy once again.

"What about this door?" he asked, indicating the rear door leading from the bedroom into the outer basement.

Malloy nodded. "Deadbolted and the knob lock and safety chain engaged."

Rizzo dropped to one knee, examining a small plastic box screwed to the wall beneath the window. He reached to the box, removing its cover. A nine-volt battery sat in place against a small circuit board. A gray wire ran from the side of the box to a pressure switch installed on the window jam. He replaced the cover and stood.

"Poor man's alarm system," he observed. "If this thing is turned on and the window opens and releases the pressure switch, the box sounds a warning." He bent slightly and pointed to the box. "The switch is in the off position."

D'Antonio moved across to the other window and bent to examine the second alarm. "This one is on, Joe," he said.

Rizzo rubbed his chin. "So the guy is safety minded enough to buy a couple a cheap window alarms, an expensive deadbolt for the front door. And he's got the rear door leadin' to his landlord's basement bolted, locked, and chained. All that, then he leaves the front deadbolt unlocked and turns off one window alarm?" He paused. "This is startin' to give me a fuckin' headache."

"How about this, Joe?" Priscilla suggested. "Junkie breaks the window, climbs in. The alarm was off 'cause the victim was about to go to bed, so maybe he's planning to open the window and get some air. Junkie comes across vic, they struggle, he strangles the guy, then lets himself out through the front door. The doorknob locks automatically, but you need the key to lock the deadbolt from the outside, so it don't get locked."

Rizzo smiled. "Yeah," he said. "Okay. Case closed."

Priscilla shrugged. "I'm just sayin'."

"Yeah, I know. But I'm thinkin' if the bottom window is alarmed, you open the top window when you wanna get air. And if you break into a place from the rear, you exit from the rear. Why risk runnin' into Joe Citizen out front on the street?" He turned to Malloy. "How do I get out to this backyard?"

Malloy beckoned to Rizzo. "Follow me."

D'Antonio reached into his jacket and removed his cell phone. "I'll see you later," he said. "I wanna get some help down here, get a street search and canvass going."

Once outside, Rizzo had a clear view of all the backyards serving the complex of one-family houses surrounding the victim's home.

"This backyard is pretty secure," he said. "The attached houses on the next street form a solid wall, no access points other than through the houses themselves. And this yard is fenced in pretty good. Seems an unlikely target for a burglar. Hell, you go to either end of the block, you could walk down half a dozen driveways and get behind twice as many houses. Why come all the way up here? There's nothin' special about this place."

Malloy shrugged. "Stupidity, probably."

"Yeah," Rizzo said with a nod. "We can never rule out stupidity."

The area surrounding the ground-level broken window was covered with worn, cracked cement. After carefully examining the surrounding yard and the window itself but turning up nothing of value, the three cops returned to the apartment to search for anything that might prove useful. While they did so, the Crime Scene Unit arrived and began their slow, methodical process— photographing, measuring, and dusting the scene. After CSU completed the portion of their investigation that centered on the corpse, it was carefully placed into a black rubber body bag and removed by morgue personnel.

Later, Rizzo and Priscilla sat at the landlord's kitchen table, the elderly man and his wife staring at them with pale, grim faces.

"So," Rizzo asked, "Mr. Lauria was your tenant for over ten years?"

The landlord, Victor Annasia, nodded gravely. "Yes," he said, his voice strained with tension. "Eleven, it would have been, this January coming."

"Tell me about him," Rizzo said.

The man shrugged. "There isn't much to tell. He lived alone, a bachelor. Didn't seem to have any friends, none at all. In ten years, except for a cousin of his, I don't think he ever had a visitor. Quiet as a mouse, always paid his rent early, in cash, never a problem. The perfect tenant, really."

Mrs. Annasia spoke up, her eyes moist. "A very nice man. Such a terrible thing to happen."

"Try not to let it upset you too much," Priscilla said gently.

"How could it not?" the woman said with resignation. "A murder in my own home. My God, this world is becoming more and more evil. Sometimes," she said sadly, "I'm glad to be so old. So I won't see things get worse than they are now."

"Mr. Annasia, do you have this cousin's name and address?" Rizzo asked.

The old man nodded. "Yes, it's with the lease, in my desk. She was his emergency contact person."

"Before we leave, I'd like that information," Rizzo said. Then, after a pause, he continued his questioning. "Did Mr. Lauria work?"

"Yes."

"Where?"

"On Eighty-sixth Street, at that big shoe store. The one near Nineteenth Avenue."

Rizzo jotted it down, then, without looking up, asked, "Did he seem to have much money?"

"No, not much at all. But he paid his rent, bought his food. He has no car, no real expenses that I saw. I guess he got by."

Rizzo looked up. "Do you think he could afford a really expensive wristwatch?"

"Oh, that Swiss watch, the gold one? No, Sergeant Rizzo, that was his dead father's watch. Was Robbie wearing it when he died?"

"No," Rizzo answered. "It was on his nightstand."

"Well, I'm glad the thief didn't get it," the old man said. "Poor Robbie was very proud of that watch. It was the most important thing he owned."

"Not that he owned very much," Mrs. Annasia added. "Always going from job to job, out of work for months at a time, no friends or family. No woman. A very sad life, Sergeant. Very sad."

Rizzo nodded. "Yes," he said thoughtfully, then resumed his questioning. "As far as you know, did he have any enemies, anyone who maybe could have done this?"

Annasia frowned. "You mean on *purpose*? Not just a burglar, but someone he knew? Absolutely not," he said. "I told you, Sergeant, he had no one in his life, just that cousin and her family. This was not a man with enemies, Sergeant. This was a man alone. A man killed by a thief, a random thief." After a pause, Annasia continued with a sheepish glance at his wife. "Let's be honest here, Sergeant. Robbie wasn't right, he was an odd duck—almost a recluse, a very sad man living a sad, empty life. I hope he's at peace now with God. I hope he's with his parents, somebody to love him again."

The man paused, reaching out a veined, liver-spotted hand and placing it gently upon his wife's hand.

"Otherwise, Sergeant, there's no point." He looked at his wife once more, then met Rizzo's eyes.

"Without someone to love, somebody to love you . . . there is no point."

RIZZO DROVE the Chevy slowly toward the precinct house. He turned slightly in the seat, speaking to Priscilla's profile as she scanned her notes.

"The guy is dead for at least a week, probably longer, and there's not one message on his answerin' machine," he said. "Not even a call from his job. Didn't they wonder where the fuck he was?"

Priscilla shrugged. "Why don't we stop off and ask 'em?" she asked. "It's not far from here, and it's only three o'clock."

Rizzo turned back in the seat. "Yeah, okay. What avenue was it?"

"Nineteenth."

They identified themselves to the young store manager, explaining the reason for their visit. She gasped, raising a hand to her mouth.

"Oh my God," she said, her eyes tearing suddenly. "How awful! That poor man, he never hurt a fly, never had a bad word to say. Oh my God," she repeated.

Priscilla spoke. "We were wondering, Ms. Gallo. Lauria was killed some days ago, yet there were no messages on his answering machine. Didn't you wonder what happened to him? When he didn't show up for work, I mean."

The young woman looked puzzled. "Work?" she asked. "No . . . We've been slow the last few months and I . . . I had to let him go. Unfortunately, Robbie was my newest hire. You know, 'Last hired, first fired.'" She looked from Rizzo to Jackson, taking in their somber expressions. "I . . . I intended to rehire him, of course. As soon as the holidays kicked in and business, presumably, picked up. I definitely planned to hire him back. He was a great worker, always on time, polite to everyone, really no trouble at all. You didn't even know he was here, he was so quiet." She scanned their faces. "He kept to himself, you know."

"So we're findin'out," Rizzo said. "When exactly did you let him go?"

She thought for a moment. "Exactly?"

"Yes," Priscilla interjected. "Exactly."

She had to check her records before she could answer them.

"October twenty-eighth. It was a Tuesday, that's our end pay-week day. I gave him a week's salary plus commission and eight severance days."

Rizzo thanked her. After a few more routine questions, the two detectives left.

As they reached the Impala, parked beneath the elevated train tracks on Eighty-sixth Street, Rizzo spoke. "Guy gets fired, takes his severance pay and squares his rent the same day."

Priscilla nodded. "Yeah. Then he's hanging around his apartment every day and he's so quiet, so unobtrusive, the landlord doesn't even know he's no longer working."

As Rizzo dropped into the driver's seat, starting the engine, he wondered aloud, "But for how long? We don't know when he got whacked."

"What now?" Priscilla asked, as she hooked her shoulder harness.

"Back to the house," Rizzo said with a shrug. "The Swede has Bobby Dee and his partner doin' a street canvass and the uniforms gathering plate numbers and lookin' around the area for the murder weapon. We need to get Lauria's phone records and contact the cousin, maybe first get her local precinct to do the death notification so we won't have to. And Vince told me the fax came in from Rosen. I wanna go over all his notes. Tomorrow, after that stink airs out some, we'll go back to the scene. I want to look around again carefully, see what's what. We need to go through the guy's stuff, then talk to the cousin. Maybe she can point us at someone."

"You goin' premeditated on this, Joe?" Priscilla asked. "What happened to our junkie burglar?"

He shrugged. "If it was a junkie burglar so strung out he missed that watch, chances are he dropped his prints all over the joint. CSU will make the prints and that'll be the end of it."

"And if there are no prints?" she asked.

"Well, in that case, we're up against it. An untargeted, random break-in homicide like this one is the toughest. No motive, nothing, just a random series of bullshit that ends up with some poor schmuck like Lauria gettin' his throat crushed. Cases like this usually get solved when some street stoolie gets jammed up on an unrelated case and uses his info to cut himself a deal. You know how it works: the perp brags to his lowlife buddies what a hard-ass he is, how he whacked Joe Citizen for givin' him some grief, struttin' around like he's John fuckin' Dillinger. And then when he gets ratted out, he's perplexed, don't know what happened." Rizzo shook his head. "I'm gettin' real sick of these dumb fucks, Cil. Real sick."

"Yeah, I hear you. I don't find 'em quite as amusin' as I did in my rookie days, either."

"Yeah, but to answer your original question, I am going premed on this. At least for now. We got a week or ten-day cold trail already, we can't afford to jerk around. We look at it like there's a reason, a motive, we check that out right away. Then if we dead end and it *is* just a break-in, we hope for a print or DNA hit or some rat bastard to give the perp up. That's about all we can do, Cil."

She nodded. "So we go through the motions."

"Yeah, for the time bein', anyway. Besides, this guy Lauria didn't leave much of a footprint behind. I'm thinkin' we can cover his whole history in one or two days. If we don't get pointed at somebody, we go with the junkie burglar theory. Or the local teenage asshole route, or the transient b and e man." After a moment, he added, "Just don't get your hopes up. This is probably just gonna waste our time and fuck up our other cases."

"We might get lucky, Joe. You never know."

"Yeah," he said without conviction. "But I tell ya, that watch—that fuckin' watch—still bothers me. I can't stop comin' back to it. I don't know squat about watches or any kinda jewelry, but one look at that Breitling and even I knew it was big bucks. Hell, a blind man could *smell* the heavy gold, *see* those friggin' diamonds. There ain't a

junkie or b and e man in the city woulda missed it. He'd have pocketed
it no matter what. That watch more than paid for his night's work."

She nodded. "Well," she said, "let's just see where it goes."

ONCE BACK at the Six-Two, Rizzo placed a call to the community
policing officer at Canarsie's Sixty-ninth Precinct. A car would be
dispatched to the home of Robert Lauria's cousin, they would make
the official notification of his death. The cousin would be asked to
identify the body at the Kings County Hospital morgue. Contact
information for Rizzo and Jackson was to be left with the woman.

The balance of the afternoon was spent reviewing Detective Sergeant Art Rosen's notes and speaking via phone to the CSU detective who conducted the crime scene investigation. A report on
preliminary findings was promised within twenty-four hours.

By five-thirty, the two detectives were ready to leave for the day.
Rizzo waved good night to Priscilla as she gathered her things and
left the squad room. He was just about to call Jennifer and tell her he
was on his way home when his direct line began to ring.

"Rizzo, Six-Two squad," he said into the black mouthpiece.

"It's me, Rizzo," a voice said in terse, flat tones. "Zee-Boy."

Rizzo frowned, glancing up at the wall clock. "What can I do for
you, kid?"

"You can stay the fuck away from me for a while," Zee-Boy said
bitterly. "After this call, stay away from me."

"Tell me," Rizzo said.

"Just sos we're clear here," Zee-Boy said, "I give you the name of
the kid you're lookin' for, you keep me out of it, right?"

"Yeah, kid, just between us."

"Us and that mullinyom partner you got," Zee-Boy replied.

"Whatever," Rizzo said.

"And when the collar does go down, there's no mention at all this
kid was hangin' with The Rebels, right?"

"Right."

"But if it ever does come up, if Louie Chink gets word of it, you'll
square it, right? Convince the old prick I did the righteous thing
here, right?"

Rizzo grew impatient. "Give me the fuckin' name, kid. I told you, you're off the hook. Just give me the fuckin' name."

After a pause, Zee-Boy said, "Jamesy Doyle. Lives with his donkey mother in the building on the corner of Sixteenth Avenue and Sixty-fifth Street, apartment two-B. He's new to the neighborhood, Joe. He don't know how it is. Just got here about six months ago from some shantytown in Ireland. He's a fuckin' immigrant and one crazy motherfucker."

"Yeah, well, thanks, Zee-Boy. Anything else I should know?"

"Yeah," Zee-Boy responded. "One more thing. The kid's only thirteen."

"Are you kiddin' me?"

"No, Joe, no shit. Thirteen. A fuckin' juvenile offender." Zee-Boy paused. "Get ready to nursemaid this shit-head through Family Court. Maybe get that black Mammy of yours to wet-nurse him. Good fuckin' luck." The phone went dead in Rizzo's ear.

Rizzo dropped a finger on the telephone's cradle, then lifted it, the dial tone coming through. He began to punch in his home number.

A fucking thirteen-year-old, he thought. Just what he needed. A fucking babysitting job.

CHAPTER TWELVE

THE NEXT MORNING, TUESDAY, Rizzo arrived at the Six-Two just before seven-thirty, a half hour before the start of his day tour. Two fellow detectives, Mark Ginsberg and George Parker, were alone in the squad room at Parker's desk, sitting out the last thirty minutes of their morning tour. Rizzo crossed the room, pulling up a chair and greeting the two men.

"How was your night?"

Parker shrugged, huge shoulders straining against his thin cotton shirt. "Quiet," he said. "All the white folk were sound asleep, nice and peaceful."

Ginsberg laughed. "That's why I told you to transfer over here, George," he said. "We're gettin' too old for excitement."

"Yeah, I know the feelin'." Rizzo glanced at his wristwatch. "Can you give me a minute, guys?"

"Sure," Parker said. "What's on your mind?"

"Those two street robberies you guys are carrying. And the Hom case, the third robbery me 'n Jackson caught."

"What about 'em?" Ginsberg asked.

Rizzo smiled as he answered. "I got a name."

"No shit?" said Parker. "From where?"

Rizzo shrugged. "Came to me in a vision."

"Oh," Ginsberg said. "Like that, eh?"

"Yeah, Mark," he replied. "Like that."

Parker spoke next. "So, it's the same perp on all three? The way we had it made?"

Rizzo nodded. "Yeah. Same guy."

Ginsberg smiled as he spoke. "Well, it's kinda late for Yom Kippur and too early for Christmas, so what's this, a Thanksgiving present you're handin' us?"

Rizzo shook his head. "Who said anything 'bout a present, Mark? But bein' today's Veterans Day, let's call it a transaction. A transaction between three old vets."

Parker snorted. "Shit, you call Mark's three years in the fuckin' Coast Guard telling dames on yachts to put their bikini tops back on being a veteran, Joe?"

"Hey, it's the Jewish navy, what can I tell you?" laughed Ginsberg.

Rizzo rubbed his hands together. "Let's talk," he said.

Parker sat back in his seat. "Talk to my attorney here, Joe. I let him handle all our negotiations."

"And I let George pick out the rib joints we eat at," Ginsberg said.

"Me and Jackson caught a homicide," Rizzo began, watching both cops nod their understanding. "So we're gonna be busy for a while. I came up with a name on the robberies. But here's the thing: the perp is thirteen."

"Shit," Parker said. "That'll kill a couple a days for the arresting."

"Exactly," Rizzo said. "I lock this kid up, either me or Jackson gotta sit with him durin' the whole process, right through to the fuckin' Family Court appearance. Then we hafta transport him to Spofford or wherever the fuck they ship 'im pending disposition. It could take two days, not to mention havin' to kiss his mother's ass the whole time." He looked from one to the other. "I ain't got that kinda time right now, guys."

"I hear you," Parker said. "So, whaddya got in mind?"

"I'll cut a deal," Rizzo said. "I give you the name. You make the pinch, walk the kid through, or maybe get Olivero to do it for you—he's the friggin' youth officer. Then me and Jackson get sole credit on the Hom case, shared on your two cases. That gives me and her three cleared cases, a cushion for us to work this homicide. We just cleared a shooting and that dick-waver case, so with the robberies, that's five in—what?—five, six weeks we been partnered? It's more than good enough."

Parker and Ginsberg exchanged looks, then Ginsberg leaned toward Rizzo.

"How do we know the name's good?" he asked.

Rizzo shrugged. "Try it out. Go talk to the kid. Squeeze him, lean on the mother. She's an immigrant, ask her for her green card, scare her a little. If the kid don't cop to it, line him up and bring in the vics. I bet one or more can make the kid." He looked from one to the other, noting the interest in their eyes. "If it don't work out, nothin' lost, nothin' gained." He paused, allowing a smile to come to his face. "I got a feelin' it's gonna work out, though. A good feeling."

After a moment, Parker crossed his hands on his broad, flat midriff and said, "You know, I been at the Six-Two less than a year, but I hear good shit 'bout your little deals, Joe." He turned his hard brown eyes to his partner. "Whaddya think, Counselor? Sounds like a plan to me."

Ginsberg turned his gaze to Rizzo. "I'll say yes. I have faith in Joe's . . . *vision*."

Rizzo slipped a piece of paper from his jacket pocket and tossed it onto Parker's desk. "Good," he said. "That's the kid. Lives with his mother, and word is he ain't wrapped too tight, so watch out when you pick 'im up. Don't let his baby face fool you."

Rizzo stood. "One more thing." The two detectives turned their eyes upward to meet his.

"This kid might be wearin' Rebel colors," Rizzo said in a serious tone. "If word gets around the neighborhood he's a Rebel, we got a very serious problem."

The two cops furrowed their brows for a moment. Then, a sudden awareness appeared in Ginsberg's green eyes.

"I smell some diarrhea, Joe," he said cheerfully, "and I think it's runnin' down Zee-Boy's leg. Am I right?"

Rizzo shook his head gently. "No squeal on The Rebels, Mark," he said. "They don't exist, far as this case goes. If you convince Olivero to help out, make sure he gets that, too."

"Done," Ginsberg said. They shook hands and Rizzo once again glanced at his wristwatch. The bargaining hadn't taken very long.

"Go on, guys," he said. "Take off. I got the squad covered. Go on home."

Parker stood, his six-four frame towering above Rizzo.

"Pleasure doin' business with ya, *paesan*," he said, laying a large hand on Rizzo's shoulder. "Truly a pleasure."

LATER THAT morning, Rizzo and Jackson sat at a small table in the detective squad interview room, across from Detective Second Grade Robert Dellosso, known around the precinct as Bobby Dee.

"Tough way to get started in the precinct, Cil," Dellosso said, "catchin' a cold homicide."

"Somebody's got to do it," she said.

"Bobby," Rizzo said, "Vince told me he had you and Kenny do a canvass at the scene."

"Yeah, we did. Four and a half friggin' hours and all of it on straight time."

"Thanks. How'd you make out?" Rizzo asked.

"Waste a time. Tough enough to canvass for info when you don't know the date of the crime, but then factor in this guy Lauria, it's fuckin' impossible."

"Why's that?"

"This guy was the Invisible Man, Joe. Not one person off the block knew who we were askin' about. And maybe two, three people on the block itself knew him, and them only 'cause they were friendly with the homeowners, the Annasias."

Rizzo ran his hand through his hair. "Yeah, I'm not surprised. Seems the guy was a loner, kept to himself."

"Big time, Joe. Even the local shopkeepers couldn't place the guy. Me and Kenny had a picture of Lauria we took outta the apartment. Even that didn't help."

"Well," Rizzo said, "thanks for tryin'. And thank Kenny for me."

"Hey, no problem," Dellosso said. "I owe you plenty a favors. Anyway, I'm almost done with the DD-fives, I'll give 'em to you when they're finished."

"Thanks," Rizzo said. "And do me one more favor, if you don't mind. Give me that picture of Lauria, too. Cil and I can use it."

"Sure."

"You're sure it's him, right, Bobby? The picture, I mean. You're sure it's of Lauria?"

"Hey, Joe, me and Kenny ain't that stupid. We had the landlord I.D. it before we showed it around."

"Yeah, well, I know. Just thought I'd ask, that's all."

"What now?" Priscilla asked, when Dellosso had left the room.

Before he could answer, a uniformed officer assigned to the squad room opened the door and stuck his head in.

"Hey, Joe," the cop said. "Call for you on three-five."

"Thanks, guy," Rizzo said, standing and leaving the room, Priscilla following. He took the call at his desk, gesturing for Priscilla to sit down.

"Rizzo," he said.

"Hey, Joe, good morning," he heard. It was Detective Dan Schillings from the CSU team.

"Hey, Dan, mornin'. What's up?"

"Some prelims on that Lauria case," Schillings said.

"Tell me," Rizzo replied.

Schillings cleared his throat. Rizzo heard a faint rustle of papers coming through the line.

"Two sets of prints in the apartment. One was the vic's, the other belonged to MaryAnn Carbone, thirty-eight-year-old female, last known out in Canarsie."

"The cousin I been hearin' about," Rizzo said. Then a thought came to him. "Why were her prints on file, Dan?"

Again Rizzo heard the shuffling of papers.

"Hold on . . . here it is. She works as an aide in the public school out on Rockaway Parkway. They print for that job."

"Okay. Where'd you find her prints?"

"Various, mostly kitchen and bathroom. Nothin' in the rear bedroom, nothing out of the ordinary."

"Okay," Rizzo said. "Just those two sets, that's it?"

"Yeah, that was it, print-wise. But we got lucky."

Rizzo's eyebrows raised. "Tell me."

"We had a mutual fiber transfer hit. We found what looks like a foreign fiber on Lauria's T-shirt. I sent a couple a guys out to the scene. They're taking samples of all the clothes in the apartment. In a few days, I'll be able to tell you if this fiber is from a piece of Lauria's clothing or possibly from the perp. It's a start."

"If we ever I.D. a suspect, that fiber can help nail the guy," Rizzo said.

"Yeah, could happen. We'll see."

"Anything else of value?" Rizzo asked.

"Not yet. Backyard was clean. In fact, the whole scene was pretty clean. There were clear prints on the inside and outside doorknobs of the front door. So they weren't wiped down."

"The vic's prints were on the knob?" Rizzo asked.

"Yeah," Schillings said. "And the first cop, Malloy. His prints were on the outside knob."

"So no strange prints or wipe downs, the perp either had gloves on or used a handkerchief or whatever while he was in the apartment."

"Yeah, most likely. Nothing seemed to have been wiped down, nothing we could find. Looks like the perp went out of his way to keep it clean."

"Okay, Dan. Anything more?"

"Nope. I'll be in touch about that fiber and anything else that turns up."

"Alright, buddy, thanks."

The line went dead. Rizzo replaced the receiver and turned to Priscilla. He quickly filled her in.

"So you figure the no-print angle is significant?" she asked.

"Do you?" he asked with raised eyebrows.

"What's this, a pop quiz? Okay, then," Priscilla said. "Let's see, now. The lack of prints and the no wipe down means the perp wore gloves. That could mean he came to the place with murder in mind, or it could mean it was just a burglar, a pro, a guy who wears gloves and doesn't break in carrying a firearm. So, when the thing went down, he had to strangle the vic because he carried no weapon. So, we still got nothin'. Am I right?"

Rizzo shook his head. "Cil, I gotta tell you, you once told Vince you weren't as pretty as Mike, but you were smarter. Well, you were wrong."

He leaned in toward her and gently patted her knee.

"You're *way* prettier *and* a damn sight smarter, too," he said with a wink. "Now follow through on what you just said. If it was a pro b and e man, a guy with gloves, no firearm, all that, how'd he miss that watch?"

Priscilla twisted her lips. "Again with the freakin' watch?"

Rizzo smiled.

"Yeah," he said. "Again with the friggin' watch."

WHILE SITTING in the Impala eating their Burger King lunches, Rizzo filled Priscilla in on the arrangements he had made with Ginsberg and Parker regarding the Hom robbery.

"Sounds like a good deal," she said. "We get sole credit for the Hom case and shared with the other two, they get to do the dirty work." She bit into her burger. "I can get used to that."

Rizzo nodded. "Plus they owe us now. We solved two cases for them. We'll cash those chips someday."

"You make stuff simple, Joe. I can use some of that."

Rizzo noticed a somberness in her tone. He turned in the passenger seat, facing her more fully.

"Now that didn't sound like the usual sharin'-a-burger bullshit-chitchat. What's goin' on?"

"You really wanna hear it?" she asked, dabbing ketchup from the corner of her mouth with a crumpled napkin.

"Sure," he said.

"Okay, you asked for it. I'm havin' breakfast yesterday with Karen. Very nice, I cooked her eggs, she's all happy, everything is cool. Then all of a sudden, things get all melodramatic. She says, 'We need to talk.'"

Rizzo winced. "Ouch. That usually means trouble in paradise."

"Yeah, well, this wasn't the first time we had this conversation. See, Karen is very close to her parents, they've been really cool with her ever since she came out to them in high school. It's impossible for her to relate to my situation with my own crazy-ass mother. So now it's the holidays, this friggin' Thanksgiving, and Karen's folks are going away on a cruise. She figures this for the perfect opportunity to mend my fences, have a little down-home Thanksgiving with my old lady."

She sat silently for a moment, shaking her head as the scene replayed in her mind.

"She means well, Joe. But she just don't get it. I don't *have* a mother. All I got is some drunk who dumped me out in the backseat of a gypsy cab 'cause she was too fuckin' stupid or disinterested to get her ass to a hospital on time. But Karen figures we invite her over, sip some sherry, eat some turkey, and exchange decorating ideas for the apartment. Blah . . . blah . . . blah, Upper East Side bullshit. I swear, sometimes I think Karen sees the whole world as some Vassar sorority round-table jerk-off club."

"So," Rizzo said. "How'd you leave it off?"

"I told her no friggin' way. That old lady just doesn't exist for me, Joe. Not after the hell she put me through till I got the fuck outta her grasp."

"Sounds like you're not kiddin'."

"Damn right I ain't. But now I gotta deal with all this. . . . You know what Karen told me? She said she expects me to be the person I am, not just some hard-ass cop I like to pretend to be. She expects me to do the *right* fuckin' thing with this. And do you know what the right thing always is, Joe? What *she* wants me to do."

They sat in silence for a moment before Rizzo spoke. "Yeah, Partner," he said. "The *right* thing. I know all about the *right* thing."

"Can you imagine? I mean, I love the girl, but, Jesus, can her head be any farther up her own ass? Does she really figure my old lady is gonna drop her gin bottle and bake me and my girlfriend a pumpkin pie for Thanksgiving?" She shook her head. "Jesus, girl, get real."

"This is the stuff people gotta hear, Cil," Rizzo said, allowing himself a small smile.

"What stuff?" Priscilla asked.

"This stuff," he said. "It's so routine. It's the same-old same-old everybody's gotta deal with. I mean, that decorator thing you told me about, and how Karen's old man wants to hook you into corporate city, and her mother wants you off the cops. Now this, this crap about your mother. It's the same stuff couples been dealin' with since Eve boosted that apple and fucked everything up."

"We *are* a couple, Joe. We ain't fuckin' Martians."

"Exactly," Rizzo said emphatically. "That's what the boys in pink and the pain-in-the-ass lesbos gotta start publicizin'. Get this stuff out there, you'll have the sympathy of every straight man and woman in the world."

Priscilla shook her head. "Hell, I'm not looking for any sympathy from any-fuckin'-body. I'm just looking for some peace. Get Karen off my back with this bullshit. My mother is fucked up. Totally. And nothing is ever going to change that." She let air out from between her lips. "Now these goddamned holidays gotta be a freakin' issue."

She turned full face to Rizzo. "Please tell me we're working Thanksgiving, Partner. Please."

Rizzo shook his head. "Sorry. I checked the duty board through New Year. We're off Thanksgiving, Christmas, *and* New Year's Day. That's three fuckin' arguments you can have with Karen. Ain't the holidays fun?" he asked, his brows raised.

"Yeah, a freakin' riot."

After a moment, Rizzo spoke again. "Why don't we do this? I'm having Thanksgiving at my house. Just my girls, Jen, her mother and mine. Why don't you and Karen come? You can tell her you feel obligated, new partner, you gotta say yes, like that. You can push off this reunion from hell showdown for another month. Think about it. It'll be fun watchin' my mother and mother-in-law watchin' you and Karen."

Priscilla laughed. "Yeah, that sounds just great, Joe."

"No, seriously," he said. "It'll be fine. Plus, maybe you and Karen can do me a favor and try to talk Carol out of goin' on the cops. Hell, maybe Karen can get her old man to hook Carol up with some nine-to-five big payday bullshit job."

"Okay, Joe, I'll think about it." After a pause, Priscilla spoke again. "Actually it may not be a bad idea. Karen would like to meet you." She smiled at him. "I told her what a broad-minded, liberal Democrat you are, but somehow I don't think she believed me."

"Yeah, broad minded," he said. "Though I gotta tell you, broads ain't been on my mind as much as they were when I was younger."

"Well, good for you," she said.

They ate in silence for a while, watching pedestrian traffic move along the avenue in front of the Burger King's parking lot.

Then Priscilla spoke once again, her tone neutral, her face expressionless.

"I gotta say, though, you did surprise me a little."

"Oh, when was that?"

"In Lauria's kitchen. With that black M.E. When you so diplomatically reminded him to check the corpse's eyes for whatever. In case the guy was too stupid to think of it himself. You know . . . maybe since he was black and all."

"Well, well," Rizzo said with a laugh, "did that get your panties all bunched up?"

"A little bit, yeah," she said.

"Cil, you need an explanation, I'll give you one. But it's not gonna break my heart any if you don't believe it, so don't hurt yourself tryin'."

He turned full face to her, speaking carefully.

"There's a few M.E.s out there who do it for the science, for the love of it. Those are the fucked-up ones, the head cases who like carvin' up bodies, pokin' around the maggots for clues. They're like dysfunctional high school science nerds tryin' to invent a better jerk-'em-off machine. But most M.E.s, the guy at Lauria's place more'n likely, are guys with medical degrees who can't get licensed to practice or can't pass their boards or whatever. Some can barely speak English, guys from Puke-istan or some other shit-hole somewheres. They take the M.E. job for the steady paycheck, benefits, and a pension. Same reason guys become cops or garbagemen or work down at the DMV. They ain't exactly consumed with ambition, you know? *That's* why I reminded the doctor to get potassium levels from those eyes. I didn't figure him for a slacker 'cause he was black. I figured him for a slacker 'cause he was an M.E. End of story." He sat back in the seat, taking up his burger.

"Okay, Joe," Priscilla said, turning to her own food. "I was hoping it was something like that."

"All right, then," Rizzo said. "Let's skip the awkward silence, okay, and get back to business."

"You got it," she said. "Tell me."

"Jesus," he said, shaking his head. "Now she's gonna start talkin' like me. A fuckin' Frankenstein I'm creatin' here."

"That invite for Thanksgiving still stand?"

"Sure," he said. "If you decide to come, I'll tell Jen to fry you up some chicken. You know, sos you'll have somethin' to eat."

Priscilla tossed her crumpled napkin at him. "Okay, Joe. I get it. Okay."

Chapter Thirteen

LATER THAT AFTERNOON, Rizzo and Jackson arrived at Lauria's apartment just as the two plainclothes CSU officers sent by Detective Schillings were leaving. The officers held fiber samples from the victim's wardrobe labeled and packaged in clear plastic evidence bags.

Once inside the apartment, Priscilla opened some windows and let the cold November air breeze through, further dispelling the lingering odor of rotting flesh.

"Let's start in the bedroom," Rizzo said. "Anything you find of cash value, make a note of it. Maybe this cousin of his can tell us if anything he owned is missing."

"What exactly are we looking for?" Priscilla asked.

He shrugged. "Don't worry. Whatever it is, we'll know it when we find it. We gotta get to know this guy, Cil. If it turns out he was killed by a burglar, this is just a waste a time, but, if it was premeditated, or the killer was somebody he knew, maybe there's somethin' in here that'll point us somewhere. Maybe the guy was a closet case—gay, pedophile, s and m dude, somethin' like that. Maybe he was a skell gambler. Whatever. If he had a secret, if there's somethin' more to this guy than just a sad-sack loser life rolled over, we have to find it.

"And when you're tryin' to find somebody's secrets, remember this: start lookin' in the bedroom."

Yesterday's search of the apartment had been cursory, surface deep, a search for the clues and debris of the crime itself. Now the two detectives methodically went through drawers, rummaged through bundled stacks of paid bills, legal papers, books and magazines. After a while, Rizzo moved to the large closet at the far wall. He slid open one of the doors and looked in.

Some moments later, he called to Priscilla.

"Hey, come check this out."

She came to stand beside him as he knelt on the worn, brown carpeting, "What you got there, Joe?"

He looked up at her. "It's a typewriter—in the original case. Friggin' thing's gotta be thirty years old. It's an old IBM Selectric. Years ago these were standard issue in all the precincts. It's a goddamn antique."

Priscilla shrugged. "Okay, so what?"

Rizzo stood, wiping carpet lint from his hands. "Take a look at it," he said. "A close look."

She knelt, eyeing the machine carefully. "What am I lookin' at here, Joe?"

"Fuckin' thing looks like it came outta the factory last week," Rizzo said. "Look at the ball—the letters have hardly any ink buildup. Check out the cartridge, it's been used, but it isn't very old. And look under the cover—freshly oiled parts, no dust stuck all over everything. This machine was worked on and very well maintained."

Priscilla examined the machine. "Yeah, okay. So what?"

Rizzo shrugged. "So . . . I don't know. But like I said, we gotta get to know the real Robbie Lauria. And since we can't go have a few beers with the guy and shoot the shit, this is how we gotta do it. By pokin' around his life and finding stuff like this."

Priscilla pursed her lips. "So okay, the guy has a functioning thirty-year-old typewriter. What does that mean?"

"I don't know yet. See, we *detect* stuff. That's why they call us *detect-ives*."

"Okay, Joe, I got it. We keep looking."

"Yeah," he said. "Let's."

Against the inside wall of the closet stood a large, green Samsonite hard-shell luggage case.

"This guy liked old stuff," Rizzo said. "I had a Samsonite just like this, same color and everything. Me and Jen used it on our honeymoon. I think it's up in our attic somewheres full of the girls' baby clothes."

Priscilla leaned into the closet, brushing against Rizzo, and grabbed hold of the handle of the suitcase.

"Wonder if he's got some of his stuff in here," she said, tugging on the case. She stumbled forward against its unexpected weight. "Wow, goddamn heavy."

"Easy," Rizzo said, as he took hold of her arm to stabilize her. "Let's get it out here."

Once they'd wrestled the case out of the closet, Priscilla placed it down flat on the brown rug and opened the two clasps securing it.

"What the fuck is all that?" Rizzo asked from over her shoulder as she lifted the top and they looked in.

"Looks like manuscripts," Priscilla said. "Typewritten manuscripts."

Rizzo crouched beside her, reaching into the suitcase and taking hold of a stack of eight-and-a-half-by-eleven-inch papers, tightly bound by thick rubber bands. He thumbed through the first few pages, nodding his head.

"Yeah, that's what it looks like." He rubbed at his eye, examining the pages. "Must be five hundred friggin' pages in this one alone."

"This one, too," said Priscilla, holding a second bundle.

The two detectives sat on the floor, rummaging through the contents of the case. It held six separate, book-length manuscripts, each carefully typed and double-spaced, apparently on the old Selectric. Each bundle was secured with multiple rubber bands, and each contained a title page with Lauria listed as the author, his address and phone number beneath his name. There were one or two duplicate copies of each manuscript and nearly a thousand pages of shorter works, each dated in ink with a neat, precise hand.

Rizzo shook his head. "This guy's been writin' this crap for over twenty years."

Priscilla looked up from the page she had been reading.

"This isn't necessarily crap, Joe. From just what I've read, the guy's got the basics down pat. He may even be pretty good."

Rizzo dismissed her assessment with a disinterested shrug. "Yeah, well, anything sittin' inside a closet for twenty years in a thirty-year-old suitcase is crap, far as I'm concerned."

He stood, dropping the bundle he held back into the Samsonite. "I'm gonna take a look around the living room. Why don't you finish checkin' this closet."

"Okay," Priscilla said, barely looking up from her reading. "In a minute."

Rizzo entered the small parlor. Its floor was covered with the same worn, brown carpeting as in the bedroom. An old sofa sat against one wall and faced a small wooden table that held a nineteen-inch television. A stereo turntable stood on a second small table in the corner. He opened the lid and looked in. A Frank Sinatra Reprise LP sat on the turntable, the black vinyl shining against the light of the room, its surface unmarred by scratches. It looked as if it was brand new.

"Fuckin' guy," Rizzo said to himself. "More of a dinosaur than me."

He crossed the room, dropping into a battered easy chair beside a small lamp table. He switched on the light and slid open the table's lone drawer. He looked in, poking objects aside with his pen and examining them—a three-week-old *TV Guide*, an old *Popular Mechanics* magazine, a nail clipper set in a cheap black plastic case, an empty Dr. Scholl's bunion pad package, a clear plastic vial of toothpicks, a *New York Times* crossword puzzle book, three Bic pens, and a short number-two pencil.

Rizzo slid the drawer closed, then took out what he firmly believed would be his very last pack of Chesterfields. He lit a cigarette and sighed.

"Come on, Robbie," he said softly. "Help me out a little. Give me somethin'."

He rubbed a forefinger at his eye.

"Any goddamned thing."

LATER, THE two detectives sat at Lauria's kitchen table, glancing at the dark bloodstains and yellow coroner's chalk marks on the pale green vinyl flooring.

"I got a feelin' this guy spent a lot of time putzin' around this apartment in his pajamas," Rizzo said, drawing on a second ciga-rette. "So your theory 'bout Lauria getting killed making himself a cup a tea in the morning or late night doesn't necessarily hold. If it was a burglar, though, and the perp did come in through that back window, we can probably figure it happened at night. Too many houses and windows lookin' down on that backyard to take a chance breaking in during daylight."

"*If* it was a burglar, and *if* that's how he got in," Priscilla said.

"Okay, let's hear it," Rizzo prompted.

She shrugged. "I don't know. This is making less and less sense to me, this burglar angle."

"Tell me," he said.

"Let's walk through it. Possibility one: It's nighttime, Lauria is in his kitchen getting some tea. Perp breaks the rear window and climbs in. Why doesn't the vic hear it? Why doesn't he go see what hap-pened? How does he wind up rear-strangled in the freakin' kitchen?"

"I don't know," Rizzo said.

She went on, "Okay, possibility two: Lauria is in bed, asleep. Perp breaks in, somehow Lauria doesn't wake up. Perp searches the bed-room, quiet as a mouse, ransacks it like we found it. Then he starts checkin' out the rest of the place. Suddenly, Lauria wakes up, goes to investigate, and gets his ass choked to death in the kitchen."

Rizzo challenged her. "So the perp searches the bedroom, but he don't see the big prize, the watch on the nightstand?"

"Exactly," she said. "The bedroom *was* ransacked, either before or after the killing. But the watch was left."

He nodded. "So our burglar perp is either the most incompetent asshole in the business, or he found somethin' else. Something better'n that watch, something so valuable he couldn't believe his luck, and he was content to leave with it—get the fuck outta Dodge."

Priscilla's lips pursed. "Or, he found exactly what he was looking for. What he had come for."

Rizzo looked at her. "Like what?"

"Beats me, boss, beats me good," she said. "From the looks of this place, Lauria didn't have anything worth stealing. What could this poor dude possibly have had that was worth killing over?"

Rizzo dragged on the cigarette, then expelled smoke away from Jackson, rubbing his eye.

After a moment, he spoke again. "That shoe store dame, the manager. She said she paid Lauria a week's salary plus commission and eight days' severance. Annasia told us Lauria paid his November rent in cash on October twenty-eighth. I saw a bank passbook in the bedroom. It showed no deposits made around the twenty-eighth. Last entry was back in mid-September, a hundred-dollar withdrawal."

Priscilla frowned. "A passbook, did you say?"

"Yeah, a passbook. Guy still had a friggin' passbook account. Like my seventy-eight-year-old mother's got. He's a freakin' fossil. Makes me look like a today kinda guy."

Priscilla reflected, then spoke. "So the guy cashes his paycheck, takes his dough, and pays the rent."

Rizzo dipped his head to the side. "Yeah, but the rent wasn't much. I came across the receipts. He'da had lotsa cash left."

"So where is it?" Priscilla asked. "It's not in this apartment."

Rizzo shrugged. "In the burglar's pocket. You know, the burglar neither one of us seems to feel was here."

Priscilla took a breath and said, "Joe, this isn't getting us anywhere. It could go nine different ways. If the guy that killed him *wanted* it to look like a burglary, he'da tossed the place, grabbed the cash, and left."

"There's nothing else worth stealin' in this place except that watch," Rizzo said. "Lauria never even got as far as the eight-track stage, he's still playin' vinyl records. If it was me tryin' to make this look like a burglary, I'da tossed the place, too. And grabbed the cash so the cops wouldn't find it. But I wouldn't be lookin' for anything else. What the hell could have been here, Cil, Ed Sullivan's fuckin' autograph?" He leaned forward.

"And that could explain the watch. The guy missed it 'cause he really didn't care about finding anything of value. He broke in specifically to kill Lauria. Assuming, of course, that he did break in. If he came in the front door and then staged that broken window, the whole thing coulda been unplanned, just a fight between two screwballs."

Priscilla shook her head. "A guy walking in and out the front door just to pay a visit woulda left prints, Joe. Or wipe-downs. *If* the murder was unplanned. And besides, you heard Annasia. Lauria only had one person visiting him over the years. His cousin."

"Yeah," Rizzo said.

She frowned. "You think it was *her* coulda killed him?"

"Doubtful," he said. "Women don't strangle—they poison, they shoot, they stab. They'll even push you out a fuckin' window if the need arises. It takes a lot of strength and a cold heart to strangle somebody. And you usually cut your hands up pretty bad. If Lauria's neck bled, so did the killer's hands, unless he wore real heavy gloves. Remind me to tell Dr. Rum 'n Coke-mon to check for multiple blood specimens from the body and floor samples."

"Yassa, boss, I's surely gonna re-member dat," Priscilla said in a high pitched singsong.

"Don't start with that shit again, Priscilla. I already explained my doubts about the guy, remember?"

"Yeah, Joe, relax. Just kiddin'."

They sat quietly, each reviewing the case at hand.

"So," Rizzo said after a while, "what have we got?"

"Whatever we want," she said with resignation. "We got a burglar, we got a pretend burglar, we got an invited guest, an uninvited guest, a premeditated murder or a spontaneous spat between two nerds arguin' over who's cooler, Superman, Batman, or Captain fuckin' Kirk. Take your pick."

"You know, this reminds me of some wisdom once passed on to me from my uncle Jim," Rizzo said.

"Yeah? What's that?"

He stood and moved to the sink. He ran water over the stub of his cigarette, then dropped it into the trash. Leaning against the small refrigerator and crossing his arms, he smiled at Priscilla as he spoke again.

"It was the day of my Confirmation. I was lined up outside the church wearin' my new shiny blue suit with a red arm ribbon, me and all the other kids and their sponsors. My uncle Jim, he was my godfather, he christened me, so he served as my sponsor. Well, we're waitin' outside, and I'm startin' to squirm around, gettin' all nervous. So Uncle Jim asks me, 'What's the matter, Joe?' and I tell him, 'Well, the nuns said the bishop's gonna slap us. They said we gotta kneel down at the altar, and then he's gonna slap us across the face. And I don't wanna get slapped.'"

Priscilla shrugged. "Sounds reasonable to me."

Rizzo nodded. "I thought so. Anyway, Uncle Jim kneels down right on the sidewalk in his good suit, probably the only one he owned. He puts his hand on my shoulder and gets real serious, looks me right in the eye. 'Kid,' he says. 'Relax. This is just to make your mother happy, that's all. So just relax. At the end of the day, it's all just bullshit.'"

"What an upliftin' Christian message of hope," Priscilla said.

"Wasn't it, though? But this here Lauria case. It brought old Uncle Jim to mind."

Priscilla's brow furrowed. "Why? I don't get it."

Rizzo reached for a third Chesterfield. "I dunno, Cil, maybe 'cause that's what this case looks like. Maybe, at the end a the day, it's all just bullshit."

He lit the cigarette, eyeing her through the smoke.

"All just bullshit," he said again.

AT SEVEN o'clock Tuesday evening, Jennifer Rizzo took a seat next to her husband on the double recliner in the den of their Brooklyn home. She turned and smiled into his dark brown eyes, noting the TV listings in his hand.

"I'm very proud of you, Joe," she said.

He looked puzzled. "Proud of me?"

"The invitation," she said. "To Priscilla and Karen for Thanksgiving. You've come a long way, baby. You're maturing nicely."

"Maturing? I'm eighty friggin' years old."

Jennifer shook her head. "Not quite. Let's not rush things, time is flying by fast enough. But I am proud of you. And impressed with your bravery."

"Bravery?"

"Yes, Joe, bravery. The girls and I will welcome your guests with open arms. But we will also disavow any and all responsibility for their presence. As far as my mother and your mother are concerned, this will have been your idea and yours alone." Jennifer paused, smiling again. "It takes a very brave man to face that. Just remember: there's a difference between bravery and stupidity."

Rizzo wrinkled his brow. "What?"

Jennifer raised a pointer finger as she replied. "Inviting them was bravery," she said flatly. "Not checking with me first—that was stupidity."

CHAPTER FOURTEEN

WEDNESDAY MORNING AT SEVEN-FORTY, Jackson sat at her desk in the Six-Two squad room. She fingered some precinct crime reports, scanning them perfunctorily, initialing them with an absent mind.

Her mother. Priscilla shook her head slightly, frowning at Karen's continued insistence on a reconnection.

"Can't reconnect somethin' never was connected to begin with," she said softly.

In the chaos that had been her childhood, the one facet of Priscilla's character and personality that had proven instrumental to her ultimate survival had been her deeply ingrained pragmatism. At an age when most young girls were hanging posters of pop stars and gossiping on the telephone, she had been dealing with her mother's alcoholism and all its inherent baggage. Priscilla had soon come to a self-preserving conclusion: the act of birthing a child was merely the physical manifestation of the biological rules of nature. In and of itself, it conferred no special powers or privileges, talents or virtues. It was the simple culmination of an earlier physical act, unrelated and even alien to any professed blessings of maternal love.

An actual mother, Priscilla realized, was a woman who loved you unconditionally, stood by you, taught you, nurtured you. A woman who would never abandon or hurt you by virtue of careless acts of indifference and selfish neglect.

By Priscilla's definition, the reality of her own life was that she never had a mother. Not as a child, not as an adolescent. And certainly not as an adult.

Priscilla sighed heavily. Her partner, she realized, could never come to such a conclusion about her own life. Karen had bestowed the magical, mystical qualities of a child's love upon the woman who had given her birth. She could never understand the consequences—the torment, the anguish, the agony—Wanda Jackson's maternal failures had imposed.

An empty coldness spread slowly within Priscilla's chest, memories straining beneath veils of darkness, struggling to reach her consciousness. She willed them away, forcing them into the abyss of the deepest corner of her soul.

"Fuck it," she said aloud, bitterly.

"Fuck what?" she heard.

Raising her eyes, she found herself looking into the curious face of Joe Rizzo. He stood at her desk, his approach having gone unnoticed.

"You okay, Cil?" Rizzo asked, concern tugging at his tone. "You look like you just swallowed a rotten clam."

She shook her head, clearing it. "These freakin' precinct reports," she said, indicating the papers before her. "Pain in my ass readin' all this, signing off on 'em like it makes a rat's ass bit of difference if I see them or not."

Rizzo's face remained impassive, and Priscilla realized he didn't believe her answer. "Okay," he said. "Whatever you say."

Later, Priscilla watched as Vince D'Antonio crossed the squad room to Rizzo's desk and sat down, conferring briefly with her partner.

Rizzo raised his eyes in her direction, meeting her gaze. He gestured across the room, summoning her. Priscilla rose and walked to his desk.

"Pull up a chair," Rizzo said. "We need to work out some details."

She slid a chair from the unoccupied desk near Rizzo's and sat down. "Mornin', boss," she said to D'Antonio.

"Good morning," the lieutenant said. "I just need a few minutes to get this straight. Rizzo tells me you're going to interview Lauria's cousin tomorrow."

"Yeah," Priscilla said. "The M.E. released the body and she's tied up making funeral arrangements."

D'Antonio turned to Rizzo. "Refresh my memory: What's your schedule look like?"

"Later today I've gotta be at court for a grand jury thing. Tomorrow we got the cousin, then me and Cil are RDO till we start midnights Sunday into Monday, then midnights all next week. Tough to work a homicide from midnight to eight, Vince. Some people like to sleep those hours."

D'Antonio considered it. "Look, let's do this. I'll reschedule you both for steady days to work the Lauria case. Take RDOs Friday, Saturday, and Sunday. After your interview of the cousin, prepare a laundry list of grunt work you figure needs doing—license plates, phone reviews, and junkie roundup. Somebody needs to check out the relatives of the landlord, see if there's a potential perp among them. I'll have the squad handle it all while you're RDO, then DD-five the results for you by Monday morning. You come in fresh and go to work."

Rizzo shrugged. "Monday I've got to be at the range, Vince. I already postponed it twice and if I don't requalify, they rubber gun me and stick me on a desk. I can't work a homicide from a desk."

"So, Tuesday then," D'Antonio said. "On Monday Cil can review the reports of what the squad got done and work the phones to follow up. Then Tuesday you both hit the streets on it."

"I never seen this happen on television, guys," Priscilla said with a tight smile. "Not even once."

"Yeah, well," said Rizzo. "The world don't stop turning 'cause two cops caught a homicide. Only people who think that are the ones putting those shows on. And you'll have to use Monday for more than just Lauria. That counterfeit prescription case, for instance. Those phony Rx's are turning up all over the borough. Try and get a lead on that girl who worked in the doctor's office for two weeks, then disappeared. We find her, we find our stolen script pads *and* our writer."

Priscilla stood up. "Okay, Joe, what now?"

D'Antonio also stood. "I'll leave you guys alone. Talk to the cousin. Get me that list of things you need done. The squad'll pitch in."

He turned and crossed the room to his office.

THE FOLLOWING morning, a cold gray November day, with heavy, dark clouds and the faint scent of a threatening early snowfall, the two detectives were speeding eastbound on the Belt Parkway, Priscilla at the wheel.

Closing the notepad he had been scanning, Rizzo said to Priscilla, "Vince means well, but the squad won't accomplish nothin' over the next three days."

Priscilla glanced at Rizzo. "Oh? Why's that?"

"Well, for one thing, checking out plate numbers is a waste of time. Only reason for it is to see if some out-of-neighborhood car was parked near the scene, maybe the killer's car. But those plate numbers were taken November tenth, after the body was layin' in the apartment ten, twelve days. It don't mean a goddamned thing whose car was parked where on the tenth. We need to know who was there the date of the murder."

"A date we don't even know," Priscilla said.

"Yeah, exactly."

"Well, what about Lauria's phone record?" Priscilla asked. "Vince said the squad would get it for us."

"Yeah. That might help, but I doubt it. We'll see."

"Maybe," Priscilla said tentatively, "we should cancel our RDOs, come in the next few days."

Rizzo shook his head. "No, let the squad do some of the work, it won't kill them. It has to be done, even if it won't help us. I especially don't want to do the junkie roundup. Let them handle it. After I qualify at the range Monday, we can focus on Lauria. One day at a time."

"Whatever you think, Joe."

They rode in silence until they reached the house in Canarsie. It was a two-story, semiattached one-family home. The house was neatly kept with a concrete driveway on the left side leading to a detached one-car garage.

Priscilla glanced at the dash clock. "Right on time," she said. It was eleven a.m.

MaryAnn Carbone, Robert Lauria's first cousin, was a thirty-eight-year-old housewife and part-time school aide. She was expecting them, and once the three were seated at the large kitchen table, Rizzo spoke across to the sad-eyed woman.

"We'll try not to take up too much of your time, Mrs. Carbone," he said. "Just some routine questions."

"Of course," she said. "I understand. I hope I can help somehow . . . I wish my husband were here." Her voice trailed off. "It's just unbelievable. I mean, you hear about this stuff, read about it . . . but . . ."

"Yes," Priscilla said. "It's a shock. We understand."

Carbone nodded. Then she said, "I can call my husband, if you'd like. He can be here in fifteen minutes."

Rizzo cleared his throat, slipping the Parker from his inner jacket pocket and flipping open his notepad.

"Hold off on that," he said. "We'll call him later if we need to. Let's get started. We'll ask some questions, you answer as best you can, okay?"

Still silent, the woman nodded again.

"When was the last time you saw Robbie?" he asked.

"About two months ago, maybe. No, wait, I went to his place around Columbus Day, that weekend. My internist is in Bensonhurst, and I was in the area, so I stopped in to see Robbie."

Rizzo glanced at the calendar page of his notebook, then raised his eyes to Mrs. Carbone.

"Columbus Day was celebrated Monday, October thirteenth. When did you see the doctor? Saturday, the eleventh?"

She thought for a moment. "It must have been. He doesn't have hours on Sunday, just half-days on Saturday. It must have been."

"How was Robbie that day?"

"He was Robbie," she said. "He was always the same. Quiet. Polite. In his pajamas, by himself." She sighed. "He was just Robbie."

"I see," Rizzo said.

"Did he have anyone in his life who could have done this to him,

Mrs. Carbone?" Priscilla asked. "A friend, an acquaintance, a coworker—anyone like that?"

Carbone seemed confused, glancing from one cop to the other.

"I don't understand," she said. "I thought it was a break-in. A burglar."

"Who told you that?" Rizzo asked.

"The young cop who came here. He told me there was a break-in and that Robbie had been killed."

Priscilla nodded. "That's what it looks like, ma'am."

"But you don't seem to be convinced," she said.

Rizzo interjected. "We need to check all the possibilities, Mrs. Carbone," he said. "Did your cousin have anyone like that? Anyone who could've gotten mad at him, mad enough to kill?"

She shook her head forcefully. "Absolutely not. Robbie was a lost soul, Sergeant. As far as I know, he didn't have a single friend, not since he was a young boy. The only kids he ever played with were me and my brother and another cousin or two."

Rizzo jotted a note, then raised his eyes to Carbone. "Has your brother stayed in touch with Robbie?" he asked.

"My brother hasn't seen Robbie in ten years."

"Oh?" Rizzo said.

"My brother's in the Air Force, Sergeant. Has been for over twenty years. He's currently stationed in the Middle East in Kuwait. He's been there for six months."

"What's your brother's name?" Rizzo asked.

"My brother didn't murder Robbie, Sergeant Rizzo," she said without anger.

"Of course not," Rizzo agreed. "I just want to give him a call. In Kuwait. Ask him a few questions, like I'm doin' here with you."

The woman laughed. "*Non mi pisciare sulla gamba e poi dirmi che sta piovendo,*" she said.

Now Rizzo replied in kind. "*Non farei mai una cosa del genere, Signora Carbone,*" he said casually.

The woman appeared stunned. "Oh. I didn't realize you spoke . . . you would understand . . ."

Rizzo waved a casual hand at her.

"Forget it," he said pleasantly. "Happens all the time, but I'd like your brother's name and contact info, if you don't mind. And those other cousins you mentioned, and maybe you should call your husband now."

"I'll get it for you, and call him. He can be here in a few minutes," she said, still flustered. She stood and quickly left the room.

Priscilla leaned inward toward Rizzo. "What'd she say?" she asked in low tones.

Smiling, Rizzo replied. "She said, 'Don't pee on my leg and tell me it's raining,'" he said happily. "I told her I'd never do anything like that."

Priscilla laughed. "I've heard that expression," she said. "Sounds a lot classier in Italian, though."

Rizzo chuckled. "Cil," he said with a wink, "*everything* is classier in Italian."

When Mrs. Carbone returned, calmer now, they continued their questioning.

"How often did you see your cousin?" Rizzo asked.

"Not very often. Holidays, mostly. Robbie would come here." Her eyes filled with tears. "He was supposed to be coming for Thanksgiving."

"Was he ever married?"

"No. I don't think he ever even had a girlfriend."

"Was he heterosexual?" Jackson asked.

Carbone raised her shoulders. "Well," she said, "if I had to guess, I'd say he was—what'da you call it?—no sexual?"

"Asexual," Priscilla said.

"Yes. Maybe that. I don't know. But definitely not queer. I'd have known that. I can always spot them."

"How'd he spend his time?" Rizzo asked, with a glance at Priscilla. "Any hobbies, interests, anything like that?"

She looked from one to the other, settling her gaze on Rizzo, but avoiding eye contact.

"No," she said, a casual lilt in her tone. "Not that I know of."

Priscilla leaned forward. "What about his writing, Mrs. Carbone?" she asked pointedly.

The woman seemed surprised. "Oh, that . . . You know about that?"

"Yeah, we do," Rizzo said. "We found a suitcase full of manuscripts in his closet. They date back over twenty years."

Jackson spoke up. "And a shoe box of rejection slips, too. In his dresser drawer."

Rizzo tapped his pen against the notepad. "You know, Mrs. Carbone, your obligation to Robbie is to help us out here. We can't be pullin' teeth on every little detail. You've gotta help us find out who killed him, not protect secrets that died with him. Anything from his personal life could be relevant if he was killed deliberately and not by a random burglar. I been doin' this a long time, Mrs. Carbone, and even I can't guess what may or may not be important. So please, don't you try. Just answer our questions as fully as you can. Okay?"

"Of course," she said. "I understand. But Robbie told no one about his writing. Only me. It was a very personal thing for him, a secret."

Priscilla spoke warmly, trying to establish a bond of trust with the woman. "Well, that speaks highly for you. I know how private a thing like that can be. Believe me. He must have respected you a great deal to confide in you like he did."

"I'm not sure about that, Detective Jackson," Carbone said with a sad smile. "Robbie liked me, of course, and in his own way, maybe he loved me. I was really his only relative. No one else in the family has seen or spoken to him in years, except for the occasional holiday when they may have seen him at my house."

"Well, believe me," Priscilla said, "if he let you in on his writing, he had to think you were very special."

Carbone dipped her head from side to side. "Personally, Detective Jackson, I think it was more about storage space than anything else."

"Oh?" Rizzo asked. "What do you mean?"

"Well, Robbie needed a place to safeguard his manuscripts. See, in addition to his other idiosyncrasies, he was a little paranoid, always worrying that his apartment might burn down and his writings would be destroyed. So he'd bring copies of his works here. For safekeeping. That's probably the only reason he told me about his writing."

Priscilla spoke. "So you have some of his belongings here, in the house?"

"Well, not really belongings. Just manuscripts, stories, stuff like that." She looked from one cop to the other. "They're in the garage. In an old suitcase."

After a moment of silence, Mrs. Carbone continued. "It's so sad," she said, her eyes welling up again. "Robbie wasn't a bad guy, just odd. But he was family." She looked from Rizzo to Jackson. "And that's what's important, you know."

They nodded at her, remaining silent.

"My kids called him uncle. Uncle Robbie. He liked that. Even my husband, who doesn't trust anybody, was comfortable with Robbie being around the kids. You know, these days . . . sometimes with relatives . . . But Robbie was just a big, dopey, gentle guy who didn't want anything out of life except to see his name on the cover of a book someday.

"You know," she said sheepishly, "I have to admit, I was curious and I went out to the garage one day. I read some of Robbie's stories." She shrugged. "I'm not much of a reader, I'd rather see a movie or whatever, but I have to say they seemed pretty good to me. I don't know, maybe if he had had some guidance . . . I think he just didn't know how to go about it. Getting himself published, I mean. Maybe if someone had helped him . . . Who knows."

With a sigh, she went on. "Or maybe he just aimed too high. Imagine? The guy couldn't even hold a menial job for more than a year or two at a time. And he aimed too high." Resignation came to her eyes. "Imagine that?"

AFTER NEARLY an hour of further questioning Carbone and her newly arrived husband, the two detectives made their way down the concrete driveway toward the detached garage. Wispy snowflakes floated before their eyes, the sky growing darker, the air crisper.

"Last winter was bad enough," Rizzo said. "Now it's gonna start snowin' before Thanksgiving?"

"They're just flurries, Joe, relax. But I gotta ask, why are we checking out here? We already saw this stuff, in his apartment. These are just copies."

Rizzo glanced at her as they reached the garage. He raised the borrowed key, unlocking the weathered doors.

"Remember Tucci, Cil? That kid who got shot in the foot? Remember him?" he asked, swinging one hinged door open.

"Yeah, I remember," she answered. "What?"

Rizzo reached into the garage, throwing a switch and flooding the musty interior with bright, buzzing fluorescent light.

"I'll tell you what," he said. "We were all set to call out the cavalry, pushin' Vince to get a sketch artist, remember? Then Vince tells us to talk to the vic first, get the whole story before we start draftin' help. And what happened next? The vic turned us on to that dental angle, we followed it up and made the case."

"Okay," Priscilla said with a nod. "And this is like that how?"

Rizzo looked around the garage. No car was present on the worn, oil-stained concrete floor, the parking area surrounded by sundry family items and outdoor furniture stored for winter.

"We're doin' it by the book, Cil. Bein' thorough. Just because Carbone told us there's nothing here but copies of manuscripts don't necessarily make it so. Let's take a look and make sure."

He turned to face her. "Thoroughness," he said. "Ga-peesha?"

"Yeah, Joe," she said. "I ga-peesh."

Minutes later, the two detectives were seated on the cold concrete floor, another old suitcase open before them. They leafed slowly through its contents.

Rizzo thumbed through a thin, weathered manuscript, the pages stapled together. He knitted his brows.

"Hey, Cil," he said. "In that other suitcase, the one we found at Lauria's place, were there any plays?"

Priscilla looked up from the book-length manuscript she was examining, a duplicate of one she had seen at Lauria's.

She shook her head. "No. Why?"

Rizzo held the pages in his hand out to her. "Look at this," he said. "It's a play Lauria wrote. I didn't see anything like this in his closet."

Priscilla took the script from him and skimmed through some pages. Minutes later, she whistled softly and raised her eyes.

"Jesus," she said. "This is strange."

"What?" Rizzo asked, looking up from another manuscript.

"This play, the play that wasn't in the suitcase in Lauria's apartment." She held it out to him.

Rizzo dropped the papers he'd been examining onto the floor and took the play back from Priscilla and began to read.

"What about it?" he asked.

"I'm not sure. Give me a few minutes, let me read this from page one."

"Knock yourself out," Rizzo replied, shrugging. "I'll write up my notes on the Carbone interview while you read." He handed the stack of pages back to Priscilla.

After twenty minutes, Priscilla called to him, her dark eyes wide and sparkling in the bright light of the small garage.

"Remember I told you me and Karen saw that Broadway play, the last play Avery Mallard wrote? The Pulitzer Prize winner who was murdered eleven, twelve days ago?"

Rizzo's eyes narrowed. He dropped his gaze from Priscilla and looked down to the pages in her hand.

"Yeah, I remember that."

Priscilla laid a hand on his forearm. She leaned in closer.

"This is the fuckin' play," she said. "The same play me and Karen saw on Broadway."

She pointed to the top page of the script. "Look at the date, Joe."

Rizzo looked to the inscription in what he recognized to be Lauria's handwriting, then raised his eyes to meet hers. "Over three years ago," he said.

"I'm almost sure of this," she said. "The characters have different names, there's no love interest like the Mallard play has, and it's set in New York, not Atlanta. But it's the same story, the same conflicts, the same ending. Hell, even a lot of the same dialogue." She handed it to Rizzo. "That in your hand is *Mallard's* play, Joe."

Rizzo fingered the pages. "Or, if you're right, Mallard's play is Lauria's." His eyes narrowed. "What the fuck, Cil?" he asked.

"I don't know. But I've read about Mallard. He came off a long dry spell with this play. He told Charlie Rose he wrote it over a two-month span while he was in the Hamptons, maybe two years ago. Those pages in your hand are dated a year earlier than that. Shit, the play's only been runnin' a couple of months, three at the most."

Rizzo scratched his head, then rubbed at his right eye to soothe the nervous tic as he spoke.

"Coincidence? One play. Two separate murders within a few days of each other. Maybe both vics tied to the play."

He touched lightly at Priscilla's cheek.

"There ain't no coincidences like that, Partner," he said.

Then, reaching for the last of his cigarettes, he dropped the play back into the open suitcase.

"No fuckin' way," he said.

CHAPTER FIFTEEN

RIZZO AND JACKSON GAZED THROUGH the windshield at the choppy, white-capped waters of Jamaica Bay. The Impala sat parked in the sprawling, nearly deserted parking area of the Canarsie Pier. Rizzo had sat silently as Priscilla Jackson gave the play a fast, careful re-read.

Having given the reluctantly cooperative Mrs. Carbone a written receipt, they had removed the suitcase from the garage, and it was now secured in the Impala's trunk.

The car's heater blew warm air against their legs, chilling winds howled softly outside the tightly closed windows. Light snow flurries danced across the gray hood.

"Now I'm sure of it," Priscilla said quietly, coming to the last page and resting the manuscript on the steering wheel. "With a few changes this is the play I saw on Broadway. What are the possibilities here, Joe?"

"Top of my head? Mallard somehow plagiarizes the play from Lauria. Lauria calls him on it, and Mallard goes to Lauria's place, strangles him, searches the apartment, and takes every copy of the play he finds."

"So you honestly figure this Pulitzer Prize winner was capable of strangling somebody to death?" Priscilla asked.

Rizzo laughed. "Yeah, well, think about this. Yasser Arafat won a fuckin' Nobel Peace Prize." He paused. "You think maybe he had any blood on his hands, Partner?"

"Okay, so then who kills Mallard?"

Rizzo shrugged. "Somebody who knew the situation, somebody who knew about the play and figured Mallard whacked Lauria. Somebody close to Lauria."

She shook her head. "There *was* nobody close to Lauria, 'cept Carbone. You can't figure her for a murderer. She just wasn't the type."

"Yeah, well, Carbone's husband looked clean, too. Maybe this brother she claims is in Kuwait." He shook his head. "That's unlikely, though. It would have to be somebody else, somebody we don't know exists yet. Everybody's got *somebody*. Maybe even this guy Lauria."

"I don't know, Joe," she said. "Sounds pretty freakin' weak to me."

"Don't it, though?" said Rizzo, reaching for a Nicorette. "But you never know. We gotta dig deeper into the vic's life. Turn up an old buddy, maybe a butt-buddy, or some screwy writer Lauria hung around with. Somebody."

Priscilla wrinkled her brow. "How 'bout this?" she speculated. "Lauria was frustrated and bitter from years of failure. He sees Mallard's play, writes almost a carbon copy, changing it just enough to make it look legit. He types it on some old paper, dates it three years ago. Then he tries to run a swindle on Mallard, says Mallard plagiarized *his* play. Tries to get Mallard to use his connections and get Lauria published somehow."

Rizzo followed through. "Yeah, they have an argument and Mallard kills the guy. Okay. But then who kills Mallard?"

She shrugged. "I don't know. Your phantom butt-buddy, I guess."

Rizzo placed the gum in his mouth, chewing it slowly before responding.

"Or maybe it *is* just some coincidence—not the murders, the plays. Maybe each guy wrote his play independent of the other, but Lauria figured Mallard stole his idea, and it all led to the murders."

"No way," Priscilla said. "The two plays are absolutely the same. I'm tellin' you, not in a million years could two strangers write two such similar works. No freakin' way."

Rizzo nodded. "Okay, so maybe they weren't strangers to each other. We gotta look at Avery Mallard's life. See where it intersects with Lauria's. Look for someone they both knew."

"*If* their lives intersect," she said. "Do you remember any of the details of Mallard's murder, Joe?"

"Not really. I only read one news article about it. I'm pretty sure it happened in his apartment. And, now that I think about it, it mighta been a stranglin'."

Priscilla sat back, facing Rizzo, her shoulders against the driver's window.

"Jesus Christ, Joe, if that's true, and the murders *are* connected, we got us some doozy here—and just one killer."

Rizzo smiled. "Yeah," he said. "A real doozy."

"We can check online for the articles. Get more info on the Mallard case."

"Fuck online. You forget we got us a pal over at the Plaza? Pretty Boy McQueen? Mike could run inside access computer checks and pull up the whole Mallard investigation. We can look over Manhattan South's shoulder, see what the college boys and girls been doin' with the case. Get all the contact info we need."

Priscilla's lips compressed tightly before she spoke again.

"Yeah. I forgot about Manhattan South." She paused. "What's the protocol here? Are we supposed to tell them about this Lauria angle?"

Rizzo shrugged. "Probably. If we develop it any further, definitely."

"Shit," she said dejectedly. "They'll grab the two cases and send us both out for coffee."

Rizzo raised his brow. "Not if I don't let 'em, they won't."

"What you got in mind, Partner?" Priscilla questioned.

He reached out and gently patted her arm. "Makin' you a star, kiddo—and me, too. If this Lauria case is related to Avery Mallard's murder, we can run with this ball pretty far before we gotta worry about any 'protocol.' Pretty damn far."

"How smart is that?" she asked.

"Well, you know it could backfire, bite us real bad if we fucked it up. But we're too sharp to fuck it up."

"It can do more than bite us, Joe," she said. "We sit on this link and get found out, we could be looking at an obstruction charge. That's no joke."

"Obstruction? Who are we obstructin'? We *are* the fuckin' cops, Cil. We can't obstruct ourselves."

She shook her head. "Please, don't fuck with me. You know what I'm sayin' here. We deliberately conceal this link between the two homicides, they can nail us for obstruction *and* official misconduct."

"Relax, okay? Nobody's nailin' us for nothing. Hell, if you hadn't seen that play with Karen, we never would've made the connection. And besides, it's nothing but speculation so far. Let's take a look, nose around a little, that's all I'm saying. A couple of unlikely misdemeanor charges shouldn't right away put our tails between our legs. Let's just look into it."

She considered it. "How about this, Joe? How about while we're 'considering' it, the killer strikes again? Suppose it *is* the same guy who whacked Lauria and Mallard? We don't know why, other than maybe something connected to the play. There could be a third party somewhere, some other big shot like Mallard or another schmo like Lauria, and the killer decides to get rid of them, too. That makes us accessories. Accessories to fuckin' *murder*. Think about that."

Rizzo shrugged. "Million-to-one shot. Besides, if the killer had a third target, it's already too late. He took out Lauria and Mallard within a day or two of each other. I don't think he's been sitting on his hands for two fuckin' weeks to take out a third guy. If there was another party, he's dead already. Done deal."

She sat silently fingering the pages she held.

"It'd be blood on our hands if it did happen, Joe," she said after a moment. "Even if we never got jammed up for it, it would still be blood on our hands."

Rizzo turned in his seat and faced his young partner. A tired smile came to him. "Cil, listen to me. I've been doing this a lot of years. Now I'm near the end. I been laboring in obscurity for a long time, just the way I wanted it. No flashy squad, no silk stocking precinct, just me and Brooklyn, for better or worse. And I managed to build a solid rep anyway. Cops all over the city have heard of me and all the bosses know how good I am at this, but you know what, Cil? It's gettin' a little old for me. Sometimes, lately, I kinda feel like I'm the greatest chef in . . . in Ireland. At the end of the day, nobody really gives a damn who boiled the fuckin' potatoes.

"But . . . if we develop this, if we tie into Mallard, break that case, I go out on the A-list."

Rizzo leaned close to her. "And you. What about you? Your stock goes way up. You'd have the friggin' politicians tripping over their mistresses rushin' to get you promoted. You could call your own tune. Think about it."

Priscilla held his dark brown eyes. A moment elapsed.

"And if somebody else *does* get killed, Joe. That'd be okay with you?"

He shrugged. "I explained that already. Nobody else is getting killed. And besides, what do you think, we hand this over to Manhattan South and they solve it in twenty minutes? With the resources Mike can provide us, you and me got the same chance as Manhattan does. Hell, we got a *better* chance." He paused and turned back in his seat, once again gazing out at the snowflakes dancing across the car's hood.

Priscilla spoke to his profile. "Because you're smarter than they are. Right?"

He nodded without turning to her. "Your call, Cil. I'll leave it up to you. I want to poke around some, see where it goes. I told you why. I'll leave it up to you."

After a long moment, she spoke, her tone pensive. "Okay, Joe. We'll take a look. But if it's starts getting heavy, we gotta reconsider."

Rizzo reached for his shoulder harness, pulling it forward, securing it.

"Okay then, let's go. I'll tell you how I think we should handle it."

"Where to?" she asked, as she turned and secured her own shoulder harness.

"Well, first, back to Lauria's place. We need to get that suitcase and the box full of rejection slips. And anything else related to his writing, even that old IBM. It could all be evidence. I want the suitcase dusted for prints, even though we were pawin' at it without gloves on. Maybe the killer got careless when he searched it for Lauria's copy of the play and left some prints on it. We have to inventory the contents of both suitcases, the one from the apartment and the one from the garage. Then we'll secure them in the precinct evidence locker. The chain of possession is fucked up enough already, we gotta start stabilizin' it, recording everything. So, we'll go to Lauria's place, then the precinct."

"Okay," she said.

"But first," he added, "head back up Rockaway Parkway. Find me a candy store."

He smiled into her questioning eyes.

"I gotta pick up one absolutely *last* pack of cigarettes."

AFTER THEY had secured all the gathered evidence in the precinct's property locker and were seated at Priscilla's desk in the squad room, Rizzo asked her for one of the two copies of Lauria's play she had run off.

"I guess I'll have to read this crap," he said absently. Then he pulled the notepad from his jacket and dropped it onto her desk. "Do me a favor. Contact the Air Force and get confirmation that Carbone's brother's been overseas at least the last couple a months. Check if he had any leave in October or early this month. All the names and numbers are in my notes."

Priscilla nodded, glancing at the notepad. "Okay, and I'll call the cousins on Long Island and over in Jersey, size them up a little. Like we did with Carbone and her husband."

Rizzo nodded. "All right, thanks. See if they can point us at any other relatives or family friends who mighta had any kinda relationship with Robbie. Anything at all they can add to this."

"I'm on it, boss," she said. Rizzo moved back to his desk, checked his address book, then punched Mike McQueen's work number into the phone.

"Comstat, Detective McQueen," he heard through the line.

"Hello, Mike, it's Joe."

"Joe, hi, how are you?"

"Couldn't be better, kiddo, couldn't be better. You got a minute?"

"Sure, what's up?"

"Well, me and Cil got us a situation here. I'd like to discuss it with you. Face-to-face."

There was a pause. "Everything okay?" McQueen asked, the caution in his tone not fully disguised by the superimposed casualness.

"Right as rain, buddy, right as rain. You workin' tomorrow?"

"Yeah, Joe, I'm steady eight-to-fours, weekends off."

"Well, good for you, banker's hours. Good for you. Listen, how 'bout lunch? Down at Pete's maybe, like last time, or I can come into the city. I'm off tomorrow."

"Sure, Pete's is fine, just five minutes across the bridge from the Plaza. How about one o'clock?"

"Great. Looking forward to it. See you then."

"Okay," McQueen said. "Is Cil comin'?"

Rizzo hesitated. "Not this time, Mike. Next time, maybe."

Now it was McQueen who hesitated. "Okay," he said. "But everything is all right?"

"Yep, everything is just fine," Rizzo said. "But we don't need Cil along this time."

Another hesitation. "Well, okay, Joe. See you tomorrow." The line went dead.

Everything *was* just fine, Rizzo thought. Just fine.

FRIDAY AT one o'clock, Rizzo smiled across the table in Pete's Downtown Restaurant. "Well, you sure look fancy today, Mike. Another new suit?"

"Yeah," McQueen said. "To celebrate my bump up to second grade." He waved for a waiter, then turned to Rizzo.

"Double Dewar's, rocks?" Mike asked Rizzo.

"Sure."

With drinks before them and their lunch orders placed, Rizzo raised his glass.

"To us, Partner. And to the future."

After sipping his drink, McQueen rotated the Manhattan glass slowly between his fingers, then asked, "So, what's up?"

Rizzo filled him in on the Lauria case, stressing its possible connection to the murder of internationally acclaimed playwright Avery Mallard.

"Think about it, Mike," he said softly. "What other explanation could there be for Lauria having that play stashed at his sister's, and not one copy of it in his apartment? What possible explanation could there be for the *existence* of that manuscript? No matter how you slice and dice, it comes back to one simple fact: Lauria and Mallard were somehow connected. Connected by that play. And whoever killed Lauria most likely searched the apartment, specifically lookin' for the play, found it and took it. Lauria was a real low-tech guy, there ain't any cyberspace copies of that play floatin' around. The killer felt confident he had the situation under control."

Rizzo smiled at McQueen. "We just fell into it, kid."

"Well," Mike replied, "it may be quite a lucky stumble for you."

"You bet," Rizzo said. "Like Yogi Berra once said, I'd rather be lucky than good."

McQueen laughed. "Or better yet, good *and* lucky."

Rizzo took a sip of his Scotch, then continued.

"If this is Mallard whackin' Lauria, and then somebody evening the score by killing Mallard, or even if it's just an interested third party killed them both, there's gotta be a link between the two victims."

McQueen nodded. "Yeah, well, good luck with that. Some Brooklyn loser and a celebrated Pulitzer Prize–winning New York playwright. Shit, I studied Mallard in English lit class at NYU. The guy is—was—a friggin' living legend."

"Yeah, so I hear." Rizzo drummed his fingers on the tabletop. "So what's the word at the Plaza, Mike? About the Mallard case."

"Not much. Manhattan South is on it, with some Major Case support. The brass is all over it. Lots of pressure to nab somebody, and time is passing. The case is getting cold."

Rizzo nodded. "What angle are they playin'?"

"Far as I know," McQueen replied, "they make it as a break-in. Perp came in a window at Mallard's brownstone on a Sunday night, there was a struggle, Mallard got strangled. Manhattan South is rousting junkies and b and e guys all over the city. They're squeezing stoolies and getting the word out to the jails. Any skell lookin' for a deal comes forward with a name on this case, the guy can write his own friggin' ticket. According to my A.D.A. friend, Darrel Jordan, the Manhattan D.A. would sell his only child to make this case. He's got his eye on the governor's chair, and he thinks prosecuting this case will help put him there."

"Yeah, figures," said Rizzo. "Better government through better bullshit. Same ole, same ole." He took a sip of his drink as the waiter reappeared, placing their appetizers before them. When he left, Rizzo continued.

"Let's get to the point, Mike. I need the Mallard file. I want the contacts—the guy's wife, mother, girlfriend, boyfriend, all of it. I wanna try to cross his path with Lauria's. I do that, I got a lead to the killer. Or killers. The M.O.s are the same. There's a connection between these cases, I'd bet two years of Marie's Cornell tuition there is. And I wanna be the one makin' that connection."

"Yeah, I'll bet." McQueen reached for a fork, looking casually down at his stuffed shrimp. "Now I've got a question, Joe."

"Yeah, I figured," Rizzo said. "What's in it for you? Let me answer that. You get me the file, raid that computer you're drivin' all day. Me and Cil do the leg work. If it breaks right, we tie you into it. Success would force the brass to overlook the—let's call it, unofficial—help you gave us. Mike, we crack this, Cil writes her own ticket—Homicide, Task Force, whatever she wants. I finish up my career a fuckin' superstar, the guy who cracked the Pulitzer Prize murder case. They get Joe Hollywood to play me in the movie of the week."

He leaned across the table. "Just thinka how proud my mother'll be, Mike."

"Yeah, I can see that." His face turning serious, McQueen added, "But I gotta tell you, I see myself maybe out in the cold here. Officially, I'll have had nothing to do with it. Plus I might have a pissed-off supervisor to deal with, maybe some other brass, too."

Rizzo waved a hand.

"Bullshit. It's me and Cil taking all the risk. If this goes well, anybody remotely near you will be wrappin' his arms around your shoulder and lookin' for the nearest photographer. There'll be plenty of glory to go around, Mike, real and invented. Believe me."

McQueen frowned. "You really think so?"

Rizzo took a sip of water, then put the glass down and folded his hands, leaning in on the table, closer to his former partner. He lowered his voice.

"Let me tell you a story, Mike. A story about this lazy, not-too-bright patrolman from the Six-Two. It was way back when, before my time even. Son of Sam was runnin' around the city, shooting kids parked in cars on lovers' lanes. The last shooting was in the Six-Two, down by the highway. This patrol cop, he tags a car parked by a hydrant around midnight, just before the shooting went down. So he writes his ticket, rides back to the house, and goes home. Forgets all about it. Next day, the detectives are canvassing the neighborhood and they see a woman walkin' her dog. They approach her. Yeah, she says, she was out with the dog last night. 'Round midnight. No, didn't see nothin' suspicious. Is she sure? Yeah, she said. All she saw was some fat ol' cop writin' a ticket for some car parked near the johnny pump about a block from the scene. So the detectives go back to the precinct and pull the house copy of the summons. They run the plate through, and guess what? The car ain't local. It belongs to some guy David Berkowitz, lives in Westchester County, north of the city."

Rizzo paused, draining his Dewar's.

"And that's how the case got cleared. The patrol cop was too dumb to make the connection, but the brass bumped him up to detective third grade anyway. For writin' a parking ticket he never even realized the significance of."

He looked at McQueen. "What do you figure they'll do for you when I crack this case and tell 'em how I'da never been able to do it without your help?"

A slow smile had formed across Mike's face. "I don't know, but I'm beginning to think I'd like to find out."

Rizzo laughed. "Yeah, I bet. And you know, it was a detective named Zito made that Son of Sam case. Half the cops working today, including you, weren't even born yet when Zito made that case, but plenty of them know the name. You never know, Mike," Rizzo added affably. "Maybe forty years from now some cops'll be schemin' out a scheme somewhere and one of them'll bring up Joe Rizzo." He waved for a second round of drinks.

"Now I see why you didn't want Cil along today, Joe."

"Oh?" Rizzo said, arching his brows, "and why's that?"

Lowering his voice, McQueen said, "Daily. Councilman William fuckin' Daily. We pull this off, we're untouchable. We couldn't discuss that aspect of all this in front of Cil. But you and I know, we pull this off, we could nail that prick Daily and not give a goddamn if anybody realizes it was us who did it. *That's* your motivation here. We'd be fuckin' untouchable."

"Okay, kid," Rizzo said with satisfaction. "You're a good learner. We find Mallard's killer, we're the fair-haired boys of the news media. There ain't a boss or a politician in the whole fuckin' city who'd tangle with that. Not just to avenge that scumbag Daily."

He gazed across the table and into the intent, steely blue eyes of McQueen.

"Get me that file, Mike," he said. "Without it, I'm blind."

McQueen pursed his lips. "Okay, I'll do it. But it'll take me a few days to figure out how to do it clean, so no one notices and starts asking questions."

The waiter appeared once again and placed fresh drinks on the table, then moved away. Rizzo raised his second Dewar's in another toast to McQueen.

"Just get the file, Mike, and leave the rest to me.

"Me and Cil, that is."

CHAPTER SIXTEEN

SATURDAY MORNING, NOVEMBER 15, the gray chill of the last two days gave in to bright, crispy, late fall splendor. Returning from the supermarket, Rizzo unloaded the trunk of his Camry, glancing upward at the deep blue, cloudless sky.

"Beautiful day outside, Jen," he said as he set the bags down in the kitchen. "We should go down to Shore Road, take a walk along the water."

Jennifer looked up from her seat at the kitchen table, notepad before her, pen in hand.

"Good idea. I've just about completed the Thanksgiving menu."

Laying his hands on her shoulders and peering down at the notepad, he asked, "How's it look?"

"Great. The girls and I will make the antipasto and the turkey with all the trimmings. Your mom is bringing the manicotti, mine is doing the gravy meat—sausage, meatballs, and braciole."

Rizzo nodded. "Don't forget the watermelon for Cil," he said, smiling.

Jennifer slapped at his hand. "Stop it," she said. "I told your mom to make some extra manicotti, so there'll be plenty to go around. I'm glad Priscilla and her friend are coming."

"Yeah, so is Cil. It helps her sidestep that whole mother situation."

"That's a shame, really," Jennifer said, with a shake of her head. "I hope they can work that out someday."

Rizzo frowned. "Yeah, well, mind your own business. She hears enough shit from Karen, so don't be takin' sides. Stay out of it."

He glanced at the clock. It was ten-thirty a.m. "You think Marie's up yet? I have to call her."

Jennifer shrugged. "Probably. Try her."

Rizzo went to the den, dropping into the leather double recliner. He picked up the cordless and punched in Marie's number at her dormitory.

"Hey, honey, it's me," he said.

"Hi, Daddy. What's going on?"

Rizzo smiled into the mouthpiece, visualizing his oldest daughter's dark beauty.

"Not much," he said. "We'll see you on the twenty-sixth?"

"Yep. Figure about three o'clock."

"Good. I'm off that day, I'll pick you up at Grand Central."

"Great," she said. "Saves me a subway ride."

"Okay," he answered. "I'll tell you why I called, honey. I need a favor."

"Really? What?"

"Well, I'm on a case and I need something. A copy of a play. I stopped at Barnes and Noble this morning, and the guy told me it hasn't been put into general release yet, since it's new on Broadway, but it went out to some of the universities. It's that new play by Avery Mallard, *An Atlanta Landscape*."

"Yes, I've heard of it." Marie paused. "Are you working on his murder, Daddy? The graduate lit majors are totally bummed about it."

Rizzo shook his head. "No, not exactly. It's somethin' else, it's complicated. I'll tell you about it when you come home for Thanksgiving."

"Okay, Dad, I'll stop by the English department and try to track one down." She paused. "You know, if Jess gets it at Hunter, you can have it sooner. She could give it to you by Monday."

"I know, I asked her yesterday. Hunter doesn't have it yet. I figured maybe Cornell does."

"Okay, Daddy, I'll call you later and let you know."

"Good, thanks." He hesitated. "And Marie, one more favor: Don't mention this to Carol, okay?"

"Why not, Daddy?" she asked flatly.

Rizzo answered with a sigh. "The last thing I want right now is for Carol to start helpin' out with police work. No matter how superficial. And if she finds out I asked you and Jessica and not her, I'll have more trouble with her than I already got. So it's our secret, okay?"

"Sure, Dad," Marie said. "Stay in denial. That'll help."

"Okay, kiddo, back off. Just get me the friggin' play, okay? Please?"

"Of course, Dad. But as far as Carol is concerned after that blowup you had, you really have to just—"

"Okay, honey, thanks," Rizzo said. "Your mother's callin' me, I gotta go. See you on the twenty-sixth." He hung up gently.

Everybody's got an opinion, he thought. Everybody.

MONDAY MORNING, as Rizzo stepped into a point at the police range during his annual firearms qualification cycle, Priscilla Jackson sat at her desk in the Six-Two squad room, a full day of work before her. The fingerprint team was on its way to dust the suitcase, its contents and some other items she and Rizzo had secured in the precinct property office on Thursday.

Priscilla needed to prepare and finalize DD-5 reports for her confirmation of the unbroken Air Force deployment of Lauria's cousin in Kuwait and the apparent noninvolvement in any aspect of the case by Lauria's Long Island and New Jersey relatives.

She also needed to update Vince D'Antonio with carefully worded half-truths on their continuing investigatory work on Lauria's possessions. When the print team was finished, she would then have to inventory, label, and resecure the confiscated items, carefully preparing a paper trail, detailing the chain of possession for what might eventually develop into key pieces of evidence—evidence which must maintain its integrity throughout any courtroom challenges that might be raised by a competent defense attorney.

Priscilla dropped her eyes to the faxes on her desk. Some additional reports from the Medical Examiner's Office put Lauria's time of death as not before Wednesday, October 29, nor later than Saturday, November 1. Priscilla learned that Avery Mallard's date of death had been established as Sunday, November 2.

Samples taken from Robert Lauria's clothing and the kitchen floor revealed blood from only one human source. If, as Rizzo had indicated, the killer's hands had been cut by the garrote, traces of his blood would probably have been found at the scene. The absence of blood tended to confirm that the killer wore gloves, helping to eliminate possible DNA evidence.

Police lab results provided by CSU indicated that a blue fiber strand found on Lauria's T-shirt was an imported blend of high-quality cotton mix. Concentration levels of water repellent chemical substances indicated a strong probability that the fiber came from an expensive, top-of-the-line raincoat. Further cross-referencing had found the fiber and chemicals to match both Burberry and Theory brand coats at the uppermost end of their product lines. None of the samples of Lauria's wardrobe matched the blue fiber.

Next, Priscilla turned to the DD-5 reports prepared over the last three days by various detectives from the Six-Two squad. As Rizzo had predicted, they showed meaningless results for license plate runs on vehicles parked in the vicinity of the Lauria apartment on the day the body was discovered. Follow-up neighborhood canvasses were equally unproductive for leads or significant information, as were field and squad room interviews with known local drug addicts. A computer scan of criminal records indicated none of the private homes surrounding Lauria's apartment housed any known criminals. An additional interview of the Annasias and subsequent criminal background checks had failed to produce a potential suspect within the circle of family and friends of Lauria's landlords.

Beneath the DD-5s Priscilla found a computer printout of the prior month's phone calls made to and from the number registered to Robert Lauria. She scanned it quickly, noting its sparseness and repetitive pattern, and put it aside for later analysis.

The print team arrived and approached her desk. She rose to greet them, making a small note to revisit the shoe store manager and workers where Lauria was last employed. She was hoping to develop a lead to someone who might fit the role of Lauria's phantom friend and thus be considered an avenging copy cat murder suspect in the Avery Mallard homicide.

As she shook hands with Detective Cynthia Morrow, fingerprint technician, Priscilla silently wished that Joe Rizzo hadn't been absent on this of all days.

The weight of the investigation, she was finding, was too great to be borne by one set of shoulders. Although she was appreciative of the team effort mounted by the squad, she felt Rizzo's absence more keenly than she would ever care to admit.

TUESDAY MORNING, Priscilla greeted Rizzo.

"Never thought I'd be so glad to see you, Joe. I had myself a hell of a day yesterday."

"Well, if that ain't the most half-assed compliment I ever got," he said cheerfully. "But, what the hell, I'll take it." He shook his head. "My day wasn't much better. Two hundred friggin' rounds through my Colt, a twelve-year-old cop on each side of me on the line, blazin' away with those goddamned Glocks. I swear, Cil, I ever get shot on this job, it's gonna be at the friggin' range by one of those kids."

"I hear you. They're gettin' younger every year."

"Yeah," he said, "and stupider, too."

He dropped his eyes to the reports Priscilla had given him. He sighed. "Don't make me have to read all this crap. Tell me."

Priscilla quickly filled him in, responding to an occasional question, pointing to a DD-5 or lab report when necessary.

"And Vince?" he asked.

She shrugged. "He seemed okay with what I told him."

"Which was?" he asked.

"What we talked about, that Lauria was a closet writer, had a buncha stuff in his apartment we figured maybe we could use to turn up a lead to a friend or somebody who might have more info or somebody we could make as a suspect in his killing."

Rizzo nodded. "Good. Vince is no dummy, though. He may start smellin' Mallard eventually, but, for now we can leave him outta this."

Rizzo picked up the sparse telephone record obtained by Detective Bobby Dellosso. "Guy barely needed a friggin' phone. You I.D. these numbers?"

Priscilla leaned inward, pointing a finger to the computer printout.

"This is the shoe store where he worked, that one's his cousin, MaryAnn Carbone. This one here's his bank's automated line, the other two his doctor and a pharmacy. I checked it out, he had a sinus infection back in early October."

Rizzo nodded. "No cell phone, right?"

"None that I could find," she said. "But see that one incoming call on October thirtieth at eight-o-five p.m.? That's from a pay phone up on Fourteenth Avenue. That could be the perp calling to see if Robbie was home."

"Last outgoing call was made on October thirtieth, too, at eleven a.m. That's twenty days ago." Rizzo shook his head. "Friggin' Dellosso. I told you, he takes great witness statements but he ain't the most thorough detective in town. He shoulda got at least two months of these records. Lauria's been dead since God knows when, and Dellosso figures this is good enough. We need to go back further." He paused, looking again to the telephone record. "What's this one?" he asked. "And these three."

"Those three nine hundred numbers are phone sex lines. You know, pay your money and get some sixty-year-old grandmother to talk dirty to you in a sexy, young voice. The other one is the Magic Massage Emporium."

"Let me guess," Rizzo said. "For thirty bucks you get half a massage, for a hundred you get some immigrant to blow you."

Priscilla gave a wide smile. "Exactly, Joe. The joint is over in the Six-Oh, near the aquarium. I called the squad, and they told me it's run by some Russians. The Six-Oh is waiting for Borough to bust it and try to close it down."

"Well, I guess old cousin MaryAnn was wrong about Lauria's sexuality," Rizzo said wryly. "Now we need to check out the joint, show Lauria's picture around, see if any of the hookers can help us out."

Priscilla shrugged. "Waste of time, if you ask me."

"Probably, but it's gotta get done. We need to find somebody in this guy's life, Cil. *If* there is anybody, that is. And if there *isn't*, well, we need to establish that, too."

"Okay," she said. "I had a thought yesterday. Want to hear it?"

"Sure."

"Well, that coat fiber they found at the scene. The lab says it doesn't match any of Lauria's clothes, and there's no junkie runnin' around in a thousand-dollar raincoat. No b and e men workin' in them, either. That could point to Mallard."

"Yeah," Rizzo concurred.

"But it could also point to a pro," she said. "Maybe Lauria was leanin' on Mallard about this play situation, so Mallard hires a pro to whack Lauria. Mallard pays the pro and figures it's over and done with."

Rizzo picked up. "But then the pro figures he don't need some screwy artistic genius a witness to his crime, so he takes Mallard's hit money, then whacks him, too."

"Exactly," Priscilla said.

"We can look at that," he replied.

"How?"

"Manhattan South probably got an access order for Mallard's finances. Pretty standard in a homicide, even if they figure it for a random break-in murder. Hell, I put in a slip to legal to get us access to Lauria's finances, though I don't expect to see anything. Anyway, I'll give Mike a call, see if Mallard's account had any unusual cash activity last two or three months."

"Okay, Joe."

"Far as the big ticket raincoat, we'll have Mallard's address in the file once Mike hands it to us. Then we can go check out his place, look for a blue raincoat. If we find one, we grab a sample and let the lab check it out. If it matches, we got the Lauria end of this case solved."

Priscilla smiled broadly. "There'd be some headlines for that one," she said. "'Famous playwright slays unknown writer—film at eleven.'"

He laughed. "Yeah, I guess. But the big question would still be out there: Who killed Mallard? If we backdoor it by solvin' Lauria's case and hangin' it on Mallard, Manhattan South boots our asses out of the picture and goes forward with that end."

"I guess it's like they say, Joe: That's showbiz."

"Yeah. Showbiz." He paused for a moment, thinking. "And you got nowhere at the shoe store?"

"No," she said. "It's like he was a ghost. They sensed he was there, saw him even, but nobody connected. He said hello, he said good-bye, he said it looks like rain, it's a nice day, Merry Christmas, Happy New Year, yes sir, no sir, and out the door. Never even went to lunch with any of his coworkers."

"Okay," Rizzo said, "so, I'm thinkin', this guy is a legit loner. We'll spend a day or two on it, but it ain't gonna go anywhere. There's no avenging butt-buddy gonna turn up here, Cil, but we still gotta look."

"And where's that leave us?"

Rizzo shrugged. "Interested third party killin' both vics, your hit man theory, maybe amateur hour. Or maybe Mallard and one of *his* butt-buddies go kill Lauria, then the buddy starts thinkin' about it too much and figures, 'Fuck Mallard, I gotta protect my own ass,' so *he* kills Mallard."

"What's the motive for an interested third party?" Priscilla asked. "How would a third party benefit from two such totally different people dying?"

"Beats me," Rizzo answered. "But one thing's for sure: if this ain't the biggest, most improbable, coincidental bullshit ever happened in the history of time, it's a double homicide tied together by that friggin' play. That's the key, the play. That's the motive, whether the killer was Mallard, Lauria's imaginary friend, a hit man, or the ghost of William fuckin' Shakespeare. The play is definitely tied to the motive in this."

Priscilla shook her head and sighed. "Jesus, Joe, we don't even know when this guy got killed."

Rizzo picked up the medical examiner's report, scanning it briefly, then dropped it back to the desktop.

"Doctor Voodoo puts the date of death between October twenty-nine and November one. October thirty-first was a Friday night. Not a good time to plan on killin' anybody 'cause street traffic is heavier than durin' the week. Plus, it was Halloween—the little kids would be out in the daytime, the older kids at night, trick or treatin' and throwing eggs at one another. November first was a Saturday, plenty of pedestrian traffic day *and* night. The last outgoing phone call from Lauria's apartment was to his bank on the thirtieth at eleven a.m. So I'm going with Thursday, October thirtieth, some time after the incoming phone call at eight-o-five p.m." He paused for a moment. "We should do a weather check, see when it was raining. Let's assume that fancy raincoat wasn't just a fashion statement. Let's assume the killer wore it 'cause it was actually raining."

Priscilla stood. "I'll go online, get the weather for those few nights. Bet it rained on the thirtieth."

"Okay," he said. "I'll call Mike, get an ETA on the Mallard file. Then we can take a look at his finances and check out his place for a match on that coat. The rest of today, we'll take a look at that cathouse in the Six-Oh, see where that goes. Plus, we still need to follow up on that prescription fraud case. I got a feeling we can clear that one soon. While you're on that weather, I'll order those additional phone records for Lauria. And I wanna call Mark Ginsberg at home, see how those street robbery cases went down with that kid Doyle. I heard it was clean, the kid copped, but I need to hear the details from Ginsberg myself."

Priscilla stretched her arms and neck muscles. "Okay. And I gotta say it's real good to have you back, baby."

"See, it's like my grandfather always said, Cil." Rizzo leaned forward, winking at her. "Every little gal needs a man in her life."

Priscilla smiled sweetly, then bent slightly, sliding a top side drawer from Rizzo's desk. Slowly and deliberately, she dumped the messy contents onto his lap.

"Get your grandfather to help you clean that shit up, Joe," she said, smiling and returning Rizzo's wink.

⋆ ⋆ ⋆

THE MAGIC Massage Emporium stood in a double storefront in the Brighton Beach section of Brooklyn, a few blocks from the New York City Aquarium.

Rizzo and Jackson stepped into the dimly lit interior and crossed to the small reception area. An attractive middle-aged woman at the counter smiled as they approached. Rizzo flipped his shield case open, briefly displaying its contents.

The woman's smile broadened.

"So," she said cheerfully, "now they are to send the mean-looking police and the pretty one, too?" Her words held a distinct Russian accent.

Rizzo glanced over his shoulder at Priscilla, then back to the woman.

"Yeah," he said, leaning both forearms on the countertop. "Now that you mention it, she *does* look sorta mean."

The woman gave a genuine laugh, bending and placing her own forearms onto the counter, positioning her face level to Rizzo's.

"I am Nadia," she said, her beautiful violet eyes shimmering in the dim lighting. "How is it for me to be of service for you, Sergeant?"

"Well, Nadia, I'm Sergeant Joe Rizzo, this here is Priscilla Jackson. Detective Priscilla Jackson. Are you the owner of this establishment?"

"Ah, Sergeant," she said, moving her face a bit closer to his, her musky perfume dancing around his nostrils. "That is very complicated in America, yes? In America, only sometimes the lawyers can figure it out who is owner."

"But—it's possible—you may be one of 'em," Rizzo said with a smile.

Nadia shrugged. "Is possible," she answered pensively.

"Yeah. Well, who can I speak to who can help me out?"

Her eyes twinkled. "It is to be my pleasure, Sergeant. I will help you out."

Priscilla sounded a derisive laugh from behind him. "You need me to go get you a bottle of wine here, Joe?"

He glanced over his shoulder at her and winked, then turned back to Nadia, producing a photo of Robert Lauria. He laid it down on the counter, turning it to face the woman and sliding it closer to her.

"Take a look, Nadia," he said. "Then tell me."

She looked at the photo, then raised her eyes to Rizzo. "I do not like to discuss the business of peoples, Sergeant. This man, this man in the picture, he is an American, no? He has all the rights, no?"

"Yes, he does," Rizzo said pleasantly. "Now how about you weigh his rights against your business license, take another look at that picture, then tell me."

Nadia bobbed her head. "Ah, yes," she said. "I remember him now. His name is Robbie. He has been here three or four times a year, since around time we open."

Rizzo smiled. "And when was that?"

"Three years, almost. Two and half."

"What's his story?" Priscilla asked.

Nadia glanced at Priscilla, still smiling, then cupped her chin in the palm of her hand and moved her eyes back to face Rizzo. He caught the sweet scent of peppermint permeating from her mouth when she spoke.

"Very nice man, very nervous," she said sweetly. "Always want same girl. If she not here, he leave and come back tomorrow. If she busy, he wait for her." Nadia let her smile deepen and her violet eyes widen. "She give *very* good massage, I think," she said to Rizzo playfully.

"Yeah, I bet," he said. "Who is this girl, what's her name?"

"Name Bogdana. Is Ukrainian name." Nadia glanced at Priscilla. "Means 'given by God,' " she told her.

"He ever come in here with anyone else?" Priscilla asked. "A buddy, maybe?"

"No. Alone all time. Nice man, very quiet. Not like some to come to here. Have respect for place. Nice man. But always come alone."

Rizzo interjected. "Anybody else ever work this counter, Nadia?"

"Just is me or Efim only."

"Efim?" Rizzo asked. "Is that a male?"

"Yes, is male." She smiled. "Like you."

"Is he here?"

"Yes, in back, with the meal before he start to work. I leave now soon for the day."

Rizzo nodded. "I'd like to speak to him, and to the girl. What was her name? Bogna?"

"Bogdana," she said. "Yes, she is too here. I will get them. But you tell me, okay? Why are you asking these about Robbie?"

"Well," Rizzo said, "I'll tell you all about that. *After* I talk to the two of them."

Nadia straightened up and turned to leave. "Okay, Sergeant. I will get them." She paused at the doorway leading to the rear, turning over her shoulder and smiling warmly at Rizzo.

"Be nice please to Efim," she said. "He is husband to me. *Very* jealous."

She fluttered her lids and then left the room.

Rizzo turned and looked at Priscilla.

She shook her head, her lips pursed.

"Women," she said. "Jesus H. Christ."

THAT EVENING, seated on the recliner in his home, Rizzo opened the FedEx package which had arrived at the house late that afternoon. Marie had obtained a copy of the play.

Rizzo smiled at the handwritten note from his daughter that accompanied it. Although he had not asked her to, he was glad Marie had gone the extra mile and FedExed the package to him.

"Good kid," he muttered, opening the bound copy and beginning to read the three-act play.

The story was set in modern-day Atlanta, Georgia, and centered around an old-money family headed by an aged patriarch. His two sons, his wife, and the daughter of a family friend who was romantically involved with both brothers rounded out the cast of characters. The father's emotional, physical, moral, and legal corruption drove the plot. The older son was complicit in the business and personal ambiguities of the father. This, and the idealism and alienation of the younger son, combined with the ultimately tragic love triangle and the quiet desperation of the unhappy matriarch, completed the drama.

When Rizzo finished reading the play, his head ached slightly. He had a vague, nagging feeling that the story was familiar: characters, setting, plot, all of it. And not from anything Lauria had written, since Rizzo hadn't yet read his copy of Lauria's *A Solitary Vessel*. No, Rizzo thought. It wasn't Lauria.

"Damn," he said aloud with sudden realization. "It's Tennessee Williams." Reincarnate a thirty-year-old Paul Newman, and he could play either brother, Rizzo thought. An equally young Joanne Woodward or Elizabeth Taylor could be the female lead.

Jennifer entered the room, her hair tied behind her head, flannel pajamas loose about her body.

"Coming to bed soon, Joe?" she asked.

He glanced at the small clock on the table beside him. "Wow, I didn't realize so much time had passed."

Jennifer moved closer and sat on the arm of the recliner, placing a hand on his shoulder and peering down at the play on his lap.

"It must have been pretty good to hold your interest," she said. "The last thing I saw you reading was . . ." She thought for a moment. "I can't even remember."

"Not really," he said. "Reminded me of some old movies I've seen. But, according to Cil, the critics loved it, and it's a sure thing for the big awards. They can't print the tickets fast enough on Broadway. Probably make a friggin' movie in a couple a years." He shrugged. "Like I said, sounded a little old to me, familiar. Sorta like, 'Screwballs on a Hot Tin Roof,' if anybody asks me."

Jennifer laughed. "Well, I don't think anyone *will* ask you." Her smile faded. "And once more, just for the record, I'm against this scheme of yours. If these two cases are connected, you should report it to D'Antonio. Let him make the call on it. Cover your butt."

"Vince would punt this whole thing right over to Manhattan South, with a cc to the Plaza."

"As well he should," Jennifer said sternly. "Haven't you had enough excitement lately? Haven't we all? That whole Daily business and the I.A.D. thing with Morelli? Wasn't all that a close enough brush for you? I swear you're like a reckless teenager with a new car, tearing around like a lunatic, defying the odds. I'm just saying . . ."

Rizzo reached up and stroked her cheek. "I know, hon, you already said what you had to say. I get it. But I'm on top of this, believe me. Cil and I struck out today on trying to find a life for this guy Lauria. We'll follow up, but I'm not expecting anything to turn up. Next, we'll start to look at Mallard. On the Q.T. Then, we'll see. We can always drop it in Vince's lap. But first, let's see how it goes. Okay?"

She shook her head. "No. Not okay."

"Think about this for a minute, Jen. I'm not being reckless, in fact the complete opposite. If I nail Mallard's killer, I'm gold. It buys me a pass with that whole Daily situation, the thing that has you so worried. Don't you see that? Mallard is my insurance, mine and Mike's. It's not reckless, hon. It's just good business."

"My God, Joe," she said softly. "Are you really that callous? What about Priscilla? What about her? You're exposing *her* to serious risk: This is not just about you and Mike. What about *her*?"

Rizzo sighed. "Go to bed, hon. I got enough problems trying to keep her on board without complicating it with too many explanations. And I *do* have her best interest at heart, too. After this is over, if it all works out, her career is made. Believe me, and just trust me, okay? I know what I'm doing. Now I just wanna look over Lauria's play, convince myself it's the same as Mallard's. I'll be up in about a half hour, forty minutes."

She glared at him, anger rising in her eyes. He held out a calming palm toward her. "Relax, Jen. Don't make me regret tellin' you about this stuff. Okay?"

Jennifer slid off the arm of the recliner, removing her hand from his shoulder.

"Whatever," she said coldly, turning and leaving the room.

Rizzo picked up the photocopy of Lauria's manuscript and began reading.

CHAPTER SEVENTEEN

ON WEDNESDAY, RIZZO AND JACKSON spent most of their tour continuing to search through the fragments of Robert Lauria's life, using names and numbers culled from the worn, black address book retrieved from the murder scene. Other than family members already spoken to, the few remaining entries consisted of former landlords, employers, doctors, dentists, and the occasional tradesman or business number. Nothing pointed them in a meaningful direction.

Robert Lauria had been as isolated and unconnected as any person living in modern-day New York City could possibly be.

By late in the tour, both detectives were convinced.

"Joe," Priscilla said as they sat at Rizzo's desk sipping coffee from paper cups, "Lauria may have been murdered by Mallard, or somebody connected to Mallard, but this guy definitely had no one close enough who'd whack Mallard for revenge."

"Yeah, it sure looks that way. I think we've invested enough time on this. We checked everything we could. There ain't no best buddy here, no lover, no outraged relative. Whoever killed Lauria, alone or with Mallard, that same guy wound up killin' Mallard, too. It couldn't be any clearer."

She nodded. "Over the play. Somehow, it all comes back to the play."

"I still can't get over how similar they are," he said. "Mallard's play had the love interest with that rich dame screwin' both brothers, and Lauria's didn't. But everything else—the old man, the mother, the family history, the friggin' dialogue, everything; it's one play in two slightly different versions."

"Never any doubt in my mind from when I first read it," Priscilla agreed.

Rizzo's phone rang, and he reached for it absentmindedly.

"Six-Two squad, Rizzo," he said.

"Joe? Mike."

Rizzo smiled, gesturing for Priscilla's attention.

"Hey, Mikey, what's new?"

"I've got something for you," McQueen said. "I can leave work a little early today, maybe about three-thirty, three forty-five. I'll swing by your house and give it to you, if you want."

"That'd be great, Mike," Rizzo said, "but I can meet you some-wheres, maybe in the city. I hate for you to . . ."

McQueen cut him off. "It's no trouble. I can say hello to Jen."

"Okay, kiddo," Rizzo said. "Plan on staying for dinner."

"No thanks, I can't tonight. Another time. Why don't I meet you at the house around four-thirty or so. Will you be home by then?"

"Sure thing, I'll make it my business to be there."

"Bring Cil along," Mike said. "I'd like to see her."

"Okay, I'll ask her. See you then."

He hung up and smiled at Priscilla.

"Mike's got the file," he said. "The Mallard investigation. Prob-ably ran a complete dupe off the computer."

She frowned. "You're gonna see him this afternoon?"

"Yeah, my house. Around four-thirty. He wants you to come along."

"Okay, only I gotta be outta there no later than five. I'm meeting that agent for a drink tonight."

"The one your writing teacher turned you on to? The one that liked your stuff?"

Priscilla's smile lit her entire face. "That's the one. Robin Miller. She called me last night and said she sold one of my stories."

Rizzo reached out and they slapped palms. "Good for you, Cil, good for you. That was pretty friggin' fast, it must be some good story."

"Well, good enough for this la-di-freakin'-da literary magazine nobody actually *reads*. And it may seem fast to you, but I've been tryin' to sell a story for ten years."

"Well, then, it's about time, that's great." Lowering his voice, he asked, "Is it SOP to go out for drinks after a sale, or is Miller lookin' for a little somethin' else?"

"There you go again, Joe, back in lesbian fantasy heaven. No, it ain't SOP, but, no, she's not on the make. Far as I know, she's as straight as you are. She said she wants to discuss some ideas about my book. Imagine that? This chick figures I can sell a freakin' *book*."

"If she's a pro, Cil, she's probably right. Hear her out."

"I intend to, Partner. The money I'm getting for this short story'll barely cover the drinks tonight. I hope they're on her."

"Maybe you should just buy your own booze. Go Dutch, it'll be safer that way."

Priscilla stood, waving a dismissive hand. "Relax, I'm tellin' you, nothing going on here with this chick. Hell, I'm thinkin' of bringing Karen along."

"Might not be a bad idea," he said.

"Well, I'm gonna go follow up on that prescription case, call over to the Eight-Four. See if our lead panned out."

"Okay," Rizzo said. "Cil—I keep forgettin' to ask you—how'd that weather check turn out?"

"On October thirtieth, it rained all day and all night. Stopped around midnight in Bensonhurst, later in the city."

"So maybe that raincoat wasn't just a prop," Rizzo said. "Our killer's a dapper fucker, ain't he?"

"Hell," she said, "if it's a dapper fucker we're after, maybe we oughta ask Mike where *he* was on the night of October thirtieth."

They were interrupted by a uniformed officer assigned to the squad room.

"Hey, Cil, this just came in for you and Joe," he said, handing her a fax from Plaza Legal.

It was the follow-up report Rizzo had requisitioned on Lauria's home telephone activity for the two-month period predating the one Detective Dellosso had obtained. Priscilla scanned it quickly.

"Do you have that other telephone record Bobby Dee got for us?" she asked.

Rizzo rummaged around on his desk, finding the dog-eared fax and nodding. "Right here," he said. "Why?"

Priscilla took the first report from his hands. "I don't seem to remember any calls to a two-one-two area code, do you?" she asked.

Interest came to Rizzo's eyes, and he leaned forward, scanning the two reports she held. "No," he said. "There weren't any calls to Manhattan. Every call comin' in or goin' out was in the seven-one-eight code."

Priscilla smiled, pointing her finger to an entry appearing on the newly arrived fax. "Well, check this out."

Rizzo's eyes followed her finger, then returned to her face. Intrigued, he said, "Get a make on that, Cil. I'm thinkin' it comes back to someone we're gonna want to talk to."

Priscilla went to one of the squad computers and sat, working quickly. The number showing on Lauria's record belonged to the Samuel Kellerman Literary Agency located on Irving Place in Manhattan. She pulled up the agency's Web site and clicked on "Clients."

"Ready for this?" she said, returning to Rizzo's desk. "The number belongs to Mallard's agent."

"Well, whaddaya know?" Rizzo said happily. "Our first murder suspect."

"Let's go talk to the guy, Joe."

He held up a calming hand. "Take it easy, relax. We gotta think this through. Mike said Manhattan South was pretty convinced Mallard's killer was a burglar, but they would still have had to check out his life, so you gotta figure they already talked to the agent."

"Sure, but they don't know the play angle," she said, her dark eyes glistening with excitement. "*We* know that's the key here, the freakin' play."

"Yeah, we definitely need to talk to the guy, and we will. But first let's take a look at that file Mike is givin' us. See what the agent told Manhattan South. We need to move slow here, Cil. Be real careful. We only get one shot at this before Manhattan South catches our scent and leans on us. Remember your gut feeling on this—obstruction, official misconduct, accessory to murder—like that. We need to use our heads."

Rizzo saw her frustration and said, "Trust me here, kid. One step at a time."

He took the fax into his hand, looking again at the 212 number. Then he slowly raised his eyes to meet Priscilla's. "Our first suspect," he repeated. "Don't that make you feel all warm and fuzzy?"

SEATED AT the metal desk in his basement home office, Rizzo frowned across to Priscilla, then Mike McQueen.

"Manhattan South confirmed the agent was in Paris the night Mallard was killed. He flew outta Kennedy on Monday, October twenty-seventh, returned Tuesday, November fourth. That alibis him for both homicides."

He tossed the thick computer-generated file onto his desk. "Real convenient for him, don't you think?"

Mike shrugged. "There's a ton of stuff in that case file, Joe; I looked it over pretty carefully. The task force working the Mallard case is pretty convinced it was a break-in. From what's in the file, you can't blame them. That play of Lauria's is a key piece of evidence they're not aware of. We're all sitting on dynamite here."

"Hell, Mike, relax," Rizzo said. "If Cil hadn't seen Mallard's play on Broadway, we'd never even have made a connection here. No one can pin anything shady on us, believe me. Later, after we poke around a little in the city, maybe then they'll catch on. And we'll just say we were fishin', just on a hunch, whatever, then hand them the play angle. So relax."

"Yeah, Mike, relax," Priscilla said. "Worst this old man can do is get us all locked up for twenty fuckin' years."

"Yeah," Mike said uneasily. "I basically stole this file from the Plaza's database."

"How exactly did you handle that anyway?" Rizzo asked.

"Very carefully," McQueen said. "I pulled up the Lauria homicide, then I hit the files for a pattern match. Any similar crime committed anywhere in the city, based on method, scene, age, race and sex of victim. The computer spit out a half dozen cases, Mallard's one of them. Then I piggybacked Mallard onto Lauria and ran it through under the Lauria case number. It won't stand up to a close look, but it won't catch anybody's eye, either. As long as no one goes looking for a problem, we'll be okay."

Rizzo nodded. "Good. Tomorrow, after I go through this file, me and Cil will start on the Manhattan end. With the agent, probably. Size up the guy."

"We found a box full of rejection slips in Lauria's closet," Priscilla told Mike. "We confiscated it along with the manuscripts. When we got the hit on Kellerman's telephone number, we checked through the box. Lauria's play was rejected by three agencies, but none of 'em was Kellerman."

McQueen nodded. "So no direct connection."

"Other than the phone call itself, no," Rizzo said. "But there's a connection all right, we just need to find it."

Priscilla glanced at her wristwatch and stood. "Speakin' of agents," she said, "I gotta get going. Sorry I missed Jennifer, Joe, I'll meet her on Thanksgiving."

Rizzo nodded, moving to show her out. "Yeah, sorry about that. I forgot it was open school night."

Priscilla bent to kiss Mike's cheek, waving at Rizzo. "Sit," she said. "I can find my way out."

LATER THAT night, Rizzo sat back in his desk chair, the Mallard file spread before him. He rubbed at his tired eyes. The only sound he could hear was the humming of the basement's fluorescent light above him. Jennifer and Jessica had long since retired for the night.

Rizzo opened a package of Nicorette, a fleeting image of the Chesterfields, hidden in the gray Impala's glove compartment, appearing before him. Sighing, he put a piece of gum into his mouth and began chewing.

One of the task force cops had printed out an online encyclopedia biography of Avery Mallard, and Rizzo now knew more about the man than he had ever known about any literary figure.

After graduating from New York's Fordham University, Mallard had set out for Los Angeles, attempting a career in television and screenwriting. After six long years of failure, he returned to New York City, supporting himself as a copywriter at a well-known publishing house. It was through connections there that he met Samuel Kellerman, an up-and-coming agent specializing in literary novels and stage plays. Soon afterward, Kellerman represented Mallard on a novel he'd written while in California. The book eventually sold, receiving wide critical acclaim but little commercial success.

Then, when he was thirty, largely due to Kellerman's efforts, Mallard's life had flared into the bright, dizzying heights of success. A play he had scripted appeared off-Broadway, where it was seen by a powerful producer and ultimately restaged at Broadway's Cort Theatre. The play was a huge success, earning Mallard great sums and garnering the first of his many prestigious awards, including the Tony and New York Drama Critics' Circle Award.

Mallard's first marriage dissolved as a result of his sensationalized affair with the play's leading lady, a Hollywood starlet rarely seen on Broadway. After a quick Las Vegas wedding, their marriage lasted only two years, also ending in divorce. Mallard would suffer two more failed marriages before his untimely and violent death at age sixty-one.

Except for his six years in Hollywood, Mallard had been a lifelong resident of New York City. He often appeared in the news for his flamboyant and opinionated political pursuits and passionate social activism.

Rizzo picked up the printout of the man's biography.

"Pain in the ass, this guy was," he thought, then tossed the paper back down on his desk.

Rizzo ran the details of the slaying through his mind again, committing them to memory. He grudgingly acknowledged the professional and thorough job Manhattan South and Major Case had done so far.

But results had been scant.

Rizzo had reviewed all the reports, DD-5s, and photographs. Everything about the case was eerily similar to Lauria's, right down to the relative security of Mallard's rear yard, thus making his home an unlikely target for a random break-in. All prints at the scene were accounted for, no physical evidence had been found. Rizzo dismissed a passing thought: how nice it would have been if a stray fiber from a blue raincoat had been found on Mallard's body.

The playwright had been largely inactive in recent years. Rizzo learned from the file that Mallard had been involved in small venue revivals of his former works in other cities, even adapting two of his old plays for television specials. But *An Atlanta Landscape* represented his only original work in nearly a decade. The task force had investigated those idle years but came up dry. They had interviewed Mallard's ex-wives, a number of former girlfriends and all his poker buddies, as well as fellow writers and various literary hangers-on.

It had only led them back to their original theory, a random burglary gone awry.

Rizzo contemplated his advantage. He and Jackson could now simply discount any and all relationships Mallard might have had except those connecting him to Lauria and both writers to the play itself, the seemingly plagiarized version of Lauria's *A Solitary Vessel*.

A distinct advantage if played correctly, but an advantage wrought with great peril.

Rizzo understood that Priscilla's fears were grounded in cold, hard fact: it was a very dangerous game they were playing.

If a third murder were to occur, their roles in it would be hard to ascertain. Rizzo knew the procedural requirements were clear. He, as the senior detective in charge of the Lauria case, was under an absolute mandate to report the existence of any possible link between it and the Mallard murder. If anything went wrong with either case, he and Priscilla would be hard pressed if confronted for explanations.

In fact, the only vaguely exculpable excuse they could formulate was one of mere stupidity. Rizzo would have to look some boss straight in the eye and say, "Sorry, I just never saw the connection."

He stood, switching off the desk lamp and stretching out his tired back muscles. He shook his disquieting thoughts away and squared the file off, then slipped it into the large, non–police issue manila folder.

Rizzo left the basement, quietly retiring to bed, a nervous excitement simmering beneath his fatigue.

He looked forward to the morning and whatever the new day would bring.

CHAPTER EIGHTEEN

BY NINE-FIFTEEN THURSDAY MORNING, Rizzo and Jackson were speeding toward the Brooklyn Battery Tunnel, on their way to Avery Mallard's Manhattan home. Priscilla wove the gray Impala deftly through the thinning rush-hour traffic.

"So," she said. "If we turn up a blue raincoat at Mallard's, and the fiber is a match to the one found on Lauria, we caught us a murderer."

"Yeah," said Rizzo. "A *dead* murderer. We clear our case, but it'll be next to impossible to stay involved with the Mallard murder. Manhattan will jump on this new angle and brush us off like crumbs on a table."

"I guess," she said with a shrug. "But then we'd be off this hook we're hanging ourselves on. And at least we'd have solved the Lauria case. They couldn't take that from us."

"Big fuckin' deal," Rizzo said. "I want the *Mallard* case."

Priscilla glanced at her partner. "So, maybe we'll get lucky and not find a coat."

"Yeah," he grunted. "Maybe."

After a moment, he spoke again.

"Here's what we got, Cil, from me readin' the case file. There was no unusual activity on Mallard's financial resources. So it's unlikely he hired a pro to kill Lauria. All the ex-wives come back clean. Believe it or not, Mallard was on good terms with all four of 'em, even that screwball actress. Anyway, none of that connects to Lauria. Way

215

I see it, we got his agent, the producer of the play, and maybe the director. Long shot is that friendly neighbor a his that found the body. Him and Mallard were pretty buddy-buddy. Equal long shot, some other pal Mallard mighta had. Any one a those guys coulda helped Mallard kill Lauria, then later on killed Mallard, or maybe killed 'em both on his own for reasons unknown to us. But their alibis are good all around for the Mallard case, and they've all flown under the radar with Manhattan South. With the agent, his alibi covers both killings: he was in Paris. Manhattan South didn't need to alibi anybody for the possible dates of the Lauria killing 'cause they weren't working it as connected, never even heard a Lauria."

"What *are* the alibis?" Priscilla asked.

Rizzo looked to the notes he held in his hands.

"Agent in Paris, producer havin' an early dinner at the Marriott Marquis with his mistress, then in a room with her till midnight. Mallard got whacked about nine. The director was at the theater for the play's matinee, then the regular evening show. The neighbor was home with his wife, went out for cigarettes 'bout nine-thirty, saw Mallard's front door ajar, checked it out, found the body, called nine-one-one from his cell."

"How'd they establish time of death?" she asked.

"M.E. got to the scene by ten-fifteen, no rigor mortis yet, so he ballparks it no earlier than eight-thirty. Neighbor claims he found the body nine-forty or so. The M.E. runs some more tests, puts time a death around nine p.m. Sunday, November second."

Priscilla nodded. "So the only alibi we know of covering both killings is the agent's, and the weakest alibi in the Mallard case is the neighbor's."

"Yes," Rizzo said. "He coulda gone out for smokes, killed Mallard, set the scene up to look like a burglary, then called the cops. But what's that got to do with Lauria?"

Priscilla speculated, "Mallard and the neighbor killed Lauria to shut him up about how Mallard stole his play. After the fact, Mallard starts to pussy out, neighbor gets scared and whacks Mallard."

Rizzo nodded. "The boys and girls at Major Case did have some inclinations toward the neighbor. They squeezed him a little, but he stood up to it. Even demanded a lie detector test, just like on television. Everybody's satisfied the guy is clean."

"What about the others, Joe?"

He shrugged. "The other three were just routinely canvassed. Without the plagiarized play angle, there was no reason to do much more than that. And their alibis tested out."

"Okay," Priscilla said.

"By the way," Rizzo said as an afterthought. "The producer? When we talk to him, steer clear of *his* alibi. Let me handle it. The cop interviewin' him gave a confidential statement amendment." Rizzo smiled. "Seems the guy's afraid his wife might get a little unreasonable with the community property if she hears about his night at the Marriott with the girlfriend."

Priscilla pursed her lips. "Thinkin' with his dick, just like the rest of you guys."

Adams Mews was a short, narrow passageway that ran between Jane Street and Eighth Avenue in the West Village. The alley was lined on both sides by two- and three-story attached houses. Each structure was a converted stable, some dating back to the eighteenth century, most from the mid–eighteen-hundreds. The street itself was unevenly paved in Colonial-era stones.

Priscilla carefully pulled the car's right wheels onto the narrow north sidewalk in front of number ten Adams Mews, former home of playwright Avery Mallard. She opened the driver's door to examine the position of the Chevrolet, satisfying herself there was enough room on the stone roadway for vehicle traffic to squeeze by.

Mallard's home had a white stone facade, two stories high, with portions of the building spider-veined with thick, leafless tangles of vines. Fronting the ground floor were a narrow entry door and permanently sealed large carriage doors which had formerly served as the stable entrance. A small window stood between the two doorways; three larger windows, two bearing covered air-conditioning units, were evenly spaced on the second floor.

The building, although now a crime scene, was still private

property. Rizzo had learned from the file that keys to the home had been left by Mallard's attorney with a local Realtor. Rizzo's detective sergeant badge convinced the Realtor to turn over the keys. Now, with those keys in his hand, he eyed the building, then scanned the street to his left and right.

"Let's take a walk around before we go in."

The two detectives came across a gated alley on Eighth Avenue that provided access to rear gardens for the homes located on the north side of Adams Mews. The gate was padlocked, but only six feet high, and ornately decorated in heavy wrought iron.

"A cripple could hop this fence," Priscilla observed.

They found a similar entry point on Jane Street, this one providing entry to the rear areas of the south side structures on Adams. Rizzo and Jackson retraced their steps along Jane Street, again noting the five- and six-story buildings backing up to the rear yards of Adams Mews' north side.

"Lots of windows facing the back of Mallard's place," Rizzo said.

The detectives then walked back to Eighth Avenue, turned right, continuing to Adams Mews and the Mallard home. Rizzo unlocked the door, eyeing the remnants of yellow crime scene tape still clinging to the door frame.

They entered the building.

From his careful reading of the file, Rizzo knew that anything resembling an address book, personal calendar, or diary had been removed and tagged by Manhattan South's investigators. He and Jackson were there for three reasons only: to search for what could be a fiber-matching raincoat, to examine the physical layout of the home to ascertain the likelihood of a break-in, and to see if there was anything connecting Mallard to Robert Lauria or his play *A Solitary Vessel.*

Two hours later, they left and returned the keys, then drove slowly northward toward a quick lunch and then a scheduled appointment with Avery Mallard's literary agent, Samuel Kellerman.

"So," Rizzo said, sipping coffee at the counter of the sandwich shop on West Fourteenth Street. "What'd we learn?"

Priscilla opened her bottled water, pouring some into a glass. "We learned that we shoulda've been playwrights instead of cops. Some cool house that dude had."

Rizzo laughed. "Yeah, and right in the middle of the city; it was like a country house somewheres. Very cool."

She sipped her water. "We also learned that Mallard's place is just as middle-of-the-block as Lauria's. Why would a burglar jump that back alley fence, then walk past five other buildings just to break into one of a line of similar residences?"

Rizzo shrugged. "I don't know."

Priscilla continued. "We learned that for a guy with a lotta dough, Mallard had a pretty shoddy wardrobe—and no fancy blue rain-coat."

"Yeah," Rizzo said with a laugh, "when I was lookin' in his closet, I thought somebody mighta put *my* friggin' clothes in there."

"Seriously," Priscilla said. "And did you see the pictures of Mallard with all those different women? Guy was a regular c-man, Joe. Wall-to-wall."

"Wall-to-wall awards, too," Rizzo commented. "First Pulitzer I ever seen."

She nodded. "Somebody better get them outta there before one of 'em sticks to some cop's fingers."

"Yeah, tempting," he said. "One of those Tonys almost stuck to mine. Funny how none of 'em stuck to the burglar, though, ain't it?"

"I was thinking the same thing," Priscilla agreed. "Even if Mallard surprised the guy, and they fought and the skell strangled him, you gotta figure a junkie to grab *something*. Those awards looked real valuable, and some strung-out asshole junkie woulda grabbed them for sure. Then he'da hocked 'em and got himself locked up the next day."

"Manhattan South did an inventory, Cil. Every award was ac-counted for. The only ones not in the display case were the three Mallard gave his ex-wives. There was no cash in the house and just a coupla pieces of jewelry missing."

Rizzo and Jackson ate in silence. Then, as he waved for another cup of coffee, Joe glanced at the wall clock. "I'll drink this fast, Cil. Let's not alienate Kellerman by being late."

*   *   *

SAMUEL KELLERMAN'S tenth-floor office looked out over the corners of East Sixteenth Street and Irving Place, his broad, dark cherry-wood desk situated cross corner at the left rear of the office, facing both windows.

Rizzo estimated the man's age from mid-sixties to late seventies—it was nearly impossible to tell. Kellerman had sharp, clear blue eyes and rich sable hair, finely sprinkled with touches of gray. He was tall and lean, carrying the self-confident air of a successful athlete or very wealthy man. He wore a simple black silk shirt open at the collar, cotton Dockers, and black leather loafers. Rizzo was acutely aware of the chance he and Priscilla were taking. By meeting with Kellerman, they were risking exposure to Manhattan South. But at this point in their investigation, if they wanted to move forward, it couldn't be avoided.

"So," Kellerman said, "why are two detectives interested in seeing me today? Is it something further on Avery's murder?"

Rizzo opened his notepad. "Your office number came up on a case we're working, Mr. Kellerman," he said. "We have a question or two."

The man nodded, looking from Rizzo to Jackson and then back to Rizzo.

"And these questions were answered less than satisfactorily by the person you found in possession of my number, I presume?" he asked pleasantly.

"Well, about that," Rizzo said. "The case we're on is a homicide. The guy who called your office was the victim."

Kellerman blinked twice in reaction, but remained silent. After a moment, he spoke again. "So I am now on the periphery of two homicides," he said. "Am I right to suspect that homicide investigators look upon such coincidences with skepticism?"

"Yeah, a little bit," Priscilla said.

"Who was this man who was killed?" Kellerman asked.

"Robert Lauria," Priscilla answered. "Does that name mean anything to you, Mr. Kellerman?"

After a moment's consideration, he shook his head. "No, I don't believe it does."

Rizzo jotted a note in his book. "Any record of incoming calls kept, sir?" he asked. "Like a log? Anything like that?"

Kellerman shook his head. "No, Sergeant. When was this call made?"

Rizzo consulted his notes, then supplied the date. Kellerman frowned.

"That long ago?" he said. "Well, unless the man distinguished himself in some way, I can't imagine my assistant remembering the call. Perhaps this man—Lauria, did you say?—is a friend or relative of Joy, my administrative assistant." He reached a hand toward his intercom. "Shall I ask her?"

Rizzo held up a hand. "Not just yet, if you don't mind. We'll talk to her about that on the way out."

"Very well."

"Let me ask you something, Mr. Kellerman," Priscilla said. "This guy lived over in Brooklyn. He was just an average Joe. Would a guy like that have any reason to call your office? Do you have any ideas about that?"

Kellerman raised his eyebrows. "Was the man a writer, Detective?" he asked. "Established or aspiring?"

"He was a laid-off shoe salesman," Rizzo interjected. "Like Detective Jackson said, just an average Joe."

"Well," Kellerman explained, "besides our usual course of business calls, we do field about ten or fifteen inquiries a day from the general public, Sergeant. Most are regarding representation or submission guidelines. My staff has been told to refer such callers to our Web site or a publication called *The Writer's Market Place*. You see, I no longer accept unsolicited manuscripts; it requires too much staffing and effort for what usually proves to be of little value."

"I see," Rizzo said. "So if somebody calls looking for representation, they get brushed off by your secretary."

Kellerman smiled. "I'd rather call it 'referred,' Sergeant. Unfortunately, the net result is quite the same."

"Any other reason someone like Lauria might call your office?" Priscilla asked.

"Yes, certainly, Detective. I represent three dozen authors with

millions of copies in print and scores of staged works—both per-
formed and printed. Sometimes we get calls from people requesting
addresses or phone numbers for the writers. Fans, usually, most very
harmless. But a few kooks as well, as you can imagine."

Rizzo chuckled. "Yeah, we can imagine. But tell me, what's your
policy with those calls?"

"My staff is instructed to first discourage such requests. Then,
and only if they believe the caller a true admirer of the author, the
request must be received by us in writing, and we see that it's forwarded to our client."

"And do you actually do that?" Rizzo asked.

"Yes," Kellerman answered.

"Are records kept of communications you receive and forward?"
Priscilla asked.

Kellerman shook his head. "No. If it's one of our more popular
authors, we hold the intake until we have a bunch, then send them all
together. For our more obscure clients, those receiving five or ten
such communications a year, we forward them as they are received.
A few of our more tempermental or eccentric clients have asked that
we simply destroy any such material as it comes in."

"Do you or any of your staff ever read this stuff, screen it?" Rizzo
asked.

"No, Sergeant. We are simply the clearinghouse."

"What about Avery Mallard, sir?" Priscilla asked. "What were his
instructions about mail you received for him?"

Kellerman smiled. "I assume, Detective, that you have conferred
with your colleague, Detective Sergeant McHugh? He was here after
Avery's murder, and he took my statement."

"Yeah, we know, Mr. Kellerman," Rizzo said reassuringly.
"You were in Paris the whole week, you're not a suspect in anything. Forgive us if we gave that impression. This is all very routine, believe me."

"Of course," Kellerman said genially. "To answer your question,
Avery had a very liberal policy. He wanted any and all correspondence we received forwarded to him immediately. I believe he even

responded to much of it. Avery was deeply appreciative of his public and grateful for his talent." Kellerman's face clouded, the blue of his eyes softening. "He was a warm, wonderful man," he said wistfully. "I was the only representative he ever had, from his first attempts as a novelist to his early playwriting successes and his eventual Pulitzer."

Then he looked from one detective to the other. "He was my dear friend, Officers, as well as my client. I miss him terribly already."

His eyes grew colder as he spoke.

"I hope you find his killer."

Rizzo tapped his pen slowly on his notepad and sighed. "Well, I can appreciate that, and I'm sorry for your loss, but we're actually lookin' for Lauria's killer, Mr. Kellerman."

The three sat quietly for a moment. Then, to break the silence, Priscilla spoke.

"I heard Mr. Mallard had been inactive for a few years, not producing much."

"That's true," Kellerman responded, conversationally, matching Priscilla's tone. "Avery had a long dry spell. Not for want of effort, mind you. He just couldn't get restarted. He feared he had lost his ability, his creative edge. I must say, I was beginning to wonder myself."

"So where'd *An Atlanta Landscape* come from?" Rizzo asked.

"Who knows?" Kellerman answered. "I've been in this business over forty years, Sergeant, and I still can't explain creative talent. I imagine no one can. *Where* does it come from? Where does the sun come from?"

Rizzo nodded. "My partner here, Priscilla, writes a little. Just hooked up with an agent herself."

Kellerman turned to Priscilla. "Really? May I ask the agent's name?"

"Robin Miller," she said with some pride.

Kellerman's face lit up. "Really? I know Robin, she's wonderful. You can't go wrong with Robin, believe me."

Priscilla looked away awkwardly. "Yeah, well, sometimes my partner here talks too much. My writing is sorta private."

Kellerman nodded. "Most good writing is *very* private, Detective. Don't ever apologize for that."

"Well, to tell you the truth," Priscilla now said with a smile, "I had no intention of apologizing."

"Take it easy, Cil," said Rizzo. "I only brought it up 'cause you mentioned how Robin helped you out. You know, with your story and the ideas she has for the novel you're working on." He turned to Kellerman. "I'm curious, Mr. Kellerman. Did you ever do that sort of thing? Help your clients with the actual writing? Mr. Mallard, maybe?"

"Many times, Sergeant. Many times. It's what a good agent does. *Part* of what a good agent does, that is."

Rizzo nodded. "So what about *Atlanta*? You help him out with that?"

Kellerman shook his head. "No, actually, I didn't. Well, no, that's not entirely true."

"Oh?" Rizzo asked. "What do you mean?"

"Well, you see, at some point Avery was faced with a dilemma. Are you familiar with the work, Sergeant? One of the characters, Samantha Sorensen, has simultaneous affairs with two of the main male characters. Avery felt very strongly about that story arc, but apparently an acquaintance of ours and the eventual producer, Thomas Bradley, didn't. He saw the work as stronger without the love interest angle."

Rizzo gave Jackson a discreet glance. Her face remained neutral.

"No kiddin'?" he asked. "So the guy didn't want the female character in the play?"

"No, actually the *presence* of the character was acceptable to him. Thomas just didn't want any *romantic* involvement for her. Anyway, Avery brought the problem to me. He said he'd be bound by my decision—in or out with the love angle?"

Rizzo shrugged. "From what I hear, the play is gonna sweep some awards, so I guess you made the right call."

Kellerman laughed. "Awards are marvelous, Sergeant, the backbone of egotism needed in theater, but filling the seats . . . now that's truly gratifying."

Rizzo smiled. "And sex sells," he said.

"Ah," Kellerman said, "how I admire the pragmatism of police-men. Yes, Sergeant, sex does sell. The director has even managed to work in a nude scene. It's quite titillating. But you see, Bradley thought the love triangle detracted from the intensity of the conflict between the father and his two sons, which he felt to be the heart and soul of the play."

"And did it?" Rizzo asked.

"Absolutely," Kellerman answered. "And still does." He smiled conspiratorily. "But as you say, now the play has sex and nudity."

Priscilla spoke up. "From what I hear, business is pretty good. I saw the play a couple of months ago. Now there's a three-month wait for tickets."

Again, Kellerman's face clouded up. "Yes, apparently tragedy is as good for box office as nudity. Since Avery's death, the wait has actually swollen to almost a year. It is, after all, the final work of an American master. In fact, I've been fending off phone calls from Hollywood—everyone is lining up to option the work for a movie." Kellerman smiled sadly. "One fellow even guaranteed me an A-list actor in the role of the father." He sighed. "Can you imagine? Cast-ing the movie and Avery still warm in his grave?"

"So I guess you haven't made the deal yet?" Rizzo asked.

"No, Sergeant, I'm not that ghoulish. Besides, I suppose I'll have to clarify my legal standing. Avery and I operated on a handshake for over thirty years. Now I imagine I'll have to reach some written agree-ment with the estate lawyers before I sign any contracts of option."

After a few more moments of silence, Rizzo spoke up again. "Well, at least Mallard broke out of his writer's block. He went out on top of his game."

Kellerman's face brightened. "At least it *was* finally broken, and Avery got to enjoy one last hurrah before . . . before his *very* last hurrah." After a pause, Kellerman spoke once more. "But, forgive me, I must ask, what has all this to do with the case you're working on?"

"Not a thing," Rizzo said, allowing a small smile. "You see, Mr. Kellerman, sometimes, cops just get nosy."

* * *

BEFORE LEAVING the office complex, Rizzo and Jackson briefly interviewed Kellerman's administrative assistant, Joy Zimmer. No, the name Robert Lauria meant nothing to her, and she certainly had no recollection of so distant a phone call. Yes, over the years, she had forwarded much correspondence to Avery Mallard, particularly since the opening of *An Atlanta Landscape*. When shown Lauria's photograph, she denied ever having seen him, as Kellerman had earlier.

"Do you remember anything bulky coming in for Mallard?" Rizzo had asked her. "Something in a large envelope, maybe eight-and-a-half-by-eleven with a bunch of papers in it?"

No, she had answered. And in today's climate, any such bulky package from a stranger would have caught her attention. There had been no such arrival.

Later, as they sat in the idling Impala parked in a no-standing zone on Irving Place, Rizzo jotted in his notepad. Priscilla fidgeted in the driver's seat, her finger tapping nervously on the wheel.

"This guy would be a *great* suspect, Joe," she said. "If it wasn't for that, 'Oh, by the way, I was in Paris,' alibi."

"Yeah, well, that's a pretty good friggin' alibi," Rizzo said, without looking up.

"How 'bout this?" she suggested. "Kellerman flies to Paris, then turns around and flies back to whack Lauria, then Mallard. 'Cause Lauria sent *A Solitary Vessel* to Kellerman for representation, but instead Kellerman slipped it to Mallard to break his writer's block. And when the shit hit the fan with Lauria, Mallard got panicky. So panicky that Kellerman is willing to whack his A-list client. Next thing you know, two dead bodies. Then Kellerman flies back to Paris."

Rizzo stopped writing and looked at his partner. "What the hell is that, Cil? Some old rerun of *Columbo* you saw back in high school?"

Priscilla shook her head. "Did you see that silk shirt?" she asked. "Hadda set him back a buck, buck and a half at least. And those loafers, they were Italian, three bills minimum."

"So?" Rizzo asked.

She shrugged. "So, a big ticket raincoat would be standard in a guy like Kellerman's wardrobe."

Rizzo nodded. "Yeah, probably."

Priscilla turned in her seat. "So, except for the Paris thing, Kellerman looks good on this."

Rizzo laughed. "Yeah, and except for the son of God thing, Jesus was a hippie."

"I'm serious here, Joe," she said.

"Yeah, that's what's scarin' me. Look, it's good you're thinkin' about this, but let's stay grounded, okay? The guy was in Paris. And there ain't no evil twin, either. Kellerman *was* in Paris. Now, he might be behind the killings, maybe in concert with someone else. Or he mighta hired a pro. We can try gettin' a look at his finances, just not right now. That would be tough without tippin' Manhattan to what we're up to. Maybe down the road, if we develop anything else. We'll see. Relax."

Priscilla turned back in the seat, eyeing the street scene on East Sixteenth. "Yeah, Joe," she said with resignation, "okay. Guess I'm a little wound up with all this. But . . . one more thing. Kellerman may be old, but he's in real good shape." She turned to face Rizzo. "I don't see him havin' a physical problem strangling these two guys, no problem at all."

Rizzo nodded while finishing up his notes, then flipped the pad closed. "Okay, duly noted. But most likely, Lauria sees Mallard's play or he reads about it, whatever. Realizes it's *his* play. Then somehow he finds out Kellerman is Mallard's agent, so he calls and tries to get to Mallard. Joy Zimmer says, 'Send us correspondence, we'll get it to Mallard.' So that's what Lauria does. When Mallard gets Lauria's letter, the rest of it plays out."

"Yeah, okay, Joe, so that leaves us right back where we started."

"Yep, that it does," Rizzo said. "But seein' Kellerman was pure gold. Pure fuckin' gold." He smiled and tapped his temple. "You find me a ratty, old, pissed-on raincoat to wear, I'll be your Columbo."

Priscilla grunted and pulled the column lever into drive, glancing into the mirrors and easing away from the curb.

"It's almost three o'clock," she said. "Let's go do the DD-fives and call it a day. I need to think about all this."

"Well, we got two RDOs. You've got till Sunday to think." Rizzo then leaned over, laying his left hand on Priscilla's shoulder, speaking in an exaggerated tone of formality.

"There *will* be a quiz."

———

CHAPTER NINETEEN

WHEN PRISCILLA ARRIVED AT the squad room on Sunday morning, she found Rizzo rummaging through various materials recovered from the Lauria apartment. She crossed the empty room and sat next to his desk.

"Morning, Joe," she said.

"Good mornin', Cil."

She thrust her chin at the papers in his hand. "Whatcha got there?"

"Copies of those three rejection letters Lauria got on *A Solitary Vessel*," Rizzo said. "They're all dated within an eight-month period. Seems like he sent the manuscript to some agents, got these three turndowns, then put it aside."

Priscilla craned her neck, scanning the letter in Rizzo's hand. She smiled. "Yeah," she said. "I know how that works. After all those years sending out short stories, I have a drawer full of letters like that."

Rizzo frowned, his right eye twitching slightly. "Yeah," he said distractedly, "but, what I'm wonderin' is, how'd this play get out there to where Mallard or somebody close to him coulda gotten a look at it?"

"Well," Priscilla suggested, "off the top of my head? Maybe by one of those agencies he sent it to."

"Yeah, that's exactly what I'm thinkin'. Tell me something: How does a guy protect himself against this kinda scam?"

"I don't know, exactly. I just used to mail stuff out and hope for the best. Then, once I hooked up with Karen, she advised me to use the poor man's patent on anything I sent."

"The what?"

"Poor man's patent," she repeated. "See, you take a copy of your work, mail it to yourself certified mail, return receipt requested. Then, when the post office delivers it, you never open the package. If it ever should become an issue, you put it before a judge with the dated receipt, and he opens it with everybody's lawyers present. Then they have a copy to compare to the published work you figure somebody stole from you. It's not perfect, but it's better than nothing."

"Yeah, I guess," Rizzo said, "but we didn't find anything like that in Lauria's place or in his cousin's garage."

She nodded. "Yeah, well, if there was a sealed package somewhere in Lauria's apartment and the person who whacked him was in the business, he'd have known enough to take it."

"I figure if Lauria had a package like that, he'da put it in the garage and we'da found it," Rizzo said.

"Or locked it up in some safe-deposit box somewhere," she said.

Rizzo continued to rummage through the Lauria material, pulling papers free from the pile on his desk and scanning them. "Well," he said, "we ran all his banking and finances. There *is* no safe-deposit box."

"Figures," she said. "Guy probably never even heard of the poor man's patent thing. Only reason I did was 'cause I was hooked up with a lawyer."

Rizzo dropped the financial reports, again picking up the rejection letters. "First thing tomorrow, we call these three agencies. Better still, we go up to their offices. These letters are all signed. We'll talk to the signers, see if we can develop a link between any of them and Mallard or anybody associated with him."

She nodded. "Okay, Joe, so what's on for today?"

"Well," he answered, "first, we spend an hour or two on the phones working our other cases. They're getting backed up. Then we have two appointments in the city."

"We do?" she asked.

"Yeah. On my RDO, I made a couple a calls. We're gonna meet Mallard's last girlfriend today. First, though, we're goin' to see the director of the play. I got him on the line Friday. It's all set up."

"Okay," Priscilla said. "I'll get started on the prescription case and that auto vandalism thing on Ovington Avenue. Call me when it's time to roll."

NEW YORK'S August Wilson Theatre was located on West Fifty-second Street between Broadway and Eighth Avenue. Rizzo and Jackson sat comfortably in two leather chairs before the small desk of the director's office.

Larry Thurbill, forty years old, had parlayed several successful off-Broadway musical productions into an opportunity to pursue his first love, legitimate dramatic theater. Now he was the overseer of Avery Mallard's final work, *An Atlanta Landscape*. Thurbill smiled across his desk at the two detectives.

"How is the coffee?" he asked.

"Great," Rizzo said over the rim of his cup. "Coffee always tastes better when it's served in really good china."

"One of the perks of a big hit show," the director said. "Believe me, I've had my share of coffee in cardboard."

Rizzo placed his cup down onto its saucer, then pulled the note-pad from his jacket.

"Well, Mr. Thurbill," he said, "it was good of you to see us, we'll try not to take up too much time."

Thurbill waved a hand. "Take all the time you need, Sergeant, the matinee begins at three, run-through at twelve. I have tons of time. And please, call me Larry."

"Okay, Larry," Rizzo said clicking his Parker. "I'm Joe, this is Priscilla."

Rizzo began a slow, informal questioning, subtly reinforcing the deliberately misleading impression he had given the director, that he and Priscilla were merely revisiting the Mallard murder. They had identified themselves only as NYPD detectives, without mentioning precinct, allowing Thurbill to make assumptions.

After nearly a half hour, Rizzo moved more toward the ground he had come to tread. Thurbill, relaxed and comfortable with the two amicable cops, answered readily.

"So, the producer," Rizzo asked. "What's his name again?"

"Bradley," Thurbill said. "Thomas Bradley. He heads the group of investors who backed the play, so, technically, he's the producer. But they all claim a bit of that role. Rightfully, I might add."

"Yeah," Rizzo said, "there ain't no art without the cash, I guess."

"Succinctly and quite accurately put, Joe," Thurbill said.

Rizzo continued. "I don't know very much about this kinda stuff, Larry, but I think I read somewhere that directors and producers butt heads a lot on these kinda things. You know, plays, movies, television."

Thurbill nodded. "Yes, we do. I'm afraid our motivations are often at odds—a director's quality and integrity of product versus a producer's concern for commercial viability. It does become difficult at times."

"I'll bet. How 'bout here, with *Atlanta*?" Rizzo asked. "Any problems between you and Bradley?"

Priscilla leaned forward. "My partner gets nosy sometimes, Larry," she said.

"No, no, not at all," Thurbill said. "I'm sure it's one of the perks of *your* job. Obtaining inside info on a variety of professions and fields. Actually, to answer your question, there was a problem or two, but, of course, Avery was alive then and very much involved in preproduction, particularly with casting and story arc. Plays are not like movies, Joe. Hemingway once said the best way to sell your book to Hollywood was to go to the California-Nevada border, have them toss you the money, then toss them your novel. With a play, on the other hand, the author is very much involved, has quite a say. It is, after all, *his* vision which brings us all here."

"Yeah," Rizzo said, "I can see that. So, you had a little problem with Bradley, and Mallard straightened it out?"

"Not exactly," Thurbill said. "Thomas Bradley is quite easy to work with actually, from a director's point of view. In fact, we sort of reversed traditional roles a bit in one particular instance. It was more a . . . I don't know, let's say a situation, between Thomas and Avery.

Thomas seemed to be pushing a bit, in my opinion. Overstepping his bounds, I think. He was adamant about the love triangle being written out of the play, and he pressed Avery right up to the actual start of rehearsals last year. It was interesting to watch the interplay. They seemed more coauthors than author-producer. Of course, in the end Avery prevailed, as he should have."

"So you figure the love angle added to the play? Artistically?" Rizzo asked.

Thurbill smiled, leaning forward in his seat, speaking in an exaggerated tone of conspiracy.

"Ah, Joe," he said, his eyes twinkling. "I never actually said that, now did I? No, the love angle's merely fluff. To help fill seats. It's a time-honored tradition in theater. Shakespeare himself inserted one or two superfluous scenes into his works. Some risqué lines and what passed as sexuality in those days. To fill the pit, you see, the area in front of the stage where the proletariat class would stand to view the production. It was good business then and remains so today.

"Avery was hungry for a hit, and, frankly, so was I. Circumstances have delivered a successful run of *musicals* to me." He smiled more broadly, fluttering his hands in parody of an excited, stereotypical gay male.

"Keeping me in character, you see," he said cheerfully. Then he grew somber. "But my goal has always been serious direction. I require meaningful works to direct. *An Atlanta Landscape* is meaningful. Maybe Pulitzer caliber. No, if Avery's little sexual triangle would get the play seen, get it some attention, that was fine with me. I encouraged Avery, and so, yes, I did bump heads with Thomas a bit. But by that point, I was pretty well entrenched, I enjoyed Avery's full support as director. I wasn't afraid of Thomas's firing me. So"—he shrugged—"I could afford to make a noble gesture and give my support to Avery and his agent. The love affairs remained."

Rizzo sat back in his seat. "You really thought Bradley might want to fire you over it?"

Thurbill stood and came around the desk, pouring fresh coffee for the two detectives. "Oh, yes. He may be easy to work with, Joe, but he's also quite ruthless, you see."

* ★ *

MAGGIE RICHARTE was thirty-two years old, a successful and influential buyer for a world-renowned New York fashion house. She had met Avery Mallard, nearly thirty years her senior, two years earlier while she was on a buying trip to Milan and he was touring Italy. They had become lovers, and their affair continued until six months prior to his death. The breakup had been amicable, and they remained friends.

Maggie smiled sadly across the airy living room of her East End Avenue co-op apartment.

"Is that what the fussy little wuss told you?" she asked with a laugh. "That Bradley is 'ruthless'? My God, I'll never get used to these people, no matter how many of them I work with. Larry Thurbill is a nice man, Sergeant, but he's not the toughest Marine in the platoon, if you know what I mean. Avery and Thomas were at odds over that one aspect of the play, but Thomas certainly didn't kill Avery because of it."

"I don't think that's crossed anyone's mind, Ms. Richarte, unless maybe yours?" Rizzo asked.

"No, Sergeant, not at all. Believe me, Thomas Bradley had nothing to do with Avery's murder, and when last I spoke to Lieutenant Lombardi about this, he seemed convinced it was just a horrible, random killing. Just a wasteful, stupid, stupid thing." She shook her head, her eyes moistening.

Priscilla cleared her throat. "That's the theory, ma'm. We're just double checking."

Richarte nodded, dabbing lightly at her eyes with the tip of her pinky finger. "Avery was a genius, you know, a true genius." After a small pause, she smiled sadly.

"And the most wonderful lover I've ever known," she added wistfully.

ARTHUR WAIN sighed, looking from one detective to the other, then meeting Rizzo's eyes.

"I've already been through this," he said wearily. "More times, and for too many hours, than can possibly be necessary."

Rizzo and Priscilla stood at the front door of Wain's home at number twelve Adams Mews—the building next door to Mallard's former residence.

"I can appreciate that, Mr. Wain," Rizzo said politely, "and I know Manhattan South is satisfied that your involvement was limited to having found the body. I just have a question or two, that's all. It'll only take a few minutes."

Wain scowled. "Well, I don't mean to be rude, Sergeant, and I know it's chilly out here, but my wife has had quite enough of all this. She was very fond of Avery, and all these police inquiries have served only to magnify her stress level. Can you ask your questions here? Without coming inside?"

"Sure," Rizzo said, "no problem. First off, take a look at this." He produced the photo of Lauria, the same one he had shown to Kellerman, Thurbill, and Richarte. "Ever see this man, Mr. Wain? With Mr. Mallard, maybe? Or hanging around the street, near the house, anything like that?"

Wain looked carefully at the photo. "No," he said after a moment, "I can't say that I have." He raised his face back to Rizzo, a faint glimmer evident in his eyes. "Is he a suspect?" he asked hopefully. "Do you think he might be Avery's killer?"

Rizzo shook his head. "No, I don't think so. Just someone who maybe can point us in the right direction. It's a long shot."

Wain replied with a sad, ironic smile. "A long shot," he said softly. "How appropriate."

Priscilla raised her eyebrows. "Oh? Why's that?"

Wain shook his head, then explained. "Every August, my wife and I would go up to Saratoga to the racetrack with Avery and whichever wife or girlfriend he was involved with at the time. We shared a liking for the horses, you see."

"And?" Rizzo asked.

Wain sighed, extracting a cigarette from his shirt pocket, searching absentmindedly for his lighter.

"Well, Avery always liked the long shots, Sergeant," he said. Then, with another sad smile, added, "And I must say, quite often they came in for him. Quite often."

235

CHAPTER TWENTY

MONDAY MORNING THE TWO DETECTIVES once again returned to Lauria's former home. There, they showed a recent photograph of Avery Mallard to the Annasias. Neither remembered ever having seen him in Lauria's company or in the vicinity of the house.

As Rizzo drove once again to the Brooklyn Battery Tunnel, Priscilla commented from the passenger seat, "I like workin' Brooklyn, Joe. I get to spend lotsa time in Manhattan."

"Yeah," Rizzo said. "And the tolls are on the city."

Her face grew serious. "I still think we shoulda called first. This could be a waste of time. These people may not even be in today . . ."

"Yeah, could be," Rizzo said, "but I wanna catch 'em cold. I don't want them with any time to think about this, why two cops are comin' to see them. With Kellerman and Thurbill and the others, they already talked to cops, they knew they were involved. These people at the agencies, they have no reason to think cops are coming to talk to them. It's better this way, trust me."

She nodded. "Well, when you put it like that . . . I guess so. Okay, so we'll just drop in." Her face brightened. "We can say, Oh, we were just in the neighborhood and figured we'd stop by and ask, 'Hey, you kill these two guys? You know who did, maybe?' I can deal with that."

"Yeah, exactly," Rizzo said. "Catch 'em with their alibis all up in the air." He shrugged. "We'll see."

The first literary agency they visited was located on Columbus Avenue at West Seventy-first Street. A little research by Priscilla had shown that this particular agency was well known for its representation of stage drama. The eventual letter declining the work had been signed by an Evelyn Myerson.

Ms. Myerson was twenty-six years old, employed by the agency as a first reader, and assigned to what was referred to as the "slush pile," a myriad of eclectic unsolicited works received by the dozens each month. Myerson had obtained her B.A. in English literature from a small local college in her native Midwest, then relocated to New York City for a career in author representation.

After a short interview, it was clear to both detectives that the surprised, pleasant young woman had no recollection of Robert Lauria or his play. It was apparent to Rizzo that the woman had, most probably, scanned the work only briefly before returning it to the unproven, unknown Brooklyn playwright.

The second agency, at Ninth Avenue and Fifty-third Street, proved to be a dead end as well, also involving a young, inexperienced first reader serving more as a clearinghouse worker than literary representative. She, too, gave the detectives the impression that she hadn't read *A Solitary Vessel* before mailing out her rejection letter.

Rizzo had deliberately started the interviews in the northernmost location of the city, working southward and nearer to Brooklyn as the day progressed. He and Priscilla left the Impala parked on Seventh Avenue and Twenty-seventh Street, stopping at a panini shop for a quick lunch.

The last of the three agencies was located in a tall office building on Seventh between Twenty-seventh and Twenty-eighth Streets in Chelsea. They rode the elevator and entered the third-floor office complex.

A young receptionist examined Rizzo's badge and I.D., her eyes growing wide.

"Oh," she said. "Is everything all right?"

Priscilla smiled. "Yes, everything is fine," she said. "We just need to speak to Linda DeMaris. Is she in?"

"Linda?" the young woman asked. "Linda doesn't work here anymore, Officer."

"Oh?" Rizzo asked. "Since when?"

"I'm not sure . . . If I had to guess, maybe about a year."

"Okay," Rizzo said. "Was she a first reader here?"

The woman shook her head. "No, not when she left. Maybe she started as one, but I wouldn't know."

"So what was Ms. DeMaris?" Priscilla asked. "An agent?"

"No," the woman said, her voice lowering, her eyes widening once more. "Is Linda in some kind of trouble?"

"No, nothing like that," Rizzo said. "We just need to ask her about something, no big deal. But tell me . . . *was* she an agent?"

"No, sir, she was an administrative assistant. To Helen."

"Helen?" Priscilla asked.

"Yes, Helen Crothers, one of the agents here."

Rizzo nodded. "Do me a favor, will you? Get ahold of Helen. We'd like to speak to her."

The woman reached for the intercom. "Sure," she said. "Helen's usually out to lunch at this hour on Mondays, but she happens to be here today. I'll get her."

HELEN CROTHERS was in her mid-fifties, sharp-eyed and intelligent-looking, her black hair short and dabbed in gray. She smiled across her desk at the two detectives.

"So," she said. "How can I help you?"

"Well," Rizzo said, "we wanted to speak to Linda DeMaris, but we understand she no longer works here."

"Yes, that's correct. She left about a year ago."

Priscilla spoke up. "She was your administrative assistant?"

"Yes, that's correct." She frowned. "Is Linda okay? Is everything all right?"

"Far as we know, yeah," Rizzo said. "We just need to ask her a question or two."

"Is there anything I can help you with?" Crothers asked.

"Maybe you can," Rizzo said. "Let me ask you, as an administrative assistant, did Ms. DeMaris screen incoming manuscripts? You know, unsolicited stuff the agency receives for representation?"

"Sometimes, but not very often. Actually, Linda resisted those assignments." She smiled. "She'd spent more than a few years as a first reader, Detective. Her promotion to A.A. was somewhat long in coming."

"So she did have a history here as a reader?" Priscilla asked.

"Most definitely," Crothers answered. "As I said, for a good number of years, until about fours years ago."

"And, as your assistant, she'd still occasionally read submissions that came in unsolicited?"

"Yes. Occasionally."

"Ms. Crothers, you ever hear of a guy named Robert Lauria? From Brooklyn? Wrote an unproduced play called *A Solitary Vessel*?" Rizzo asked.

The woman frowned, then shook her head. "No, those names are not ringing a bell. Why?"

"His name came up on a case we're working," Rizzo said. "It turns out he submitted a play to this agency and it was rejected by Ms. DeMaris. We were just hoping maybe she had some additional info on the guy."

"That would be unlikely, Detective," she replied. "We process hundreds of submissions each year."

"So we've been learning," Priscilla said. "Do you keep any record of them?"

Crothers tossed her head from side to side. "Yes and no. When a first reader turns down a work, generally no record is kept. But when something goes beyond the first reader and receives serious consideration, it will often be entered into our databank." She turned to the computer on her desk. "What were those names again?"

After keying in the information, Crothers shook her head. "No," she said. "Neither is showing here."

Rizzo nodded. "Okay, thanks, we'll just talk to Ms. DeMaris. Do you know where she's working now?"

"Oh, yes, Detective, I can help you with that. You see, Linda left us for a marvelous opportunity that opened up for her."

"Oh?" Priscilla asked. "And what was that?"

Crothers's smile broadened. "A personal assistant position for a very important and influential man."

Rizzo crossed his leg, sitting back in his seat. "And who might that be, Ms. Crothers?"

"Thomas Bradley," she said. "The Broadway producer. Have you heard of him?"

Rizzo turned to Jackson, and they exchanged smiles. Turning back to Crothers, he began to stand as he answered her.

"Oh, yeah," he said. "His name does ring a bell."

SEATED IN the Impala on Seventh Avenue, Rizzo turned to Jackson with a smile.

"It's always the last place you look, Cil," he said, "every time."

Priscilla started the engine. "And of all the suspects, you left Bradley for last."

"Yeah," he said. "Bradley looked good to me almost from the beginnin'. Remember when we talked to Kellerman, Mallard's agent, and I told you speaking to him was pure gold?"

"Yeah, I remember," Priscilla answered.

"Kellerman was the first guy to mention the rift between Mallard and Thomas Bradley, you know, how Mallard wanted that female character to be screwin' the two brothers and Bradley didn't. That's what tipped me. Lauria's play, the one that Bradley seems to have stolen, had *no* love triangle. Mallard put it in there on his own. He was a horny son of a bitch, wasn't he? Four wives, all those girl-friends, the guy's life revolved around women. Lauria, on the other hand, saved his nickels and dimes for phone sex and blow jobs at the massage parlor. The play idea appealed to Mallard, but he wanted to spice it up with the sex angle. Bradley wanted to keep it pure, the way Lauria originally wrote it."

"You think Mallard and Bradley were in it together?" Priscilla asked.

He shrugged. "I dunno. Could be. But more likely it was just Bradley, and he spoon-fed it to Mallard."

"Why you leanin' that way, Joe?"

"It makes the most sense. Bradley steals the play, feeds it to Mallard. Bradley knows the play's good, great even. He also knows he's got no chance in hell of raisin' a few million bucks to stage a Broadway production of a play written by some asshole from Brooklyn. But, if he gets Avery Mallard's name on it, and he hypes it as a second Pulitzer by the American master, all the fat-cat art patrons in the city start liquidatin' assets and tossin' cash into Bradley's hat."

Priscilla nodded, easing the car out into the speeding downtown traffic. "So Bradley originally got the play from Linda DeMaris."

"Bingo. DeMaris spent years eatin' shit at that agency, then finally she gets a promotion. But every once in a while, some boss, maybe Crothers, says, 'Hey, Linda, you ain't doing anything, go help out with that slush pile.' DeMaris gets pissed, but she's gotta do what she's told. So she grabs something off the pile and actually starts reading it. And it's fuckin' great. So, what to do with it? Hand it over to Crothers, then go out and get coffee for the big agents' meetin' that afternoon? No, DeMaris has a lead in to a big Broadway producer. Maybe she was sleepin' with the guy already, maybe not, but she takes the play to him, and this plot to reject Lauria and spoon-feed Mallard gets hatched." Rizzo smiled.

"Dollars to fuckin' doughnuts, Cil, we get Mike to access the uncensored copy of the 'confidential' statement Bradley gave Manhattan South, that alibi mistress of his turns out to be Ms. Linda DeMaris."

"So, Mallard comes up clean here?" Priscilla asked.

He shrugged. "My money says he does, and here's why. When Lauria learns about *An Atlanta Landscape,* he freaks. He *knows* it's his work, only with a sexy female screwin' the brothers tossed into the mix. Then he finds out Kellerman is Mallard's agent, and he sends a letter, through the agency, to Mallard. Mallard reads it, and in his heart, he knows it was Bradley who spoon-fed him the play under the guise of just helping him write it. I'd bet my pension Mallard never once saw the actual Lauria script. It seems unlikely a guy of his stature would deliberately plagiarize so blatantly. So he goes to Bradley and says, 'What the fuck?' He demands an explanation. Maybe threatens goin' direct to Lauria. Bradley says, relax, it's just a nut trying to make a score with some phony plagiarism claim. But Bradley's still worried. He *knows* Lauria wrote the play, and maybe the guy could prove it. Maybe with one a those whaddaya-call-its? Poor man's patents. So Bradley sees his entire career goin' down the shitter. And Mallard's, too. Bradley'll forever be known as the guy who destroyed Avery Mallard's literary legacy."

Priscilla picked up. "So Bradley whacks Lauria."

"Yeah," Rizzo responded. "And he grabs all the incriminatin' evidence he could find in the apartment, all the copies of Lauria's play. Only he misses that box of rejection letters, and he never even knows about the duplicate manuscripts in Carbone's garage in Canarsie."

"But Bradley knows enough about the business to realize something like that *could* exist somewhere," Priscilla suggested.

"Yeah, and he also knows a full-blown motive-based homicide investigation could turn it up, so he makes Lauria's murder look like a break-in, just a random killing."

Priscilla interjected, "But he still can't relax. Mallard might still try and reach out to Lauria in response to that letter. Bradley figures if Mallard learns Lauria's been conveniently murdered, the shit could still hit the fan."

Rizzo continued. "So Bradley figures Mallard's washed up anyway, been dried out for ten years already. Bradley can best protect himself by killin' Mallard. That explains the time frame of the two murders. He had to act fast, so he kills Lauria on the thirtieth of October, Mallard on November second. Then he uses that DeMaris dame to alibi him for the one murder the cops would question him on: Mallard's. Nice and neat."

"So when do you figure they'll be fishin' DeMaris outta the river?" Priscilla asked.

"No, Cil, not gonna happen," Rizzo said, shaking his head. "He whacks her—he's the married man, she's the *goumada*—and he becomes number one on the suspect hit parade. Once his alibi witness turns up dead, Manhattan South starts takin' another look at the Mallard case, only now with Bradley the target." He smiled. "This is real life. The only people find themselves involved in different murders all the time are TV characters on those old shows like *Murder She Wrote* and *Diagnosis Murder*. No, DeMaris is safe for now. Maybe not indefinitely, but at least for now."

"This is great, Joe," Priscilla said in frustration. "We solve both cases, but we can't write a freakin' dis-con summons on the evidence we have, let alone prosecute some showbiz hot shot for a double homicide."

"Yeah, tell me about it," Rizzo said. "We've got zero chance for an indictment. Tomorrow, we'll go talk to Bradley. Rattle his cage a little. We play dumb on the DeMaris angle at first, like we never saw the confidential part of his statement where I bet DeMaris is named as the alibi, and we don't know she's relevant. Then we drop her name on him and let the guy simmer a few days over Thanksgivin'. After that . . . we'll see."

Priscilla pursed her lips. "What about Manhattan South, Joe? We been stringin' D'Antonio along with our verbals and vague DD-fives, but now we might have to come clean."

"Bullshit," Rizzo said. "All we got is a lead on the Lauria case. That's *our* case, Cil. And we're just too stupid to make the Mallard connection."

Priscilla looked skeptical. "We're jugglin' hand grenades here, Partner."

"Maybe," Rizzo said. "And if one of the pins falls out, we might have to run for cover. But for now, it's okay. Believe me, Cil, stupidity is always your best defense on this job. There's no regulation says a cop can't be too stupid to see the nose on his face."

"This is not just about covering our asses," she said. "You gotta see that, for Christ's sake. If we screw up here, even a little bit, somebody gets killed. I know you think you can handle this—"

"No, Cil, I don't *think*. I *know*. Believe me, if I start having doubts, we'll bring it to Manhattan. But like I said before, it's not like we're riskin' some innocent citizen. DeMaris is part of this, she's dirty, same as Bradley. *She* put her ass on the line here, not me."

"Even if you're right about that," Priscilla said, "there could be something else, some angle we're not seeing. Maybe some citizen *is* at risk here. I'm just saying—"

But Rizzo was adamant. "I know what you're sayin'. You either trust me on this or you don't. I told you before I'd leave it up to you, and I'm telling you now I can handle this. *We* can handle this. Manhattan South isn't some magic bullet gonna solve this overnight. Hell, by the time we fill them in and they get up to speed, whoever the fuck you're so worried about can already be dead. We're close to the end here, Cil, believe me. The safest way to go now is for us to stay on course. The time to turn this over to Manhattan may come, but for now we're committed. We just need to ride it out."

After a moment she responded. "Okay, Joe. I'll stick with it if you say it's still cool. But try to remember, I can't retire in less than a year like you're gonna do. I need this job. And the last place I want to end up is in state prison with blood on my hands."

"I hear you," said Rizzo as he dug his cigarettes out of the glove compartment. "Just for your information, though, me and Mike had a very similar conversation back around August or so." He turned to her, winking.

"And look at Mikey now. Plaza big shot with fancy new suits and everything."

AT FIVE o'clock that afternoon, Rizzo sat at the desk in his basement office, cell phone in hand. McQueen answered on the third ring.

"Hello, Mike," Rizzo said. "I'm glad I caught you home."

"Yeah, well, I was just about ready to leave," McQueen said. "My folks are coming in for Thanksgiving. I'm on my way to pick them up at the airport."

"Okay. This'll only take a minute."

"I'm listening."

"The Mallard file, the one you downloaded for us. There's a statement in there from a Thomas Bradley. The guy's married, and he alibied himself with a girlfriend he was supposedly bangin' at the Marriott Marquis. The cop from Manhattan South confidentialed it to protect the guy. The downloaded copy was censored, referred to the girlfriend as 'companion,' then, at the end where she was named, it was blacked out. And the reports on her interview were censored, too."

"So?" Mike asked. "Is it important?"

"I wouldn't be burnin' up my weekday minutes if it wasn't, Mikey. I need you to take a deeper look into the file for me. I wanna know if the alibi witness is a broad named Linda DeMaris. If it's not her, get me the name and contact info for whoever it is."

"Okay, I can do that easy enough," McQueen answered. "I'll call you tomorrow with it."

"Thanks," Rizzo said.

"So what's the latest?" McQueen asked. "Is this going anywhere?"

"Oh, yeah, Mikey, that it is. Just make sure you keep your hair trimmed, they might be takin' your picture sooner than we figured."

McQueen laughed drily. "I just hope it's not for a fuckin' mug shot."

"What is it about you young cops?" Rizzo asked. "Cil's shakin' in her boots, too."

McQueen sighed. "I'll call you tomorrow, Joe."

"Okay, kid, tomorrow."

CHAPTER TWENTY-ONE

EARLY MONDAY EVENING, Carol Rizzo swung her ten-year-old Civic into the driveway of the Rizzo home. She parked in front of the small, detached garage beside her father's Camry. Switching off the engine, Carol stretched out her arms, weary from the traffic-clogged two-and-a-half-hour drive from the Stony Brook campus on Long Island's north shore.

Entering the house, she was surprised by her father as he came through the basement door and into the kitchen.

"Hey, hon," he said in greeting. "We didn't expect you till tomorrow."

Carol shrugged, crossing the room to exchange a perfunctory kiss with him. "I left early," she said. "I only have one class tomorrow—sociology. The other two were canceled for Thanksgiving break, but my soc professor refused to capitulate to the crass celebration of the exploitation of indigenous peoples."

Rizzo smiled, reaching out to brush brown strands of hair from his daughter's face.

"So you canceled him. Good for you," he said. "Welcome home."

Carol dropped her travel bag to the floor and walked to the refrigerator, removing a Snapple. She opened the bottle and turned to face her father.

"So," she said, injecting a casual tone into her voice. "When is Marie due home?"

"Wednesday. I'm picking her up at Grand Central. Maybe you can take a ride with me."

Carol shook her head. As she crossed the kitchen to the travel bag, lifting it from the floor, she twisted her lips as she spoke.

"Doubtful," she said. Then she left the room, making her way toward the staircase and the small upstairs bedroom she shared with her sister Jessica.

Rizzo shook his head slowly, running a hand through his hair.

"Damn," he said softly.

THOMAS ROSS Bradley was forty-nine years old, a native of the section of London known as Kingston-on-Thames. After a voluntary stint as a British Army Commando with Special Air Services, he had pursued, with assistance from his wealthy, influential family, a career as a producer of London theater. He had emigrated to New York City fifteen years earlier, carrying with him a stellar reputation in the theater world and finding quick success with a string of Broadway shows, followed by a rather rocky and unproductive five-year period, which had come to an end with the success of Avery Mallard's *An Atlanta Landscape*.

Bradley gazed across his neat, glistening black desk to Rizzo and Jackson, his gray eyes clear and probing. It was Tuesday morning, November 25.

"There's no need to be apologetic, Sergeant Rizzo," he said in the clipped accent of the British upper class. "I'm fully aware of the complexities in the nature of your work. I would imagine follow-up interviews are often necessary." He paused, looking from one to the other. "This would be my third interview, Sergeant," he said. "May I feel confident this one will suffice?"

Rizzo shrugged, taking out his notepad and pen. "Yeah, let's hope."

Bradley sat back in his seat, his expression stoic.

"Yes," he said. "Let us hope." He paused before continuing. "I'm afraid I must insist on brevity, Sergeant. I've an appointment of rather great importance in less than an hour's time."

Rizzo shrugged. "If you're gonna insist on it, then you better tell me what it is," he said with a smile. "Brevity, I mean."

Bradley's eyes moved from one detective to the other, then fell on Rizzo. His own smile appeared forced as he replied.

"Conciseness, Sergeant," he said pleasantly. "Condensation of language. I'm in a bit of a push, you see. Short of time."

Rizzo nodded. "Oh," he said, slowly turning to Priscilla. "Did you know that, Cil?" he asked. "Did you know what 'brevity' meant?"

"Yes," she said with a shrug, her eyes on Bradley.

Rizzo nodded again. "That works for us, too. Now we can skip all the polite public relations bullshit and get down to the questions." He leaned inward toward Bradley. "Fair enough?"

"Yes, Sergeant," Bradley replied. "Quite fair."

Rizzo flipped open his pad. By coincidence, the notebook fell open to the page where, earlier that morning, he had made a notation of what McQueen had reported: Bradley's uncensored statement to Detective Lieutenant Dominick Lombardi, Manhattan South, confirmed that Linda DeMaris was Bradley's mistress as well as his alibi witness.

Rizzo raised his eyes once again to meet Bradley's. It was time to begin rattling the man's cage.

"So, you're from England, eh?"

"Yes. Kingston-on-Thames."

"Where's that?"

"In London, Sergeant."

Rizzo nodded. "Really? Must be quite a fancy neighborhood."

Bradley arched his eyebrows. "Oh?"

Rizzo shrugged. "Well, you ask most people where they're from, they say, New York, Chicago, Paris, like that. You said Kingston-on-the-whatever, not just London. So I'm guessin' it's a fancy place, a place you're proud of."

"Yes, Sergeant," Bradley answered with a tight smile. "I do take pride in it, actually. However, in Great Britain, it's common practice to refer to one's locale quite specifically. A cultural practice, if you will."

"Is Ms. DeMaris in?" Rizzo asked.

Bradley blinked. "Pardon?"

"Linda DeMaris," Rizzo repeated. "Your personal assistant. Is she here today, at work somewhere around the office?"

Bradley shook his head, his face without expression. "No, she's taking today off."

"Sick day?" Rizzo asked. "Vacation? What?"

Bradley remained silent, holding Rizzo's eyes. Rizzo smiled at him.

"You wanted brevity?" He shrugged. "I'm figurin' this is it."

Still expressionless, Bradley answered. "Ms. DeMaris worked all day yesterday, Sergeant. At the theater as well as here in the office. It was a very long day. So, in compensation, she is not working today."

"Okay," Rizzo said, jotting in his pad.

With a frown, Bradley spoke once again. "Just what is your interest in Ms. DeMaris, Sergeant?" he asked, his accented tones sounding cool.

"Interest?" Rizzo asked, looking up from his notes.

"Yes, Sergeant. Interest."

"Nothin' special," Rizzo said. "Just followin' the same lead to her that we followed to you."

Bradley laid his hands palms down on his desk and leaned forward. Annoyance tugged at his facial muscles as concern dawned in his eyes. Rizzo took notice, still smiling benignly.

"Perhaps you should explain yourself, Sergeant. What is this 'lead' you mention?"

"Well," Rizzo responded, cocking his head to one side. "Do you know a guy named Samuel Kellerman?"

Bradley's brow furrowed, and he sat back in his seat. "Sam? Yes, of course, I know Sam very well. He's a dear friend, in fact."

"Really?" Rizzo said, raising his brows. "Funny, he didn't put it like that when we spoke to him."

Bradley's eyes narrowed, and Rizzo noted slight color come into the man's cheeks.

"Sergeant," he said, glancing pointedly to the Rolex on his wrist. "I must insist you get to whatever point it is you are here to make. As I told you, I have an appointment. If it becomes absolutely apparent that I must, I shall call Lieutenant Lombardi, whom I assume to be your superior officer, and have him intercede in this. I have had his assurance that certain factual information I provided to him is confidential and for his eyes only, and now you are indicating that . . ."

Rizzo held up a hand, palm outward, his smile turning cold. "Take a beat, Bradley, okay? I'm just doin' my job, that's all. I don't even know this Lombardi guy, and I don't know what you're talkin' about with 'confidential.'"

Bradley's face flushed, his effort to maintain composure becoming obvious. "Explain yourself, Sergeant," he said, his voice tight with surpressed anger.

Rizzo nodded, lowering his hand, allowing his smile to fade.

"Sure. And as you requested, with brevity." He cleared his throat and began. "We're workin' this Brooklyn case, and Kellerman's name comes up, so me and Detective Jackson here, we follow it up. It leads us to a few other people—you, for instance. And this DeMaris woman who works for you. And so, here we are."

Bradley's expression remained neutral as he looked from one detective to the other. Priscilla remained silent, allowing Rizzo to play his line out.

"Brooklyn case?" Bradley asked. "I had assumed you were here inquiring into Avery Mallard's murder."

"Oh?" Rizzo asked. "What gave you that idea?"

Bradley shook his head. "Well, when you called to set up this appointment, you identified yourself as a police officer, so I assumed—"

Rizzo looked up. "I couldn't help but notice that picture, Mr. Bradley," he said, indicating with a tilt of his head a black-and-white, eight-by-ten photo hanging on the wall to his left. "You in that fancy combat uniform. See, once, when I was in the Army, I had this sergeant, tough old son of a bitch, tell me, 'Young man,' he said, 'never assume *nothin*'.'" Rizzo leaned forward.

"Didn't they ever tell you that, Mr. Bradley?" he asked in a low, threatening tone. "In the service, I mean?"

Bradley glanced at the photo showing him in full S.A.S. Commando combat dress, face darkened with grease, automatic assault weapon in hand, his eyes shadowed by the Kevlar-and-steel helmet on his head.

"What is this inquiry about, Sergeant?" he asked softly.

Rizzo continued. "Like I say, we have this case in Brooklyn we're investigatin'. Some sad-sack semirecluse type got himself murdered. Looks like just a break-in, same as what happened to Mallard. We found somethin' in the guy's apartment leads us to Kellerman. He was Mallard's agent, matter-of-fact. See, that's why it don't pay to start makin' assumptions, Mr. Bradley." Rizzo smiled. "Like, for instance, I could start figuring Kellerman's involved here somehow. In both murders, maybe. Only that would be an assumption, and my old drill sergeant, he was pretty friggin' clear about that: you assume, you make an ass outta you and me."

Bradley became impatient. "How am *I* relevant here, Sergeant? *Please* explain yourself."

Rizzo shook his head. "Far as I can see, you aren't relevant," he said. "We're just takin' a look around Kellerman and his associates, that's all. He mentioned you're the producer of Mallard's last work, this play on Broadway. What's it called, Cil?"

"*Atlanta Landscape*," Priscilla replied.

"Yeah, right." He looked back to Bradley. "I hear it's pretty good."

Bradley nodded. "A typically American understatement. This play is a very serious work of art, Sergeant, rendered even more remarkable when you consider its contemporaries currently in production. Restagings of tired musicals from other eras, mindless chronicles of faded pop stars, recycled film works, and even, God help us, comic book characters." He smiled sadly. "*An Atlanta Landscape* is Broadway at its best, Sergeant. *Theater* at its best, as it was meant to be, not merely drivel designed to amuse tourists from Iowa and God knows where else. This work rates amongst *All My Sons, The Iceman Cometh, The Glass Menagerie, Angels in America.*"

"Yeah," Rizzo said, nodding. "I saw those movies."

Bradley looked at Rizzo, his lips pursing. He shook his head. "I fear the death of Avery Mallard is a tragedy unfathomable by the superficial fabric of your rather sad American culture, Sergeant," he said. "Now, if it had been some bubbleheaded blonde pop singer in between rehabilitations, *that* would be considered a true American tragedy, I've no doubt." He shook his head once more. "That would be something you people could take to heart."

Rizzo laughed. "You know, it amazes me how many foreigners I run into bitchin' about the U.S." He allowed a moment to pass, then continued. "Makes a guy wonder, how come they're over here bitchin'? Why didn't they just stay the fuck home, where everything was so perfect?"

With growing anger, Bradley responded. "Once again, Sergeant, get to your business. My appointment cannot be delayed."

"Okay, relax," Rizzo said. "Here we go: Kellerman ever mention a guy named Robert Lauria to you? A shoe salesman from Brooklyn?"

Bradley shook his head, his face now without expression. "No," he said.

Rizzo smiled. "Just like that? 'No'? You don't even have to think about it?"

"No, Sergeant. I do not have to think about it. Sam never mentioned *any* shoe salesman to me. From anywhere."

"Maybe in some other context, some other reference? Robert Lauria." Rizzo spelled the last name.

"No. Never."

"Okay," Rizzo said, as he wrote in his pad.

"What's the connection between Sam Kellerman and this murdered shoe salesman, Sergeant?" Bradley asked.

Rizzo looked up from his notepad. "Oh, that's kinda confidential, Mr. Bradley," he said lightly. "You know, like whatever you got goin' with your lieutenant, that guy Lombardi." He paused. "And did I say Lauria was the murder victim? I don't remember saying that." He shrugged. "Guess you're assumin' again. Only this time . . . you happen to be right."

Bradley did not respond.

"I understand you helped Mallard out with writing that play," Rizzo said. "That *Atlanta* thing."

"Your understanding being based on what information exactly, Sergeant?"

"Oh, I dunno. Something Kellerman said, I think."

Priscilla interjected. "It had something to do with the plot."

"I assure you, Officers, my only assistance with the script was in allowing Avery to utilize my cottage at Southampton while he crafted the play." He smiled coldly at Rizzo, then Jackson. "If I were capable of contributing to so majestic a work, I daresay I would author one myself."

"Where were you on October thirtieth?" Rizzo asked.

Bradley again looked from one to the other, settling his gaze on Rizzo. "Pardon?"

"Yeah," Rizzo said offhandedly. "That's when Lauria was probably killed, or maybe the twenty-ninth. Just a routine question, you know. I gotta ask it. For the record."

Bradley seemed to ponder matters for a moment. "I cannot answer that, Sergeant," he said coolly. "You're talking about nearly one month ago. I have no idea where I may have been."

"See, Cil?" Rizzo said, turning toward Priscilla. "It's like I said, who knows where they were a month ago? Nobody." He turned back to Bradley, lowering his voice, again leaning inward. "Kellerman knew where he was right away," Rizzo said. "Claimed to be in Paris at the time."

"I see," Bradley said.

Rizzo nodded. "Yeah, always gets my attention, these instant alibi answers. But you, you weren't sure. Had no idea where you were. Hell, I got no idea where *I* was those two days, either."

They sat silently for a moment before Rizzo continued.

"Well, Mr. Bradley, unless you can think a somethin' you wanna add about Kellerman, I guess we're done here."

Again Bradley made a point of looking at his wristwatch. "No, Sergeant. I have nothing further to add."

Rizzo stood, Jackson following his lead. He reached across the desk, shaking hands with the producer, noting the dryness of the man's palm.

"Thanks for your time," he said. "Maybe we'll stop by after the holiday, next week sometime. Just to have a word with—what's her name, your assistant?"

"Linda DeMaris," Bradley said, releasing Rizzo's hand.

"Yeah. DeMaris." Rizzo turned to leave. "We can find our own way out, Mr. Bradley," he said. "No need to get up."

"Fine," Bradley said. "Good day to you both."

"Yeah," Rizzo said on the way out. "And I hope your Lieutenant Lombardi finds Mallard's killer."

"Yes," Bradley said curtly, his eyes dark. "As do I."

At the door, Rizzo turned once more, remaining silent and making eye contact with Bradley, the gesture designed to prod the man to speak one last time, to impose a sudden and unwanted obligation on Bradley. Awkward seconds ticked by.

"And, Sergeant," Bradley finally said. "Good luck to you as well, with your Bensonhurst murder."

Rizzo smiled. "Oh, yeah," he said. "Thanks."

ON THEIR way out, Rizzo and Jackson stopped at the reception desk and showed Robert Lauria's photograph to the young woman there. She shook her head.

"No," she said. "I've never seen him here."

Afterward, the two detectives bought coffee from a shop in the building's lobby, then sat in the Impala on Fifth Avenue, drinking and reviewing their notes.

"Bradley's our killer, Cil," Rizzo said. "No fuckin' doubt about it."

Priscilla frowned. "He sure looks good, Joe, but *no doubt*? How you figure that?"

"Remember his little, 'In Great Britain we use our specific area, not just the city we live in,' bullshit?"

"Yeah, he's from Kingston, not just London. So what?"

Rizzo sipped his coffee. "Point of information," he said, "for when you're dealin' with a cool character like Bradley. And he *was* cool, believe me. His palm was dry as a stone in the desert, even after that completely unexpected dance around DeMaris and Lauria he had with us. See, guys like him, they think one step ahead, they anticipate, form their answers before they speak. They're not street skells, blurtin' out whatever bullshit pops into their heads. Not as a rule, anyway. He was one step ahead of my next question for most of the interview. But as we were leavin', I turned slow and stared at him. He's calm on the outside, but wound tight inside his chest. He sees me starin', he figures I'm gonna ask him somethin' else now, after he thought we were all done. And he can't imagine what I'm gonna say. So he's gotta buy himself some more time to think, and he finally *does* just say what pops into his head. Any damn small talk chitchat."

Priscilla furrowed her brow. A moment passed, then her eyes widened. Rizzo smiled, again sipping his coffee.

"Holy fuck, Joe," she said softly. "*Bensonhurst*. How did Bradley know Lauria got killed in Bensonhurst?"

"Bingo. The guy didn't even know we were from Brooklyn till I tole him, let alone Bensonhurst. And we never mentioned the Six-Two, either, not that some limey would know it's in Bensonhurst anyway. No, Cil, this guy's a foreigner, probably never been over to Brooklyn before, or if he has, just the trendy neighborhoods like The Heights and Park Slope. When he was plannin' Lauria's murder, he'd have resorted to what's native to him. He'd have checked a map of Brooklyn, maybe Googled Lauria's address. When he saw it was in Bensonhurst, from habit he mentally converted 'Brooklyn' to 'Bensonhurst.' Just like 'London' to 'Kingston-on-Thames.' Then, under the pressure of my parting stare, it slipped out, and he didn't even realize its significance."

Priscilla shook her head. "He's a double murderer," she said.

"Yeah, that he is," Rizzo said. "And from the getup he was wearin' in that photo on the wall, he was some kinda special forces guy, Royal Marines or S.A.S., somethin' like that. Bet he got plenty a training in strangulation. Piece a cake for Bradley to kill *these* two guys. Neither one of them was a tough guy, that's for sure."

Priscilla nodded. "And did you see that suit he was wearing, Joe? Musta set him back a grand, at least. Outta the four of 'em—Kellerman, the director, the neighbor, and Bradley—he's the most upscale dresser. A guy like him would definitely own a high-priced raincoat."

"Yeah," Rizzo agreed. "Like every other well-off London dude."

"So why'd you piss him off so much, Joe?"

He smiled. "Mostly 'cause I could. He figured me for some not-too-bright reactionary cop type. I could see it in his smug expression.

I didn't wanna disappoint the prick. Plus, it made it easier for me to switch gears, rattle him, maybe force a slipup."

"Yeah, let him get all comfortable with that," she said. "This way, when we shove the arrest warrant down his throat, he'll never see it coming."

"Yeah," Rizzo said softly, "but we're a long way from an arrest warrant, Cil. We got a ton of circumstantial evidence, enough to convince most people Bradley's our man. But it's still not worth much in a courtroom. We can't *prove* anything. Not yet."

Priscilla countered, "But we throw a fiber match from his raincoat onto that pile of circumstantial, we got a conviction."

"Yeah," Rizzo said. "But we need a search warrant to get to the coat. And I can't see a judge signin' one. Not based on what we got so far."

"I disagree," Priscilla said. "We got a clear track for Lauria's play to Bradley through DeMaris. We got the Bensonhurst comment, and we got Bradley's ties, motives, means, and opportunities on both Lauria's *and* Mallard's killings."

"Normally I might take all that to a judge," Rizzo said. "Take a shot, cut DeMaris a lesser charge. She takes back that alibi, Bradley sinks with Lauria's *Solitary Vessel*. But we go to a judge with the Mallard tie-in now, we risk losin' it all to Manhattan South. We need to work it just from the Lauria angle, which is too weak for a warrant. Or we gotta have an open-and-shut slam-dunk against Bradley on *both* homicides."

"Sounds kinda tough."

"Yeah, it should. It *is* tough, but I'm thinkin', what's Bradley's next move?"

Priscilla thought for a moment. "He has to warn DeMaris. Or kill her."

"Exactly. He's gotta protect himself before we talk to her some time next week, like I told him we'd do. He's got to make sure she's prepared to stonewall us. We don't know how deep she is in all this. We can certainly figure she stole the play from her former job and gave it to Bradley. She knows it's plagiarized. Then she alibied Bradley for the night of the Mallard killing, so she probably knows, or damn well *should* know, he's the one killed Mallard. She may not know about the threat Lauria posed, although why would she think Bradley had to kill Mallard unless she also knew Lauria had turned up claimin' he was ripped off?"

"Whatever she does know," Priscilla said, "she's up to her freakin' eyeballs in this whole mess."

Rizzo sipped at his coffee. "And Bradley has to get her past the interview with us. An interview he figures'll only focus on Lauria, and maybe Kellerman."

A worried look came to Priscilla. "I hope we didn't just sign De-Maris's death warrant, Joe. If Bradley sees her as the weak link, he might just decide she's gotta go, too, and right now."

Rizzo nodded. "Sure. As awkward a position as that would put him in—connecting him to three murders—he might figure it's better than her bein' out there with too much information and maybe not enough balls to stand up."

Priscilla shrugged. "Well, we haven't even met the woman yet, Joe. Maybe she does have the balls."

"Could be," Rizzo said. "Maybe *she's* the spark plug here, and he's just the piston. But either way, his best chance of survival might be for her to stop breathin'."

"So how should we play it?" Priscilla asked, uneasily. "We're on thin enough ice as it is, sidestepping Manhattan. We get some woman killed, we're really in deep shit. Maybe now's the time to bring it in, go to this Lieutenant Lombardi. We lay it all out for him and maybe he cuts us in for a piece of the credit. If we don't, this DeMaris maybe gets killed."

"She ain't exactly the Virgin Mary, Cil. She's an accomplice to murder. Maybe two murders." Rizzo hesitated. "Wouldn't break my heart if she did get whacked, but I see your point. That's why I figure we keep this on a short leash. We're off tomorrow, the next day is Thanksgiving. I don't see Bradley doin' anything rash. His history shows he's a careful planner, not a spur-of-the-moment killer, and he needs a new plan—he can't use that break-in routine again. He'll warn DeMaris, then assess the risk. If he decides to murder her, it won't be on Thanksgiving. Even though he's a limey, and probably doesn't give a rat's ass about the holiday, he's been here long enough to have someplace he's gotta be for turkey dinner—some friends or business associates, whoever. And DeMaris, she's the *goumada*—*goumada*s hafta spend their holidays single, tellin' themselves by this time next year, Mr. Dreamboat will have left his wife and filed for divorce. Yeah, next Thanksgiving everything'll be just peachy. But for this year, it's back to Momma's or Aunt Tillie's or whoever. No, Cil, I figure she's safe for at least a few days. We'll go see her on Friday."

Priscilla compressed her lips. "Seems a little risky to me, Joe. I don't know."

"Yeah, well, like my daughter Carol says, anything worthwhile is hard." He shrugged. "Let's chance it. It'll be okay."

Reluctantly, she agreed. "All right, I guess . . . But Jesus, I can't see myself getting too much sleep until this is over with. When we do see her, how should we play it?"

"Oh, I got a plan, Cil. I'm gonna let it percolate in my head a couple a days, then we'll talk about it."

He drained his coffee container, then tossed it to the floorboard in the rear of the car. He started the engine and smiled at Priscilla.

"We will talk about it, Partner," he said. "Believe me."

"Okay," Priscilla said. "But if DeMaris turns out to be a cool character like Bradley, this could be a tough play."

Rizzo pulled the car out into traffic. "Yeah, well, I wouldn't worry about it. Chances are, she'll turn out to be just another self-absorbed yuppie found a way to grab herself a new BMW with her stolen play idea. She probably never figured she was signin' on for two murders. My money says, we slap her around a little, she caves."

Priscilla shook her head. "Too bad Bradley didn't just put his own name on the damn play," she said. "At least then, Avery Mallard would still be alive."

Rizzo nodded. "Yeah. But you heard what Bradley said. Most of the big Broadway shows are revivals, or bio plays about Frankie Vallie or Sinatra. I'm thinkin', that kinda stuff comes with guaranteed audiences, so it makes it easy for a producer to raise money. That's why Bradley never approached Lauria in the first place. Like we figured, he knew he'd never hit a home run, make millions on a show with Lauria's name on it, no matter how good it was. And his own name wouldn't be much better. But with *Mallard* bein' the playwright, Bradley sees a built-in audience and knows he can easily raise enough dough to produce the thing, and it's Broadway here we come."

"Yeah. I forgot that," she said.

"Well, relax, kiddo," Rizzo said. "It's almost over, so don't be losing any sleep over DeMaris. Your biggest worry right now is my mother."

Priscilla looked puzzled.

"Yeah," Rizzo said. "My mother." He turned to face her. "You gotta come up with some sorta answer."

Priscilla shook her head. "Answer for what?"

"For Thanksgiving when she asks you and Karen, 'How come two nice girls like you aren't married?'"

CHAPTER TWENTY-TWO

THE TABLE IN THE RIZZO DINING ROOM, its two extension leaves in place, ran nearly the entire length of the room. Joe Rizzo sat at the head of the table, his back to the breakfront. Jennifer was to his right, closest to the kitchen, daughters Marie and Jessica to her right. Priscilla Jackson sat to Joe's left beside Karen Krauss and the youngest Rizzo girl, Carol. At the table's end were the two family matriarchs—Joe's mother, Marie Rizzo, and Jennifer's mother, Jessica Falco.

"Take more antipasto," Grandma Falco said, waving her fork at Karen. "Have some prosciutto and some provolone."

Karen, platter in hand, smiled. "Yes, well, alright," she said. "Maybe just a bit more."

Jennifer smiled. "Easy, Mom, it's a long day, there's a ton of food . . ."

She shrugged. "I'm just sayin'," she said. "She's so skinny, she should eat."

"Mom," Jennifer said, a warning in her tone.

"Look," Grandma Falco said. "Look what she's taking: an artichoke heart, two olives, one stalk of celery, and a couple of peppers." She shrugged, holding her shoulders high, almost to ear level. "What is she, a rabbit?" She turned back to Karen. "There's capicola there, and caponata. Take some pepperoni—it's imported."

"They're all skinny," Grandma Rizzo said, shaking her head. "Look at our granddaughters, Jessica, they're the same way." She placed a slice of provolone in her mouth. "Skinny, like long drinks of water."

Joe laughed. "Just take what you want, Karen, but save room for the manicotti and the meats."

"Not to mention the turkey," Carol said.

Priscilla took the offered antipasto platter from Karen, forking generous portions onto her plate. "This stuff is great, Mrs. Falco," she said. "You don't have to encourage me."

"You're too skinny, too," Falco said matter-of-factly.

Rizzo's daughter Marie leaned forward from opposite Karen. "I imagine you guys didn't realize that the Pilgrims *had* antipasto for Thanksgiving," she said, "not to mention manicotti, sausage, meat-balls, and braciole."

"I made the meats," Falco interjected. "You'll tell me if you like them."

"And I made the manicotti and the gravy," Grandma Rizzo said.

Marie smiled at Karen and Priscilla. "She means sauce. She made the tomato sauce."

"Yeah, Ma," Joe said. "The Ameri-cahns call it sauce. Gravy's for the turkey. Brown."

Joe's mother waved a hand at him. "Stop talking and eat."

He laughed, shaking his head. "One thing I said," he told Jennifer. "One thing."

Jennifer sipped her wine, then turned to Karen. "Joe tells me that you're an attorney."

"Yes," Karen said. "Corporate law. I'm mostly involved in acquisitions and mergers, conforming out-of-state business structuring to New York law, things like that."

Now daughter Jessica asked, "Do you go to court much, Karen?"

"God, no," Karen replied. "In fact, the only times I've ever been in a courtroom were to watch Cil testify on some of her cases. Professionally, I have no need to be in a courthouse."

Grandma Falco leaned over, speaking in her version of a whisper to Joe's mother.

"They send the men to court," she said.

"Mom," Jennifer said, again with a warning in her tone.

Priscilla spoke up. "This antipasto is *awesome*," she said. "Who put this together?"

"The girls did that," Jennifer said. "They've been doing it every Thanksgiving since they were young kids."

Grandma Rizzo spoke up. "I taught them how to make it," she said. "But they never use *ah-leech*. It's not as good without *ah-leech*."

Priscilla noticed Karen's look of puzzlement.

"Anchovies," she said softly. "*Ah-leech* is Brooklyn-Italian slang for anchovies."

Karen nodded. "Oh," she said.

"*Scommetto che quella le mangierebbe*," Joe's mother said to Jennifer's mother in low tones, referring to Priscilla.

Joe shook his head. "No Italian, Mom. It's rude."

"I won't talk," she said, shrugging and feigning insult.

He nodded. "Good idea, probably."

Later, with simmering plates of pasta, sausage, meatballs, and pork braciole dominating the table, Priscilla gave a hearty laugh.

"I had no idea the Pilgrims ate this good, Joe," she said.

"Yeah, well," Rizzo countered, "the Indians probably brought this stuff. I don't think the Pilgrims were noted for their cuisine."

Grandma Falco spoke up. "No, but the Italians are."

Grandma Rizzo chimed in. "And for their art, and their literature, and science, engineering, medicine—"

Carol broke in. "And their mobsters."

Grandma Falco shook her head. "Never mind, Carol, we get hit on the head enough with that from television and books. And from the movies. If it was anybody else, there'd be lawsuits, riots, and God knows what else."

"Okay, Mom," Jennifer said.

"No," Grandma Rizzo interjected, "your mother is right, Jennifer. It's not okay. She's right to say it." She glared at Carol. "And you, you be quiet. You bring that up in front of strangers?"

"They ain't strangers, Ma," Joe said gently. "Priscilla's my partner."

Grandma Rizzo spooned manicotti onto her plate and reached for the gravy boat. "But still not family," she said. "And don't say 'ain't.' What are you, a *strattone*?"

Joe turned to Priscilla and Karen. "The secret to an Italian Thanksgiving dinner is in the pacing," he said. "One dish of antipasto, two manicottis, a couple of meatballs, a little braciole and sauseech, a few pieces of Italian bread. Then we take a break, watch a little football before the turkey comes out." He shrugged. "Turkey's overrated, anyway. Best way to eat turkey is tomorrow, in a semolina hero, with mayo and provolone and roasted peppers."

"I was around eighteen before I even tried a piece of turkey on Thanksgiving Day," young Jessica said. "By the time it would come to the table, I was always full."

Grandma Falco snorted. "Turkey," she said. "Ameri-cahn." Then she glanced sheepishly at Karen. "Which is good, too. But . . . try my braciole. Go ahead, try it. Then you'll see." She shook her head. "Turkey," she repeated, baffled.

"So," Carol said to Karen, "when did you and Cil meet?"

Karen smiled. "About two and a half years ago."

Grandma Rizzo muttered. "Oh, *ma-don*," she said.

Priscilla smiled down the table toward her. "This manicotti is unbelievable," she said. "Best I've ever had."

The elderly woman's face lit up. "Really? You think so?" she said. "Take another piece, don't listen to my son, you can have more than two, there's plenty. I made extra."

"I may just do that, Mrs. Rizzo," Priscilla said.

Beaming, Grandma Rizzo waved a hand at Priscilla. "Eat, eat, and call me Marie, dear. Please."

Priscilla broadened her smile. "Like Joe's oldest? Marie?"

She nodded proudly. "Yes. My granddaughter, the doctor."

"Not yet, Grandma Rizzo," Marie said. "Not quite yet."

Jennifer's mother leaned forward. "And Jessica is named after me," she added. "Try the meatballs, Priscilla," she added. "They're delicious. *I* made them."

LATER, WHILE coffee and dessert were being prepared in the kitchen and Joe dozed in his recliner in the den, Carol, Karen, and Priscilla gathered in the living room.

"It doesn't make sense, Cil," Carol said, her face set in anger. "He works with a female cop every day, then he tells me it's not a job for a woman. And after a lifetime of listening to him preach about equal opportunity . . . Apparently it was all just bullshit."

"Carol, your father means well," Priscilla said. "Believe me, his heart's in the right place. And to tell you the truth, if *I* had a kid, girl or boy, I'd probably steer him away, too. It's not the right choice for a lot of people. It's complicated. It's not just about male or female. And what he's not telling you is, he's just plain scared. Afraid you'll get hurt, shot maybe. He doesn't want to say it. A lot of old-time cops believe saying it out loud is a jinx. Believe me, he's scared."

Karen added, "Cil and I may have a child of our own someday, and I wouldn't want to see him or her become a police officer, either. Your father only has your best interest at heart."

"And what *I* want isn't important?" Carol said.

"Nobody's even suggestin' that," Priscilla said calmly. "That's just your defensiveness talking. But here's what I think you should do: hear your father out, weigh what he's got to say. And keep in mind, he's tryin' to do right by you, his motives are good. You know, after all those years on the job, Joe knows what he's talking about. Hear him out, and you respect his opinion." She shrugged. "But keep in mind, it's your life. Ultimately, *you* gotta decide. And when you do, he'll go along with it, either way."

Carol leaned forward. "What about you, Cil? Do you regret having become a cop?"

"Not for one second," Priscilla said with a smile. "Your old man would ring my neck if he heard me tell you this, but the truth is this is the greatest job on the planet. I love it."

Priscilla reached out and patted Carol's knee. "I think I know this guy, Carol," she said, "in ways you never can, bein' his daughter and all."

She leaned back on the couch, pursing her lips. "When all is said and done, if you come on the job, he'll be there for you. I guarantee it."

LATER THAT evening, after the guests had gone, Rizzo went down to his basement office, cell phone in hand. He sat behind the desk, taking a Nicorette from his pocket, absentmindedly calculating the remaining hours before morning when he would once again have access to the Impala and its secret glove compartment stash.

Rummaging through the desk, he found his phone book containing the number he needed.

The call was picked up on the third ring.

"Hello?" he heard.

"Hello, Dan, Joe Rizzo here. From the Sixty-second Precinct."

There was a pause. "Hello, Joe, how are you?" the man said. "Is everything all right?"

"Yeah, Dan, couldn't be better. How was your Thanksgiving?"

"Great, just great. And yours?"

"Perfect," Rizzo said.

"Glad to hear it, Joe. So what can I do for you?" Dan asked, a slight tone of resignation barely apparent.

"You're still with the *Daily News,* right?" Rizzo asked.

"Yeah. My seventeenth year."

"I thought I still saw your byline." After a slight pause, Rizzo continued, his voice pleasant, his tone even.

"So, Dan, remember that little favor I did for you couple a years back? You know, with your son?"

Rizzo could hear a slight sigh come through the line. "Of course. How could I ever forget that?"

"Yeah, well, I guessed you would remember," Rizzo said in the same pleasant manner. "See, at the time you said how grateful you were, how if there was ever anything you could do, I shouldn't hesitate to call."

"Yeah, Joe, I remember."

"So I can assume you meant that?"

"Yes. Of course I did."

Rizzo smiled into the phone. "Okay then," he said. "So, here's the thing . . ."

CHAPTER TWENTY-THREE

AT EIGHT-THIRTY THE FOLLOWING MORNING, traffic was lighter than usual as Priscilla Jackson drove the Impala toward Manhattan.

"I still say there's a good chance DeMaris won't be home when we get there, even if she is still breathing," Priscilla said to Rizzo. "Friday after Thanksgiving, long four-day weekend."

"Maybe," he said, "but we know the office is closed, so she isn't workin' today. Like I told you when we went to the literary agencies, it's best we catch this broad cold, unannounced. It'll scare her." He paused before continuing. "And that's how we want her—*scared*. The scareder the better."

"*Scare-der*?" Priscilla asked. "You mean *more* scared?"

"Yeah, okay, Professor, whatever the fuck," Rizzo replied. "You get my point. See, by now Bradley had to warn her we're comin', but not until next week sometime, so he probably hasn't face-to-faced with her yet to firm up her story. If we catch Ms. DeMaris in her hair curlers and skivvies, cup of coffee in her hand, her blood pressure is gonna spike, Cil, believe me."

"So: bad cop / worse cop?" Priscilla asked.

"Yeah, like we discussed," he said, enjoying himself. "If she proves to be what most murder-for-profit people are—a spoiled, conniving, self-centered bastard—we lean on her hard. Both of us."

Priscilla responded. "Which one am I?"

Rizzo pondered it for a moment. "Bad cop," he said. "I know the script a little better'n you do, so I'll be worse cop."

"Okay, boss, whatever you say. I just hope we don't find this chick lyin' on her kitchen floor with her eyeballs poppin' out."

As she accelerated onto the Williamsburg Bridge, Priscilla was silent. After a few moments, she said, "Imagine the luck of this poor guy Lauria? There had to be—what?—six, seven book-length manuscripts in his apartment? Plus God knows how many short stories? Thousands of freakin' pages."

"Yeah," Rizzo said. "So?"

Priscilla shook her head. "So he decides to write *one* damn play, and it winds up a big smash under some other guy's name, Mallard's name. *And* it gets them both killed."

She turned to face Rizzo briefly. "Lauria couldn't get anything published in over twenty years of writing. Then, his play hits the big time, and he's dead. It's just sad, man. Really sad."

Rizzo pondered it. "Well, I guess. Sad life, sad death. Some guys get dealt a hand like that. And who knows, maybe some of those other books a his are just as good as the play's supposed to be. If we learned anything from this case, it was that it helps to have some big name on a play if you're lookin' to get it produced." He shrugged. "Maybe it's the same with getting a book published. Maybe we should take one of Lauria's manuscripts and put Norman Mailer's name on it, hype it up like a newly discovered work of a deceased American master. We might come up with a best seller."

Priscilla pursed her lips. "If we can tie Lauria's murder to Mallard's, and it breaks big in the news, Lauria gets his fifteen minutes. I oughta take those manuscripts to my agent, Robin Miller. Maybe the poor schmuck *will* get published after all."

"Or maybe we should just steal 'em," he suggested. "Put *your* name on them if they're any good. Better yet, put *my* friggin' name on them."

"We can do the same thing Bradley did, only this time everybody who needs killin' is already dead," Priscilla said.

"Yeah, Cil," Rizzo said. "We can be grave robbers."

They both laughed, and she added, "What other job can offer that kind of opportunity? And you tryin' to keep Carol away from all this fun."

He chuckled. "Yeah. Imagine that."

"Which reminds me," Priscilla said. "Yesterday at dinner, your mother said something in Italian to your mother-in-law. I got the impression it was about me. What'd she say?"

"You *sure* you wanna know, Cil?"

She shrugged. "Sure. I can take it."

Rizzo replied. "Okay. You had just explained to Karen that *ah-leech* is Brooklyn-Italian slang for anchovies."

Priscilla nodded. "I remember."

"Well," Rizzo said, "I think my mother had the impression your prim and proper WASPY girlfriend wouldn't put an anchovy in her mouth if her life depended on it."

"Yeah, probably right," Priscilla said. "So what'd she say in Italian?"

Rizzo laughed. "She said, referrin' to you, 'I bet *this* one would eat them.'"

Priscilla laughed. "Damn," she said. "Don't bother to explain, Joe. I get it."

THE FEAR in Linda DeMaris's eyes was reassuring, Rizzo thought, as he and Jackson sat across from her at the kitchen table in her small, Lower East Side apartment.

"Recognize that?" he asked deliberately, jutting his chin at the paper he had placed before DeMaris.

She dropped her eyes to the sheet of paper, color coming to her cheeks.

"Pick it up," he said softly. "Look at it."

DeMaris, thirty-seven years old with long, jet-black hair and large, beautiful brown eyes, reached a pale hand to the paper, her fingers trembling as she obeyed Rizzo's order.

"Recognize that?" Rizzo repeated.

Steadying the paper in both hands, she placed it back on the table. "No," she said.

Priscilla leaned forward. "No?" she said. "Did you just say 'no'?"

DeMaris nodded and turned toward Priscilla, avoiding the dark coldness in Rizzo's eyes.

"It's . . . it's a letter," DeMaris said.

"Yeah," Rizzo said. "It's a letter. A letter from the literary agency where you used to work. And with your signature on it."

DeMaris nodded but remained silent.

"'Course," Rizzo continued, a transparent casualness in his tone, "that's just a photocopy." He sat back in his chair. "We got the original in the precinct evidence lock-up. In a plastic bag. See, at some point, we're gonna lift prints off that letter. One set will be Robert Lauria's. We gotta figure the second set will be yours."

Rizzo smiled. "You know who Robert Lauria was, don't you, Ms. De Maris?"

She shook her head. "No, I . . . I can't say that I do," she said. "I see the letter is addressed to him, but I handled hundreds of letters like that, maybe a thousand over the years. I can't be expected to re-member—"

Priscilla cut her off. "Lauria is dead," she said. "Murdered."

DeMaris's anxiety seemed to intensify. Rizzo could only specu-late how much or how little Bradley had told her in anticipation of this interview.

"Yeah," Rizzo said. "And in the same way Avery Mallard was murdered."

DeMaris sat back in her seat, eyes wide, breathing shallow. "Why are you here?" she asked in a strained, tense tone.

"Do you wanna tell her or should I?" Rizzo asked.

"Go ahead, Joe," Priscilla said. "Ruin her day."

Rizzo folded his hands on the table, hunching his shoulders and leaning slightly forward, closer to the frightened woman.

"We're here because you stole Lauria's play *A Solitary Vessel*. You rejected the work, then took it to your boyfriend, Thomas Bradley. Or maybe you took it to Bradley *before* you rejected it, I don't know. But you knew the play was pure gold. Maybe in the beginning, you were legit, who knows? Maybe you figured you and Bradley would just cut the agency out. But then, somehow, Lauria got cut out, too. Then Bradley spoon-fed the play to Mallard—word by word, scene by scene, act by act. Mallard was desperate, blocked for nearly ten years. He was more than willin' to use what he believed was Bradley's inspiration. Of course, Mallard did get a little creative, throwing in the love story on his own initiative, and he and Bradley bumped heads over it. So Mallard went to his agent, Kellerman, and got backing for the love triangle; Bradley had to give in."

Rizzo sat back. "And everybody lived happily ever after," he said. "Except for Lauria, of course. He got fucked good. And when he contacted Avery Mallard to complain, Mallard went to Bradley and demanded an explanation. Then, one rainy night, Bradley rides over to Brooklyn. He calls Lauria from a pay phone on Fourteenth Avenue and tells him he represents Avery Mallard, and asks if he can stop by for a few minutes. To discuss the play. Lauria says sure, come on. Bradley rushes right over, Lauria doesn't even have time to put up some tea and get dressed. Bradley walks through the front door and strangles the guy." He paused, smiling coldly. "Maybe his original plan was to just blow Lauria off if he ever turned up bitchin' about how his play got stolen. Buy him off or accuse him of runnin' a scam. But once Mallard got wind of it and refused to cooperate, Bradley had to take some drastic action.

"But . . . what was one little man in the face of all a this? Who's more important: Lauria, you, Bradley?" Rizzo leaned in again. "I'm thinkin' you figured you were, Ms. DeMaris. You and your boyfriend. The only thing left to threaten you both was Avery Mallard. Maybe Mallard kept insisting on doing right by Lauria. So Bradley had to kill him, too. And convince you to alibi him for it."

DeMaris looked from one cop to the other, her heart racing in her throat, her palms growing moist with perspiration.

"I want a lawyer," she said hoarsely.

"Yeah, I bet you do," Priscilla said.

Suddenly Rizzo stood up. "You want a lawyer," he said harshly. "See, Cil, like I told you, no use tryin' to be nice to her." He turned hard eyes back to DeMaris. "You want a lawyer, you can get one at the precinct. You can call one from there. You want a fuckin' lawyer, you can have one for when we're grillin' you. We can get you some kid from Legal Aide." Now Rizzo placed his hands down on the tabletop and leaned forward, bending to bring his face closer to DeMaris.

"But understand somethin', lady," he hissed. "I ain't some college boy cop from Manhattan South. You're comin' to *Brooklyn* now. And I don't give a fuck who killed Mallard *or* Lauria—you *or* Bradley. For all I know, Bradley's clean and you killed 'em both. Maybe *he's* alibiing *you* for the night of the murder. I pin this all on you, I clear two cases and still walk away a hero. So if you're thinkin' this is about justice, think again. Far as I'm concerned, real justice would be somebody stranglin' you *and* Thomas Bradley. *That's* fuckin' justice. Anything else is politics, lady, just politics. And maybe I figure it's my turn to get elected."

DeMaris shrank in her seat, perspiration glistening on her forehead. Desperate, she turned toward Priscilla, her eyes imploring the female detective for help.

Priscilla smiled at her, then raised her gaze to Rizzo's face.

"You know, Joe," she said in a cold, low tone. "I think maybe she *did* kill 'em both."

"No," DeMaris said loudly, her voice cracking. "I didn't kill anyone, I swear."

Rizzo shook his head slowly. "Understand me, lady: it don't mean shit to me. You want a lawyer, fine. We go to the precinct, you call a lawyer. I arrest you on suspicion of murder, second degree, two counts. Then the lawyer can handle it. If he's good, better than your lover boy's lawyer turns out to be, he gets both murders pinned on Bradley. You take a fall on two counts a conspiracy, second degree. You do maybe ten, fifteen years. Bradley does twenty-five to life, twice." He shrugged. "Best you can hope for. And only if your lawyer is better than lover boy's."

After a moment, Priscilla stood and walked around the table, laying a hand on DeMaris's shoulder. She bent slightly, speaking in a soft, even tone into the right ear of the frightened woman.

"Or maybe you'd like to hear what me and Sergeant Rizzo can do for you?" she asked.

LATER, RIZZO and Jackson sat at a table in the small interview room of the Six-Two squad room, a pale, tired-looking Linda DeMaris opposite them.

"Like we promised, Ms. DeMaris, I deliberately kept your statement vague," Rizzo said. "Far as anyone can tell from readin' it, you brought the play to Thomas Bradley 'cause you recognized it to be a masterful work. Bradley convinced you to let him handle it, told you to turn down Lauria on behalf of the agency. You were unaware of any problems that occurred later on, after Mallard got the letter from Lauria and confronted Bradley. You were not further involved until Bradley asked you to alibi him for the night of the Mallard murder." Rizzo paused. "Lucky for you, I'm not a real good statement taker, Ms. DeMaris. The way your statement reads, it's a little unclear exactly *when* Bradley approached you for the alibi. Coulda been before he killed Mallard, coulda been after. Better for you, of course, if it was after. We'll let your lawyer, when you get one, clarify that. As to Lauria, your statement is a little unclear there, too. Seems like Bradley told you Mallard was wise to the plagiarism, but Lauria himself never came up as bein' the specific source of Mallard's knowledge and possible anger about the whole situation. Not to you, anyway. So, reasonable doubt could certainly exist as to whether or not you could have known any harm would ever come to Lauria. Far as anybody's concerned, it could seem reasonable that you didn't even know about Lauria's murder till this mornin' when me and Detective Jackson told you about it."

DeMaris opened her mouth to speak, but Rizzo held up a hand to silence her.

"No need to comment," he said. "I got all I need, and I know more about you than I want to. Let me be blunt, Ms. DeMaris. Far as I'm concerned, you're a thief and a callous, calculating, coldhearted bitch who's gettin' away with murder. Let's just leave it at that."

The door to the interview room opened and Detective Morris Schoenfeld stepped in.

"Here you go, Joe," Schoenfeld said, handing some papers to Rizzo. "Signed, sealed, delivered."

Rizzo glanced at the legal papers he held. "Thanks, Mo," he said.

Schoenfeld nodded, turning to leave. "This little favor squares us for that counterfeit prescription case you handed me and Rossi. We're pickin' up the perp tonight."

"My pleasure," Rizzo said. He turned to Priscilla as Schoenfeld left the room. "Here, take this court order. Call Homeland Security, give 'em the order number so they can put a freeze on Bradley's passport." He waved the other papers at her. "These are the warrants."

Priscilla left the room. Rizzo turned back to DeMaris, speaking in a softer tone. "I called a friend a mine over at Brooklyn South Homicide. He's got some juice at the D.A.'s office. They got hold of the homicide bureau chief. He's comin' down personally to hear you out, and once he sees that half-assed statement I took, he's gonna want you to give him a better one. You refuse and speak to him *only* after your lawyer gets here. *I'll* fill the bureau chief in. Because of your cooperation and statement, plus some circumstantial evidence I already had, Detective Schoenfeld was able to go down to court and secure a search warrant for Bradley's home. I'm hopin' to get the physical evidence I need to tie him to the Lauria homicide. Without you as his alibi, and with your testimony as a cooperating witness, he'll fall on the Mallard case, too. Any defense lawyer in the city can cut you a deal you'll be satisfied with. Bradley's my target here, he's the strangler."

He reached across the table and patted her hand. "Relax, you're doin' the right thing. If you'd have bucked me on this, I'd have gladly crucified you. And your boyfriend, too. He was done for either way, so you might as well look out for your own ass. Most you'll probably do is a couple a years."

Rizzo stood, his expression now stern. "Not too bad for stealing a play from a lonely, sad dreamer so you could line your own pockets."

He shook his head and turned to leave. "Whatever jail time you wind up with, lady, it ain't enough. Not nearly enough."

BACK AT his desk, Rizzo began making phone calls, first to Dan Cappelli, the *Daily News* reporter he had spoken to on Thanksgiving night, then the Six-Two squad boss, Vince D'Antonio. He made a perfunctory apology to D'Antonio for disturbing him at home, then filled him in with the briefest of outlines. D'Antonio said he would be at the precinct in less than an hour.

Next he called Lieutenant Dominick Lombardi at Manhattan

South. Lombardi was one of the senior investigators assigned to the Mallard homicide. Upon hearing Rizzo's summary of the situation, he promised to be at the Six-Two as quickly as possible.

As he hung up on Lombardi, Priscilla stepped up to his desk.

"Passport is frozen, boss," she said. "They got it into the computer while I was still on the line with them."

"Good, Cil," Rizzo said. "Sit down. I gotta talk fast, so let me get started. Vince is on his way, and Lombardi from Manhattan South. When they get here, I'll fill them in. Then Lombardi makes his play to push us off the case and have Manhattan pick up Bradley. That's when we bend him over and shove it up his ass."

Priscilla smiled. "Tell me," she said with a wink.

Rizzo laughed, then grew serious. "Few years back, a bunch of local teenagers jumped a black kid down by the highway. They beat 'im up a little, then chased him. Kid ran out on the highway and got hit by a car. Hurt pretty bad, almost lost a leg."

"Racial thing?" Priscilla asked.

Rizzo nodded. "Couple a nights before this happened, some old white man got mugged on Cropsey Avenue. Perp was black. So these neighborhood kids figured they'd go vigilante, even up the score, so they grabbed this poor kid. Well, the case got a lotta ink—politicians, activists, all the usual parasites. Me and my partner at the time, Johnny Morelli, we were the assigned."

"Okay," Priscilla said. "What's this got to do with anything now?"

Rizzo continued. "We locked up a bunch of kids. One of 'em wound up sentenced seven-to-ten upstate, a few others did some time, too. One of the kids, Stevie Cappelli, was the son of a guy I happened to know. Well, Stevie wasn't a bad kid, he was just hangin' around on the wrong night at the wrong time with the wrong bunch. I couldn't see ruinin' his life on account of it. So me and Morelli got a little creative with the DD-fives and the witness statements, and next thing you know, Stevie Cappelli was outta the picture."

Priscilla shrugged. "Okay," she said.

"Yeah. Okay. Anyway, how I knew the kid's father, Cappelli—he was a beat reporter for the *Daily News*. Handled the Brooklyn police blotter. Nowadays, he's a big-time feature writer and mainstream reporter. Needless to say, he was very grateful to me for savin' his kid's ass. Cappelli was always a flamin' liberal, very PC. How would it look if his son got caught runnin' with a lynch mob? So the old man tells me, 'If there's anything I can ever do for you . . .' Like that." Rizzo shrugged. "Seems like nowadays Stevie boy is a senior at some journalism college up in Massachusetts, getting all the liberal indoctrination he'll need for a career in the impartial world of print news."

"So," Priscilla said, impatient, "you saved the kid's life."

"Yeah, sorta. With a little help from his SAT scores and his old man footin' the tuition bill. Anyway, I been sittin' on this payback for a lotta years, Cil. It's not something I can hand off or pass down to anybody, and Morelli retired to the bottom of a vodka bottle. So the time to cash in is now. It's why I asked Schoenfeld to run down to the courthouse for those warrants and the court order freezing the passport instead of sendin' you to do it. See, Cappelli's gonna show up here at the precinct. And he's gonna wanna talk to Vince. Seems as though an anonymous source down at the courthouse tipped him off to the warrants and this impending bust on the Mallard case. Maybe it was the cop who applied for the warrant, maybe one a the court officers on Cappelli's payroll, a court clerk—who knows? But Cappelli learned that two Six-Two cops are about ready to break open the infamous Avery Mallard murder. That would be us, Cil, me and you."

Priscilla laughed. "So when Lombardi tells Vince to pull us off the Lauria case so the Plaza can cut us out of the Mallard case, this reporter, Cappelli, tells them, 'Not so fast, guys, I already wrote the story.'"

Rizzo nodded, smiling. "Exactly. Cappelli gets his liberal righteousness all in an uproar. 'How dare you bureaucrats attempt to deny the citizenry of its right to know the full truth. If Sergeant Rizzo and Detective Jackson—African-American *female* Detective Jackson, I might add—are not given their due desserts by the NYPD, the *Daily News* will demand, in headlines, to know exactly why not.'"

"So Cappelli makes a deal," Priscilla added. "He'll hold off on breaking his exclusive story until *after* we lock up Bradley, and the Plaza is forced to let us plant the flag on both cases."

"Bingo," Rizzo said. "Everybody and their brother'll figure we leaked it to Cappelli, but they can't prove shit. They're stuck with us. Best they can do is capitalize on my generosity for even *callin'* this guy Lombardi. That call will take the edge off, pacify them a little. They can get their pictures in the papers, too." He paused. "And bottom line, Cappelli *still* owes me. After all, I'm gettin' him an exclusive on the Mallard murder."

"Sounds good," she said. "Now let's hope the search warrant turns up a blue raincoat that matches the fiber found on Lauria's corpse."

"Oh, it'll be there, Cil, and it'll match. But even without it, now we have DeMaris's testimony. And she's damn lucky we grabbed her so quickly. Once the pressure started to build on Bradley, he'd have come to one conclusion, that he *had* to kill DeMaris, just like you've been scared of since all this started."

Priscilla shook her head. "Always treat murder like a solo act, boys and girls. A partner in crime'll get you busted every time."

"Amen, sister," Rizzo said. "Amen."

"So now?" she asked.

Rizzo shrugged. "Now we wait for everybody to get here. Let the D.A. bureau chief make his preliminary arrangements with DeMaris's lawyer. Then we talk to Vince and Lombardi, and don't forget to look surprised when Cappelli walks in." He stood up. "But right now I want to calm DeMaris down a little, tell her what to expect. I don't think she realizes she's gettin' locked up tonight, maybe for two nights before bail is set and posted. Come on, Cil, come with me, I need a witness in there so she can't claim I copped a feel of her sweet-lookin' ass."

"Just give me a heads-up before you do, so I can look away. That way I won't be lying when I tell I.A.D., 'Hey, I didn't see nothin'.'"

VINCE D'ANTONIO, his face tight with anger, glared across the desk at Rizzo. They, along with Priscilla, Lieutenant Lombardi, and Assistant District Attorney Raymond Kessler were in D'Antonio's office.

"Damn it, Joe," D'Antonio said, "you shoulda told me about all this, you shoulda kept me posted from day one."

"This aspect of it just come up, boss," Rizzo said lightly. "Check the DD-fives; everything we had is in there. We just didn't see the whole picture till now. We followed the leads and next thing we know, we're lookin' at this Mallard thing."

D'Antonio shook his head sharply. "That's bullshit. You knew where this was goin' from the moment you and Cil first found Lauria's play."

"You're givin' me too much credit here, Vince. I ain't that sharp."

D'Antonio frowned and began to speak, then suddenly changed his mind. He glanced to Priscilla.

"You got anything to add here, Jackson?"

"Not really, boss," Priscilla said. "It's like he told you: we just followed our noses and kinda tripped over Mallard."

D'Antonio held her eyes for a moment, before turning to Lieutenant Dominick Lombardi.

"What can I tell ya?" he said to Lombardi. "It's the first I'm hearin' about any of this."

Lombardi, a thirty-year veteran of the NYPD, smiled. "Yeah, I got that impression."

"Well, whatever," Rizzo said, addressing Lombardi. "What's done is done. We should drop the warrant on Bradley and look for that raincoat. We got enough in DeMaris's statement to lock him up right now. Then we wait for the lab test on the fiber. Should be a slam dunk."

Lombardi's face brightened. "We?" he said. "I'm not followin' you here, Sergeant. What do you mean, 'we'?"

"I mean, we, like us," Rizzo said. "Like me and my partner. And, of course, you're welcome to come along." He reached into his shirt pocket, extracting a packet of Nicorette. "Being how it *was* your case and all."

Lombardi laughed. "I like a guy with balls, Rizzo," he said. "Refreshing change from most of the Plaza boys and girls. But, in this particular case, I gotta say, you're outta line."

"Yeah, well, I can see where you might figure that, Loo. But you can ask Vince here—I don't go outside the lines."

Raymond Kessler, the Homicide bureau chief from the Brooklyn District Attorney's Office, interjected from Rizzo's left.

"Maybe you do and maybe you don't, Rizzo," he said curtly. "But you could use a little work on your statement-taking skills."

Rizzo responded, wearing a puzzled look. "Oh?" he asked. "And why's that?"

"Oh, I think you know," Kessler said. "That statement you took from DeMaris has more holes in it than Swiss cheese. A kid straight outta law school could convince a jury DeMaris was just in it for the plagiarism angle, didn't know shit about the murders. She can practically walk away from this. The prosecution will have to spit nickels for even a conspiracy count to stick, let alone felony murder."

"Yeah, Rizzo," Lombardi said. "If a guy didn't know better, he might figure you lobbed it in for DeMaris to get her to bury Bradley for you."

Rizzo turned to Lombardi with a hard expression, his eyes hooded. It drew a shrug from Lombardi.

"*If* a guy didn't know better," the lieutenant repeated.

Rizzo let his expression soften. "Well, whatever," he said. "It's moot now, water under the bridge. Me and Cil made this case, with help from Mike McQueen. Least you can do is accept that, and let's just move on."

Lombardi shook his head. "You two are out," he said simply. "And whoever McQueen is, he's out, too. As of now, Manhattan South is takin' jurisdiction on the Lauria case." He paused before adding, "Sorry, Joe, that's how the brass wants it."

Rizzo leaned over toward the man. "You know, Dom, I made a call on you," he said softly. "Looks like twelve days from now, you get promoted off the captain's list. If you break the Mallard case, next stop for you is deputy inspector."

Lombardi shrugged. "Could happen," he said.

Rizzo turned to D'Antonio. "You gonna sit there, Vince? You gonna let this happen?"

"Look, Dom," D'Antonio said to Lombardi, his tone hard. "There may be some irregularities here, and maybe you got a right to be pissed. But *my* guys broke this. Rizzo and Jackson, yeah, but the squad pitched in, too. I can't let you walk in here . . ."

Lombardi held up a hand. "Who you need to hear from, Vince?"

he asked casually. "Inspector Kelly? The PC? The fuckin' mayor? Let me know, I'll make the call."

Color came to D'Antonio's face. He shot an annoyed glance at Rizzo, then turned back to Lombardi.

"Don't lean on me, Dom," he said. "Don't try and push me aside. It pisses me off."

Lombardi sighed. "It's a tough business, Vince. I'm just a cog in the wheel, is all."

A tense silence developed, broken after a moment by a knock on the closed door of D'Antonio's office.

"Sorry to interrupt, boss," a uniformed officer said as she stuck her head into the room. "There's some guy here to see you, says it's important."

"Not now," D'Antonio said, his face still flushed with anger.

She hesitated, then spoke again. "Guy's from the newspapers, boss," she said, her voice low. "Says he's here about the Avery Mallard murder. Says he wants to talk to the two cops who broke the case." She glanced around the room.

"He says he's writin' the article now, and he needs to talk to the two cops right away," she said to D'Antonio. Then, looking at Rizzo she added, "You know, boss. Rizzo and Jackson."

Chapter Twenty-four

SATURDAY MORNING, RIZZO SPED the Impala along the Gowanus Expressway, once again heading for Manhattan. Priscilla Jackson sat in the front passenger seat, Detective Lieutenant Vince D'Antonio in the rear behind her.

"You have the warrants?" he asked Rizzo.

Rizzo sighed. "Yeah, boss, for the third time, I have the warrants. Relax, okay?"

D'Antonio shook his head. "Yeah, relax," he muttered. "Easy for you to say. Tomorrow, you and Jackson are the stars of the city, media darlings of the week. But I get Plaza brass chasin' after my ass with giant hard-ons in their hands."

Priscilla chuckled. "Don't you just hate when that happens?" she said sweetly.

D'Antonio glowered at her profile. "Jesus Christ," he said. "Just what I need. A female version of Rizzo to deal with."

"You won't have to deal with her for long, boss," Rizzo said. "Next stop for Cil is Major Case, Brooklyn Homicide, Manhattan South, wherever she wants to go. And me, I'm outta here in about nine months."

D'Antonio shook his head. "Nine fuckin' months," he grumbled. "Like a goddamned pregnancy."

After a moment, D'Antonio spoke once again, his tone now conversational. "I gotta admit, though, Joe, runnin' Cappelli past Kessler and Lombardi, that was pure genius. Did you see their faces

280

when he quoted tomorrow's headlines? 'Brooklyn Cops Crack Mallard Murder'?"

Rizzo shrugged. "Wasn't me, boss. Somebody down at the courthouse must have tipped Cappelli, remember?" He turned slightly to Priscilla. "You didn't have anything to do with it, did you, Cil?"

"Innocent as you are, Partner," she answered. "I never even heard of Cappelli till he walked into Vince's office."

"Well, whatever," Rizzo said, then addressed D'Antonio. "Like I told you yesterday, these personal accusations, suspicions, where's it all get ya? No place. Let's just go get this prick Bradley. That's our main goal here."

D'Antonio laughed. "Yeah, Joe," he said. "Spoken like the true public servant you are."

Rizzo met D'Antonio's eyes in the rearview mirror. "Whatever you say, boss," he said.

THOMAS ROSS Bradley sat impassively on his sofa, his gray eyes cold. His wife, pale and fidgeting, sat beside him, a bewildered, frightened look on her face. Lieutenant Lombardi led a team of Manhattan South detectives through the sprawling Midtown apartment. The warrant Rizzo had served on the Bradleys authorized a search of the apartment in any area reasonably expected to contain articles of clothing. It also authorized the examination and seizure of any inner or outer garment reasonably resembling a blue or partially blue article of men's clothing, as well as any and all pairs of gloves found in the home.

Rizzo, with Jackson at his side, stood before the Bradleys, a tight smile on his face.

"You finished readin' that arrest warrant yet, Bradley?" he asked.

The man raised hostile eyes to Rizzo. "Yes," he said. "And once again, I demand my attorney."

Rizzo shrugged. "You called your attorney. He's on his way. In the meantime, I'm placing you under arrest for the murders of Robert Lauria and Avery Mallard. You have the right to remain silent. You have the right to an attorney, and to have an attorney present during all questioning . . ."

When he finished the Miranda warning, Rizzo took the arrest warrant back from Bradley and smiled down at him.

"There, now all the little technicalities of our shallow American culture have been taken care of." He turned, leaving Bradley under guard of two uniformed officers from the host Manhattan North Precinct.

"Does that make you feel better, Mr. Bradley?" Rizzo asked, as he moved away.

PRISCILLA JACKSON sat in the Six-Two interview room with Thomas Bradley and his attorney. She carefully completed Bradley's pedigree for the preliminary paperwork on the Lauria homicide. She would later transport the suspect to Brooklyn Central Booking to complete the process. From there, Rizzo and Lombardi would transport Bradley to Manhattan Central Booking and prepare the Mallard paperwork. Bradley would presumably be arraigned on Sunday in each borough, and, as was customary in murder cases, be initially remanded to the Department of Corrections without bail.

At the same time, Rizzo sat in D'Antonio's office, smoking a cigarette in defiance of the New York City ban currently in force for all public buildings. Lombardi sat to his right.

"Well, let's hope the coat we found is a match," Lombardi said. "That'll be the last nail in this guy's coffin."

"Be nice if they get Lauria or Mallard's trace blood off a pair of those gloves, too," D'Antonio said.

"Let's not get greedy, Vince," said Rizzo. "Blood or no blood, this guy is so busted, the Queen's teeth must be fallin' out."

"Yeah," D'Antonio said, chuckling. "I bet."

Lombardi cleared his throat. "I wanna go off the record, guys," he said.

D'Antonio shrugged. "Okay."

"Sure," Rizzo agreed.

Lombardi again cleared his throat. "Just so you know, you ain't fooling anybody here, Joe. We know what you did. Almost from day one you ran your Lauria case to get to the Mallard case—for the perks that collar would bring. You kept Manhattan South in the dark and deliberately withheld evidence from us."

Rizzo opened his mouth to protest, but Lombardi held up a silencing hand. "Easy, guy, take it easy. We're off the record here, remember?"

Rizzo thought a moment. "So what's your point?"

Lombardi responded. "My point is you broke every fuckin' rule you came across. Includin' doing DeMaris's attorney's work, creating her escape route on felony murder charges with that half-assed statement you wrote. All so you could nail Bradley, Joe. You gambled big, and I guess you won big, but I want you to know, you ain't fooling anybody. I don't care what Cappelli says, his 'confidential' source at the courthouse is sittin' right here next to me."

"Off the record or on, I deny that," Rizzo said with a shrug.

"Good for you," Lombardi answered. "But whatever, that angle covered your ass. Nobody at the Plaza will buck a crusading reporter who's backing your play. It's better to just eat shit and smile, so that's what'll happen."

"I'm still waitin'. What's your point?" Rizzo repeated.

Lombardi's tone softened. "Well, my point is—and we're still off the record—I do appreciate what you did on the bottom line. The phone call to me, I mean. I know you've got the balls to end-run us completely, so you tipping us to the situation, even at the risk of getting cut out yourself, that was righteous. And I appreciate it. *We* appreciate it. Far as John Q. Public is concerned, the Mallard arrest was a team effort with you and Jackson as the MVPs. We can live with that." He paused. "What else *can* we do?"

Rizzo shifted in his seat and waved a casual hand at Lombardi.

"No big deal, Dom," he said. Then with a wink, added, "I kinda had a feeling I wasn't gettin' cut out of anything. Sort of a gut feelin'."

Lombardi laughed. "Yeah, I figured. Nothin' like those gut feelings, eh, Joe?"

Vince D'Antonio leaned forward on his desk. "I hate to break up this little circle-jerk you guys got goin' here, but how 'bout doin' *me* a fuckin' favor?"

Lombardi raised his eyebrows in question. "And what might that be?"

"Well, Dom, how 'bout taking this pain in the ass off my hands before he gets me jammed up beyond repair?"

D'Antonio's eyes moved from Lombardi to Rizzo and back again.

"How 'bout lettin' Joe do his last nine months breaking *your* balls over at Manhattan South?"

CHAPTER TWENTY-FIVE

December

SEATED AT HIS KITCHEN TABLE, Joe Rizzo sipped coffee and casually leafed through the *Daily News*. It had been just over a week since headlines had announced an arrest in the Mallard murder case.

His mind wandering, the faint sound of an automobile motor came to him from the driveway. He pushed back his chair and rose to investigate.

Reaching the window, he watched as Carol climbed out of her car. Rizzo frowned, wondering what had brought her home so unexpectedly.

"Hi, Daddy," she said as she entered the house.

He smiled at her. "Hi, hon. Everything okay? I thought you were coming home on the twentieth."

Carol crossed the room, dropping her backpack to the floor by the door. She kissed Rizzo on the cheek.

"Yeah, well, I decided to take the day off," she said. "I have some laundry to do."

Rizzo glanced at the backpack. "Okay," he said. "Seems like a long drive for one load of wash, but . . . okay."

Carol smiled, her pretty features lighting Rizzo's eye. "Is that sarcasm or skepticism I detect?" she asked, her tone light.

"Neither, Carol," he replied. "Just an observation, that's all."

Carol went to the coffeemaker, taking a mug from the cabinet and filling it. She moved to the refrigerator, gathered milk and apple pie, then sat at the table. As she gestured for him to join her, he returned to his chair.

As Carol forked some pie into her mouth, she said, "We need to talk, Daddy. One awkward holiday was enough; let's not ruin Christmas, too."

Rizzo smiled at her. "Was Thanksgiving ruined? I hadn't noticed."

"Okay, maybe not ruined. But awkward. Definitely awkward."

He nodded. "Settled. *Awkward* is what we'll call it."

Some moments passed, Rizzo sipping his coffee, Carol eating her pie.

"So, kiddo, how'd you do on the police exam? Any feelings about it?"

"Well, I just took it a couple of weeks ago," Carol answered, shrugging. "Naturally, I haven't heard anything yet. But it was pretty easy. I think I maxed it."

"Okay," Rizzo said, his eyes on hers. "So what's next?"

"You know how it works, Daddy: written test, medical, physical agility, psychological. Then into the Academy."

Rizzo began to drum his fingers on the table. Carol reached out a hand, laying it on his to stop the drumming. She smiled as she spoke, her voice soft.

"Relax, Dad," she said. "You can handle this. So can Mom."

Rizzo turned his hand under hers, taking hold of it and massaging it gently in his grasp. For reasons unfathomable to him, memories of her First Holy Communion day wafted across his mind's eye.

"Yeah, Carol," he said, his voice the equal to hers in softness, "I guess we could." He paused. "You know, it's not about your mother and me, honey. I understand it's hard for you to accept that, but it's always been about you. About what *you* could handle, about what was right for *you*."

Carol placed her other hand over the one Rizzo was holding. "Yes, I do know. I've always known that. But this is what I *really* want. I've just spent the entire week reading about you and Cil, how you solved the Mallard case. I have the *Newsday* article framed and hanging in my room at school. I'm very proud of you, Dad. That's why I had to come home and straighten all this out. I don't like us being mad at each other."

Rizzo shook his head slowly. "Carol, I've never once been mad at you your entire life."

Carol's eyes twinkled. "No? Never? Not even that time I found bird crap on the fender of your car and used one of Mom's emery boards to file it off? Along with some of the paint?"

Rizzo laughed. "Okay," he admitted. "One time, maybe."

Carol removed her hands from his and stood, moving toward the coffeemaker. Refilling her cup, she returned to her seat.

"So," she said, her features set, a grimness affixed to her expression. "Would you like to hear what I came to say?"

Rizzo sat back in his seat, his eyes falling to the table. "Probably not."

Despite herself, Carol's expression softened. "Well, you're going to anyway. My mind is made up. I'm going on the cops as soon as they call me."

Rizzo raised his eyes to meet hers. "And so you decided to drive two hours to come home and tell me this today?"

"Yes, Dad. Today is as good as any. I know you and Mom still plan on talking me out of this, turning me around somehow. I want it resolved now. I want it behind us. I need you to just accept it."

"But what's the urgency, kiddo? This coulda waited till . . ."

Carol shook her head. "No, it couldn't. All week I've been reading about you, how you broke that case, how you and Cil put a murderer behind bars. And I've been wondering, how can he be so against me going on the cops? So now, I'm asking you: Why? Is it the danger? Are you scared? The most dangerous job in America is convenience store clerk. Did you know that? Not cop, not firefighter, not race-car driver. Seven-Eleven night clerk. It's just life, Dad. You can't protect me from it. I'm an adult, you have to accept that."

Rizzo rubbed at his jaw, considering it all. Then he sighed before leaning inward toward his youngest daughter.

"All right, Carol," he said, weariness apparent in his voice. "All right. You read about your big hero father and his gangbuster partner in the newspaper, how they locked up the bogeyman. Well, I think you need to hear the *real* story, kiddo, not just the news. The real truth."

Rizzo sat back and gave Carol a sad smile. "I solved the case, okay, solved the crime. But the truth is, to do it, I took a big chance with someone else's life, I risked a third murder. Then I falsified a sworn statement. I promised a coconspirator, a person just as guilty as Bradley, that if she played ball, cooperated and recanted her phony alibi story, I'd write a statement for her with more leaks in it than the *Titanic*. I practically guaranteed she'd have the basis to walk on two homicides, probably just take a fall for a low-weight felony, maybe only a couple a misdemeanors. Then I perjured myself in official sworn court papers. And I'll do it again when I testify at the trial, if there is a trial. I *broke* the damned law, Carol, because that's what I had to do to *enforce* the law. It's *crimes* cops deal with. *Just* crimes. Not people. I break as many laws as I enforce. Maybe more. That's how it's done. Wait. You'll see. If you go ahead with this quest of yours, you'll see. Believe me."

Carol seemed confused. "What are you saying, Dad? That it's a bad arrest? That this guy Bradley is getting railroaded?"

Rizzo shook his head. "No. I wish it was that simple. The arrest is good, tight as a drum, and the guy is guilty as hell. I just needed that woman's cooperation to give me the legal ammunition to secure a search warrant for Bradley's place. Once I did, we had him. We found the physical evidence we needed to throw on top of the cir-cumstantial we already had. Bingo—case closed." He paused, giving his daughter time to digest what he had just told her, see it for what it was.

"Pretty heroic, isn't it?" Rizzo asked softly.

Carol sat silently looking at her father. Then she sighed and gave a slight shrug. "Seems to me, Dad," she said, "you did what had to be done. It is what it is." She was silent for another moment before continuing.

"You know, Dad, human civilization is built on a foundation. And in this country, we've built a lot on our foundation: a free press, great universities, churches, ballets, museums. And do you know what that foundation consists of?"

Her father shook his head. "Sometimes I think I don't know much of anything, kiddo. Not really."

Carol continued as though he hadn't spoken. "The foundation consists of security, Dad. Security and law and order, put there by soldiers, put there by cops. Some people look down on them, criticize them, betray them, feel superior to them. But without those soldiers, without those cops, without the foundation built with their blood and sweat, there *is* no free press, there *is* no freedom, there's nothing. Nothing but tyranny and chaos and crime and violence."

Carol stood slowly and walked behind her father, placing her hands gently onto his shoulders. She bent her face to his ear, speaking softly into it.

"Maybe it's not always pretty. Maybe a cop's job can get dirty. But the truth remains. No cops, no foundation. No foundation, no civilization. It's the only thing I want to do. Just let me work on that foundation. Let me help keep it sound, let me repair some cracks. If I have to get my hands dirty in the process, so be it. I can do what you do, Dad. I can fight fire with fire. You just watch me."

Carol stood erect, her hands still on Rizzo's shoulders. He turned his head, his eyes finding hers as she spoke once more.

"I need you to be there for me on this. I could always count on you. Don't change on me now. Please, Dad."

Rizzo, his eyes moistening, smiled up at his daughter.

"Okay, kiddo," he said. "Okay."

THE AFTERNOON of Friday, December 12, was slate gray and bitterly cold. A harsh northerly wind swept along Smith Street, buffeting scattered pedestrians as they hurried along the sidewalks.

Rizzo climbed from the Camry and pulled his coat collar over his ears and neck. He crossed diagonally to the Non-Combat Zone and pressed the doorbell. As he waited for a response, he glanced at his Timex: three-thirty sharp. Right on time.

"SO, MY friend," Father Attilio Jovino said happily. "You've had quite a two weeks, I see."

"Well, yeah, Tillio, I guess I have," Rizzo said.

Reaching across to accept Rizzo's offered Chesterfield, Jovino said, "You must tell me all the inside dirt, all those tantalizing details which somehow never quite make it into the news reports."

Rizzo leaned forward with his Zippo, lighting Jovino's cigarette, then sat back to light his own.

"Well," he said, blowing smoke down at the desktop, "there's not much to tell, I'm afraid. That reporter from the *Daily News*, Cappelli, he had a good source. He grabbed a pretty nice scoop for himself."

Jovino widened his eyes. "And how very convenient for you," he said with a smile. "I would imagine the higher-ups were all poised to steal your thunder for themselves. Cappelli's headlines may just have kept them honest."

"You'd have made a hell of a cop, Til," Rizzo said matter-of-factly.

"God forbid," the priest answered, crossing himself. "I have all I can handle right here, thank you." He paused, drawing on the cigarette. "But really, nothing to share? No inside tidbit?"

"Well, in a day or two, the story'll break that the fiber found on Lauria's corpse matched Bradley's Burberry coat. Plus, the lab pulled trace elements of blood from Bradley's leather gloves, and it's Lauria's. That shuts the door." He paused. "There were some problems with DeMaris's initial statement. It was sorta vague and poorly framed as to the extent of her involvement, and she may get outta this cheap, but her pulling the alibi story did a good job of nailin' Bradley on the Mallard case. And there'd be no reason for him to kill Lauria other than to protect his plagiarism and the fortune he was reapin' from the play, so once we prove Bradley killed Lauria, DeMaris's testimony makes the Mallard case a no-brainer. He's goin' down on both of 'em."

"May God forgive him," Jovino said in a neutral voice.

"Yeah," Rizzo said coldly. "Let's hope."

Jovino's face brightened. "So, I saw your picture in the paper. You and Detective Jackson, with our dear mayor and illustrious police commissioner. I understand the *Daily News* may run a full feature on you in a future Sunday magazine."

Rizzo gave a short laugh. "Yeah. Unless some ditzy pop singer loses her drawers again. Then I'm yesterday's news."

"Quite possibly, Joe," Jovino said, laughing. "Quite possibly."

"Well, it's been fun. The attention, I mean. Nice way to finish up my career. Plus, Mike got a big boost from it, too, and Cil can probably write her own ticket. Everybody wins."

Jovino frowned. "Except those two dear souls who were murdered and the misguided souls who murdered them," he said.

"Yeah," Rizzo said. "Except them."

The two men sat in silence for a few moments, smoking. Then, Jovino leaned forward, cigarette smoke curling around his head, his hands now crossed before him on the desk.

"So shall we discuss it?" he said. "The reason for your visit today?"

"Yeah, sure, Til, but relax, okay? I'm not bailin' out on you."

The priest smiled at him. "I hadn't suggested you were."

Rizzo sat back in his seat. "Oh, yeah, you sorta did. It's in your eyes."

"Set my mind at ease then, Joe."

Rizzo reached into his pocket and extracted a small Panasonic tape recorder/player. From another pocket, he removed a microcassette.

"There'll never be a better time for me to get this out there," he said. "Me and Mike are bulletproof now. Maybe not forever, but all we need is right now. You got about a half hour to spare, Father? I got somethin' I want you to hear."

LATER, AS Jovino showed Rizzo the door, they paused and shook hands.

"I'll personally deliver the tape to the United States attorney for the Eastern district. First thing Monday morning."

"Good," Rizzo said. "They'll have no trouble believin' some runaway left it here at the shelter. Once they start nosing around and find out Daily's daughter was once a runaway herself, they'll see the logic of it."

"Of course they will," Jovino said, his eyes twinkling. "And despite the rather less than stellar conduct of some few of my colleagues, most people still do trust priests, Joe. They'll believe me all right. Don't concern yourself about that."

Rizzo nodded, lifting his collar in anticipation of stepping out into the dark, cold evening. "Good," he said.

Jovino shook his head, a sadness coming into his eyes. "I always knew Councilman Daily was something less than noble, Joe. But this . . . this tape. It's an outrageous betrayal of trust. Of dignity. Of *democracy*."

Rizzo shrugged. "Do yourself a favor," he said. "Keep it simple. What we got here is a crime, Father. Forget about what's right, what's wrong, what's a betrayal."

Rizzo opened the door, the cold wind intruding immediately, biting at the exposed skin of his face.

"What we got here is *illegal*," Rizzo said, his eyes kind, his tone soft.

"A crime, Father. Just a crime."

APR - 2011